The Best Of Becky Freeman

The Best Of Becky Freeman

*Worms in My Tea and
Other Mixed Blessings*

———

Marriage 911

———

*Still Lickin' the Spoon and Other
Confessions of a Grown-Up Kid*

Three Bestselling Books Complete in One Volume

Becky Freeman

INSPIRATIONAL PRESS

NEW YORK

CONTENTS

Becky Freeman & Ruthie Arnold

Worms in my Tea

And Other Mixed Blessings

Dedicated with love
to our children and grandchildren:
Zachary
Ezekiel
Rachel Praise
and Gabriel

Contents

Acknowledgments

First, we must thank the incredible men in our lives: Scott, Becky's husband, and George, Ruthie's husband, who were our first and most enthusiastic cheerleaders in the project. They allowed us to sit about nine inches from their faces while they read portions of the manuscript, allowing us to observe every twitch, every raised eyebrow, and every grin as they read, knowing we wouldn't be able to stand it long before blurting out questions.

"What? What part? What part did you think was funny? *How* funny? Too funny, or just right funny?"

Good, patient men.

Without Zach, Ezekiel, Rachel Praise, and Gabriel, this book would not have been written. So thank you, children and grandchildren, for the great material.

Other family members gave us the applause we needed while we dwelled in "unpublished purgatory." Beverly Freeman, Scott's mother, penned our first rave review on flowered stationery. Scott and Rachel St. John-Gilbert, Ann Bietendorf, and Jamie Patterson—all know how to gush when you need them.

We owe a particular debt of gratitude to Etta Lynch, Ruthie's sister and Becky's aunt, who is the first professional writer in the family and who gave us invaluable pointers and suggestions.

Mary Rusch contributed a lot to the book, not only in terms of material, but as a continuing inspiration. "Becky," she observed one day, "you *have* to find time to write a book, even if you *do* have the dirtiest floor in America." True words of encouragement.

We feel a sense of gratitude to people in the publishing world who gave us just enough encouragement to keep us plugging along. Mr. Bill Wallace, award-winning children's author, critiqued the earliest manuscript and sent his remarks: "I think it will go. I won't tell you not to be discouraged while you wait, because you will be."

Also to Larry Hampton, a seasoned editor who gave us a great boost when he liked our book, as did Ken Petersen. Ed Wichern, man of God, retired writer, beloved Sunday School teacher, who, along with his wife, Betty Lou, put up with numerous phone calls for advice, each time encouraging us to keep writing and leave the results in God's hands.

Lisa Spaight, Lou Wayne McQuirk, and Jim Wilde may not think of themselves as answers to prayer, but their help with typing, cranky computers, and print outs came just in the nick of time.

And finally, thanks so very much to Vicki Crumpton and the people at Broadman & Holman Publishers who believed in *Worms in My Tea* and felt the time had come to serve it up to the public, so to speak.

We were truly blessed.

∿

Worms in My Tea

Some mothers use TV as a babysitter. Not Becky Freeman. No sir. The first thing every morning, I run outside our lake-side home, look for any small creature that breathes and moves, pop it in an empty butter tub, poke holes in it (the butter tub, not the critter), and my three-year-old, Gabriel, is set for the day.

There have been days, however, when I probably should have fallen back on the TV. One such day began as I sat folding the morning's wash. I noticed with a sense of unease a strange bulge in the pocket of a pair of Gabe's jeans. Gingerly, I forced myself to explore the warm, dark interior of the pocket, reminded of the feeling I had had years before when the bigger neighborhood kids would blindfold us little kids and force us to stick our hands into a bowl of cooked spaghetti, all the while assuring us the bowl contained either brains or guts. I realized, as I explored the pocket under discussion, that I hadn't matured all that much.

My hand enclosed an object that could have been a piece of bark. Feeling false reassurance, I extracted the mysterious bulge.

Can anyone know how black and shriveled and—well, bark-like a frog can be unless they have seen one washed, rinsed, and fluff-dried?

This event set the tone for the morning. Later that same day I turned from loading the dishwasher in time to see Gabe holding a baby turtle by the tail with one hand, scissors poised in the other.

"Whoa, Gabe!" I managed. "What do you think you're doing?" His reply had a "Why do you ask?" tone to it.

"This turtle needs me to cut his ponytail."

That turtle owes me one.

Toward evening that same day, things quieted down entirely too long. (Have you ever wondered why six minutes of peace and quiet feed the soul of a toddler's mother while seven fill it with terror?) On the seventh minute I dropped my chopping knife with a clatter and ran out to the back porch to check on Gabriel. All was strangely calm. In fact, he seemed to be meditating, his gaze fixed upon a styrofoam ice chest waiting to be stored away. Our eyes met when I heard a thumping sound issuing from the closed ice chest.

"There's a cat in there," Gabe said matter-of-factly, jerking his thumb toward the chest. I was not unduly alarmed for the safety of the cat at this point, since I could see the lid of the chest rise and fall with the thumps, but I did move to liberate the animal. As I lifted the lid, I realized with shock that Gabe had managed to fill the chest with water before depositing Kitty. I grabbed the saturated feline by its neck and estimated her to be on about her ninth life. I turned horrified eyes on my son. Like George Washington, he did not lie.

"I put her in there," he confessed. But he had a reason. "She was really thirsty."

Time passes, wounds heal (both to cats and to moms), and life goes on. For several days after that, nothing particularly unnerving transpired. Then one evening at church I looked down from my hymnal to discover that Gabriel clutched yet another wilting frog in his warm little hands. For some unknown reason, Gabe chose this moment to ask in a loud whisper, "Something smells! Is it you?"

Needless to say, I, Gabe, and the frog all needed "Amazing Grace" to survive that service.

But Gabe, our baby, is growing and is now big enough to dig for fishin' worms. What *I* wish is that he was big enough to go *fishing* with them, because he so hates to see them go to waste. Believe me, there is no experience that quite compares with downing the last of a big glass of iced tea only to discover a grayish worm squirming among the cubes at the bottom. "Just look," Gabe cooed sweetly as he showed me a sand pail containing a number of worms he had not yet invited to tea. "See how they love each other! They're hugging!"

But Gabe *is* maturing. Just yesterday he confronted me, hands behind his back with the look of love and pride other children have when they bring their mommies a hand picked flower. Beguiled, I extended my hand where he lovingly deposited a snail, complete with slime.

"It's for you," he beamed. "I love you, Mommy!" Then he kissed me straight on the lips.

Take it from a woman who knows. Snails and worms aren't so bad. Really.

How many are your works, O Lord!
In wisdom you made them all;
the earth is full of your creatures.

PSALM 104:24

Motherhood:
A Can of Worms?

"Have you had a chance to read *My Little Bear*?" inquired my friend, Mindy, who holds a degree in pre-med.

"No, I haven't," replied I, a card-carrying member of the National Honor Society. "But have you read *My Little Bunny* yet?"

What was happening? Did we go brain dead when our children were born? Our hearts had long since convinced us to forego careers, if possible, in order to "stay at home" (any housewife will chuckle at that expression) with our children, at least until they started school. But then, as I observed my husband Scott studying the best-seller, *Dress for Success*, I also observed myself, dressed in standard, faded purple, Porky-Pig sweats and felt qualified to write my own version: *Dress Like a Mess*.

That was the night I decided to write a book. A real one. I wasn't motivated so much by the desire to make my mark as I was the need to put down on paper for myself—and maybe others—the reasons I believe making a home and building a family is important and worthwhile. I had seen a demonstration of that in the family from which I sprang (sprung?) and I feared such families are getting scarce as hen's teeth.

Beyond that, I wanted an excuse to share the fun of the simple, yet profound, children's chatter that makes up so much of my days with my four little people. I also had in mind that the project might help keep my gray matter from permanent atrophy while I put my college education on hold. I figured it might even keep some other mom from thinking *her* atrophy is permanent or from prematurely throwing in the towel.

If nothing else, I figured I'd have something to read when it's all been said and done and I must pass through the valley of the shadow of the empty nest syndrome, which the experts all agree I must endure if I don't develop a life of my own. Personally, I expect at that time to be busy dancing a jig and going out to dinner every night with a deliciously adult husband, like my own parents are now doing.

It occurred to me that Mother might give me a few pointers. She had pounded the typewriter on and off through my teen years, writing Sunday School curriculum and other things that had gotten into print. It didn't look all that hard, so I broached the subject by phone.

"Mother? I just read the funniest book. I think it's called *Stick a Geranium in Your Hat and Smoke It*. Wanna write a book with me?"

She seemed to hesitate for a moment, and I may have heard her sigh before she answered, "Sure. Why not?"

We decided to begin with the subject of motherhood and branch out from there. There *are* tricks to the trade of mothering and I have a few of my own. In order to see mothering from the most positive perspective possible, rather than as a can of worms,

5

I invented a mental game to play with myself. I pretend I am Erma Bombeck and write down each disaster as if it could—someday—be funny. So you see, I already had quite a stack of notes for My Book.

Not everything my little people have said and done has been a disaster by any means. On some days I have felt certain that, just as Mary Poppins said of herself, they were "practically perfect in every way." Such was the day I took our third child, three-year-old Rachel, to the bathroom at Burger King. From inside the bathroom stall I heard, "I love you, Mommie. Aren't we *both* so sweet?"

Remembering another occasion with Zeke, our second born, I can still feel his grubby little hands gently caressing mine as he said, ever so kindly, "Your hands are getting a little old, Mommy. But they're not as crumbly as Nonnie's." He was lost for a moment in his dreamy world, but then finished, "I still love *her.*"

And I melt. Perhaps having a glamorous career isn't nearly as gratifying, after all, as being sweet and crumbly.

Whoever loses his life
for my sake will find it.
MATTHEW 10:39
&

Curbin' Their Wormin' Ways

Everybody knows that children must be disciplined. That is, everyone except the children. What parent has not faced down the toddler who declares through his outthrust bottom lip, "You not the boss of me!" Then ensues a scene not unlike the shoot-out from *High Noon*. Hopefully, Mom (or Dad) is the one left standing.

Now, discipline has never been my strong suit, partly because of my Erma Bombeck vow to try to see the humor in a given situation. I also find it impossible to frown and laugh at the same time. I knew I had a problem with discipline long before the day I discovered my first-born, Zach, age three, engrossed in the contents of my make-up kit. With proper anguish and indignation, I confiscated his supplies and began the scrubdown.

Suddenly, he pointed his chubby finger at me and said in a voice that would have put Isaiah *and* Jeremiah in the shade, "I'm gonna tell God you took that make-up away from me!"

"Well," I responded firmly, "God sees everything and He knows you took my make-up without asking me."

Silence. Then very quietly he admitted, "Oh. I not be frazy bout that."

Ah, discipline. Ain't many of us frazy about it. And kids know all the angles. The important thing, say the experts, is not to let them worm their way out of it.

At age two, reasonableness was not Zach's strong suit. If I failed to cut his peanut butter sandwich into a perfect right triangle, he would throw himself to the floor thrashing, screaming and nearly foaming at the mouth. To handle the situation without getting physical, I was faced with the prospect of hiring a professional draftsman to bring his protractor and Xacto Knife™ and cut the sandwich. The other possibility was to call the folks at the zoo to come with their tranquilizer guns.

Neither alternative seemed really practical, so I faced the showdown, shades of *High Noon*. However, he must have seen the spanking coming because he stopped the tantrum virtually in mid-air. He wrapped his chubby little arms around my knees and lisped, "I wuv you. I give you big kiss."

What's a mother to do? Spit in his eye?

The books tell us the goal of disciplining children is to teach them to become self-disciplining. A few weeks after I had determinedly dealt with Zach's sandwich syndrome, I made the mistake of cutting his sandwich diagonally from top left corner to bottom right rather than vice versa. I was pleased and surprised when instead of throwing his usual tantrum, he said with great restraint, "This is *not* funny, Mother."

Being new to motherhood and partial to any "natural" philosophy of raising children, I bought into the whole Earth Mother ideal. It goes without saying that I was one of those women who breast fed their babies until they were old enough to cut their own meat.

But when I got the literature on "The Family Bed," I felt relieved and reassured, since Zach spent most of his nights in our bed. Little did I dream how crowded our nuptial bed was destined to become. When Zeke made his appearance, I decided one night to try to persuade at least Zachary to sleep in his own big bed, offering an inspired suggestion.

"Zachary, wouldn't you like to snuggle up with this nice big Pooh Bear™?"

He took one look at the teddy bear bait and tearfully sniffled, "I'd rather snuggle up with a nice big mommy."

So, for several years following, the children would file one at a time into our bedroom at night like silent sleepwalkers muttering, "I had a bad dweam," or, "I cold in my woom," knowing I was a patsy for frightened or freezing children.

Scott and I were frequently waking up with a vague feeling of never actually having slept, as we clung tenaciously to the sides of our bed in areas the size of small tea towels. The children, however, remained sprawled in our bed while visions of sugar-plums danced in their heads, so blissful were they. My husband and I, without kerchief or cap, began to dream of a long winter's nap.

Fortunately, I came to realize that a tender-hearted sucker does not always a good mother make, nor any sleep receive, and I began to move from the Back to Nature literature to the Dare to Discipline genre.

Sooner or later, however, comes a day when our children echo back to us the words of discipline we have taught them. One evening some years back before Gabe joined us, and after a late bedtime fiasco on an evening with no relief from a late working, stressed for success daddy, I had come to the end of my patience. I ordered the boys to bed, plunked Rachel on the couch and sentenced her to lie there until I could get a grip on myself. I began furiously loading the dishes into the dishwasher, grumbling to myself all the while until, like a balloon out of air, I exhausted my anger. Rachel, noticing a quieting in the kitchen, bravely peeked over the back of the couch. She smiled knowingly and spoke in a most maternal tone of voice.

"Are you ready to behave now?"

No discipline seems pleasant at the time, but painful.
Later on, however, it produces a harvest of righteousness
and peace for those who have been trained by it.
HEBREWS 12:11
∾

Mother Earth Worms

There are three kinds of people in this world: right brain creative types, left brain organizers, and people who cannot seem to locate cerebral matter in either hemisphere. I am whichever brain it is that can organize her thoughts on paper, be a member of numerous honor societies, and still manage to wear her dress inside out all day without noticing it.

People seem to be born either basically organized or artistically creative, but rarely both. My little sister, Rachel (out of admiration for whom I named my daughter), and I are prime examples of both extremes. When we were children living at home, her belongings were so organized that I could not filch so much as one M&M™ from a mammoth Easter basket without being called to account for it.

I recall a morning when I desperately needed to borrow a clean blouse from her closet because mine were all in use, piled on the carpet in the corner of my room to hide a Kool-Aid™ stain from Mother. I opened Rachel's door ever so quietly and tried to tippy-toe into her room without waking her. She never moved, never opened an eye, but said in what I thought was an unnecessarily threatening voice, "Don't even *think* about it."

Even our choice in clothes reflected our different personalities. As we grew to be teenagers, Rachel opted for a few well-tailored, quality suits. I, on the other hand, had a closet full of bargains with lots of ruffles, lace, and color.

Our courtships and subsequent marriages also revealed our right brain/left brain contrasts. Scott and I fell hopelessly in love at the ripe old age of fifteen while on a mission trip to El Salvador, digging ditches for an orphanage. We married at eighteen, full of happiness and thinking very little about the things money *could* buy—food, clothing, shelter, gasoline…We would simply live on our love, which we were certain was the greatest since Romeo and Juliet.

But my little sister kept her head about her, even in matters of courtship. First, she graduated from college and then, at a respectable age, met her potential lifetime partner, another Scott: Scott St. John-Gilbert, no less. (I like to call him Gilley.) Before rushing into marriage, Rachel and Gilley ran through a series of personality compatibility tests and endured agonizing spiritual searches to determine God's will in the matter. After their tentative budget was planned and their five-, ten-, and fifteen-year goals carefully drawn up, they plunged down the aisle with reckless abandon.

With their Five-year Plan right on track, my penny-wise sister and brother-in-law saved their D.I.N.K. earnings (Double Income, No Kids) to purchase a lovely condo overlooking a golf course. For the time being, I will describe our country home as "rustic." I see no need to draw any further comparisons with regard to housing. Rachel and Gilley soon purchased a houseful of Ethan Allen furniture, in white. When I purchased a new couch, I chose a tan and burgundy print for its ability to blend with peanut butter and grape jelly.

One might expect that in bearing children, we are all sisters under the skin, which is true. However, no two births are ever exactly alike, and Rach and I even bore children under incredibly different circumstances. When Zach was born in the late seventies, the watchword of the young and idealistic was "Back to Nature!" Lamaze was the only way to go. Therefore, I would give birth in the warmth and intimacy of our own home. No conventional doctor, antiseptic hospital or pain blocking drugs for me, no siree.

On a Saturday morning in early December, I began to experience signs that this might be The Day. We notified our male midwife and he promptly appeared at our door, did a quick exam and agreed with our diagnosis. However, he said there was no rush to boil water or tear up a sheet for white rags. It would be a little while yet. He sounded light-hearted and wonderfully reassuring and when we asked about going out to buy a Christmas tree to decorate in order to pass the time, he thought it was a jolly idea.

We notified our folks and before they could throw down the phone and jump in the car we told them it might be as long as six or seven hours. "No rush."

That evening, ten hours later, Mother served barbecue to us and the midwife and his red-haired female assistant. (No need to worry about nausea, since I *definitely* would not be having any anesthetic.) Not much progress had been made other than a nicely decorated Christmas tree, but we were all still smiling and in a companionable mood. The lights of the tree blinked gaily in the deepening twilight. The midwife was dressed in a T-shirt and jeans, and he told us during supper that he was a former Marine sergeant.

After supper, he announced that I needed to get busy walking to speed things up. At 2:00 the next morning, Scott was literally walking me through the house, standing behind me, holding me up and moving my feet with his feet. Mother was chewing her lower lip and glancing at the back bedroom, where sounds of the midwife's snoring issued forth, making her nervous. He was confident we were in good hands with his assistant, but at 3:00 A.M., Mother decisively made her point. We called out the Marine.

We had figured things had to get tougher before they got easier, but when Mr. Midwife speeded things up, none of us were prepared for three hours of pushing. If I declined to push, the ex-Marine barked orders at me in such a way that I discovered there was one more push left in me after all. Scott's mother had dropped by for coffee eighteen hours earlier, and still had enough of her wits about her to photograph the proceedings. My own mother was gyrating between moments of deep prayer on her knees in the kitchen and babbling idiocy.

As for the prospective mother, I would have cheerfully strangled every natural childbirth expert who had ever told me that labor was not painful, just hard work. This was *PAIN*.

Scott supported my head and shoulders and coached, "Just think, the baby's almost here!"

"Just think," I shot back, "if I get out of this alive, you are going to be living a celibate life!"

At 6:30 that morning, twenty-one hours after we had so blithely welcomed the first signs of impending birth, the midwife laid my 9 lb., 2 oz., son in my arms. Maybe the fact that I am five feet two and small boned accounts for Zach's taking his good old time to arrive, but it was suddenly all very worth it. So much so, that we managed to keep having children. And having them. And having them.

The birth of Baby Number Two seemed like a piece of cake in comparison to Baby Number One. Zeke arrived at mid-morning on a rainy June day, assisted into the world by a highly competent midwife and her two assistants. (As an aside, I might mention the Marine had made the front page of our metropolitan newspaper, having been arrested. This is a true story.)

Baby Number Three would have none of making her appearance on a warm summer morning. The holiday season seems to be the first choice birthing season in our family, and Rachel Praise chose to make her debut three days after Christmas in 1983, one of the coldest winters in the history of the United States. Condensation froze on the windows *inside* the house, and snow and sleet fell in heavy sheets outside our tiny home. My parents and my sister, Rachel, eighteen at the time, were visiting for the holidays, and they all needed to return home. I was overdue, and felt like a watched pot waiting to boil. I had already imagined several instances of labor pains about which we had notified our female midwife (a good friend by this time), but so far, I had been unable to produce a grandbaby and a niece/nephew for my audience. But at about two in the morning on December 28, I woke Scott to tell him I was in labor.

"Go back to sleep," he yawned. "I don't even think you're pregnant anymore." The interesting thing is, I managed to do it, but when I next woke up, there was absolutely no doubt. I *was* pregnant, but I wouldn't be for long.

The scene that followed was like a choppy Keystone Cops episode. I yelled orders while Scott scrounged in the closet for the box of supplies I had assembled for use by the midwife. I realized the box was now the "Do-It-Yourself Birth Kit" because the midwife was thirty minutes away in *good* weather. So much for the LaBoyer method I had wanted to try.

Daddy got on the phone to the midwife, relayed messages to Mother, who hollered them to Scott, who was the most qualified at this point to officiate since he had assisted at the first two home births we had hosted. In the meantime, Rachel took careful notes in the section of her looseleaf organizer entitled, "Things I Must Never Do." Then she dived in like a trooper, ready to boil rags or tear up sheets, though we never figured out what we should have needed either for.

When the baby was born into Scott's waiting arms, he tearfully announced it was another boy. A few seconds later, Mother said, "Scott...um...I think you were looking at the umbilical cord there." We named her Rachel Praise, meaning "God's Innocent Lamb of Praise."

The midwife arrived in time to tie the cord, and Scott, now full of pride and self-confidence, allowed as how he might offer a free baby delivery with each new home he built thereafter.

Three years later, Gabe arrived, and the birth happened so swiftly and smoothly that my mother didn't make it in time for the actual event, to her everlasting gratitude. During my recovery, she managed the three older kids and our household just fine, but Gabe was a little hard on her back. He had weighed in at ten pounds plus. Talk about your grand finale.

On the first day of February 1992, my sister, Rachel, gave birth to her first child—her way. She went into labor after a full night's rest at about seven in the morning on her day off. Seven and a half hours later, she called me from the exquisitely beautiful and home-like birthing room at the hospital to tell me in graphic detail of the two painful contractions she had endured before calling for the epidural.

"After that," she reported enthusiastically, "it was great. We all sat around and laughed and played Gin Rummy." That evening when I called to check on her and her new son, she could hardly talk because she was chewing steak from the candlelight dinner the hospital had served her and Scott. She apologized for cutting me short, but she had to call the gym and make her next racquetball appointment before it closed.

Good grief! I mentally ground my teeth. *She has managed a Yuppie childbirth!*

As memories of my totally natural Lamaze, LaBoyer, LaLudicrous births swept over me, all I could think was, *What was I thinking?*

In retrospect, I draw some comfort in wondering if the modern way of giving birth in those beautiful birthing rooms with loved ones about would ever have happened if a generation of Mother Earth devotees had not put their collective foot down. Maybe I had a tiny part in helping to make my sister's childbirth experience one she will always cherish. I hope so.

And as time progresses, I fully expect that my new nephew will sleep through the night throughout his infancy, develop into a child prodigy at the piano, and as a teenager frequently ask, "What else can I do to help you, Mother?"

In reality, however, it is the differences between my sister and me that keep us fascinated with each other's lives. As women, we have grown to admire and love each other more with each passing year, due to a good deal of acceptance and understanding. She has always loved Scott, me, and our children unconditionally with abounding enthusiasm.

So even though Rachel *does* have a twenty-two inch waist (I honestly don't know how she does it), had a quick, painless childbirth, and owns furniture that doesn't stick to the seat of her guests' pants, how could I help loving her?

The body is a unit, though it is made up of many parts;
and though all its parts are many, they form one body.
So it is with Christ.

1 CORINTHIANS 12:12
☙

From Grub Worms
to Grandeur

The scene is the Dallas-Fort Worth Airport, Summer 1974. Scott's mother, Bev, and my mother, Ruthie, are standing near the boarding ramp watching their teenage offspring depart for a summer mission experience. As the plane shrinks to the size of a toy in the warm Texas sky, Mother turns to Bev, and sighs deeply.

"I feel better knowing that Becky is with Scott. She needs someone to look after her because she'd lose her head if it weren't attached."

"Mmmm," said Bev.

"Mmmm?" said Mother, registering concern. "Mmmm what?"

"Actually, I was hoping Becky might help Scott keep up with *his* things."

The two mothers grip the guard rail a teensy bit tighter, suddenly realizing their fifteen- and sixteen-year-old children are headed for El Salvador to help construct a church building, and neither can be trusted to keep up with their shoes, let alone their passports.

Meanwhile, up in the air, I was having my own thoughts. They went something like this:

Lord, I'm so excited. Scared, too. I'm glad Scott will be with me on this work team. He's in good shape so he can probably show me how to dig or saw or whatever it is I'm supposed to do. I did do a couple of sit ups this morning. I think I feel stronger already. I checked to be sure no one was watching, flexed my best muscle, then passed some time trying to locate it.

Too bad I'm not going with his big brother instead. I'll just never get over Kent, no matter how hard I pray. It hurts even to think about the moment he broke up with me. And that was ages ago.

Maybe this mission trip will help me focus on You, Lord. I really do want to learn to love You more—and my teammates, and all those little brown skinned children I plan to adopt someday.

Scott tells me his thoughts went something like this: *YES!!! I have Becky Arnold with me for seven weeks! YES! YES! YES!!!*

Scott and I had known each other for several years, getting to be buddies in our youth group. My folks knew his folks from church also, but the church was a big one and they hadn't spent a lot of time together. What I did not know is that Scott had spent several afternoons visiting with my mother, trying to find out what it might take to win some points with me.

"I hated to tell him he needed to grow at least another ten inches taller," she later laughed. As it turned out, he did manage another eight, and, in the space of a few months, zoomed from five feet four to six feet. And I hardly noticed. But, back to the summer of 1974.

Before we could leave for our final destination in El Salvador, we had to go through a type of boot camp somewhere in the swamps of Florida. When we arrived at what appeared to be a refugee tent city, I turned to Scott hopefully. "Where do you suppose is my condo?"

He grinned and squashed a mosquito the size of a small chihuahua feeding hungrily on my arm.

"This is *great!*" he beamed, and I realized with awe that he actually meant it. Soft spoken, mild mannered Scott Freeman transformed before my very eyes into MacGyver and Rambo combined. And I, Miss Teen Femininity, would soon find myself living in denim overalls and army boots. Little did I realize how long it would be before I enjoyed a hot bath or air conditioning again. At the moment, only one of us was a genuinely happy camper.

I soon found my quarters for the next week, a tent filled with girls from as far away as Hawaii and Canada, most of whom looked as bewildered as I. A beautiful Hawaiian girl, Canaca, sped up the female bonding by sharing a forbidden bar of chocolate from the islands with all of us. Strengthened by the sugar and her kindness, I decided to open up real communication.

"Thanks for the candy! Where're all of y'all from?" I drawled. A bouncy blond was the first to respond.

"I'm from New Yoik." Talk about fascinated. To me, she sounded exactly like a cab driver in a movie I'd seen. Apparently she found my accent equally entertaining. She looked at me as if I were an alien from another planet.

"Hey, Tex, is that accent for *real?*" she squealed.

Before I could drawl "Yep" to the miniature "New Yoikuh," the dinner bell rang, and we trudged to the soup line arm in arm.

I was famished. But as soon as the server handed me my tin bowl of chili, I tripped over my new boots and deposited most of my one course dinner on a fellow teammate's back. I did the best I could to scrape the beans off his shoulder with my spoon.

"I guess that's why they call it the mess hall," I offered, but he didn't see the humor of the situation. Looking around to see who had observed my graceful dive, I saw Scott grinning at me from his seat in the corner of the makeshift dining hall. I blushed clear down to my steel-tipped toes.

I had lived to the ripe old age of fifteen, and accidents like spilling chili down a stranger's neck were already fairly common. I usually took them in stride, but this time was different. A whole new set of thoughts tripped into my dithered head.

Scott looks so tall. Has he always been so handsome?

He stood up slowly, stretched to his full six feet, glided toward me with the litheness of a cat—and slammed face-first into a tent pole.

Oh, my goodness! my heart beat wildly. *He's perfect!*

After dinner I wandered exhausted through the sea of green tents, trying to remember which one was home. Eventually I found my pillow and, after saturating myself with insect repellent, I fell soundly asleep. Minutes later, or so it seemed, I heard a voice in the dark outside the tent.

"Time for calisthenics! Up and at 'em!" I recognized Scott's voice as he bounded by our tent. Any romantic thoughts I had entertained the evening before evaporated. The only difference between me and a rattlesnake in the morning is that I bite with less provocation.

"Just let me at him!" I growled to myself. "I'd like to personally give that boy a root canal—minus anesthetic."

I yanked my overalls on, inside out and backwards, and managed to crawl out the tent opening. I squinted toward the red ball peeping over a palm tree in the east.

So that's where the sun comes from, I thought groggily.

Scott was merciless, leading our team in a workout that left me feeling like a wad of silly putty. Too late I remembered he had taken gymnastics for years, which may have accounted for the Adonis build. Even in the dim light of dawn, I had to admire his tan, his perfect white teeth, the straight golden brown hair falling over his brown eyes, the square chin…At the moment, however, the girls in my tent desperately wished I had brought along a fat Texas couch potato named Bubba instead.

That was on Monday. By Friday, Scott had whipped us into shape and the physical obstacle courses had united our rag-tag group into a real team. During the day we learned to tie steel, mix concrete, and lay brick under a blazing sun. In the evening, camp meetings inside the big tent under the stars were precious times of worship and refreshment. There was one night in particular I will never forget.

It began after an especially moving devotional. I was kneeling at the front in prayer when I glanced behind me and saw Scott kneeling at the altar, too. I looked into his face, and he into mine, and it seemed as if the dirt floor became holy ground. Like some ethereal dream, everything around us stopped and quieted and blurred, except for what was clearly happening between the two of us. A strange thought shot through my mind. *This young man will be your husband someday.*

Then Scott reached for my hand and held it for a few seconds, our eyes unwavering.

"I love you, Becky," he whispered. "I always have."

"I love you, too." My lips formed the words before my mind could talk my heart out of it. Could it be that I was falling in love with a friend? A buddy? *Kent's little brother?*

As I walked back to my tent in a world that had changed forever, I found myself thinking with wonder, *Little brother has grown up.*

I was shaking when I slipped into my sleeping bag, and to calm myself I reached for my Bible under my pillow. I fumbled for my flashlight and opened to Jeremiah 24:6-7: "My eyes will watch over them for their good…and I will build them up and not tear them down; I will plant them and not uproot them. I will give them a heart to know me, that I am the Lord. They will be my people, and I will be their God, for they will return to me with all their heart."

Somehow I knew that those verses were especially for me and Scott that night and that good things lay in store for us in the days ahead, perhaps even in the years ahead. Now one might say, "We are talking about a fifteen-year-old girl and a sixteen-year-old boy here!" And I would agree. Serious relationships almost never begin, and even more rarely last, at those ridiculous ages. But sometimes, miracles do happen.

The week in boot camp passed and the day finally arrived when we were to leave the Florida swamplands for the country of El Salvador. The plane flew over emerald-green hills decorated with beautiful patchwork fields, then passed over Lake Illapango shimmering in the sunlight. Once on the ground, I fell in love with the people immediately. I couldn't understand a word they were saying, but I did my best.

"¡Bienvenidos!" greeted the dark-haired hombre who met our plane.

"Sí," I responded politely. "Picante salsa chili con enchilada," I said, quite pleased with my perfect Spanish accent. The man looked impressed and was wonderfully warm and welcoming. I still cherish the warm feelings of affection in my heart for the hospitable people of Central America.

Our team of about thirty teenagers and three married couples found our accommodations to be much more luxurious than at boot camp. We girls were housed in a chicken shack, a great improvement over tent city, and I think the boys got the goat barn. Our mission? Prepare a huge foundation for a Christian camp for native children, without the aid of any modern equipment. I developed a new empathy for the children of Israel in Egypt, building pyramids for the Pharoah after first building their own bricks.

Because we had had to pack so sparingly, the toughest part of the summer for me was spending almost every day in my huge, smelly overalls. Our days started at 5:30 A.M. and were filled with mixing concrete by hand, digging endless chunks of dirt from the sides of a mountain, wheelbarrowing, and tamping, which meant pounding dirt for the foundation with cans of cement attached to a broom handle. I must confess, I perspired. Actually, I sweated. In fact, I could hardly stand the smell of myself. I thanked God everyday that our chicken shack home had no mirror so I did not have to see my own reflection during those weeks.

Most of the time I was a trooper. When a rat ran across our beds one night, I did not keep screaming on and on and on like some of the girls. Although I had to get up before the sun and had been on ditch-digging duty from dawn to dark, I did not complain. But I *hated* those overalls. They made me cry. Every day. In a way only a fifteen-year-old girl can. Daily, I washed them with bar soap like the native women. I poured an entire bottle of perfume over them. Still, they smelled like rotten eggs and made me look like a hayseed.

One morning during devotions, I caught a whiff of myself and my overalls, and off I went into a crying spell again. I felt sorry for myself a good long time, and then I reached for comfort again. The Lord reached back to me this time through the book of Job: "Even if I washed myself with soap and my hands with washing soda, you would plunge me into a slime pit so that even my clothes would detest me" (9:30-31).

Job and I had become soul brothers in whining, and it was then, at a young and tender age, I realized God must have a sense of humor. I wiped my tears and grinned. After that, the overalls were a little easier to bear.

On Saturdays, we enjoyed glorious freedom, except that boys and girls were not to pair off. Our chaperones allowed us to roam the markets and villages by ourselves, once we had walked the five miles to town. I think they figured we'd be too exhausted to stir up much trouble after a long hike in the El Salvadoran sun.

I immediately bought a beautiful, floor-length, turquoise-colored dress, richly embroidered with red roses and deep-green leaves. I was already anticipating the day I would wear it: the day of the farewell banquet. On that day, hunting season would be opened and guys and girls would be allowed to pair off for the first and last time. I knew one thing for sure: I intended to start a raging fire on that day—with denim, buckles, and snaps!

After several weeks in the camp at El Salvador, the adult staff decided to transfer my half of our team to a village in Guatemala for a building project there. Once again, I marveled at the picturesque scenery and the beautiful people in their colorful, hand-embroidered costumes. I felt especially drawn to the young mothers with long dark braids, their black-eyed "papooses" peeking out from snug bundles attached to their backs.

I thought, *What quiet, reserved people!*—until they went to church. There we discovered that the local Guatemalans had only one volume for singing hymns—excruciatingly, ear-splittingly, loud! We wondered if there was an unannounced competition to see which small, unassuming Guatemalan Christian could puncture the most eardrums. Not only did they have a penchant for singing loud, but they also sang long. My ears rang for hours after every service.

After one of these exhausting services, my ears still ringing and my stomach growling with hunger, I trudged the last few yards alone toward "home." The girl's dorm in Guatemala was actually a two-story adobe house with, praise the Lord, indoor plumbing.

As I have said, I was tired and famished when I happened upon a tree with little green apples. They looked delicious. Reminiscent of Eve, I blatantly ignored one of the "Teen Commandments": Do not eat that which does not abide in a can or a bottle.

I ate of the fruit and I thought I would surely die. Now I know why the songwriter wrote, "God Didn't Make Little Green Apples." It's hard to believe a benevolent, loving God would create something so malevolent. For three days I alternated between agony on my cot and moaning in agony near the, praise the Lord, indoor plumbing.

Then came the good news. We were to board an unaircon-ditioned, unbathroomed bus for a six-hour ride over and under, and over and under, hills and valleys back to our main camp in El Salvador. At the mere thought of it, my stomach lurched.

Then came the *truly* good news. The team leaders felt so sorry for me they declared open season early so I could legally lean on Scott during the journey. And lean I did. The only time he let go of me was when I had to visit the roadside outhouse. When I emerged I promptly passed out into his waiting arms. Sick as I felt, I was delightfully aware of Scott's strong arm around me, his hand caressing mine as he prayed for me to get well.

Miraculously, I began to feel much better even though I was still very weak. We were young and in love and eager to explore the world around us together. Once, in a quaint courtyard, Scott decided to take pictures, and he positioned me among the pigeons strutting about the stone yard.

"Smile, Becky," he coached, "try not to faint for just one minute!"

I still have that snapshot, now framed and displayed in our home. I never want to forget the day when I was fifteen years old, reeling with an intestinal virus among a dozen Spanish-speaking pigeons, and at the same time, euphorically happy.

When we arrived back at home base in El Salvador, I and my stomach settled down. I even managed to be somewhat useful to the work crew for the waning days of the mission. Then, at last, the day of the farewell banquet arrived. That afternoon, I did indeed build a bonfire, and together with my girlfriends, watched the overalls go up in smoke. To my surprise, none of us were overcome by toxic fumes.

After the ceremonial burning of the overalls, I reached into my duffle bag for "The Dress." Scott had bought me a red carnation from a street vendor, so I combed out my dark braids and pinned the flower in my hair. When I stepped out of the chicken shack, my date met me at the door. He was wearing a white Guatemalan shirt and a broad smile of approval.

"Let's go for a walk," he said softly as he reached for my hand. It felt tiny in his strong, yet gentle grip. Together we walked toward the hill overlooking Lake Illapango.

It was supposed to be a romantic walk and it was, except that, with the long dress, I kept falling and stumbling into potholes. Halfway up the hill I gave up the struggle, picked up my skirt, and began trudging up the mountain like an El Salvadoran farmer. I heard Scott laughing behind me.

"You remind me of your mother," he chuckled.

Mother? Hmm-m-m.

At the top of the hill, Scott and I stood together looking down at the foundation our team had somehow managed to complete. We absorbed what would be our last view of the hills and the lake. We would miss it, but we would especially miss the people we had met, our brothers and sisters in Guatemala and those on the team from all over the world.

The evening sun decorated the sky, sending a brilliant burst of purple, red, and orange to celebrate the end of a summer and the beginning of love. Scott turned me to face him, then reached into his pocket and produced a tiny gold band which he slipped on my right ring finger. I later discovered he had bought the ring with all the money he had left, twelve dollars. It was a perfect fit. So were we. Then he kissed me softly for the first time ever, and I thought to myself, *I might as well die and go to heaven right now because I will never be any happier than this on earth.*

A rustle of movement from behind a nearby bush pulled us back to reality, but pleasantly so. Two barefoot El Salvadoran children giggled and darted from behind the bush and down the hill. We laughed with them and reluctantly started back down to the banquet.

Two years later, Scott slipped that very same gold band on my *left* hand. This time he vowed to love, honor, and cherish me as long as he lived, of which I remind him every time I bring home a new dent in the car. My twelve-dollar wedding ring is my most treasured material possession. For our engagement, he gave me a more expensive diamond ring which I lost behind the refrigerator for three years. He lovingly replaced the ring for Christmas. I subsequently sucked it into the vacuum cleaner. Though I found the ring among the lint, the tiny diamond was gone forever.

Since Scott has lost twenty-eight sets of car keys and five pairs of glasses during our marriage, he is not intolerant of my problem. Every Christmas he continues to replace jewelry that we eventually find in the yard, down the drain, or behind a major appliance. But I have prayed for God's eyes to watch over my precious, twelve-dollar wedding band inscribed "Jer. 24:6-7." The memories it represents, and the promise it still holds, are of the most precious gold.

I will build them up and not tear them down;
I will plant them and not uproot them.
I will give them a heart to know me, that I am the Lord.
JEREMIAH 24:6-7

Wedding Ring Worms

I returned from El Salvador by plane (though I probably could have flown without one) and deplaned at Dallas-Fort Worth Airport with Scott much as we had flown away. His folks and mine stood on tiptoe, watching for us to emerge from the plane. We left with a lot of daylight between us, we emerged from the plane as one entity.

Daddy drove me home to our nice brick house on a cul-de-sac in Arlington, Texas, where I had grown up. After weeks in El Salvador, it seemed like the Taj Mahal. I spent so long in the bathtub my toes and fingers turned into twenty prunes.

That evening, the family took Scott and me out for a spaghetti supper, and then we all came back to our house. We spread out on the floor and talked, and talked, and talked. I had come to take this kind of easy communication for granted, hardly remembering what it had been like at our house before the summer of '72.

At that time, the Country Squire panel wagon glinting in the afternoon sun had made the statement to the world that we were "The Arnolds—the Fam" was intact, parked, and stable. But around the olive-green, self-cleaning oven and down the rust shag in the hallway, there was "a whole lot of shakin' goin on" in the hearts of Mom and Dad. There were also quite a few tremors occurring in the nation as a whole.

The sixties had left their mark. Free love changed the 1950s' adage of *Father Knows Best* into the question, "Who *is* my father and *where* did he go?" Something dreadful had happened to Jim and Betty Anderson's America and it was much more serious than little Kathy breaking a window with a baseball. Unbridled freedom had arrived, bringing a total lack of boundaries. Common sense and morality seemed relegated to quaint old black and white reruns. Nothing made much sense anymore.

The women's movement suggested housewives look for fulfillment in outside activity. Mother, not one for being labeled unfulfilled, joined two women's clubs and managed to get elected president of both. Playing bridge provided another outlet for social activity.

Mother continued to run faster and faster in the race for fulfillment. She tells about the day she suddenly realized that when one of us kids wanted to tell her something, we reached out and grabbed her skirt to be sure she stayed still long enough to hear it. Something was haywire. Bridge yielded twenty-six recipes for making anything edible into the shape of a diamond, heart, club, or spade, and the women's clubs caused indelible skin indentions from girdles and high heels, and jaws that ached from forcing a smile when everything was dark and rainy on the inside.

It wasn't long before my parents decided that if there was to be meaning in life, it had to be with God. Each in their own way and their own moment made Jesus first in their hearts and lives. Then the real adventures began in the house on the cul-de-sac in Suburbia.

For one thing, our television played less and less. Mother especially kept an eye on the TV set. She actually made a label for it with her handy little label maker which read, "This television is to be used for the glory of God. Honor Him with your choices." If something came on the screen she felt we shouldn't see, she would leap from her spot at the kitchen sink into the den in a single bound and spread her apron over the screen before we could yell, "Look out, here she comes!"

But seriously, things did change around our home, mostly for the better. As a family we "hung out" more together and spent more time just talking. Mother was always good for one more sloppy joe for a school or church friend. Gradually, our home became a "cool" place to "rap." College students began dropping by for deep theological/philosophical discussions that stretched on until midnight or until Daddy fell asleep and slid out of his recliner, whichever came first.

Daddy often sat for hours in his old rocker in his bedroom, highlighting book after book with a yellow marker—books by such writers as Francis Schaeffer, C. S. Lewis, and Elton True-blood.

Looking back, I realize our home became a kind of substitute coffee house for young people living in turbulent times and faced with tough questions previous generations of Americans had rarely asked. Though most of the talks were over my head, I enjoyed visiting with handsome college men in our living room.

Frequently, serious discussions dissolved into silly, mass hilarity, especially when it got late and our brain cells begged for sleep. If for some reason there had been a police raid, only a breathalyzer would have saved us from a night in jail. It may have also been the effect of sugar-overload, because at that time much of our fellowship centered around food, particularly chocolate. Those are precious memories, and I hope to share evenings like that with my soon-to-be teenagers. I must remember the formula: deep philosophical discussion, late hours, plenty of laughter, and frosted pecan brownies topped with ice cream and hot fudge sauce.

A few months before Scott and I were to marry, my parents called me into their bedroom for a private discussion. Daddy had asked for a leave of absence from his job for several weeks, planning to take the entire family to L'Abri, Francis Schaeffer's community in Switzerland. There, he and Mother planned to study theology and philosophy along with other seekers from around the world.

It sounded great to me. I had always wanted to leap about on top of a Swiss alp, spreading my arms and twirling about in the mountain breeze. I would lift my face toward the sun and break into glorious song, "The hills are alive with the sound of music..."

But Daddy jolted me back to reality with a very tough question.

"Are you sure you want to get married in June before we leave in October," he asked, "or would you consider postponing the wedding for the trip to Switzerland?"

The decision wasn't even hard. I'd just have to belt out my song while I spun around in my new husband's kitchen over a sink of dirty dishes. I was getting married in June! The Arnold Von Trapp family would just have to yodel-lay-he-hoo across Switzerland without big sister's soprano.

Friends and family filled the church on our wedding day that Sunday afternoon in June of 1976. The wedding was like a fairy tale come true, complete with Prince Charming. The fact that we were so young added a Romeo and Juliet quality to the celebration.

Six bridesmaids and groomsmen radiated a pastel haze of color at the front of the church where my white tuxedoed groom waited. I stood in the foyer, dressed in a flowing cloud of white lace and ruffles, my hand resting on Daddy's arm. But my heart rested with the handsome prince waiting for me at the altar.

With the swelling chords of the wedding march, I had the feeling of being carried forward on a wave I could not stop, though it was the moment we had dreamed of for at least two years.

Although I could not have known all that lay ahead (who does?), I knew full well we had made a holy vow in the presence of the living God that afternoon. And when angry words are spoken and thoughts of divorce (or murder) sometimes enter my mind, I think back to that sacred altar and the vows two starry-eyed kids made to each other.

Actually, we managed to remain The Charmings through our entire honeymoon week. Not until we got home did I discover that my handsome prince had a few warts, and the prince began to think perhaps he had accidentally married the wicked step-sister. Thus began the inevitable period of disillusionment, of which all prospective newlyweds are duly warned by their pre-marital counselors, counselors who might as well save their breath. Every engaged couple is sure *their* love will be the exception because no one has ever loved as much as they, not since the beginning of time, nor ever shall again. What we need is post-marital counseling, given about a month after the wedding day when the descent from each other's royal thrones is well underway.

As I recall, the first thing to hit me about newlywed bliss was the 103-degree weather. The only duplex we could afford to rent had no air conditioning. For us, "making whoopee" meant literally shouting, "Whoopee!" every time a breeze found its way through an open window.

Furthermore, Scott hailed from a military family, and I soon learned he liked to make little rules. Now isn't that special? Actually, a number of situations did not turn out as I had dreamed they would.

Disillusionment #1. Scott's heavy work schedule demanded he get adequate rest. This was complicated by (1) the fact that I am a talkative night person, (2) the heat wave, and (3) the fact that our bed had settled into a shape resembling an open hot dog bun due to years of occupancy by previous tenants. These conditions led Scott to make the first rule. He drew an invisible line down the center of the bed and announced that each of us must stick to his or her own side of the bed when it came time to go to sleep.

I tried to follow the instructions, I really did. I hung on to my edge for dear life but I would inevitably roll into the crevice in the center of the bed. When this happened, Scott would grunt and pinch me.

For years I had dreamed of snuggling all night with my honeybee. Instead, I learned he had quite a stinger.

Disillusionment #2. Bathtime is near sacred to me. I love lying in the tub for long periods of time, periodically turning the water on with my toes while leisurely reading a good book.

A few weeks after the honeymoon, Scott suddenly strolled in, interrupting my time and space without so much as a knock, and presented me with a copy of our first month's water bill. He then proceeded to instruct me in the details of how to take a two-minute military shower.

"That's how the Freeman family does it," he finished.

Now, I might have handled the hot dog bun rule with grace, but nobody—NOBODY—messes with my bath! He soon discovered that even small honeybees can pack a stinger, too.

Disillusionment #3. Quite a few of our difficulties seemed to center around the basic problem of obtaining nourishment. I was fairly new to the art of cooking, but I felt comfortable with Mother's tortilla chicken casserole recipe. In an effort to avoid heating up the kitchen later in the day, I prepared the dish early in the morning and left it on the stove all day, waiting for our dinner that evening.

I was shocked when Scott refused to eat my first homemade meal because of a silly worry about botulism or something. I threw the casserole *and* the beautiful baking dish (a wedding gift) in the trash. If he wasn't going to eat m*y* dinner, I certainly was not going to wash the pan.

Our fights became so spectacular that I began giving them titles; more than a few of them had to do with meals. One in particular I dubbed, "The Salad Fight."

I had made a delicious three-course meal, but Scott complained about the lack of Thousand Island dressing on the table (the Arnold Family is blue cheese). As any dutiful wife would do, I quickly whipped up some homemade dressing, poured it on his salad, picked up the dish, and walked out the door to dump the entire concoction on the hood of his car. He in turn jumped up, ran outside, and washed the mess off the car with a water hose, then followed me into the house with the hose.

Then there was the "I Can Walk Home Faster Than You" fight. For this round, we decided to eat out, and one might think that would have eased the chances of another bout. However, we had a fuss in the car on the way to the restaurant, and each determined to play the martyr and walk home. We spent some time tossing the keys back and forth like a game of hot potato; the keys ended up on the pavement between us. We took off in a dead heat race-walk, huffing and puffing down Main Street until we both ran out of breath. We eventually made up out of sheer exhaustion.

That was our first year. In between our battles royale, we had some great times, too. Somebody with a twisted mind gifted us with a pet chinchilla which we dubbed Wilbur, and, like the children we were, we enjoyed letting him run loose in the duplex. However, when we needed to put him in his cage, we discovered what a fast little bugger he was. We chased him with coats and blankets, trying to get close enough to catch him in one without hurting him, but usually we were laughing so hard we gave up and left him to his own devices in our little duplex.

We planned all our college classes together so that I could ride with Scott on the back of his motorcycle—to Mother's terror. We were almost always late, and I'm sure we made quite a scene roaring down the highway while I held on to Scott with one hand and tried to keep the hot rollers in my hair with the other.

Winter came, bringing with it a rare Texas snow. It was great fun to build a snowman and to chase each other with snowballs. For our P.E. requirement, we learned square dancing because it was the only possible athletic activity we could do together. I was delighted to discover that my husband was as graceful as he was handsome, and we both loved dancing together—until the inevitable happened and he stepped on my toe and broke it.

In our first spring we planted a garden, and, like good Earth People, tried to avoid using insecticides. We read in the *Organic Gardener* that insects are repulsed by the odor of their own kind, so we experimented with several formulas for non-toxic insect repellent, each containing organically hand smashed bugs as the active ingredient. Then we tried picking the bugs off by hand.

We had planted thirty-two tomato plants which yielded 320 plump tomatoes, our best crop. We were thrilled until we realized neither of us liked tomatoes.

In our third year, Scott finished his degree, but fourteen springs would pass before I earned mine. After three years of work toward a degree in Music Education, I dropped out because I wanted to have a baby. As hard as it is to believe, we had a little trouble getting the project under way, but once I got the hang of it...

[Love] always protects, always trusts, always hopes,
always perseveres. Love never fails.
1 CORINTHIANS 13:7-8

36

Worm with a View

I was a new bride suffering from a bad case of homesickness when I began receiving Mother's blue tissue letters from Huemoz, Switzerland. The first one read:

Dearest Scott and Becky:

Your Daddy thinks he's died and gone to heaven, studying every day in the chapel overlooking a breathtaking view of the Rhone Valley below.

That's okay, Mom. Rub it in. I, on the other hand, am overlooking a breathtaking view of unbelievably smelly laundry as I wait for my twentieth load of clothes to dry at the corner laundromat.

At noon, the budding philosophers gather in small groups at various chalets where they enjoy simple meals and complicated conversations with people from all over the world.

Scott and I are enjoying complicated meals—trying to figure out just what it is I have cooked for dinner—and simple conversations such as, "This really tastes gross, Honey," and "Shut up and eat, Sweetheart."

In the afternoon, everyone works around the community, but it is simple work, such as gardening or housekeeping.

Did she define gardening and housework as simple!?

And me? I'm a stranger in a strange land when it comes to daily shopping in the French-speaking villages. The French are not noted for friendliness and warmth toward people who do not speak French. I, being a people person, have often had my feelings hurt.

I know exactly what you mean. When I go to the bakery at Piggly Wiggly and order a "Kro-sahwn," the lady just stares at me.

Our first encounter with Dr. Schaeffer helped a great deal, because he was so kind and personal in his lectures. Daddy and I, along with David and Rachel, often gather with others in the chapel for discussions with him. He's a small man with collar-length gray hair and a goatee. He wears knickers most of the time. The first evening, he sat on the rock hearth, smiled, and asked simply, "Where would you like to begin?"

Something unusual has happened in reference to our accommodations. As you know, we're staying in several rented rooms in a converted saw mill called the Rose Farm.

Yes, I remember. With Grandpa and little Luke, was it?

Well, the proprietors left for England and asked us to take care of renting out other rooms to L'Abri visitors. We find we're duplicating our discussion nights in Texas, but with friends from around the world.

Good thing the Swiss are noted for their chocolate.

A young family from Australia rents three rooms of the Rose Farm. I served them a good ol' Texas barbecue dinner, which their four-year-old Johnny referred to as "bah be que tea."

David has entered into a new stage of contentment, having found a small boy to aggravate. Would you believe David has a job harvesting grapes in the vineyard? Your little sister's summer job is also impressive. She's herding cows at Bonzon farm.

Well, that's certainly a departure from flipping burgers and pizzas.

Rachel may have left an interesting impression about Americans on a French gendarme.

I hate to show my ignorance, but what the Sam Hill is a gendarme? One of her cows, maybe?

One morning after lacing her hiking boots and double tying the knot, she discovered she had a bee in one of her boots. As she began the fastest un-lacing job on record, she heard an insistent knock on the door. Hopping across the floor, still unlacing as she hopped, she opened the door to see the stern face of the gendarme, who rattled off something in French.

So much for the cow theory.

It was quite a scene as she frantically gestured to her boot, making buzzing sounds like a bee, indicating to him that she didn't speak his language. He, in order to help her understand, spoke louder. I'm not sure she ever found out what his business was at the Rose Farm, but she took care of the first order of business—the bee came out of her boot somewhat worse for wear. She did not wait two seconds for revenge.

I'm assuming the gendarme was somewhat less insistent after that display.

The letter ended with love and inquiries about how Scott and I were getting along as man and wife, and how we liked college and our little white duplex. I let the paper-thin airmailed letter fall to my lap and sighed as I daydreamed of Heidi and goat's-milk cheese. It all sounded so Old World and interesting. How I did miss them!

Both of us especially missed the traditional Sunday lunches at my family's house after church. For some reason, Scott's longing for one of my mother's homecooked meals had increased passionately. But at least the weather had cooled, and I eventually managed to serve a piece of meat resembling a Sunday pot roast. And with time, Scott and I began to find a new closeness. We realized that we were becoming a family on our own, just the two of us.

A few weeks later, I realized just how serious my father's quest in Switzerland was. He had been considering leaving industry, to enter seminary to prepare for full-time ministry. Several people at L'Abri had encouraged him to go ahead with the idea. A visit in the home of Edith Schaeffer helped him make the final decision. Mother wrote details of that afternoon:

Mrs. Schaeffer opened the door of Chalet Le Melez, her warm smile welcoming Daddy and me for our afternoon appointment. I recall thinking, *This is a very pretty lady!* as the petite, delicate-boned woman directed us to a sofa in the softly lighted room. Outside, mist had settled over the mountains, but inside, the fire crackled its own welcome as Mrs. Schaeffer chatted quietly and poured tea into china cups. She made a charming picture, her long, dark hair pulled into a thick bun at the back of her head. A few grey strands added softness to a face that was aging gracefully.

She asked where we were from and how we were faring at L'Abri, and if there were anything she might do to make our stay all that we had hoped it would be.

This is a very nice lady, I decided as your dad began to explain to her his thoughts about leaving his job and going to seminary.

"How old are your children, George?" she asked.

"The two still at home are twelve and fourteen," he responded. Then Edith began to talk about their years in the work at L'Abri, and about its tremendous rewards, but also about its sacrifices.

"It was not easy for our children to almost always have guests in our home. If we had it to do over again," she smiled ruefully, "we would take more time off to be together, just with our family. Your children are at such a crucial age. What you are considering would mean a lot of change for your teenagers.

"There are many opportunities for ministry open for laymen that wouldn't require so much upheaval in your family. You may want to consider something of that sort for the time being, and think of full-time ministry when your children are on their own."

At the end of our thirty-minute appointment, we prepared to leave. Our hostess cheerfully ignored our preparations and two hours later, she walked us to the door and took thirty more minutes to say goodbye.

Your dad and I walked silently together down the mountain toward the Rose Farm each thinking our own thoughts. Finally, I broke the silence.

"Honey, we'll only get one chance at raising our kids."

"I know," he answered quietly. We reached the porch of the Rose Farm and he put his arm around me, pulling me close to him. "For now, I'm convinced—our *family* is our ministry."

Early in November, Mom, Dad, David, and Rachel dropped out of the sky at Dallas-Fort Worth airport, back into our arms with a bounce and a tumble, almost as if they had not been gone. The chocolate-covered discussion/comedy nights resumed, but with a new make up of our family. Scott and I were now enrolled in a Christian college, and he had especially come alive to history, to Schaeffer's writings, and to philosophy. It was great fun to observe my husband and my parents becoming even closer friends than before.

That is not to say there were no adjustments. No indeedy. We still laugh about our first camping trip together. One beautiful morning in South Carolina, Scott loaded the van while

Mother was in the bath house. As one might expect, Scott's idea of a tidy loading job and my mother's idea were as far removed from each other as the east is from the west, to borrow a phrase.

After an exchange of words that soon grew testy, we all climbed into the van and drove toward breakfast in stony silence. Once inside the cafe, we each ordered a hearty meal, and the waitress returned to the kitchen to fetch it. A minute later, Scott swallowed hard, excused himself and went out to the parking lot. Mother followed quickly behind him, dabbing at her eyes. I sat in the booth a minute or two longer, blinking back tears until I had to give it up and head for the ladies' room.

Daddy still laughs at the look on the waitress' face when she came to the table barely able to carry all the plates of food we had ordered and found one customer to eat it all.

There have been a few other scrapes over the years, most of which we can laugh about, and one or two which are filed under, "Painful—Handle with Care." But not long ago, after a fishing trip with Daddy and our boys, Scott characterized Daddy as a "best friend." And as for Mother, if anybody went after Scott to do him bodily harm, they would have to go over her first. And I think that might include me.

He will turn the hearts of the fathers to their children,
and the hearts of the children to their fathers.
MALACHI 4:6

Yummy Worms

My struggles in the kitchen continued for more years. Some days I was lucky just to find a clean pan. Because weenies cook faster than any other cut of meat and can be prepared in such a variety of ways, I gained the reputation of being the Weenie Queen. Weenies can be barbecued, beaned, or bunned in less than ten minutes. (The one drawback of any food is that it can also be burned.) This tended to be my preparation of choice, (not really by choice), and my budding family came to expect it. One morning I noticed five-year-old Zeke busily scraping a perfectly browned piece of toast over the trash can.

"Zeke, honey," I interrupted, "I didn't burn your toast today. You don't have to scrape it."

"Oh," he replied in surprise, "I thought we always had to whittle the toast."

Not long after that, I stepped into the kitchen to find it filled with smoke, our dinner a blackened ruin. At that moment, Zach strolled nonchalantly into the kitchen.

"M-m-m-m," he remarked, "smells like Mom's home cooking."

Sometimes I worry that my children will be invited to someone else's outdoor barbeque, by-pass the food, and pig-out on the charcoal.

Since I am told that confession is good for the soul, I feel compelled to confess one of the worst results I have ever had from a dish that I created. It was a horrible day when I realized that I had actually killed Zeke's pet with a casserole.

It began when Zeke left his pet ferret in my care for a few days while he went to visit my mother. She had volunteered to keep the children while I took a mini-course at East Texas State University. I tried to get comfortable with Mousequat, who was cute and fun to watch, but unfortunately smelled like stinky feet on a warm day. He also enjoyed taking playful but painful nips at our fingers at unpredictable intervals, a habit which made me more than a little nervous.

Choosing to conquer my ambivalent feelings toward Mousequat, I picked up a copy of the Ferret Lover's Brochure, although I realized that, realistically, my affections toward him would probably only reach the level of Ferret liker. I was not surprised to read that ferrets enjoy eating people food. Since I happened to have some leftovers in the fridge, I decided to give Mousequat a special treat—a generous portion of my Mexican casserole. I watched him eat enthusiastically, and feeling proud of my benevolence, I placed him gingerly back in his cage with nary a missing phalange on either of my hands.

The ferret brochure failed to mention one important item—ferrets cannot burp. The next morning Zeke returned and went to check on Mousequat. The animal was deceased, mysteriously swollen from the size of a paper towel tube to that of a hairy watermelon with eyes. An autopsy was required to eliminate the possibility of some contagious and fatal disease, and when the vet called with the results, I felt like a murderer. The verdict? Death by Mexican casserole gas.

Only we parents who have inadvertently run over or poisoned our child's pet can understand the kind of guilt and pain that comes with this experience. For weeks I could not bear to ask Zeke to so much as take out the trash. I was afraid he'd flash those sad brown eyes at me as if to say, "I may be in therapy when I'm thirty years old coping with the lack of trust in all my significant relationships, and you are asking me to take out the trash?"

Thankfully, Zeke took out his grief in the form of a letter to Bill Wallace, best-selling author of Zeke's favorite adventure books including *Beauty, Red Dog*, and, ironically, *Ferrets in the Bedroom, Lizards in the Fridge*. I will be forever grateful to this wonderful ex-teacher and principal turned children's writer, for helping to get me off the hook with the following letter to Zeke:

Dear Zeke:

I was sorry to hear about your ferret. But I wanted you to know that I *do* understand.

When I was about ten or so, my dad got me an Indigo Snake. (They are sort of an indigo blue color, but so dark that they look almost black.) I always liked snakes and he was real gentle—never tried to bite or anything like that. He was a great pet.

When I was twelve, I went to a boy's camp near Kerrville, Texas, called Rio Vista. While I was gone, Mom and Dad were "supposed" to take care of my snake. I was at camp for a month and after they picked me up, on the drive home, they told me that my snake had died. When I asked them what happened to it, they said they fed it a horny-toad and it must have gotten stuck or something.

It made me mad, because I knew you couldn't feed that snake horny-toads. I'd done it a couple of times, because that's all I could find to feed him, but I always watched to make sure he swallowed it head first. (That way the sharp horns fold down and don't puncture the snake's insides.) My snake probably swallowed it tail-first, and they didn't watch him. After thinking about it, I figured Mom and Dad probably just didn't know.

I guess I did a bunch of dumb stuff, too. I was always breaking things or doing something I wasn't supposed to (seems like I always got caught, too). But Mom and Dad were pretty good about forgiving me when I did dumb stuff. I figured the best thing to do was forgive them like they always seemed to forgive me.

Like I said, I understand how you feel. Hope you can forgive your mom. Sometimes, parents aren't much smarter than we are—but at least it sounds like she was trying to do the right thing.

Your friend,

Bill*

Obviously, this man cares about kids and I plan to buy every book he ever writes. And yes, I'm forgiven. We can even joke about it some now. Zeke got mad at Zachary not long ago and asked me if I had some leftover Mexican casserole he could feed his brother.

Now comes the truly amazing part of this chapter. Believe it or not, I found myself looking down the gun barrel of an absurd destiny. I would one day become a food caterer.

Sacrifices and . . . burnt offerings . . . you did not desire, nor were you pleased with them.

HEBREWS 10:8

❧

*Used by permission

46

Wormy Puppies

Our dogs have eaten so many of the children's pet chicks and bunnies that I have a generic name for them: Dog Food.

I have learned not to get attached to pets, except perhaps an occasional dog. I recently read an article entitled, "Endangered Species: Millions of dogs and cats vanish every year. Will yours be next?" I'm ashamed to confess, my sinful nature leaped with hope.

Like all mothers when confronted by their child holding a puppy in their arms and begging with heart and soul to be allowed to keep it, I at first refuse to even *think* about it. Gradually, however, I am worn down, and they are allowed to keep the animal, with the standard provision.

"*You* are going to be the one to take care of him. *Do you hear me?* You've got to feed him, and keep him *outside!* And if he makes a single mess in the house, he's a goner and you may be, too!"

The standards are rigorously met for about a week, but by the end of the second week, the dog thinks your king size bed was installed just for him. Furthermore, if Momma didn't feed him, the animal would starve. Because Momma is the one who feeds him most, the animal has become attached to her, and inevitably, vice versa. I know this not only from personal experience but also from memories of pets that I and my siblings were supposed to take care of as we grew up.

Most of the time, our pets were cats, most notably a homely tri-colored female named Midnight and a handsome figure of a male we called Wallace. But my brother David was the cat charmer in the family, and, unless Midnight was in a family way (homely or not, she always seemed to find husbands), I did not generally become emotionally involved with the cats. They so obviously preferred David I knew it could only end in heartbreak.

On one occasion, Mother was in a hurry to leave the house for an appointment and quickly started the station wagon for the trip. As she drove down the drive, she heard a terrible commotion—an unnerving series of bumps and howls—howls she recognized as being feline, and probably coming from Midnight.

Just as Mother was about to go in the house and call Daddy to see if it would hurt the car to drive it with a cat in the fan belt, Midnight shot out from under the car, a one-inch strip of hair neatly shaved down the entire length of her back.

Soon after, Midnight took up residence elsewhere, and within a year, David brought Wallace home. He gazed beseechingly at Mother holding the yellow kitten in his arms. The story had the usual ending.

"You are going to take care of him. *Do you hear me?*"

By this time, we had been through several cats, and after one of them had decided he much preferred a nice, soft, carpeted corner of the bedroom to a litter box, his successors seemed to think this entitled them to the same privilege. With Wallace, David was given to understand that he had better teach him to use a litter box, and that every single mishap would be David's responsibility.

When the inevitable happened, Mother dispatched David to the bedroom corner with paper towels, soapy water, and a scrub brush. She assumed all was going as it should. However, she walked into the kitchen a few minutes later to observe David at the kitchen sink watching the garbage disposal. A strange odor filled the room. So intent was he that he jumped when Mother yelped in horror, her worst fears confirmed.

"Huh? What!" David responded, trying to figure out what all the fuss was about. After all, garbage is garbage, isn't it?

After Wallace went to cat heaven, I began to lay the groundwork for getting a pet of my own to love. I was not about to consider a cat, knowing I couldn't compete with David for its affection, but I began to read the newspaper ads to see what kind of puppies might be "free to a good home." I persuaded Mother that it was *my* turn to have a pet, since all the cats had ended up being David's. Besides, my fourteenth birthday was coming up and I couldn't think of another thing I wanted except a puppy.

At last, her sense of guilt conquered, we acquired a six-week old, half-breed Pomeranian. When we brought him home, Mother decided he looked like a thistle, a round ball of blonde fur with limpid Pomeranian eyes staring out at us. I named him Angel, Rachel named him Po Po, and David named him Weezer. It's no small wonder he was confused from the start.

We began the process of trying to housebreak the new puppy, but he couldn't quite seem to grasp what we had in mind. If he had not been adorable, he would have been gone. He was even allowed to stay on after he pulled his crowning stunt.

Mother had trimmed the fat off a ham and placed the trimmings in a plastic bag in the trash under the sink. She then left home for several hours, leaving Po Po to his own devices.

When she returned and walked in the front door, Po Po came bounding joyfully to meet her, a little heavy on his feet. In fact, he was about twice as round as he had been when Mother left a few hours earlier. Not only that, what little remained of the ham trimmings were strewn across the kitchen into the living room. About the time Mother grasped what had happened, Po Po keeled over at her feet.

You might think she would have felt it served him right, but she had a weakness for sick or injured animals. She grabbed him up, ran to the car, and roared to the vet's office, taking the corners on two wheels, not knowing if Po Po was alive or dead. She charged into the pet doctor's examining room, explaining as she went.

When she laid Po Po on the vet's examining table, he struggled woozily to his feet, and after a shot of morphine, got to spend the night in style at the animal hospital. After paying the bill, Mother was careful to remember that even though Po Po was too dumb to potty train, he was smart enough to open the kitchen cabinet with his paw and get into the trash.

As for me, I had imagined that Angel-Weezer-Po Po would follow me about the house, snuggle in my arms, sleep at the foot of my bed, and learn to love me above all others. However, he had a tendency to run the other direction when he saw me coming, and I *could* hold him in my arms, but I had to face him away from me and ignore the growling and snapping that went on. I was the only member of the family so honored, and the family would hoot and howl at the spectacle while I insisted, "See? He just *loves* me!"

He was not without his redeeming features, however, and we still laugh about some of his weird antics. We could take a towel, drag it on the floor in front of him and he would immediately latch onto it with his teeth, flatten out like a platypus, and allow us to pull him all over the house, which sent the entire family into hysterics.

He had deeply-ingrained sheep-herding instincts and spent many happy hours trying to herd beetles across our patio, his nose to the concrete as if it were the most important task in the world. Unfortunately, he had the same tendency to herd cars on busy streets every time he managed to sneak out a carelessly opened door.

Other larger, wiser dogs would have been terrified at the cars whizzing by at peak traffic time, but not Po Po. You would have thought he was a traffic cop, the way he worked the middle of the street. Usually, someone in our neighborhood who had come to know who this half-witted half-breed belonged to would call, and we would risk life and limb to dash into the traffic and drag him home.

Po Po had a number of besetting sins. If we had guests, he was so deliriously happy to see them that he made it almost impossible for *us* to visit with them. If we put him outside when guests were coming, he ran back and forth across the yard, barking a high-pitched bark that drove the neighbors to contemplate giving him a ground glass hamburger patty.

Po Po dearly loved sneaking out any open door and, on two occasions, Mother had to post signs on telephone posts and in grocery stores and pay a ten dollar reward to get him back.

One morning, I was standing with a group of friends on the high school grounds waiting for the bell to ring. I looked up to see Po Po bouncing across the grounds toward me with Mother in hot pursuit behind him wearing a bright red robe and curlers in her hair. I pretended I didn't know either of them and dashed into the building.

Meanwhile, Po Po was approaching two years old and was not yet potty trained, which is all right for a child but not for a dog. He was too dumb to potty train, yet after he had soiled the carpet, he would stand just inside the door of the room, peek around the corner, and watch for Mother to come after him with the newspaper.

Po Po's failings eventually ended his membership in our family. We were at wits end about his failure to accomplish the most elemental of skills, and we were about to get a houseful of new carpet. What to do, what to do!

On the day the carpet was to be installed, I went out the door to go to school and left it open, as I almost always did. Po Po was out the door like a shot. Mother responded in her usual way.

"Grab him, Becky! PO PO, COME BACK HERE!" and she ran for the car keys, wearing her red robe and curlers, while I cringed. As Po Po rounded the corner, she skidded to a stop at the car, leaned against it and watched him disappear from sight. For a moment she seemed lost in thought. Then she calmly found the house slipper she had lost on the way to the car, walked back into the house, shut the door, and poured herself a cup of coffee.

We always hoped Po Po found his way to a good home where people knew better than we did how to train half-witted, beautiful little dogs. He was so charming that we had no doubt he would find a good home, at least for a while.

My husband has given his heart to one—and only one—dog. Their story is bittersweet.

In the rural area where we lived, a little boy had been bitten by a wild puppy, and in order for the boy to avoid painful rabies shots, Scott found himself facing the terrible chore of finding the litter of puppies, destroying them and sending them to the state capitol for testing.

Scott took his gun and did what had to be done. It was much like the tearful scene from "Old Yeller." As he finished the hateful job, the stray mother of the pups walked to Scott, gazed sadly at the gun barrel, waiting with resignation. The executioner wiped away a tear, stooped down and put his arms around the little mutt and tenderly apologized, stroking her rough fur.

From that moment, she became his faithful, loving "Lady," following him everywhere he went and being rewarded royally with the choicest of morsels. But then, as animal stories so often end, he accidentally ran over her two years later. He buried her near the edge of a lake in one of her favorite resting spots. For the next few days when I looked out the window I often saw Scott sitting near her grave, his head on his knees.

I'll leave it to theologians to debate whether or not animals have souls. Yet, I have always believed that since Heaven is full of everything wonderful, God will have the pets we came to love waiting there to welcome us. Don't you?

But the poor man had nothing
except one little ewe lamb he had bought.
He raised it, and it grew up with him and his children.
It shared his food, drank from his cup and even slept in his
arms. It was like a daughter to him.

2 SAMUEL 12:3

Wander Worms

M y sister Rachel and I are just concluding a long distance
telephone conversation. It is 1983, and she has called
from her college dorm in Kansas to my parents' house in Texas.
There are moving boxes all around me.

"It's going to be especially hard for you to let them go, I
know," she sympathized.

"I can hardly stand to think about it," I responded. "But I
guess they know what they're doing."

This kind of conversation usually takes place among parents
of college-aged kids who have decided to see the world on a
bicycle and a shoe string. In our case, however, we were discussing our forty-five-year-old parents. Daddy quit a secure job in
aerospace and accepted an unlikely position as director of
Academic Services at a Christian university in Virginia. Never

mind that he had never worked in academia or ministry before. He had always dreamed of it, and now it looked like he was going to do it. At a third less salary. And, he was planning to take the grandmother of my children with him.

I felt a strange parental concern, as if my traditional mother and father were suddenly buying lovebeads and a Harley—off to make peace, not war.

There in my parents' empty house, I said good-bye to Rachel and slowly unplugged the phone and placed it in a cardboard box for the movers. The time had come for Daddy to begin another adventure. This time it would be Virginia, over fifteen hundred miles away.

It might as well be Europe again, I thought sadly. *Except this time, they won't be coming back soon.*

My folks pulled out of the driveway after several heart-rending embraces and farewells. Scott and I had volunteered to do some last minute cleanup in the house on the cul-de-sac in Suburbia. It was now a huge empty shell with nothing but floods of childhood memories bouncing off every freshly painted wall and undraped window.

Zachary was four at the time and couldn't understand where his beloved grandparents were going and why their house had nothing in it. Zeke, at two, realized that even the toy box in the hall closet was gone.

"Mommy," Zach asked with moisture glistening on his long dark lashes, "let's pray for Jesus to bring Granny and Daddy George back to their house now."

I grabbed him in a bear hug before he could see my tears spill down my face and onto his soft knit shirt.

Yes, it was going to be very hard to let them go.

When my parents moved to Virginia, a friend gave them a verse of Scripture, Malachi 4:2, "You will go forth and skip about like calves from the stall" (NASB). From the sound of Mother's voice over the long distance wire, the prophet had proved to be one hundred percent correct. It hadn't taken them any time at all to begin kicking up their respective hooves.

"Becky," she giggled, "Daddy and I have done it again! You know we're looking for a church home here. Well, last Sunday we visited a lovely, mission-oriented Sunday School class. They were discussing a dinner they were going to prepare for a group from Jungle Aviation and Radio Service, and they were looking for volunteers to help with the meal. When several people responded, the announcer said, 'We really appreciate you helping to cook and serve those people in JAARS.'"

"Now I ask you. Could *you* have kept a straight face?"

The laughter we shared eased the ache in my heart from knowing they were no longer close by where I could drop by with the kids. To further lift my spirits, I hung up the phone and decided to take Zach and Zeke to the mall for lunch.

I headed for the cafeteria where Mother and I used to meet for lunch on an almost weekly basis to talk and coo over the grandbabies. As I pushed two toddler-filled highchairs through the line, the uniformed lady on the other side of the counter asked, "Would you like a salad?" It was a simple question, really.

Mother and I always split a spinach salad, an order of fish and, of course, chocolate pie. Who would share my lunch this day? My two and three-year-old sons were *not* fish and spinach lovers.

In full view of several surprised blue-haired ladies, I pulled Zach and Zeke out of their highchairs, swallowed the lump in my throat and decided we'd better go to the corn dog booth instead.

A couple of weeks later, Mother wrote of *her* first experience with lunch alone at a cafeteria in Virginia. She had forced herself to go through the line, but as she pushed her tray along, an elderly lady moved along just ahead of her. When the woman neared the cash register, the cashier looked at her and at Mother.

"Are you two together?" she asked.

The elderly lady looked startled and answered, "Oh no! All my friends are dead."

Mother said she almost wailed, "And all *my* friends are in Texas!"

At the corn dog stand, I wiped ketchup and mustard off the boys and supplied each with a lollipop. I then moved steadily down the mall, children in tow, trying not to think of Mother. But then I passed a dress shop, and found myself suppressing a giggle as another "mother story" began to elbow its way into my mind.

On a warm summer afternoon, Mother was hurriedly shopping for a pair of walking shorts at the largest and most elegant mall in the city. The moving van was on its way to the house in Arlington to haul their belongings to Virginia. Time was of the essence. She developed a system of grabbing three or four pair of shorts from the rack, running into the dressing room and trying them on, throwing her lightweight jersey skirt back on, running out and grabbing more shorts, and returning to the dressing room.

She finally found a pair she liked, ran back to the rack to return the rejects, and noticed a young serviceman looking her over with interest.

Hmmm, old girl, she thought to herself, *maybe you haven't lost all your charm yet!* She dashed to the cash register stand, which happened to face broad doors leading into the length of the mall. As she made out her check, a woman moved close to her, her eyes wide in horror.

"Did you know your skirt is up in back?" she whispered. When Mother checked, the entire back of her skirt was rolled up neatly around the waist band. No wonder the young soldier had been intrigued.

Still smiling to myself, I was yanked back to the present world by a scream of outrage from Zeke. Thinking he must surely have lost a leg in an escalator, I felt somewhat relieved to discover he was staring in disbelief at an empty lollipop stick. Zach observed Zeke's outburst with both cheeks bulging, his eyes oozing innocence.

Taking my life in my hands, I went in after one of the candies and popped it into Zeke's gaping maws with nary a thought for germs. Peace descended, and Zach decided to steer the subject away from his "breaking and entering" charge.

"Can we go fwimmin' when we get home?" he asked. My mind wandered from taking the boys swimming, to swimsuits in general, to a specific swimming suit—a green bikini—worn with fur-lined boots. Another Mother story.

This time we were vacationing at Holly Lake, our favorite family vacation spot in the piney woods of East Texas. One morning Mother decided to enjoy her coffee on the porch of our rented mobile home. We kids disappeared into the woods to do our own thing, and she propped up her feet, soaking up the peace and quiet. Before long, a small dog, which looked more like a rag mop than a dog, frolicked down the path, up onto the porch and gave Mother his "jumpin', lickin', dawg" greeting. Scarcely had she wiped the slobber off her feet when the dog's mistress fell into view, breathless with apology as she attempted to corner her "naughty boy."

Mother guessed the woman to be about her age, but while Mother was clad in her robe and no makeup, this lady was clad (just barely) in a lime-green bikini and fur-lined boots. The extent of her tan indicated the bikini was her most frequent costume, which indicated to Mother that they might not have a lot in common. Even so, they struck up a conversation in which Mother became the primary listener.

The topic fell upon the lady's daughter, of whom she was extremely proud because she worked as a hostess in a famous nightclub (now defunct) in Dallas where she was required to wear a small costume resembling a small rabbit. Mother's new acquaintance expected to marry again soon, and her fiancé had a motto: "You can tell a successful man by how expensive his toys are." Furthermore, she owned her own business in Dallas, and she knew the score.

"I don't hire young, cute women," she declared, "They're nothing but trouble in an office. They fuss with each other and the men can't keep their minds on their work. I hire ugly, old, women." She then shrewdly looked Mother over, sized her up and paid her the supreme compliment: "I'd hire you."

My mouth turned up at the corners recalling how many times we three kids had teased our pretty mother about being an "ugly old woman" as a result of that famous encounter. Every time she repeated the story, she laughed hardest of all.

Sighing, I gave up on the mall and loaded my sticky, tired, whiney kids into the car and drove home. Happily, a letter from Virginia waited in the mailbox.

Once I had the boys down for a nap, I poured myself a cup of hazelnut-flavored coffee, and settled down in a rocker to read the letter while I "celebrated the moments of my life." Unless you are a mother of two pre-schoolers who are down for a nap, you will never understand the true ecstasy of a moment of quiet, a cup of coffee, and something interesting to read.

Dearest Scott, Becky, Zach, and Zeke,

Though we ache to see you all, it helps to have Rachel living with us now. Your little sister likes Virginia so well, she says we can go back to Texas if we want to—she's staying!

We are coming to love Virginia, though. We're an hour's drive from colonial Williamsburg and you know how much Daddy loves "hysterical markers." He also enjoys his work at the university—using his business skills and enjoying deep fellowship with other believers. I'm enjoying being more involved in your dad's work than I could be when he was in industry. I'm leading the University Women's Organization, which is fine. I really enjoy working with women. In fact, I love women. Of course, I love men, too. And kids aren't too bad when they're cleaned up.

Our little twenty-year-old bungalow overlooks a tree-filled yard and a gorgeous lake! The only problem is that we only have one bathroom. This is causing some stress in our marriage because Daddy rarely remembers to adjust the faucet back to "bath" after his showers, and I rarely remember to check it until I am on my hands and knees to clean out the tub and fill it for my bath. When I turn the faucet on, I am immediately doused and you know how I hate to wash my well-sprayed hairdo more than once a week!

We're still looking for a church home. Last Wednesday evening we visited another church and arrived during a video series on marriage. Since we've been at our marriage quite a while, I had a little trouble paying attention. At the end of the video, a questionnaire was passed out about the material just covered. I left mine in my lap, but Daddy began to fill his in by reflex. I gouged him in the ribs with my elbow.

"Good grief, George!" I whispered. "We've been married almost thirty years. What are you doing filling that out?"

He grinned, but finished the questionnaire. Church was dismissed and we returned home to our bungalow, where I proceeded to get ready for bed by starting my bath water, and your father went to the bedroom to turn down the covers. Once again, he had left the shower lever on, and I caught it full blast on my teased bun. Catching my breath, I rocked back on my heels and yelled, "I want a divorce!"

After a moment of silence, I heard a tap on the bathroom door, and opened it to find Daddy standing there in his pajamas, already cuddling his bedtime pillow. His expression was holy, if not holier than thou.

"If you had filled out your questionnaire like *I* did," he said ever so kindly, "that wouldn't have bothered you."

I must confess, I almost bludgeoned him to death with his own feather pillow.

By the way, Rachel is dating a tall, slender, young man with a shock of dark hair, nice blue eyes and a jaunty nose. His name is Scott St.John-Gilbert, no less.

I folded the letter and laughed out loud. Only my mother, a true writer, would use the word "jaunty" to describe someone's nose. A true word nut and reigning family champion of Scrabble,™ she recently described herself as having trouble "ambulating" without her glasses.

"Mother," I said to her over the miles, "why is it that other people simply *walk* while you insist on "*ambulating*"? With that thought, I jauntily ambulated out of my rocker, refreshed by the news and the giver thereof.

My parents remained and prospered in Virginia for nearly three years. During this time, I gave birth to Rachel Praise. They came to Texas for her birth, and we managed to see them fairly often, but we made huge sacrifices to be together.

Daddy's job, though rewarding, was beginning to take its toll. I was amused by the latest story Mother shared via Ma Bell.

During Daddy's career in industry, he had worked with programs involving millions of dollars, yet he almost always had been able to leave problems at the office at the end of the day and sleep like a baby. However, the first outdoor commencement and reception he supervised almost put him under.

He had scheduled the celebration to be out-of-doors, but nature had scheduled a hurricane not far away. The weatherman predicted high winds for their area. Daddy and his committee debated about what to do and finally decided to pray a lot and go ahead as planned.

"During the reception," Mother wrote, "I saw at least one paper plate filled with barbecue and potato salad become airborne and land smack in the back of a lady's head."

Later came the lighting of the Eternal Flame. The chancellor of the university was supposed to do this, but it eventually took Daddy, a professor, and a blow torch to accomplish the task.

The university has an annual spiritual awareness event called "Seven Days Ablaze," in which the pace equals any Daddy ever knew in industry. By the end of the week, Daddy came home dragging his coat, his tie untied, and generally looking to be on his last leg.

"I hate to make a negative confession," he told Mother, "but the registrar has crashed and burned during Seven Days Ablaze."

At the end of three years, my parents felt the Lord was calling them to, as Steve and Annie Chapman sing, "Turn Their Hearts Toward Home." There were several signals. First of all, it began to be obvious that my grandparents' time on earth was nearing an end. Our Nonnie had suffered a heart attack and stroke, Grandad Arnold had to have his carotid arteries reamed out, and Grandmother Arnold had been diagnosed with Alzheimer's disease.

When Daddy's former employer offered him a good job back in Texas, I was thrilled. I had recently discovered that baby number four was on its way and I felt a renewed need to have my parents close. There is indeed a time to be born and a time to die, and it is a great blessing to be surrounded by loved ones for either event.

It may be that Zach made the final impact upon their decision to return. Learning to read and write in first grade, he sent Mother the following note: "Grannie, my cat got run over. I am so sad."

She wrote back, "I'm ready to bust out of this house and run all the way to Highway 64, hitchhiking to Texas yelling, "'I'm coming, Zachary! Grannie's coming!'"

So it was that three-year-old Zachary, who had wanted to pray for Granny and Daddy George to come back home immediately, got his prayer answered by age six. As Granny and Daddy George pulled into our driveway, he and Zeke and two-year-old Rachel held up the welcome home banner. I, heavy with child, waddled into Mother's arms with a sense of deep gratitude and relief, and made her an offer she couldn't resist.

"Wanna go out to lunch and split a spinach salad?"

There is a time for everything,
and a season for every activity under heaven:
a time to be born and a time to die,
a time to plant and a time to uproot.
ECCLESIASTES 3:1-2

Fried Worms, Anyone?

Gabe, our grand finale, was just one year old when the recession of the eighties caused his daddy's construction business to evaporate before our very eyes. I had always envisioned that I would have the privilege of being a full-time wife and mother like my own mother had been. If I had been raising a family during the sixties as she had, perhaps it might have worked out that way. But I entered upon my career as a wife and mother in the inflationary seventies and eighties, and like so many other couples, my husband and I discovered that two incomes were now essential to provide even a minimum standard of living for our family of six.

His new job managing a private lake with a social club meant we would have a modest home provided for us on the lake, which was a dream come true for our boys. Unfortunately, it also required that someone cook for the clubhouse socials. You can guess who that someone was.

Thankfully, the children could often accompany me and were sometimes even a big help in the kitchen. I did very well generally, which is one more reason why I never doubt the existence of God, but I do remember preparing for an elegant candlelight dinner and actually misplacing a pan of marinating pork chops. I frantically searched the kitchen with no luck and finally realized guests were arriving for their pre-dinner socializing. Providentially, I had enough individual servings of prime rib in the freezer that I could go straight to Plan B. Just as I began to prepare the prime rib, I heard a female voice that resembled the quality and volume of a pipe organ behind me.

"Becky, Dahling, you *do* create the most interesting centerpieces!" I followed her soprano laugh to the dining room, where, in the middle of the romantic candles and cascading floral arrangement, sat a plastic industrial dishpan full of raw red pork chops aesthetically floating in teriyaki marinade. It looked more like I was hostessing a hog-killing than an elegant buffet. Noting the chairman of the social committee in her basic black with pearls trying gallantly to sound amused while nauseated, my faith was strengthened, not only in God, but in womankind. I discreetly transported the giant tub to the kitchen while muttering to myself, "Nothing like raw unidentifiable animal parts floating in a dishpan to whet appetites, I always say."

That was the worst that ever happened, but there were many near misses of which my clientele remained blissfully unaware. The kids love to tell about my famous wild rice. I, for one, think that weevils definitely resemble coarse ground black pepper when mixed with exotic grains of cooked rice. So, apparently, did my dinner guests. All except one man who made a neat pile of them in the corner of his empty plate. I thought it was pretty rude of him, too, when everyone else ate their weevils as polite dinner guests should. Zach added insult to injury by referring to my dish as Mom's Famous Wild Life Rice.

And of course there was the luncheon where Gabriel investigated a lettuce leaf slowly crawling off the salad bar and found a fat green worm at play. Not the sort of thing we could expect Gabe to keep under his hat, now could we?

After some time, and for no obvious reason, I began to have the feeling that I had better get out of catering while the getting was good. I examined all my abilities and assets, and realized that my resumé consisted almost entirely of an uncanny ability to attract creeping, crawling things. I even considered a possible market for fried worms. After all, in some countries people enjoy chocolate dipped ants, and in Texas, some people eat rattle snakes, though I do believe they cook them first.

My desire had been to go back to college when Gabe started kindergarten, but when faced with the possibility of a lifetime in catering, Scott and I began to seriously discuss the feasibility of my starting back to school as soon as possible. We decided it really would be in the best interest of humanity and the animal kingdom to get me out of food service entirely, though we had no idea how we could swing it. By the grace of God, Scott found a different job which did not require that his wife cook, and we began to look for another place to live.

I am fully convinced
that no food is unclean in itself.
ROMANS 14:14

The Worm Farm

"C ome on in!" I flung the door of our new home wide to admit Mary, my friend who had cheerfully dedicated almost a week of her busy life to helping me look for a house in our price range. Miraculously, we had actually found one.

"Be careful of that little electrical wire hanging over your head there," I said as I took her hand to guide her past the tools heaped in the middle of the floor of the new home we had actually bought—a thirty-year-old, 850-square-foot cabin on a huge wooded lot on the banks of the exclusive private lake where we had previously been employed.

I could almost see Mary's logical mind re-counting the six members of our family and the one bedroom in the cabin. She looked as if her knees might buckle.

"Oh, Mary," I tried to reassure her, "We just couldn't uproot the kids, especially the boys. After living in the country, we'd go bonkers living in town. So there's only one bedroom for the time being. We'll stack the kids to the ceiling in bunks and Scott and I can sleep on the couch in the living area—just for the time being. Look at that view!" I desperately tried to communicate my vision of "what was to be."

"Did you ever see such a gorgeous lake? And right out our picture window! Look at the size of those cypress trees! Running water? Well, of *course* we have running water, silly!" To myself I said, "*hot* water will come later."

"A bathtub? Not yet, but that tin box-looking thing in the corner is a shower...sort of. Did I mention the view? I did, huh?"

"Smell? Oh, that. Scott's working on the septic system." The expression on Mary's face could only be described as one of shock, and I detected a fading in my own rose-colored glasses. "Look at that spectacular bluejay!" I ventured. "Noise? Oh, the barking! Daisy finally had her puppies. Just eleven."

Mary clutched her adam's apple and this time her knees actually did buckle. Even with the shock of seeing the cabin for the first time, it seemed to me she was taking the news about Daisy's pups awfully seriously, but then I realized the source of her pain.

"Oh my goodness! I forgot to tell you to duck! We're hanging our clothes on that piece of rope 'til Scott gets a closet built." And so went the tour until the brilliant orange sun settled into the coolness of the lake in front of us with an almost audible sigh. A gorgeous display, but even that brought its own set of problems.

"Yes, it *is* getting dark in here," I admitted. "No overhead lighting yet, but it can be so cozy sitting around the glow of a fireplace in the dark, don't you think?" *Oh gosh! I'm beginning to sound like Pollyanna on amphetamines. I've got to get her out of here!* I gently took Mary by the arm to avoid shocking her further, possibly into catatonia.

"Let's go down to the lake and watch the sunset!"

I wish I could say that I felt as optimistic as I had tried to sound about our decision to live in the old cabin and renovate as we could afford the time and money. Our family of six had reached its maximum number, but it was rapidly increasing in sheer volume. Scott, my give-me-wide-open-spaces husband, is six feet tall with shoulders that strain his new business suit. Zach and Zeke were ten and nine and showing every promise of being at least as big as their Dad. Rachel was a petite six and Gabriel, three. It looked to be a long winter.

The hardest thing I remember about the winter of '89 was the tin, box-looking thing called a shower. It was inevitable that we would have trouble with each other. Under the best of circumstances, I do not like a shower. It is impossible to shave one's legs in any sort of lady-like posture while standing. However, the shower did not like me, either. All the other members of the family could bathe in the thing without any great problem, but almost as soon as I turned on the spigot, the drain would stop up and water would begin to flow out onto the bathroom floor. This did not happen to anyone else in the family.

I finally developed a technique which involved turning on the spigot for only a few seconds at a time, and so managed to survive the first weeks of winter taking showers while my heart longed for a long soak in a hot tub with a good book. I even attempted to re-create the feeling by sitting close to the furnace with my feet in a pan of hot water. Definitely not the same.

Scott was determined to solve the mystery of why the shower overflowed only when *I* was in it. He decided to observe my routine. I entered the shower, hit the spigot, got halfway through my scrub down, and sure 'nuff, water began to lap up and over the edge of the tin box. I heard Scott muttering. Poking his head through the curtain, he peered at my feet incredulously.

"Becky," he asked, "You're not standing on the drain, are you?"

When the arctic winds began to blow across the East Texas lake, I had moments when I felt it might have been wiser to have taken our chances on going bonkers in the city, and I thanked God for my El Salvador experience.

Whatever my doubts were, I had to keep up a good front because my claustrophobic husband was about to go crazy. During the winter months, he mostly just came home from work and curled up in a fetal position, biting his fingernails while his eyes darted back and forth with a look of caged terror. The children didn't seem to mind the close quarters as they jumped, wrestled, and crawled over him.

On his better days, he would uncurl himself and do a bit of remodeling. Gabriel, too young to appreciate "what was to be," found this upheaval to be very unsettling. Finally, as he surveyed yet another wall his Daddy had demolished, he gathered his coat in hand.

"I'm ready to go home now," he announced.

"Gabe, this *is* home…remember? We have a lake and everything! Just look at the view!"

He was not to be consoled. "But this house is broken!" he wailed.

When spring sprang, however, the whole family changed its tune. Gabriel discovered the incredible world of frogs, not to mention chameleons, snakes, and skunks—a veritable worm farm. Zach and Zeke spent their days exploring the woods and fishing for crappie. Rachel became a waterbug and begged to swim every day. Scott began to heal through nature therapy: bird watching. He would arise early on weekends and, with a cup of coffee and his binoculars, settle into his recliner and watch the birds in quiet fascination.

By spring, my dream too, had come true. I had a real bathtub—almost better than the view, even with the dogwood in bloom. And with the cabin almost inhabitable, we could begin to turn our thoughts toward another dream—getting Mom through college.

O Sovereign Lord, you are God!
Your words are trustworthy,
and you have promised these good things to your servant.
Now be pleased to bless the house of your servant...
and with your blessing
the house of your servant will be blessed forever.
2 SAMUEL 7:28-29

Awkworm Situations

Have you ever had one of those experiences when you wish you could just disappear? Often I want to do that, especially when I find myself in a situation where it is rude, sacrilegious, or unthinkable to do what I have an uncontrollable urge to do—laugh. Scott has been so embarrassed by my outbursts in the past that he is now skittish about sitting next to me in any formal situation. It's an awful affliction, and I honestly don't know what to do about it.

It's pure agony to try to suppress the laughter. I bite into the flesh of my cheeks, cover my mouth and nose, and still...I somehow manage to blow. I once got tickled at a prayer meeting—not a light-hearted women's prayer meeting, but a serious, down-on-your-knees, prayer meeting in Glen Eyrie, Colorado. A nice young fellow was leading us in prayer, and I know this is no excuse, but he had the most nasal tone I have ever heard from the mouth of a human being.

On top of "the voice" came a string of requests addressed to the Almighty with an incredible preponderance of "eths." "Dear Father, blesseth Thoueth the meetingeth hereeth in our presenceth." The giggle bubbled up from the belly, threatening to pour forth through my mouth and nose. I slapped my mouth and held my nose. The sound I issued resembled a suckling pig. My shoulders began to shake, and I could sense Scott's presence seething next to me. Then, there was a blessed pause, and I thought I might be saved. But no. "Andeth ifeth it pleaseth Thine heart, maketh useth…" At that point I began to wheeze. There was to be no mercy. It waseth the prayer that hadeth no endeth.

Finally, I grabbed a Kleenex™, feigned being overcome with emotion, and ran out the door pretending to sob. Actually, by the time I got out of there, I was laughing so hard I did began to weep. After the service, Scott was livid with shame and embarrassment. I apologized profusely, but then I noticed how Scott's nostrils flared when he got mad and how his ears twitched when his voice got loud, and I found myself once again in a situation where fools laugh and angels fear to tread.

Everyone I'm sure has had the experience of going into the wrong restroom a time or two. Granted, there are some of us who have done this a bit more often than others, but my mild-mannered, deeply spiritual father has the prize for the most embarrassing example of this awkward situation. The horrible part is that he was stuck in the women's restroom at no less than the prestigious Dallas Theological Seminary where he was taking a layman's course. He came to realize that something was awry when he saw a woman's purse drop down in the stall next to him. All he could think of was how he would explain his presence to Dr. Howard Hendricks if he should come strolling down the hallway just as Daddy ran in panic out of the ladies' room.

Of all of the awkward places to laugh, funerals must certainly top the list. I'm sure even the most godly of ministers have had funny situations occur at that delicate time. Perhaps a bit of laughter is a good thing at some funerals, particularly when a person has lived a full life, to a ripe old age, for the Lord. Then the service takes on an almost festive feeling, a celebration of joy at the beloved's homegoing. It would have been nice if that had been the reason for the laughter of Jamie, my willowy blond blue-eyed cousin who is my opposite in looks but my clone in nature.

Jamie went alone to the funeral of a friend of hers, a young man she had known in high school. She arrived early, taking a seat near the front of the chapel in the funeral parlor. Just seeing the coffin brought a wave of emotion, and she dabbed at her eyes with a tissue. People began filing in until the chapel was almost full.

Mmm, Jamie thought to herself, *I don't recognize any of Jeff's friends here. Well, it's been a few years since I've seen Jeff. Friends change with time.*

After an opening hymn, the minister ascended the pulpit and began the eulogy. "We are gathered here today to honor the memory of Mr. Samuel K. Whitzle..."

Mr. Who-zle? Jamie thought, *Oh, my goodness sakes alive! I'm at the wrong funeral. I am sitting here grieving for a person I have never had the privilege of meeting. And Mrs. Whitzle must wonder why a tall blond girl on the front row is grieving for her husband. I've got to find a way to get out of here.* In the end, Jamie used the old "overcome with emotion so I have to leave" ploy, covering her convulsions with her damp tissue as she left out the back door.

Shortly thereafter, we put our heads together during a visit and exchanged ways to back out of a variety of tight spots. Jamie owes me for the sobbing technique, but I owe her for helping me to perfect the stalling procedure that has saved my life a time or two. She developed it one day at a swimming pool with her beautiful little girl. A woman came up, complimented her child, and asked what her name was.

"Well, I drew a blank," Jamie described the situation, "How could I tell a stranger I suddenly could not remember the name of my own child? So I stalled, 'You mean that little girl in the green bathing suit? The one with the big blue eyes? The one calling me Mommy?' Finally," she finished, "I remembered my own daughter's name."

Thanks to Jamie's expertise, I have often used the stalling technique myself. It comes in quite handy when I make a phone call and cannot remember who it is that I have dialed. I'll say, "Well, hi! This is Becky Freeman. Do you remember me? *(Oh, how I wish I remembered you.)* Well, how in the world have you been and what have you been up to?" Usually there are enough clues in their answer that it will eventually dawn on me to whom I am speaking. It's a little awkward if you've dialed, say, the electric company, and the woman on the other end is trying to figure out why you are acting so folksy during a business transaction.

Sometimes there are entire days that come under the topic of Awkworms. One such day occurred in early fall, the first time I had planned to go to a Women's Bible Study at our church. For starters, I went out to my car and the door handle fell off in my hand. I went around, climbed through the passenger's side to the driver's seat, and managed to finally get it to start. Then the engine began to make noises that reminded me of the sound my clothes dryer made when one of my children had poured an entire bag of dog food into the tumbler. Seconds later, the car began to hiss and spurt and foam and spout. I started to ignore it, but I hated to humiliate myself by driving it down the road. I gave up and ran inside to call my friend Janna and asked her if I could hitch a ride.

"Sure, " she said, "But I have to be there early so I'll pick you up in five minutes." No problem. All I had left to do was change shoes and I'd be ready. As I reached for my shoe in the murky depths of my closet, I stubbed my toe on a cold, hard object. Taking quick revenge, I gave the thing another hearty kick and found I had just knocked over an entire gallon of white paint in the floor of my closet. I hurriedly threw an old towel over the spreading paint so I could think about what I should do next.

At that moment I heard Janna's car honking in the driveway. I took another look at the impossible mess and made my decision. *Oh, well,* I thought, *out of sight, out of mind I always say. With that towel over everything, it doesn't look that bad.* I grabbed my shoes and ran to Janna's car, slipping on my shoes as I ran. I started to tell Janna what a hectic morning I had had when she looked at my feet in horror. Little did I know that I had stepped in the paint with my hose-covered foot.

"What's that?" she asked, grimacing. When I glanced down I saw globs of white paint oozing over the top of my shoe.

We elected to go on to church where I dashed to the ladies' room. I washed off the paint to the best of my ability, but even that left visible portions of my foot with albino splotches. After Bible study, another friend, Susan, offered to take me home.

"I'd *love* to see your house—where you write—how you manage." I could feel the panic start to rise as I remembered what my house looked like when I had run out the door that morning. However, I needed the ride and it was too late to back out. Susan would just have to accept my house the way it was.

Once we arrived at my front door stop, I warned Susan that things might be a little messy. First we encountered the trail of white painted footprints leading from the front door to the closet.

"That's an interesting touch," Susan commented. Once in the kitchen, I cleared the counter of cereal bowls and warm, sticky milk and opened the refrigerator to see what I might offer Susan in the way of a snack. I have encountered many interesting things in my fridge, but this time, even I was shocked. Staring me in the face was the dead carcass of a rabbit and the pelt of a squirrel. It was not a sick prank, I realized. Zach and Zeke were big game hunters these days. I quickly slammed the refrigerator door and thought, *I can't let her see in there. She and Bill are so well-to-do. She'll think I'm related to Jed Clampit.* Turning, I noticed Susan staring at my calendar.

"Becky," she quizzed, "It's September and your calendar is still on May."

"I know, Susan," I answered, "I just like to pretend its Spring." *Like everyone keeps up with what month it is,* I thought to myself.

"Well, let me see where you work!" she said cheerily, waiting to be impressed. There was nothing I could do but show her the desk which I currently shared with Gabriel. There sat my computer next to a large ceramic piggy bank. A stack of files was graced with the remains of a peanut butter and jelly sandwich. Susan never batted an eyelash, bless her. Thankfully, I have landed in a group of people at my church who take me just as I am, without one plea.

Especially do I love and appreciate my pastor, Ralph Anderson, and his wife, Joyce. When I think about Ralph I think of the days when I catered Wednesday night meals before the evening service. My helper was Lisa, a mentally handicapped but loving little go-getter of a girl. Every Wednesday at 11:00 A.M., Lisa and Ralph participated in a little ritual that was lovely to see. Lisa had permission to buzz Ralph's study from the kitchen, and before long Ralph would show up with a deck of Uno™ cards and delight Lisa by playing several rounds with her in the dining hall. The loser always bought the winner a coke.

As I watched that scene, time and again—Ralph and Lisa laughing and playing together as the sun streamed in from the skylight above—it never ceased to touch my heart. To me, a great pastor is not necessarily an accomplished speaker or a superior leader, although Ralph has those qualities. Great is the man who quietly talks and listens to children in the halls and takes the time to show friends like Lisa that he cares. That's Ralph.

I called Ralph yesterday to ask him if he and Joyce had ever experienced an awkward moment in their years of ministry. He related something that occurred in the early years of their time at our Aldersgate Church, around 1970. When Ralph and Joyce took the pastorate, the church was very young. It had split from a Methodist church in town, and there was concern as to whether the newly established evangelical church would even survive. The first pastor stayed for only five months. To the relief of the congregation, Ralph and Joyce arrived and soon added a sense of warmth and stability to the growing church.

One night, about a year later, Ralph and Joyce awoke to the sound of glass breaking accompanied by flashes of light and searing heat coming from the industrial cleaning company next door. They soon realized a roaring fire was engulfing the building, so they bundled up their two-year-old Lisa, taking her outside to safety. They were worried that the fire might traumatize her, but their fears were obviously groundless. They watched their small daughter clap her hands with glee and belt out a rousing chorus of "Happy Birthday to Me" to the dancing firelight.

Ralph swung into action and sent Joyce to the house of Ham and Nancy Kate Hamilton, one of the founders of the church, to seek shelter and bring help. Somewhere around 12:30 A.M., Ham was awakened by an insistent knock at the door. Ham was a little hard of hearing, so it was remarkable that he woke up at all. Still in his shorts, he went to the door and heard the voice of the young pastor's wife.

Peeking out the window he saw Joyce carrying her child, frantically yelling, "Ham! We've had a fire! We've had a fire!" Ham shook his head in disbelief, ran back to the bedroom to grab his pants and wake up his wife.

"Nancy Kate! Get up! The pastor's wife and baby are out there on the front porch, and I don't know what to do."

Nancy Kate scolded, "Ham, what's the matter with you? Let her in!"

"I'm sorry, Nancy Kate, but I didn't know what to say. Just when we thought we'd found a quiet, loving couple that might stay awhile, the pastor's wife is out on our frontyard and is yelling that they've gone and had a fight."

When Ham and Nancy Kate finally let Joyce come in and discovered she had been yelling about a fire, not a fight, relief spread across both their faces, much to Joyce's puzzlement. It was years before Ralph and Joyce discovered the midnight panic that Ham's hearing impaired ears had caused, and ever since it's become one of the famous "tell-it-again" stories around campfires and retreats.

Actually, awkward situations can make for fairly tasty worms in life's cup of tea. You just have to know how to serve them. You've got to let them set out to dry awhile. After some time has passed, re-hydrate the awkworms by re-telling the story. Mmmm, delicious. Much more appetizing with time and a few garnishes on the side. By sharing your experiences, awkward situations become less threatening and unbearable. It's comforting to know that each of us will have the opportunity to deal with our own share of awkworms.

He remembered that they were but flesh.

PSALM 78:39
☙

The Worm Turns

Once we had determined I would go back to college to finish my degree, the next question became, "What did I want to be other than a mom?" What were my talents other than cooking for a crowd? Like a good mother, I discussed it with the children, and one evening around the dinner table we went on to discuss toward what heights *they* might be aspiring.

Zach wavered between being a priest or a ballerina, which I thought was interesting since we are neither Catholic nor coordinated.

Zeke's answer took me somewhat aback, given his gentle nature. "An enemy," he responded firmly. (Hey—it'll sure save on those pesky college tuition bills.)

Turning to Rachel, I posed the question in a neutral-gendered, designed-to-encourage-nonstereotypical-thinking manner: "Would you like to be a doctor or a nurse when you grow up?" After much thought, she replied in true feminist form.

"I'll have to wait and see which outfit looks better on me."

I'm beginning to feel I'm failing somewhere in this area because when I asked Zach the question, "Why do we treat women with respect?" he answered sincerely, "Because you never know when you might need to use one."

Having drawn a blank in my quest for a career direction, I agreed to teach VBS that summer, which I have since learned can often stand for Very Bad Situation. One morning, I happened to stroll by the church kitchen with a preschooler named James by the hand. The aroma of fresh baked goods deliciously perfumed the air, and seeking to make conversation with James, I remarked, "Mmmmm…what is that wonderful smell?"

James obviously possessed an esteem for his small self that needed no boosting. "It's me!" he beamed.

I loved it, and of course all the other moms loved it when I reported it to them, and that night, inspired by James, I sat down with my dog-eared journal and chuckled over the long list of questions I'd been asked at different times by my own or by other people's children.

"Mom, how do they make snakes turn into rubber?"

"What are those minnows that come in a can and that people eat?"

"Why does my finger gots two elbows?"

"Is your lap just for babies tonight?" (An excellent postpartum guilt inducer!)

"How do they squeeze people into those tiny airplanes up in the sky?"

"Are you potty-trained, Mom?"

"Can I have ice cream with chocolate chipmunks?"

"Will you put this up, Mom? I'm afraid I'm about to get into it."

"Why don't you just buy that zucchini swimsuit and let's get out of this lady store?" (Because I would need enough material to make a tent for the entire Saudi desert in order to cover up the stretch marks you gave me five years ago, thank you.)

Last but not least, as Gabe observed his first caterpillar, "What is that worm doing with a sweater on?"

I laughed that night, but realized there were tears on my face. "Wait a minute!" my heart cried. "I *need* these little critters in my life! I'm not ready to give this up!"

And so my decision to become a kindergarten teacher was partly selfish. My last baby was standing at Kindergarten's door. As a kindergarten teacher I would be relieved of the pressure of pleasing adults with discriminating tastes, and I could teach kindergartners who *love* messy food and bugs and worms.

Actually, I had always been somewhat of an educator at heart. I recall when Zeke was a baby. For a long period of time everything in his infant world was a "bean-bean." I dutifully sought to introduce him to new vocabulary, particularly days when I had him pinned in his highchair for lunch.

"Zekey," I said to my noodled, highchaired student. "This is spaghetti. Can you say spaghetti?"

He blinked two Ragu-covered eyelashes and replied in absolutely perfect English, "Spa-bean-bean!"

While we're on the subject of Zeke, I know that you have been waiting breathlessly for the chapter dealing with, "Raising the Difficult Child," or "How To Contain Your Little Wormonger." Actually, I feel uniquely qualified to discuss the problem of "Dealing with the Perfect Child," which Zeke just about is.

He did not begin life that way. He was born just eighteen months after Zach and got off to a terrible start. He had colic and cried for hours at night, even though I breast fed him and rocked him and did all the right mother-things I knew to do. I did find some comfort in a book by Anne Ortlund, *Your Children Are Wet Cement*. My mother spotted the book on the kitchen table one evening as she walked the floor with screaming Zeke.

"Are you sure that's not, *Put Your Children in Wet Cement?*" she inquired.

As Zeke became a toddler, he was like a spider monkey, able to shinny up my legs and into my arms, clinging to my neck twenty-four hours a day, seven days a week it seemed, screaming most of the time.

Finally one morning Mother called when I was at wit's end, drowning in a sea of tears and wondering if I would ever be able to enjoy this unhappy baby. I began to wail out my misgivings and then noticed the other end of the line was very quiet, which to say the least, was unusual.

"Becky," she began, and I seemed to hear something akin to awe in her voice, "something happened this morning as I was praying for you and Zekey Baby that doesn't happen to me very often. It was as if the Lord shot a message into my head. It was very clear. It was, Zeke will be Becky's blessing."

Needless to say, I took heart, and have lived to see that prophecy more than fulfilled. This is the child who received the "Most Tenderhearted" award three times in a row in school. The little guy inherited bad teeth and suffered too much for his age in the dentist's chair, yet when he overheard me complain about the high dental bills, he told me earnestly, "I'll ask the dentist not to give me a prize next time so he won't charge you so much."

Zeke loves to work alongside his Dad, has patience beyond his years with other family members, and usually gives in to their desires. He will ride happily in the car for hours, and his favorite hobby is *reading!*

I had actually begun to worry about him until I overheard a conversation between him and his older brother and younger sister. Gabe was napping and the older three were sitting around a picnic table on the back porch enjoying the breeze from the lake. I was enjoying the fact that they were all sitting. They were growing so fast, it gave me a chance to look them over carefully and see what time was doing. Where had my babies gone?

Zach was so obviously an Arnold—stocky, deeply tanned, straight dark brown hair, dark dancing eyes. Zeke, a total opposite, was so obviously a Freeman—lanky, with light brown hair, tender brown eyes, quiet and soft spoken. And Rachel Praise?—light brown curls, freckled, with an upturned nose, fair skin…What long recessant gene pool had she drawn from to be another totally different child? Whichever it was, Gabe had dipped from the same pool for his fair skin and freckles, but checked in at the Arnold's Spanish stream for his almost black hair. But it looks like his build is going to be the best from the Freeman pool, long and lean with broad shoulders.

In my meditative state, I smiled as I thought of how relieved Mother must be with the physical makeup of her grandchildren.

Years back, when she had realized Scott and I were headed for the altar, she had worried about our progeny. "Becky dear," she had asked, "what if your children inherit the Arnold legs and the Freeman arms?"

I had to admit—if the unthinkable happened, we might produce a line of humans with the posture of a gorilla, but we were so in love we were willing to risk it. There on the deck that gorgeous day I knew our worries had been groundless. They were all fine looking specimens. I was delighted with them, and with the moment.

I hadn't been paying much attention to their conversation, but Zach made a pronouncement that caught my ear.

"I'm special because I'm the oldest," he said with pride.

Rachel quickly countered, "But I'm Daddy's sweetheart because I'm the only girl." Both turned to Zeke who thought for a moment, grinned, and assumed a saint-like expression.

"Yes, but *I'm* perfect," he intoned.

No one raised a voice to contradict him.

He is the Rock,
his works are perfect and all his ways are just.
DEUTERONOMY 32:4
❧

Worms in My Mother's Coffee

Perhaps the time has come to talk about my mother, the kind of mother who would suggest you "put your children in wet cement." Obviously, she's not your average, run-of-the-mill old mother, but then, whose mother is? She tries hard to avoid becoming set in her ways, but I've noticed a number of things lately that have caused me to suspect that she is, well…shall we say, resistant to change? Months and months after a new style of clothing is in vogue, she finally notices, complains, issues a proclamation about its foolishness, and ends up buying it just before it goes out of style.

When sweat pants swept the nation, I sat with her one day at the cafeteria munching our spinach salads and gazing absently out the window. We were watching people in the parking lot, and when I glanced at Mother she seemed a little glum.

"I think it's sad," she said with an air of resignation.

"Sad? What's sad?" I inquired.

"The whole world is running around in their pajamas. Nobody ever gets dressed anymore."

I did my best to console her. "Sorry, Mother, but I think change is here to stay."

With a sigh, she gathered her packages, and we began our stroll back down the length of the mall.

A couple of years later she had to come to terms with stirrup pants. She now owns two pair, but she is still prone to philosophize. "Have you noticed," she observed, "that we now have a large percentage of women who goose step through the mall because their stirrup pants are too short?"

I made the mistake of giggling, and she felt encouraged.

"Something else I've noticed that I think is interesting. We all feel so comfy in the overgrown tops that go with the stirrup pants. We think because our posteriors are covered up, we don't have to worry about them. But when we put on a big sweater which also happens to cup in just under the bottom line, so to speak, we might as well pin a bright red bow on our backside!"

I had to laugh, even as I tugged at the bright red sweater topping my stirrup pants. "Oh, well," I offered, "It's possible that stirrup pants may virtually eliminate fallen arches and flat feet in a generation of women."

While my mother is prone to philosophize and is also an honor graduate of her high school class, this does not necessarily mean that she is a left brained, detailed individual. After all, I did not spring forth on this earth out of nothing, so right brained that I tilt in that direction when I walk. As you might expect, this almost overpowering genetic tendency has programmed both of us to look for the fun things in life and to avoid all machinery more complicated than an electric can opener.

Mother is constantly amazed by people who love gadgets and rush out to buy the newest as soon as they are available. We bought her her first microwave oven, and to her great credit, she overcame her fear of being vaporized and now wonders how she ever managed without it.

But Mother is also very aware that a refusal to learn new skills is a sign of aging, and as we have seen, she does not intend to *age*. She remembers that Grandmother Arnold never consented to use the new dishwasher in her apartment. She also remembers buying a tape player for Nonnie and how delighted Nonnie seemed to be when she opened her gift. Some years later Mother found the tape player still in the box on a top shelf in Nonnie's closet. It had obviously never seen the light of day. Consequently, she *will* eventually learn to operate the latest, absolutely necessary advance in technology. Take her new "under the counter" coffee maker for an example.

Mother used the standard American coffee pot for most of her life. She put water in the pot, put coffee in the basket, put the lid on the basket, and then plugged the cord into an electrical outlet. The pot made happy, gurgling noises while she leaned against the counter humming and tapping her fingers on the counter in anticipation. This was a comforting and satisfying morning ritual for many years, and she found no fault with it until she visited her brother-in-law and found that *he* had a new coffee pot which, when set the night before, had *his* coffee waiting for him the moment he staggered into the kitchen. He was able to have a cup even *before* his eyes were open. Could it possibly be that it was time to retire her faithful percolator, even though it was in perfect working order?

Mother decided to purchase an "under the counter" coffee maker, and I mention this only because such a coffee maker requires slightly more know-how and attention to detail than the average modern coffee maker, and certainly more than Mother's fifteen-year-old eight-cup percolator with the dark brown interior. The new coffee maker was familiar in that the operator first filled the pot with water. But the similarities ended there. In the older version the water remained in the pot. In the new version, the water had to be poured from the pot into the stand and the empty pot placed under the drip spout, where the pot (if everything has been done right) received the coffee.

The night she brought the new contraption home, Mother carefully prepared the coffee maker as directed and went to bed with visions of fresh-brewed coffee awaiting her at 6:00 A.M. The next morning, much to her dismay, she found the coffee maker silent and cold, the pot empty—just as she had left it the night before. She tried again the next night, only to awaken to the same disappointment. She decided at this point that the automatic device must be defective and was about to bundle the coffee maker up and return it to the department store. Then Daddy read the directions carefully, discovering that it was not only necessary to set the automatic turn-on for 6:00, but that it had to be set for 6:00 A.M.

And so, on the third morning after her purchase, Mother awoke to the aroma of coffee wafting down the hallway from the kitchen to her bedroom, and she congratulated herself on conquering yet another technological advance. Before long, setting up the coffee pot at bedtime became routine.

About three months after becoming accustomed to having fresh coffee almost before her eyes were open, Mother shuffled down the hall to the kitchen to find the coffee freshly made—on the kitchen counter, the kitchen floor, and a few inches into the den carpet. She had poured the water into the coffee maker stand the night before, set the pot down on the counter, and gone to bed. The next morning, the coffee maker did its thing, but there was no pot under the drip spout to catch the lovely brew.

This has happened often enough over the last two years that the varnish has come off the cabinet where the coffee runs down on its way to the den carpet. On other mornings, she has arisen to find the coffee pot sitting under the drip spout, dry and hot as a pistol—she had forgotten to put the water in. Other variations have included finding the pot full of hot water, signaling that she had failed to put coffee in the stand, and finding it too weak to wake anybody up because she had not only remembered to put the water in the stand, she had put it in twice.

She continues to get the coffee ready to perk at bedtime but has given up on setting the pot on "automatic" anymore, feeling it just can't be trusted. Recently, however, Daddy observed her sleepily pouring the water intended for the vaporizer into the coffee pot stand.

When Mother began to talk about purchasing a 160-horsepower fruit and vegetable juicer, you can imagine the wave of excitement that swept through friends and family. She had become interested in this gadget (against all her right brain programming) because it was advertised on TV by a muscle-bound gentleman in his late seventies. I suspect she took a sidelong glance at Daddy snoring in his easy chair, compared him to the gentleman on TV, and decided to have a shot at adding the juicer to their vitamin/exercise regimen.

When the juicer arrived, she installed it in a place of easy access beside her coffee maker and began the ordeal of learning to use it. Before that was accomplished, she had managed to shoot three cups of carrot pulp into the crack between her stove and refrigerator, and in a later effort, managed to run three cups of carrot juice down the side of the cabinet. Fortunately, it chose to run about the same course as the coffee usually took, thus avoiding another strip of bare wood.

No discussion of Mother's reluctance to change would be complete without mentioning her antipathy for computers, which (who?) she is convinced are not entirely mechanical but may actually be inhabited by beings from another world. Maybe this is why she finds it hard to hang up on a computerized sales phone call.

She first learned to use a computer some years ago when she purchased a Kaypro™ and taught herself to use one of the first word processing packages, treating our delicate ears to her critique of computer inventors who insisted on using five-syllable words like "documentation" when a three-syllable word such as "manual" would have worked better. (In Texas, manual is a two-syllable word.) The term "tutorial" particularly annoyed her, and she never referred to the tutorial in her computer as anything other than "instructions." She learned to use the word processing capability of her Kaypro, but never had the slightest inclination to see what else was in there. She was quite proud of this rather difficult accomplishment and assumed she would never have to learn anything more than she had already learned. Then her Kaypro died, and she learned it had become so obsolete she couldn't find anybody to repair it. She was outraged.

"Why didn't they tell me when I paid two thousand dollars for a machine that it would become an antique in eight years?" Then with a sigh of relief, she purchased a simple, compact word processor for herself, and one for me, and we wrote happily everafter (well, for a couple of years) on these relatively simple gadgets. If we needed to swap material, we never thought of using a modem, we just made a date to meet halfway between her house and mine at Big Burger with a playground for Gabe. Then, writing took a serious turn, and there were more and more deadlines, closer and closer together. Enter modern computers and fax/modems. It adds a whole new dimension to the question, "Do you do Windows™?"

For weeks Mother circled her new computer, watched other people operate it with idiotic grins on their faces, watched her grandchildren glory in it, avoided looking at Daddy's expectant face each evening as he returned from work, asking if she had used it that day. Then came the publisher's call, "We need forty *more* pages by the end of the week." She did what she always does when she has her back to the wall. She came to grips with technology, but if she loves it yet, she's not about to admit it.

The government has been attempting to overhaul the country's medical system, hoping to provide medical care for all citizens. But even before the government has had its shot at the system, Daddy's company, like most other companies, has been looking for ways to cut insurance. Recently Daddy told Mother that, if they were to be reimbursed 100 percent for medical fees, they would have to make some changes. If one of them were to need to be hospitalized, he or she would have to forego the excellent hospital just five minutes from their house, say good-bye to their dearly beloved doctor, and drive twenty minutes to a strange hospital to see a doctor who would also be a stranger to them. She responded with a shout heard almost round the world. After thinking it over, she calmed down. A few days later, she called me to discuss the situation. It took me a while to answer the phone.

"You must have been outside," she greeted.

"Well, no, actually, I couldn't find the phone."

"Pardon me?"

"Our old one kept coming unplugged in the middle of conversations, so Scott marched out last week and bought a new one, a portable one. So now it gets ported all over the house by the kids and an occasional mother. It's not unusual for it to get covered up with first one thing and then another, depending on how long it is between calls."

"Ah, modern conveniences," she said. "How'd you find it?"

"I just followed the sounds under the bedspread, but last week I had to run to the neighbors and ask them to telephone me so I could run back to the house and hear it ringing. Worked great." It hadn't struck me as particularly funny, but she was whooping and relaying the story to Daddy in the background.

My mother—she laughs at all my stories, even the ones that cost her time and money. But she was not to be diverted long from the topic on her mind, changes in their hospitalization insurance. When the steam began to subside, she did what she does so well. She found philosophical comfort.

"It's becoming clear that our generation—your dad's and mine—have had it awfully good. I'm beginning to suspect that our era has been just a blip in time when a comparatively tiny number of people on the face of the earth lived in remarkable prosperity and comfort. (*There's a lot of good Scrabble material in that sentence!*) I guess we've sort of come to expect it as our due. It takes so much more for your generation just to live. I don't know how you do as well as you do. (*Thanks, Mom.*) I hope and pray that the changes we're looking at in the medical system will mean that you and Scott and David and Barb and Rachel and Gilley—and so many others in the country who have not had it as easy as we have—will benefit. If that happens, we can adjust.

"The thing that worries me about government solutions is that they can create some very peculiar situations like the one we faced when Nonnie needed constant care. If we put her in a nursing home, Medicaid would pay all her expenses because she had no money. But there was no government aid to hire help if we kept her at home, even though it would have cost less than to maintain her in a nursing home."

I heard Mother sigh on the other end of the wire, and I knew she was struggling with the memories and the sorrows, and yes, even guilt because Nonnie had spent the last eighteen months of her life in a nursing home.

"So you can see why I have some reservations about government intervention in our medical system." She thought for a minute more and then continued, "By the way. If you have to put me in a nursing home someday, please try to remember what you did with me."

Don't be deceived, my dear brothers.
Every good and perfect gift is from above,
coming down from the Father of the heavenly lights,
who does not change like shifting shadows.
JAMES 1:16–17
ↄ

Like Death Wormed Over

What I gained in sense of purpose, self-esteem, and head knowledge as I once again entered college, I sacrificed in the orderliness and aesthetics of my life and the life of my family in general. Bear in mind that we were a family of six living in an 850-square-foot cabin which we were also in the process of remodeling, doing all the work ourselves. Perhaps I can be forgiven for failing to receive the "Garden of the Month" award even once during my back-to-college years, and for the innumerable events at which I either failed to arrive on time or managed to forget entirely.

I'll never forget my first day back at college after an absence of ten years. I suppose I had secretly hoped I might be mistaken for an eighteen-year-old coed. At the very least, I expected my fellow students to faint when I revealed to them that I was the mother of four children. The actual reaction was more like, "Just four? Any grandkids yet?"

If I seemed elderly to the college kids, they appeared barely pubescent to me. The girls were wearing ponytails and hair ribbons! I might not have passed for Homecoming Queen, but I felt I did look a picture in my sand-colored corduroy skirt, olive jacket, and burnished leather boots. It was an outfit that obviously said, "Back to School! Crisp nip in the air, falling leaves..."

Too bad the Texas weather said, "You gotta be kidding!"

I sweltered through my first class, and, just before I passed out from heatstroke, I decided to take a restroom break. Checking my autumn pallet makeup in the mirror, I was transfixed. The face looking back at me was wearing a mustache. Evidently I had wiped the sweat from my newly-made up brow, then swiped my hand across my upper lip in an agony of thirst.

"Well," I addressed the coed version of Groucho Marx staring at me from the mirror, "I'll bet *that* impressed the professor."

As I mopped up, I lectured myself. "Wipe that silly mustache off your face! You are finally in college. You are a university student. Now go cash your check at the university bookstore and get yourself a big glass of university iced tea and a collegiate salad at the University S.U.B."

I cashed my check (and sheepishly invested in a few rubber-bands and hair ribbons), filled my lunch tray, and poured myself a huge glass of iced tea, grateful for the security of knowing there were probably no surprises waiting for me at the bottom of the glass. The surprise came when I reached for my wallet to pay for my treat and found it empty at the bottom. I had had the money just ten minutes ago, but it was not there. The next surprise came when I found there was no credit to be had in the university cafeteria. I watched as the university lunch ladies took away my tray, then found a quiet corner, sat collegiately down, and cried.

Later that night, Mother called to see how my day went. She seemed to think it was hysterically funny when I told her I had lost my lunch money on my first day of school.

Back on the home front, my memory continued its downward spiral. I became so lax in my responsibilities as tooth fairy that the children were forced to try a variety of techniques to help the old girl out.

One of the children, having despaired of the tooth fairy ever remembering to look under his pillow, tried placing his tooth in a cool cup of water in the middle of the kitchen table where it could not possibly be missed. However, he forgot that Ms. Fairy was nearsighted and that she would also be thirsty at bedtime.

A second toothless child had the bright idea of tying his tooth to a string hanging from the ceiling fan above his parents' bed, thinking perhaps Mom and Dad might have more influence with the important personage they so much wanted to visit them. However, tooth fairy got too warm in the night, and the bicuspid became airborne somewhere in the wee hours of the morning and flew off into never-never land.

The older children began taking their newly shed teeth with them directly to the store where they could whip them out of their pockets while the tooth fairy was nearby with cash in hand. Gabe continued to struggle bravely on, even though he was understandably not quite clear on just how the tooth fairy system was supposed to work.

On a rare day when I had time to make his bed, I lifted his pillow and found, to my surprise (other mothers would probably have felt horror), the tooth-filled jawbone of a long deceased cow.

"Gabriel James!" I bellowed, "what is this filthy thing doing under your pillow?"

I can only describe the grin on his face as cunning.

"How much do you think the tooth fairy will give me for *that*?" he asked.

During this extremely hectic time, my personal appearance also suffered and eventually became a cause for some periods of mild depression, probably for Scott as well. My Nonnie had an expression to describe people who were not looking their very best for some reason or another. She would pronounce that "they looked like death warmed over." On the morning I had promised to chaperon Zeke's field trip at his school, I woke up with a huge red pimple on the end of my not insignificant schnoz. I thought of my grandmother's expression and decided it was incredibly apt.

"Okay," I told myself. "So you woke up with a little pimple. All right, a *huge* pimple. Why do you, a thirty-something woman, feel thirteen-something again? You will not disgrace your son: you'll be the only one who notices it. You are blowing this tiny imperfection in an otherwise flawless face out of all proportion."

Even so, after inspecting 6,737,294 different specimens of amphibia and reptilia at the Museum of Natural Creatures That Make Mothers Queazy (in the company of thirty third graders who often have the same effect), I was not feeling "good about myself," as the support groups say. And that was *before* it began to rain.

At Burger Billions for lunch break, I fell into the soggy line at the counter, jostled about in a sea of starving nine-year-olds. I caught a sympathetic glance from another field trip mom. Hoping for comfort, I confessed, "I just feel so ugly today. My hair is a wet mess…"

A bright-eyed boy named Christopher chimed in, "Yeah, and you've got a great big red mole thing on your nose, too!"

That did it! I knew the time had come when I simply had to find some time for myself. As soon as the field trip ground to its merciful end, I dropped the children off at home with their dad and headed for Mary's house. Mary is good at many things beside finding nice suburban houses. She sells a lovely line of cosmetics; she is a professional hairdresser who works from a shop in her home; and she is my best friend. That day I needed all she had to give.

Heading straight for her work station, I stepped over two toys and one kitten belonging to Mary's children, Michael and Michele, aged nine and six. I dropped into the beauty chair and sighed deeply.

"You know, you're going to think I'm silly, but I've been so self-conscious about this little blemish today."

"Really?" Mary asked in mild surprise. "Why I..." She moved in for a closer look, stepped back, frowned, clicked her tongue. "I don't believe I've ever noticed anything *that* big on your face before."

"Thanks so much," my reply dripped sarcasm. "I didn't mean to offend you with my gross physical deformity. Excuse me while I go to the bathroom to spackle over this volcano on my nose."

In the bathroom, I applied a couple of Band-Aids™ to the problem, tried to see the humor of it and returned sheepishly to Mary's chair. Attracted by the Band-Aids™, Michael and Michele crawled onto the sofa with the kitten in tow and watched as we discussed what might be a really smashing new hairdo to soothe my battered self-esteem.

"Let's try some color this time, Becky," she suggested. "Something like—Plum Brown. It has nice burgundy highlights to accentuate your red...lips," she finished carefully. Then she set to work turning me Plum Brown.

Considering the large size of the yellow gloves she wore, she deftly measured and mixed and stirred.

"Sorry about these big ol' gloves. I had to use kitchen gloves because I'm out of the thin kind." Looking back over my day, it seemed the least of my problems.

At that moment, Kitty decided to make his escape from the sofa and jumped at Mary, attaching himself to her leg with his small but efficient claws. She screamed and planted her dye-smeared gloves into my forehead, leaving three extra large Plum

Brown fingerprints, complete with burgundy highlights. In the aftermath, our eyes held.

"Nice touch," I said.

Mary apologized profusely while she applied the dye to my head, jerking and yanking at my hair with the huge plastic gloves.

"I'm not hurting you, am I?" She was really very kind, and through my tears I assured her that it did not hurt quite so much as natural childbirth. I tried to remember my Lamaze breathing. Things seemed to settle down and I began to relax and wonder just how gorgeous I might be when the labor was over. Then Mary said something I found more unsettling than what had already happened to me that day. "Uh-oh," was what she said.

"What do you mean, uh-oh?"

"Oh, nothing." Silence. More pulling. "Becky—you haven't been losing a lot of hair lately, have you?"

"No," I fought the swelling panic in my chest. "Am I losing hair now?"

"A little," Mary answered in a professional, try-not-to-alarm-the-customer voice.

"How much is a little?"

"Well…no more than you'd lose with chemotherapy."

From the sofa, Michael and Michele collapsed with glee. "We love it when Becky comes over! This kind of stuff never happens to Mom's other customers. Hey, we could give Becky a T-shirt that says, 'No Hair by Mary.'"

When you've come to the end of your rope, these are the kind of kids who would say, "Tie a knot—and put a noose around your neck."

We managed to salvage what was left of my hair, and I left Mary's house Plum Brown and plum tuckered out. As I drove wearily into the driveway of our home, Gabriel ran out to meet me and smiled his sweet three-year-old smile. He put both hands on my cheeks and gazed tenderly into my eyes.

"Mommy," he said, "you're fat."

At the moment, Nonnie's expression, "looking like death warmed over," seemed inadequate; "death wormed over" fit much better.

Sometimes I feel overwhelmed by the differences between me and the gorgeous Barbie doll look-alikes I see on TV and in magazines. The message they send is clear: "You are only wanted and desired if you look like me."

Then I get mad. How dare the media lead us to believe our worth depends on how we look? God is such a comfort to my sagging ego. He looks past my less than perfect body into my soul, which has had a complete make-over by His forgiveness and love.

Besides, I know a secret. Barbie is hollow inside. I know because Gabe takes her head off regularly. Lord, forgive me for sometimes wanting to do the same thing to real women who wear a size six.

Man looks at the outward appearance,
but the Lord looks at the heart.
1 SAMUEL 16:7
∽

S E V E N T E E N

Plump, Juicy Worms

I assume by now you know I hate the word *plump*. Only *chubby* is worse. I much prefer "a few pounds overweight," which sounds more like the condition is temporary. Why not "softly curved"? "Nicely rounded"? Or even "voluptuous"?

With each of my four pregnancies also came an enormous appetite. Food never tasted so delicious, and if it weren't for the accumulation of pounds, I would still miss the way a Big Mac™ melts in my mouth when time is measured in trimesters. As a result of this enormous appetite, I gained an average of sixty-five pounds (that is not a misprint) with every pregnancy. Luckily, a nursing infant takes seven hundred calories a day from his lactating mommy, bless him, so I lost all but five or six of the newly acquired pounds. But…4 times 5 equals 20 anyway you tally it up. Since I had a baby permanently attached to me for nourishment for nearly ten years of my adult life, I enjoyed a decade when my weight was fairly easy to manage.

Then I hit the big "3-0." I began to realize I could no longer expect to eat even the sesame seed off a Big Mac™ without it showing up on *my* buns. To make matters worse, just when I needed Mother to blame for my hereditary genes, she hit middle age, went on her health food regimen, bought walking shoes, and trimmed to a svelte 120 pounds where she has remained for some years now. To her credit, she never mentions my weight, nor suggests I go on any of her seaweed diets with her. But every now and then, she puts her foot in her mouth. For instance...

Not long ago I called to tell Mother about a small triumph. I had dashed into our local Christian bookstore, wearing sweat pants (you already know her opinion of sweat pants), old tennis shoes, and a messy hairdo that wasn't on purpose. I knew the sales lady, and she chose this moment to introduce me to all the customers in the store as a "real writer." I appreciated the attention, but it was not the way I had pictured myself looking at my author's debut. I was chuckling about the incident to Mother when she used the P word in reference to Yours Truly.

"Oh, Becky," she comforted, "those people *loved* you! And all the more because you were plump and disheveled!"

I don't remember anything else she said because I was lost in my own thoughts. *So it's come to this. I am plump.*

To make matters worse, Mother called back the next morning, wanting to make amends.

"Becky," she began tenderly, "you got quiet on the phone yesterday. I think I may have put my foot in my mouth again. I want you to know that you're hardly ever disheveled."

Disheveled? I could care *less* about being disheveled! Disheveled is a temporary, fixable condition, whereas *plump* sounds so *permanent*. Somehow I managed to get off the phone without coming through the line with bared fangs, but when I hung up the receiver I stomped my right foot.

"That does it!" I said, and hitching up my sweat pants, I marched to the mall and bought one of those plastic, cross-country skier deelymabobs that "conveniently folds flat to fit under the bed." I opened it, tried it once, folded it flat, and found it did indeed fit conveniently under my bed as advertised. It fit so conveniently it stayed there for weeks. In fact, that was the only convenient thing about it. Finally I realized it wasn't doing me much good under the bed, so I hauled it out and took it back to the store and exchanged it for a lounge chair.

As I searched for a workable way to get back to a size 8, I began reading the articles that suggested losing weight by simply (Ha!) cutting back on fat and walking—the *healthy* way! Have you seen all the wonderful low-fat products on the grocery store shelves these days? Why, there's everything from no-fat chocolate devil's food cookies to baked—not fried—sour cream and onion potato chips.

I ate all these things by the box full and didn't lose a pound. I did discover it is possible to eat enough fat-free marshmallows and angel food cake to completely negate the fat-burning benefits of walking for exercise.

Then I got really desperate. One evening when I was getting dressed to go out with Scott to a ranch style steak house, I discovered I could no longer squeeze into my favorite pair of black jeans. I tried catching the legs in a closed door and pulling on the waist to stretch them, but to no avail. Then I lay with my shoulders on the bed, sucked in my breath, and put my feet up the wall to get gravity on my side. I ended up wearing a big full skirt, and at the steak house later we watched tiny cowgirls in black jeans and boots prance back and forth with their trays of steak and potatoes. There's a saying in Texas among cowgirls that if you can get a dime into the pocket of your jeans, they're too loose, and I figured these cuties didn't have a dime to their name.

Shortly after making the sad discovery that I could no longer wear my black jeans, I did something I never thought I—nor any other self-respecting Christian woman—would do. I went to a complimentary exam to explore the benefits of liposuction. Let me just say, it was a humiliating experience.

When I got into the examining room the nurse asked me to undress and then to don a garment the size of a Kleenex™. This highlight was followed by even more fun. The nurse then took a Polaroid™ picture of my backside. Why didn't I leave then?

The next thing I knew, a dark and, of course, handsome doctor with a flawless physique entered the room. He began prodding and poking and looking back and forth from me to the Polaroid picture, describing what I could expect with lipo-suction. For starters, I could expect pain. Then there would be the bruises from my hips to my knees. Oh, and did he mention I would have to wear a full-length girdle for months? And there was that pesky little problem of folds of loose skin that might persist after the surgery and require additional nips and tucks. When he left the room I couldn't slip into my dress fast enough.

The grand finale took place when the nurse brought in the projected cost of the surgery, beautifully printed on linen paper in an elegant shade of pink. I expect Dr. Richer-Than-You sent his nurse to deliver the news so that he would be out of swinging distance. I don't care if it is written in gold-leaf calligraphy on sheets of fine pink Japanese parchment, four thousand dollars is a lot of money.

During the drive home, I mentally went through what I would report to Scott. By this point, he was like a frightened rabbit when it came to the topic of my weight. There is nothing inoffensive a man can say to his wife who wants to lose a few pounds. If he says, "I love you just the way you are, Sweetheart," she cries, "And just *what* did you mean by that? What's *wrong* with the way I am?" If he tells her to go on a diet and promises he will support her in it, she replies, "If it's that important to you, you don't love *me*. You only care about how I look." If he says, "Hang the diet. It'll just make you cranky," she will accuse, "I wish just this once you'd be *supportive!*"

By the time I pulled into the driveway, I decided I would make it easy for Scott. He was sitting in his easy chair and looked up expectantly when I entered the room. I slammed the door and walked past him, heading for the bedroom.

"Don't say a word and you'll live longer," I advised.

For a while after that humiliating day, I felt a certain amount of peace with who I was and realized how much I was robbing myself of the happiness of my romantic relationship with Scott by obsessing about my weight. I determinedly got rid of the phrases of self-condemnation playing in my head. Once I settled the issue of weight and self-esteem, what did I do? I went to Wal-Mart™ and bought a Deal-A-Meal™ kit. The morning I dealt my first cards into the vinyl carrying case, I also went to a Bible study at my church. I took a seat next to a cute little blond, one of those abnormalities of nature, and before long the subject of dieting came up, as it too often does.

"Have you seen those Deal-A-Meal™ kits at Wal-Mart™ this week?" she marveled. "What kind of people do you suppose buy those things?"

I thought it over a minute before answering, "Really desperate ones?"

I must say, I lost six pounds and, other than the constant grumbling of my stomach, the diet wasn't all that bad. And shortly after beginning the diet, another man entered my life. His name was Richard.

The day I met Richard began like any other day. I had a breakfast date with Mary, and I might just mention that Mary is knock-em-dead gorgeous. When we're together, I always feel like a wallflower. Men seemed to be drawn to Mary like ants to a picnic, and it's not unusual for men who are perfect strangers to introduce themselves to her. I often wondered what that would be like.

On this particular day, I was in a rush as usual. I decided to dash by Get-It-Kwik to pick up a pack of gum, and as I started into the store, I almost bumped into a large man, wearing baggy pants, a red flannel shirt, suspenders, and a grin as big as all outdoors. I merely smiled at him, but he stopped in his tracks, transfixed it seemed. He stared at me shamelessly.

"Ma'am," he said (Texans make two syllables of it), "you shore are purty." He raked his stocking cap off his balding head, and the expression on his face indicated he was probably hearing heavenly music.

"Why, *thank* you," I replied, flustered a little but not displeased. I hardly missed a step as I went on into the store to finish my errand. By the time I dashed back to the car, I had forgotten about it. I popped the key into the ignition and had a little trouble getting it started. Then I heard a tapping on my window. There stood my starry-eyed admirer. At this point I became flustered and not particularly pleased and began praying that my car would start immediately. The man again swept off his hat, held it reverently in his hands, and spoke to me through the window.

"Ma'am, I'd like to introduce myself. My name's Richard."

I smiled but kept the window closed and shouted through it, "It's nice to meet you, Richard!" Thankfully, the engine finally started. I heaved a sigh of relief, waved good-bye to Richard, and drove the two blocks to the restaurant, really giggling now and planning just how I was going to relay this story to Mary. When I arrived, Mary was there, having struck up a conversation with a nice looking man in the breakfast line.

"You're not going to believe what just happened to me," I said, and by now I was really tickled. "I was at Get-It-Kwik just a minute ago, and this guy..."

"Ma'am?" I heard, just slightly behind me and to my left. Hoping I had not heard what I thought I had heard, I turned to be sure. There he was, big as life, hat in hand.

"Well, hello, Richard," I said nervously and introduced him to Mary. I noticed with a bit of ridiculous pride that he hardly noticed Mary. He only had eyes for me.

"Ma'am, I work at the cafe down the street and I shore would love to buy you a cuppa cawfee sometime." Suddenly the restaurant became so quiet you could hear a pin drop. All commerce halted as every patron and employee fixed their eyes on the little drama being played out before them. Before I could break the news to him that I was a thoroughly married woman, he said the following words I will never forget. "I just never met a woman quite like you."

Mary chimed in, "Oh, lots of people say that about Becky!"

Yeah, I thought, *but I don't think they mean it the way he does! I've got to get control of this.*

"Richard," I said as kindly as I possibly could, "I'm married and have four kids, and I really don't think my husband would want me to meet you for coffee. Thanks so *much*, though." The light went out of his eyes, I presume the heavenly music stopped inside him, and his head drooped noticeably. His hat still in his hands, he turned slowly and left the restaurant. But he had left me a gift. I felt like a starlet, a ballerina, the Queen of Sheba. Mind you, Richard and I were just two ships passing in the night, and yet he had concluded in a few seconds of awestruck admiration that he had "never met a woman quite like me."

I may be struggling, I may even be plump (there, I've said it), but God never made another woman quite like me. Thank you, Richard. You may have been an angel in disguise. If I weren't already married to a wonderful guy, you just might have stolen my heart.

A few days later, Mother drove from the city to the country for a visit, bringing with her a copy of the January/February 1994 issue of *Today's Christian Woman*, one of our favorite magazines. On its cover was a big, beautiful blond woman whose very smile invited you to smile back. Mother pulled out a bar stool.

"I want to read you some of this interview with Liz Curtis Higgs," she said. "It's wonderful. This gal has written a book with a great title—*One Size Fits All and Other Fables*. Isn't that good?" she chuckled. "Listen to this," she began to read from the magazine with gusto the words of Ms. Higgs: "'I notice women in my audiences who are a little larger than average. Their facial expressions are downcast and their style of dress less than flattering...I wanted to let these women know they can be happy and healthy *now* instead of feeling as though they have to diet their way to happiness. Too often we postpone joy until we're a size 10. I've been a size 10 and was no more joyful then than I am now at size 22. Basing our happiness on what the scale says only programs us for disaster!...—*Vogue* doesn't give us the right message. Scripture does.'"

Mother laid the magazine down on the counter. "Just for the record, honey," she said, and I thought she might be about to cry, "I think you're one of the prettiest little things I ever laid eyes on. You light up my life."

Thanks, Mom. Thanks, Richard. And—thank *You, Lord.*

I praise you because I am fearfully and wonderfully made;
your works are wonderful,
I know that full well.

PSALM 139:14

The Worm-mobile

I was pleased to note that our children seemed to be growing in faith by leaps and bounds, even among the chaos, and could even seem to be almost pious at times to the casual observer. I might wish they had learned to depend on prayer in some manner other than through their experiences riding as passengers while their mother roared up and down country roads—always late to class—in an ancient and dilapidated Country Squire station wagon which we referred to as "The Titanic."

Recently I realized that these experiences had not been all bad when Scott decided to run an errand in my car, taking Gabriel along. When Scott started the motor, Gabe was aghast.

"Daddy!" he shouted, "you forgot to pray!"

Because the Titanic and I have been through so much together, I begin most trips with a simple but fervent prayer:

"Lord, please let this car start." Once I leave the driveway, I realize I should have prayed more specifically and at greater length.

The Titanic is the ideal vehicle for transporting wet and muddy boys, their fishing poles, and their worms. Considering the usual menagerie loose in its confines, we hardly notice when the worm box tips over. At one point not long ago, I had a box turtle, a blue-tailed lizard, a chameleon, and a skink running loose in my station wagon.

There are three things, however, that cause the Titanic and me to tremble: trees, country mailboxes, and country ditches. The chrome on the Titanic sticks out all over like porcupine quills, but even more pitiful is the haggard condition of the trees in our circle drive. The children like to use these trees for show-and-tell when their friends come to visit.

"See those trees without any bark on 'em?" asks Zach.

"Wow!" responds the visitor. "Beavers?"

"Nope. My mom can't back out of the driveway without skinning a tree."

My husband used to keep a supply of mailboxes in our garage to replace those of our friends and neighbors after I mowed them down trying to back out of their driveways. I once bagged three in a row, a feat of which I am not really proud, but I have become quite artistic at painting house numbers on the boxes we replace.

As for the ditches, a few months after we moved to our cabin, big white guard rails with reflectors were installed in front of every ditch from our house to the highway. Since I was hauled out of five of those ditches in those first months, I assume the neighbors got together for our mutual benefit and voted to erect the railings.

I also have something of a reputation at the drive-in bank. My car always comes to rest with at least one front wheel on the curb of the concrete island. This is not deliberate on my part, but it does permit me the advantage of getting really close to the tube sucker machine.

One of the things that surprises me about banking is how few people—other than myself—actually take the banking tube right on home with them. I am now on a first name basis with most of the tellers at our bank who, when they see me come in the door, merely smile and hold out their hands.

With this kind of reputation, you can imagine the tension that sweeps through our local Get-It-Kwik when I stop by their drive-in store for gasoline. Until recently, the owner and his employees had managed to prevent my driving away with the pump nozzle still nestled in my gas tank by running outside and waving frantically as I started my car. In spite of their best efforts, the day finally came when I pulled away from the pump with the forgotten nozzle in my gas tank. When I felt the tug and heard the pop, I slammed on the brakes and wearily slumped from my car. Numbly I extracted the nozzle and stood staring at the hose writhing in the wind like a beheaded snake. A kindly man at the next pump looked as if he wanted to weep for me.

"You must be having one of those days," he commiserated. If only he knew how many of "those days" I have accumulated.

Believe it or not, I almost repeated the incident a couple of weeks later, but three employees, watching me carefully from inside the store, sprinted outside in record time and saved the day. "Get-It-Kwik" has taken on an entirely new meaning in our town.

All these have been relatively minor incidents which did not really endanger anybody's life or limbs. But there have been several harrowing instances when Scott had to have his car towed and I have been the only one available. He usually turns whiter than the Pillsbury Dough Boy™ at the prospect of sitting atop or inside any vehicle or machine which is in turn attached to any vehicle which I am driving.

Therefore I was surprised and pleased at his renewed trust in me when he asked me to give him a tow on his riding mower about a mile down the road to where he intended to cut a neighbor's grass. After attaching the mower to the Titanic, he mounted it and I carefully began to pull him down the bumpy, oil-topped road.

Things went along very smoothly. It was a lovely day and the wildflowers were just coming into bloom. I was delighted to see how many varieties there were. Before I realized it, my foot settled into a comfortable forty miles per hour position on the accelerator.

When I happened to glance into the rearview mirror, I saw Scott's elbows flapping up and down like an injured bird in takeoff; I saw six inches of daylight between his posterior and the seat of the tractor and his mouth wide open in a silent scream.

Now, I know I shouldn't have laughed, because it's true; I could have killed him. When I finally got control of myself and brought the Titanic to a halt, the look on Scott's face was a study. It reminded me of Charlie Brown's expression when he had once again trusted Lucy to hold the football so that he could practice kicking.

For he will command his angels concerning you
to guard you in all your ways.
PSALM 91:11
ல

Early Bird,
You Can Have the Worm!

L et me make one thing perfectly clear. I don't do mornings. At least, not well. Or consciously. For me a good day begins somewhere after 10:00 A.M., after a leisurely bath and large doses of concentrated caffeine.

Before starting back to school, I could get away with getting out of bed and shuffling around the house in my robe with a mole-like expression until the school-aged children became aware of my unintelligible grunts. This was their cue to rise, dress, and choose an entree from the breakfast menu: plain bread with peanut butter, bread lightly toasted, or my specialty, whittle-your-own toast. If the third item on the menu was chosen, I could count on the smoke alarm to call any remaining little sleepwalkers into action. I did not think it was funny when Scott began to refer to the smoke alarm as the dinner bell.

On most mornings, Scott would gulp down a cup of coffee, gather the three older children in his car, and race to meet the school bus on his way to work. Gabe and I were often able to wave good-bye from the front porch, close the door, and snuggle back into a warm bed to catch another hour of sleep. Golden days. Simply golden.

Once I added a full schedule of college courses to my life, it became imperative that I become a more active participant in mornings. Unfortunately, my participation seemed to transform mornings that had previously been chaotic into mornings that became near catastrophic. One particular day, a catch-up-on-chores Wednesday sandwiched between my Tuesday/Thursday class days, I vowed to keep a clear head during the morning's activities with an eye to organizing and improving the situation in the future. If I was going to have to do mornings, I would try to do them reasonably well.

As I considered six people getting ready for school and work in one bathroom the size of a gerbil cage, the scene often reminded me of Gabey's worms writhing in the bottom of my tea glass.

Zach has reached the age when he has discovered he can make an "Elvis Wave" with his bangs, given access to the blow dryer and mirror for a mere thirty minutes.

Rachel Praise has learned that if she stands pressed between the sink and her Daddy as he shaves, she can brush her teeth—if she is careful to dodge his foamy drippings.

Zeke usually makes a few feeble attempts to dash in and find a place at the sink before muttering, "If I can just get my toothbrush, I'll brush my teeth in the kitchen."

Since Gabe is not too far removed from his potty training period, he is given undisputed first rights to essential plumbing, even though I am standing on the rim of said plumbing, weaving and bobbing like a prize fighter to get a look at myself in the mirror over the top of Zach's head and just under Scott's armpit. As a matter of fact, when Gabe comes hopping down the hall toward the bathroom, it's as if someone yelled, "Grenade!"—with bodies flying in all directions. His aim is still not the greatest.

On the morning under discussion, Zeke was rummaging through the toothbrush can, speaking calmly in a voice that, for Zeke, was complaining.

"I spent my allowance on my own toothbrush," he frowned, "and Zach's been using it."

"I did not!" came the indignant reply.

Zeke so rarely complains that I felt it demanded an investigation and just resolution. "Rachel!" I yelled into the kitchen where Daddy's Little Princess was whittling her breakfast. "Have you been using Zeke's toothbrush?"

"Not me," was the immediate response. Why do I bother?

"Okay!" I decided to get to the bottom of the matter in the quickest way. "Bring the toothbrush can to the kitchen!" I dumped the contents on the table with a flourish that would have done Sherlock Holmes proud. "All right! Quiet! All of you. Now, pick out your own toothbrush."

I was stunned. Six little hands grabbed simultaneously for the yellow one. Zeke simply sighed. "I give up," he said and trudged to his room to finish dressing.

I risked the split second required to glance at the clock, then dove for the bedroom and my closet where, I'm sorry to confess, I neglected to coordinate my winter color palette. And since it had started to rain, I completed my stunning ensemble with Scott's knee-high mud boots. Then suddenly from the kitchen I heard a noise resembling the bellow of a large pachyderm.

I made a near perfect two point landing at the table where Gabe was spooning through a jar of peanut butter, using one of Scott's disposable razors. He was in a state of rage, staring at Rachel with glazed eyes, his neck veins distended. She, on the other hand, appeared totally unperturbed, so I directed my question to her.

"So what's the problem?" I asked. Her reply was deadpan.

"There's nuts in the peanut butter and he thinks it's *my* fault."

I confiscated the razor, gave it a quick swipe with a dish towel, and delivered it to its rightful owner in the bathroom. He accepted it with a puzzled, and somewhat pained, expression.

"Smells like peanut butter."

"Think of it as beard conditioner," I suggested.

I took a quick glance at the clock and felt the usual jolt. "Head for the station wagon!" I yelled. "We're gonna miss the bus again!" Everyone started to cry and/or scream, including Daddy, who evidently did not feel up to another careening chase over country roads trying to catch the school bus before it reached the highway and picked up speed. We had even begun to suspect that the bus driver actually *enjoyed* the chase and took pleasure in trying to outrun us.

Zeke dashed by on his way out the door, and, even in the chaos, I knew that something had to be done. I caught him in mid-stride. He was wearing cutoffs, a shirt which had obviously been rolled into a wad the night before and used to shoot baskets, no socks and a tennis shoe with a loose sole that flapped against the floor in duck-like fashion as he ran.

"Zeke," I said with remarkable calm, "I only ask one thing of you when you leave this house to go to school. By your appearance, I would like you to say to the world, 'I live in a house. I do not live under a bridge.' Go change your clothes. I'll drop you guys off at school. Daddy would never be able to catch the bus now."

Scott grinned like a kid whose dental appointment had just been canceled and darted out the door before I could change my mind. I needed to make a stop at their school sometime during the day anyway to fill out multiple immunization forms for the famous and ominous-sounding Permanent Record. The school had waited for this information as long as the state would allow, and my children were in danger of being expelled.

Why had I delayed? Well, picture this. Four children, numerous shots per child, and an absent-minded mother who doesn't even remember where her checkbook is most of the time, much less under which category she filed, "children's shots." Fortunately I remembered to look under "T" for "Traumatic Experiences." By the time I got through with the questionnaires at the school, I was so pooped I think I put "Undecided" in the blank next to Name, and "Not Applicable" in the blank by Sex.

I had brought Gabriel along with me and he had been remarkably quiet and good. Just as I started to compliment his behavior, I realized he had licked and stuck an entire book of postage stamps to the school library shelves. He was beaming at his handiwork, and I decided it had been well worth the five bucks for the stamps. After all, libraries are managed by educated people; surely they could figure out a simple way to get the stamps off the shelves without removing the finish.

I scooped Gabe up in my arms and dashed for the car, muttering aloud about all that had to be accomplished that day.

"Gabe, Momma's got to stop by the grocery store and get home in time to get Daddy some underwear washed, and I *have* to get the house cleaned today..."

As I attempted to lower him into the car seat, I felt his arms tighten around my shoulders and his warm breath on my neck.

"And love on me," he whispered in my ear.

I felt as if I'd been running at top speed and hit a wire stretched across the road. I stepped back and took a deep breath of the cool autumn air. A crimson leaf danced lazily down from an oak tree in a ballerina-like pirouette. Looking down into Gabriel's upturned face, I brushed his thick dark hair back from his forehead, marveling at how soft it was. Deep gratitude washed over me for my four-year-old, who had his priorities straight.

"Yes," I answered in a deliberately slow, purposefully soft voice as I hugged him close, "and love on you."

The early bird may get the worm, and as far as I was concerned that day, he could have it. Real people, and especially little ones, need to stop and smell the flowers along the way.

But I have stilled and quieted my soul;
like a weaned child with its mother,
like a weaned child is my soul within me.

PSALM 131:2

Worms in My Apple!

A t one point in my college education, I said to myself, "Now what I really need to do is get some practical teaching experience. All I know is what the professors tell me and what I read in books. Maybe I should do a little substitute teaching to get my feet wet." Having done so, I am extremely cautious about talking to myself anymore.

In my book, any substitute teacher who completes a full day in a new school deserves the Medal of Honor. I had been warned that this was the case. But I, you see, would be different. I had A's in all my education classes.

Furthermore, I had already survived Vacation Bible School, where I had encountered Benji, the small boy who could leap tall Sunday School shelves in a single bound. In one morning alone, this pre-schooler had held me and my shivering class of four-year-olds at bay with a spray bottle of 409 disinfectant, then proceeded to feed our rare Japanese goldfish purple Kool-Aid.™

Yes, I would not be just a conqueror, I would be more than a conqueror. I would be irresistibly creative and vivacious. Firm, yet kind. I might even sew matching outfits for the children from my old drapes and teach them to sing "Do Re Me" as I entered the room strumming my guitar. I would climb every mountain, ford every stream!

Had I known what awaited me, I probably would have joined the convent.

I enthusiastically listed my name at the administration building under available substitutes, and then waited every morning throughout the month of September for the phone to ring. Every evening in September I picked out something "teacherish" to wear, my favorite being the standard denim jumper embroidered with apples and tiny black boards and sporting little ceramic buttons in the shape of yellow school buses.

Wouldn't I be a picture? With my hair pulled back in a red gingham bow, matching ankle socks and tennis shoes painted to look like watermelons, I would have that early-childhood-educated look written all over me. Kindergarten power clothes, one might say.

I could have saved myself the trouble. My nighttime ritual of laying out clothes for the next day became an exercise in futility. Scott and the children began giving me patronizing, "Isn't she pitiful?" looks as I picked out the best read aloud stories for my hoped for students.

"What cha doin', Becky?" Scott would gently probe.

"I'm getting ready in case I get called to teach in the morning," I'd answer confidently.

Then he would give an exaggerated "Let's humor her" wink to the kids and say in a voice usually used by teachers of nursery school children, "Isn't that nice."

Then it happened. On a morning early in October the phone rang.

"Mrs. Freeman? Could you be at the Junior High in twenty minutes?"

"Oh, my!" I stuttered, not wanting to appear overly eager. "This is awfully short notice. And junior high—that's a little older than I expected—but yes, I'll be there!"

I mentally began to switch gears from kindergarten level to junior high. I had been so excited about teaching young children cute finger plays. I was soon to discover that junior high boys know some very interesting ones of their own. I reluctantly hung the jumper with the yellow school bus buttons back in the closet and opted for a purple knit dress with high heels and headed for the Junior High School. My first stop was the principal's office.

"Hi, there," I cheerfully greeted the man I assumed was the principal. He did not introduce himself.

His glance at me seemed to say, "There's one born every minute," as he came from behind the counter and headed out the door.

"Follow me," he barked. I struggled to keep up with his long strides while attempting to follow the designated lines on the floors in my dainty black pumps. I longed for my watermelon tennis shoes.

Teachers lined the hallways, apparently guarding their classroom doors. I searched their faces for a glimmer of friendliness, but found their faces screwed up as if they'd had persimmons for breakfast. And they looked old, so very, very old.

The principal stopped abruptly before an unguarded door. The sounds issuing from behind it sounded like the crowd at an exciting football game. "Smiley" opened the door and indicated I should walk through it.

"Any...anything I should know?" I dared to ask.

"There's a white button on the wall in each classroom," came the clipped reply. "Press it if you need help."

What a soothing thought for a rookie sub—panic buttons in every classroom—just like the ones used in banks to foil hold-ups. I entered the room filled with seventh graders eager to chew me up and spit me out. On my desk I found a note from the regular teacher: "Check for last night's homework. Give spelling test. Good luck." It was a place to start.

"Please," I quavered to the teeming masses, "if you don't mind, would you take out last night's homework? That is, if it's not too much trouble. Please." My voice had become that of an adolescent boy.

I waited for the class to move, to hear the rustling of papers, notebooks opening. Nothing. Just awkward silence. Could it be possible that not a single child had done their homework? Finally, mercifully, a girl in glasses and braids broke the silence.

"Anyone who doesn't bring their homework back to class needs a demerit slip filled out." This helpful child approached the teacher's desk and produced the forms and indicated I was to fill them in. They appeared to be about twenty lines long, in triplicate.

"Fine," I agreed, my smile beginning to hurt. "Now. How many of you do not have your homework this morning?" Every hand in the room shot up, with the exception of my little braided helper (who also informed me she had a perfect attendance record). So, I spent the first thirty minutes of the period filling out twenty-one demerit forms while the class played wastebasket spitball. Obviously there was not going to be time today for the creative group activities and dramatic play I had planned.

At this point, the English teacher from next door poked her wrinkled, angry face into my noisy classroom and shook a bony finger at the group.

"Don't move! Don't say another word! Don't even think of asking to go to the bathroom. I am right next door and I can see through walls! Do you hear me?!"

We were all dumb struck, including the sub, and the students nodded their heads in synchronized submission. After that, it was blessedly quiet, at least for a while. I decided it might be safe to check roll, but as I reached for the grade book, sounds of scuffling jerked me back to reality.

"Mrs. Freeman!" squealed my little braided friend. "They're fighting!" Sure enough, two boys were having at it, fists and legs flying. I knew immediately this was no job for a greenhorn and I hit the panic button. At the same time I yelled across the hall for the English teacher-cum-drill-sergeant to help me pull the combatants apart.

Thirty minutes later, long after the young warriors had been subdued, the principal appeared. He apologized for the delay and explained there had been another fight going on in another classroom and the other teacher had buzzed first. An insane vision shot through my mind of thirty teachers trying to see who can hit the panic button first, just like on the game shows.

I desperately wanted to go home. In fact, I wanted my Mommy. But alas, it was only the end of first period.

At the end of the day, when the last of the canni—I mean kids, charged out the doors, I became more resolved than ever not to teach adolescents again. Even if one or two of them *did* have a perfect attendance record. Those gifted ones would simply have to manage without me. I laid my head on the desk and tried to cry, but I was too drained. Then I became aware of a figure standing beside me.

When I looked up, I was startled. Standing before me was a grandmotherly woman with twinkling blue eyes and a wonderfully gentle voice. I thought for a moment it was an angel, but she looked vaguely familiar. Could it be? Yes, it was the English Drill Sergeant with x-ray vision who had earlier helped separate the two boys locked in what appeared to be mortal combat.

"Honey," she began, "it's not your fault. You were just too nice, that's all. I'm sorry to tell you that so many kids today only understand *tough*. Their home lives would break your heart if you knew them, but as a sub, you're going to have to learn to transfix a kid with one hard look. The drill sergeant you saw this morning—that is not me. I would much rather be nice, too, but most of the time I don't dare…" While she spoke, a horrible fear knifed through me.

"Excuse me," I managed, and rushing past the transformed woman, headed for the teacher's lounge. I stared into the mirror, my worst fears confirmed. Staring back at me was only a twisted shadow of my former self. My eyes had narrowed to slits, my face was wrinkled beyond recognition, and I looked old—so very, very old.

My breath coming in sharp gasps, I found my car and gripped the wheel tightly all the way home, relieved to see my hand on the steering wheel was smooth, not wrinkled, the nails pink and manicured rather than long, sharp, and curling. Safely home, I fell in the doorway, grabbed the phone, dialed the administration building, and instructed the startled secretary to remove my name from the substitute teacher's list for all eternity.

Pride goes before destruction,
a haughty spirit before a fall.
PROVERBS 16:18

Bee Pollen and Worm Milk: The Geritol Years

Christmas Eve morning found Scott and me together shoving our youngest child into the last remaining square foot of our luggage-and-gift-packed van.

"Next year," I puffed, "let's rent a moving van, hang the expense."

Scott settled into the driver's seat. "Maybe we ought to just stay home next year," he offered, and braced for mutiny from the back of the van.

"No!" Frantic, muffled voices of children arose in unified protest. "We like to go to Grannie's house!"

Scott shrugged, started the engine, and then reached down to peel a well-licked candy cane from the seat of his brushed-denim pants. He tossed it out the window in Daisy's direction, making her day.

So, over the meadow and through the woods to Grand-mother's house we went. In reality, we were *leaving* our "Little House in the Woods" to go to Grandmother's house in the 'burbs. Once we settled into Grandmother's living room on Christmas Eve, with family strewn on the floor and "Deck the Halls" playing in the background, we knew we'd be back next year.

This was to be my first Christmas with my newly married little sister, and I looked forward to cozy chats in a back bedroom where we would spend several hours alone while Mother joyfully watched over the children. Fa-la-la-la-la, it was not to be.

Mother and Daddy had just had their physicals, complete with cholesterol tests, and Mother had discovered that all those years of chocolate-covered conversations had caught up with her. There was not a chip of chocolate in the entire house!

"It rusts your pipes," Mother informed us. "Full of fat— elevates your LDL and lowers your HDL. The LDL is bad cholesterol. You can remember it as Lousy DL. HDL is the good stuff. You can remember it as Happy DL."

"I must not be old enough to be interested," I muttered, but she was already on the way to the kitchen to get her and Daddy's cholesterol-lowering niacin tablets. She brought his to him, along with a glass of water, as he lounged in his easy chair with a look on his face that was borderline rebellious.

"They make me turn red and tingle," he protested. "I think they may be dangerous."

"That's ridiculous," she insisted. "The whole world is taking niacin to lower their cholesterol. What makes you think you'd be the first fatality?" She shoved the water and the pills at him. "Drink up!" To us she commented, "This is a man who has never had a minor illness—all major." She turned to retrieve what she expected to be an empty glass, but found Daddy still examining the large blue and white capsule in the palm of his hand, the glass still full to the brim.

"I don't think I'm gonna take 'em anymore," he said, looking as if he were prepared to deal with the consequences, which were not long in coming.

"All right!" she declared, retrieving the pill and the glass before flouncing to the kitchen. "I'm tired of arguing with you. I do not intend to chase you around the house trying to get you to take your vitamins anymore! You're on your own from this day forward!"

"I'll take my chances," he called after her. He turned to us and grinned. "I think I saw her using my tackle box to sort and store our pills in this morning."

Their fuss was about as serious as most I'd ever seen between them and lasted about as long. We spent Christmas Eve sprawled in the living room floor, playing games, working puzzles, and humming harmony to carols issuing from the stereo. Mother was in rare form with a fresh audience of grandchildren, performing her repertoire of all nine verses of, "Up on the Housetop," each verse sung in a different, and more exaggerated, foreign accent.

We had a late, light supper which Mother served on their 1950s metal TV trays. When we had eaten every morsel and crumb available to us, Daddy took his coffee cup and ran it back and forth across his metal tray in the manner of prison inmates raking tin cups across cell bars to incite rebellion.

"Is this all the swill we get?" he demanded.

"Oh, for Pete's sake," Mother shot back, "you ate it too fast. If you chew food slower, you eat a lot less. You sounded like a dinosaur in a feeding frenzy. I think I'll start calling you, 'Tyrannasaurus.'"

He flirtatiously winked his eye. "*You* can call me Rex," he invited.

While they held onto each other and laughed so hard their eyes watered, my sister and I seized the opportunity to steal away and scrounge the kitchen for *anything* that might contain sugar. We found an old crunchy fudge diet bar in the dark recesses of the cabinet and hungrily divided it between us. After one bite, Rachel handed me her half in disgust.

"That stuff tastes like chocolate-covered cat food!"

"Meow," I purred, and stuffed her reject in my mouth before she could change her mind.

Mother and Daddy went off to bed, reminding Scott and me that, in case we had forgotten batteries for any of the toys Santa was to bring, the city version of Get-It-Kwik closed at midnight.

At about 1:00 A.M., Mr. and Mrs. Santa fell into a deep sleep, dreaming of a three-layered chocolate cake with french vanilla ice cream topped with hot fudge. Dawn arrived all too soon.

Gabe was already shooting up the place with the latest superhero toy. Our only daughter had dressed and re-dressed her doll, while Zach and Zeke gazed in wonder at pellet guns. Amid the clamor, the doorbell rang and I headed in that direction.

The doorbell ringer turned out to be the neighbor from across the street, who had noticed our van's sliding door ajar and, seeing its jumbled interior, assumed it had been ransacked during the night. Scott followed him out to the street to check it out and then had to explain to the neighbor, a bachelor, that the van was exactly as we had left it the night before.

In spite of all this activity, Mother and Daddy were not up yet. The kitchen remained dark and quiet, which was most unusual.

Thirty minutes later, when Rachel and Gilley staggered into the kitchen to figure out how to operate Mother's coffee pot, Daddy emerged from the bedroom with an odd expression on his face. I couldn't figure out if he was distressed or amused.

"Your mother isn't feeling well," he said, stifling a twitch at the corners of his mouth. "She's had a rough night. She's been regurgitating excess niacin since about 2:00 this morning."

Rachel and I managed to get Christmas brunch together and Mother emerged from her niacin overdose somewhat chastened but nevertheless determined to bound into her twilight years with vim, vigor and vitality, taking Daddy with her—pushing, pulling, and dragging if necessary.

After the holidays, I went out to eat with Mother and Daddy. Mother had loved dining out in cafeterias for years, originally because they made great pies. Now, however, it was because they offered a glittering array of salads and cooked veggies brimming with vitamins and beta carotene. I observed that cafeterias seem to be primarily populated by people their age or older, and that most couples swap bites, trade food, drink each other's tea and coffee, and share plates as if they were playing a rhythmic game of musical food. At one point, Daddy directed Mother to, "Put the chicken on the bread plate," and she responded with a toe tapping, "Pickin' out dough, honor your partner and do-si-do!" They both laughed until they had to wipe their eyes with their napkins.

"The first sign of aging," I observed, "is a gradual loss of dignity and decorum." Unperturbed, they sat there grinning at each other with an air of, "Ain't Life Grand?"

They looked so happy and rested. I felt a new anticipation for the years when Scott and I would be dancing *our* jig once our family responsibilities were behind us.

"Well," I threatened, "if you two keep acting this way, they may not let you room together at the nursing home."

Indeed, if they should ever be separated, Mother will probably waste away to skin and bones. She seems to feel that food eaten from Daddy's plate will not make her fat, and coffee from his cup will not keep her awake. I have come to understand the primary reason for all this sharing of food is to cut calories and cost, and I have certainly noticed they seem a bit more cost conscious these days. They have discovered, seemingly with shock, that they are within a few short years of retirement.

Mother has begun assembling an impressive assortment of vitamin bottles to keep expensive doctors away. She suffers agony every time she must remove the cotton from a new vitamin bottle and throw it away. Such a waste! One evening, in a flash of inspiration, she decided to use the cotton to apply her skin toner.

Daddy had already gone to bed and turned out the lights when she lay down beside him. Soon his doleful voice broke the stillness.

"I knew it was going to happen."

"What was going to happen?" she demanded.

"You smell like a giant vitamin pill!"

And the man said,
the woman whom thou gavest to be with me,
she gave me of the tree, and I did eat.
GENESIS 3:12, KJV

Welcome to My Classworm!

On an unusually cool and pleasant August Saturday after-noon in 1991, I walked across a stage to accept a college diploma in elementary education. Following the ceremony, amidst joyful celebration with our family, I presented to my husband and our four children their own versions of a diploma, handmade for them by their Aunt Laura. I assured them it was not just *my* degree that had been earned, but *our* degree, and I framed and hung their "diplomas" beside my own.

It was an emotional and enormously significant day for me, and the words of a poem danced through my mind often that day and in the days that followed. It read:

The only crown I ask, Dear Lord,
To wear is this: That I may teach a little child.

I do not ask that I may ever stand
Among the wise, the worthy or the great;
I only ask that softly, hand in hand,
A child and I may enter at the gate.

ANONYMOUS

After a wonderful student teaching experience, I had regained the confidence I had lost from the experience with substitute teaching. There is nothing like hands-on experience and I felt proud to belong to a profession that encourages mentoring. You might say I was pretty idealistic, having never actually been shut up in a room alone with small children for an entire school year. A major concern at the time was whether I could keep up with my own lunch money, much less the education of twenty-plus students.

So far I had not been able to interest my own child, Gabe, in learning his *ABC's,* but I kept trying to sneak up on his blind side. After all, kindergarten with its confinement was definitely in his near future. Would he be able to accept the bit and bridle?

"Gabe," I approached one afternoon, "next year you will go to kindergarten and you will get to learn to read!"

"Yeah," he responded with gusto, "and *this* year I get to play on the dock and have fun!" Oh well, in our years at home together I *had* taught him to snap his fingers, to whistle, and to blow a great bubble.

And by the grace of God, we had some years at home together before I entered the work force. As a teacher, I would still be able to be home when the children were home. It seemed the best solution to our economic stress and we looked forward to being a two paycheck family. And to be truthful, I was eager to get a real classful of those little heartwormers and hear them say in harmonic chorus, "Good morning, Mrs. Freeman!" Wasn't *nobody* gonna burst my bubble!

With my guitar tucked under one arm, my "Teacher's Have Class" tote bag snuggled under the other, I took a deep breath and swung open the door labeled, "Mrs. Freeman's First Grade Adventurers," and turned on the light as if I had just directed the sun to rise.

The room was perfect. It was clean and bright, with discovery centers inviting pint-sized exploration. My favorite spot was the large, homey corner by the flower trimmed window. There I had placed a huge rug, a rocking chair, and a book shelf. I set the guitar down gently in the reading nook, wrote my name on the chalkboard in three-inch script, and turned to face my first day of teaching.

I was soon to discover there were a few things they neglected to cover in Education 404. First of all, twenty-five students arrived simultaneously when I had been expecting seventeen. Each of the twenty-five students was escorted by an average of five family members. I had not realized how exciting the first day of school is in rural areas hard up for entertainment.

I managed somehow to finally reassure the last momma, daddy, sissy, Aunt Elsie Pearl, and Cousin Billy Bob that Little Bubba would be in the hands of an expert. They could go home. Please.

Turning to face my new students, I planned to jump right into our getting to know you activities, but someone was knocking at my classroom door.

It was the lead first grade teacher giving me advance warning about the horrors of the first day of bus run. She strongly advised I take care of that order of business first off. As Ross Perot is fond of saying, "Here's the deal": 3,498 look-alike buses descend upon our school in the afternoon, and each of my rookie first graders would have to find his/her particular bus—with the help of his/her rookie teacher. My job was to assign each child to the correct bus, colored name tag, sidewalk picture, and bus run teacher. I approached one of my little students for a sample information-gathering interview.

"Sweetheart, do you know your bus number?"

"Yes," the little fellow replied with all the confidence in the world. "It is black and it is stuck on the side of a yellow bus. I like it." He seemed satisfied he had given me all the information I needed.

"Okay..." I persisted, "do you know where you live, Dar-lin'?"

"Yes'm. I live 'cross the street from my friend."

I kept on ringin', but this child was not pickin' up the phone. "What about your telephone number? Can you tell me that?"

"Uh-huh. 1-2-3-4-5-7-8-9. I brought a show and tell in my backpack." Surely enough, he had.

"Oh, my...a real live frog. Named Ralph, you say? That's great." Wondering how on earth I was going to get this child home at the end of the day, I asked hopefully, "Is Ralph, by any chance, a *homing* amphibian?"

Seeing the other natives were getting restless, I decided to deal with bus run later. I reached for my guitar, and re-captured their attention by strumming a chord or two. I smiled broadly and broke into song.

"Oh, what a beautiful morning," I trilled. Just before I got to my favorite line—"Everything's going my way"—there was another tapping at my chamber door. It was the principal, Mrs. Boone, reminding me to do lunch count. How could I have forgotten?

While the children entertained themselves by sampling bites of fresh Play Doh™ and playing jab thy neighbor with freshly sharpened pencils, I glanced at what appeared to be the IRS version of the long lunch form. I never dreamed there could be so many lunching possibilities. There was your free lunch, your reduced lunch, your charged lunch, your paid lunch, your brought lunch, your brought lunch milk buyers, your brought lunch with milk and ice cream, your paid lunch with ice cream, and finally, your individual milk and ice cream buyers. Each possibility came with its own cute little code.

I did my best, but my head began to throb. Mrs. Boone sent down her executive secretary with a calculator, and managed to get lunch count turned in sometime around 2:00 P.M., well after the big event.

During my much anticipated afternoon break, I learned I had a phone call waiting for me in the office. It was Scott, informing me that Gabriel had not been allowed to start school that morning because he did not have his birth certificate.

"Okay," I said with remarkable calm, "I don't know where I put it. Tell his teacher I will be by this afternoon to show her my stretch marks in lieu of the certificate."

The highlight of the day was reading, "The Gingerbread Man," to my class and going on an explore-the-school walk as we tried to find the escaped cookie boy (whom I had cleverly dropped off earlier in the school cafeteria). One of the things I like most about six-year-olds is their complete gullibility. They were very sincere as they investigated the place, asking everyone they saw in the hall if they had seen a flat, runaway boy made of sugar and spice. When we found our giant cookie friend, none of the girls could bear to eat the poor thing while the boys fought over who would get to eat his eyes and head and bite off his feet.

At the end of the longest day I had ever lived, our vice-principal, Mr. Manley, peeked in to remind me to bring my bus run clipboard along when it was time for the children to board the bus. I suppose by then, word had gotten around that I needed plenty of reminders from my superiors if disaster was to be averted.

Observing Mr. Manley, I certainly thought he was a guy who lived up to his name. He was huge, with a moustache and a bald head, and I was intimidated just standing in his presence. (I later learned he is simply an overgrown teddy bear.)

But, in the five minutes that lapsed between his stern reminder and my time to venture forth leading students to the buses, I had forgotten what it was he had said I was to bring with me. In a last minute panic, I grabbed my purse and took my place with the children outside. My purse dangled from my arm where the clipboard should have been. Mr. Manley passed by and noted the purse.

"Mrs. Freeman," he observed dryly, "you're not planning to ride the bus home *with* the children, are you?"

Two months into the term, I was still absentmindedly carrying my purse out to bus run duty on the average of once a week. In the interim, Mr. Manley had taken to calling me, "Blondie," because he was sure that underneath my brunette exterior, there was a true dumb blonde. However, I reminded Mr. Manley that there had been moments when my purse had come in handy. Once I had saved the day when he was desperate for a pencil and I dug an eyeliner pencil from the depths of my purse.

He reminded me I had also worn one red shoe and one black shoe to school earlier in the year, totally oblivious of it until my students pointed it out to me around 9:00 A.M. Black and brown he might have excused as a plausible mistake, but black and red?

He also reminded me he had lost count of the times he had called me on the intercom to pick up my now famous purse at the office. He calculated I had accidentally left it in every major room in the building at one time or another.

He then reminded me that on both of his "walk-through" evaluations of my class, the children were straightening up the room (and dancing) to the tune of "Achy Breaky Heart."

Then I reminded Mr. Manley that I had made small children and large vice-principals laugh, which must surely be worth something. The gentle giant smiled his moustached Manley smile and gave me one of his famous bear hugs.

"You're okay, kid," he said, and moved his massive frame on down the hall.

After those lavish words of praise, my feet barely hit the ground. After I was chosen teacher of the month by my peers, I knew true job satisfaction. This is what it's all about, I decided.

That afternoon after school, I lay across my bed in what had become my usual state of exhaustion, and I felt Gabe snuggle next to me. I dreamily observed he looked awfully cute in the new school clothes I had bought him with my first paycheck.

"Momma?" he asked, "would it be okay if I just lay here by you and pretend you can hear me?"

Oh, God! I cried out silently as I encircled my lonely little boy with all the strength I had left, *What am I doing?!*

Even in laughter the heart may ache,
and joy may end in grief.
PROVERBS 14:13

Glowworms

L ast Thanksgiving, our family decided to meet at a lake in Kentucky, one day's drive for each of us. David and his wife, Barb, brought their three-year-old Tyler from Indiana, but Rachel and Gilley declined to be incarcerated in their small car for a day with tiny Trevor. Tyler met Grannie and Daddy George at the door, his enormous brown eyes wide with excitement as he spied the mammoth bucket of flavored popcorn his grandparents were hauling up the steps.

Imagine Tyler's disappointment when he discovered only a few kernels left in the container. There is no such thing as sinless perfection and sometimes, Mother and Daddy descend into gluttony. Seeing our reproachful eyes, Mother tried to explain.

"How can I tell you that you cannot trust two sensible, people with ten gallons of popcorn on a long trip in a small car?"

We allowed her time to put away her coat and get a cup of coffee before we began interrogating. Her defense was inspired.

"We hadn't been on the road two hours before I began struggling with visions of caramel flavored popcorn. I reached into the back where the can occupied half the seat and grabbed a handful to share with Daddy George.

"Before long, we were filling the lid of the can one load at a time, our hands moving from lid to mouth with increasing speed. Soon the rate of speed was such that our hands could not be seen—similar to the blades of a helicopter in flight; two rotors are in motion, but only a blur is visible." (By this time our four children and Tyler were open mouthed, and Mother warmed to her story.)

"Finally, with so many trips to the back seat for refills, the car started to wobble on the highway. My accomplice suggested I try to get the entire can into the front seat with us, but I was not willing to hang out the door in order to accommodate the can. When he suggested I do so, I knew we had to get control of ourselves." She paused dramatically and gazed at the kids.

"I reminded Daddy George of you *dear* children. Our rotor blades slowed and again became hands as they finally sputtered to a belching halt. But then, we made a terrible mistake." She paused for effect.

"We were thirsty and stopped for a tall glass of water. The popcorn, acting like a million tiny sponges, swelled up until only one of us could ride in the car. Daddy George had to tie me on top of the car for the rest of the trip!"

The kids loved it, but Zach and Zeke, so close to being worldly-wise, groaned a lot. "Awww, Grannie…" We may not have been able to transport a turkey to Kentucky for our Thanksgiving table, but there was plenty of ham to go around, thanks to Grannie.

We had a great time, with a snowfall sufficient to build a slightly muddy snowman, but insufficient to deter the fishermen. They sat hunkered down on the dock in the falling snow, pulling in dumb fish who didn't know it was too cold to bite. We fried their catch on Friday night, as Uncle David did his stellar imitation of a Cajun chef.

"Fuhst, you take 'bout half a pound a buttuh dat what cum from da she-cow…" Barb became Mother's "extra pair of hands" as Mother liked to describe her, while I loved up on Tyler.

"I've decided," Mother announced, "that if we checked Barb over thoroughly we'd find a label somewhere that reads, 'Made in heaven especially for David.'"

Saturday morning we packed and loaded the cars and then gathered in the living room for a precious tradition. The kids lounged on the rug, we grown-ups sat in an easy circle, our eyes meeting and holding one another's, storing up pictures of dear faces we would not see again for several months. Quiet settled over us, and Daddy reached for Mother's hand on his right, my hand on his left and the circle became connected.

"Lord Jesus," he began, "we're grateful for You and Your presence here with us. We know you've enjoyed it as much as we have. We ask that You go before and behind us on the road; surround each of us with Your protection. Bless our children with continued love and laughter. Draw them close to Your heart. Prosper their way. And may our grandchildren grow as You grew—'in wisdom and in stature and in favor with God and men.' We love You, Lord. Amen."

And Israel beheld Joseph's sons, and said, Who are these?
And Joseph said unto his father,
They are my sons, whom God hath given me in this place.
And he said,
Bring them, I pray thee, unto me, and I will bless them.

GENESIS 48:8-9, KJV

Weary Worms

By mid-term, I had come to see life more clearly than ever before. I now knew what I truly wanted. After a full day of dealing with first graders, I had only two desires: (1) sleep, and (2) being left alone.

I was rarely privileged to be alone, even at the grocery store, which may have been for the best because I could never remember where I parked the car. If the children could not remember, then our poor sack boy was doomed to roam the parking lot with us, pushing a cart sufficiently full of groceries to feed a family of six robust eaters for two weeks. On one occasion, our sack boy paused momentarily to wipe the sweat from his brow, and in the awkward pause, I felt I should say something.

"I bet this happens to you all the time—people not remembering where they parked their cars?"

"No, ma'am," he replied politely.

I did develop a system of grocery shopping such that I could remain in a state near to dozing. I pass it on to other exhausted moms; use it with my blessing.

The method requires no menu planning at all. I call it "Zombie Shopping." I amble into the supermarket, lean against a post until a sharp-looking mother with apparently healthy children pushes her cart down the aisle, and I then fall in behind her. Whatever she puts into her basket, I put into mine. After all, her children look well-fed.

I had grocery shopping down but my marriage was leaking at every fitting and threatening to blow sky high under the pressure. My vision of Scott and me jogging happily together in our middle years began to seem remote indeed. We weren't even laughing between fights anymore, they were coming in such rapid succession. We were both heartsick, scared to death it would never be wonderful again.

It was a dismal winter, reminding me of another difficult winter two years before when my Nonnie died. She had lived to be eighty-six years old. The last eight of those years had brought senility and illness, and eventually she had to live in a nursing home. She had changed so much physically and mentally that it would have been impossible for someone who had known her in the past to recognize her. Even so, it was hard to let her go.

Mother's big family re-assembled itself in the small West Texas town where they had all grown up. We gathered in the church where Nonnie had been a faithful member for fifty-two years. Because Nonnie's home place had been sold, and there was no house where we could all be together, we stayed in motels the night before the funeral. On the day of the funeral, those people in the church who had known the family for half a century served us a wonderful meal in the church fellowship hall, and opened their large, lovely parlor for us to use for the afternoon.

In the few minutes before we were to enter the sanctuary for the service, Mother put her arm around my shoulders and looked down the aisle we would soon walk to where Nonnie lay in state at the front of the flower-laden room.

"Becky," Mother whispered, her eyes brimming and her voice husky. "She is lying in almost the exact spot where Daddy and I were married thirty-six years ago. What memories this place holds!" As I thought of what was happening with Scott and me, the contrast with my parents' happy marriage was almost too painful to think about.

Then the music began and the usher signaled the family to move into the sanctuary and take our seats. After a small, hidden choir of Nonnie's friends sang two of her favorite hymns—"No Tears in Heaven," and "Where the Soul Never Dies,"—Daddy stepped to the podium to read the eulogy Mother had written two days before.

In an era when the concept of a woman totally dedicated to motherhood is rapidly fading from memory, it would be supremely wasteful to allow the passing of Elsie Jones to occur without thoughtfully savoring what it has meant to be her child, or her grandchild, or her great-grandchild.

In an era when the world is starving for a friend who can simply be there for us when we need them, who knows what it means to listen with complete self-forgetfulness, and who somehow brings comfort by their very presence, it would be a great loss not to pause and reflect on the life of Elsie Jones and her example of being this kind of friend.

Her six living children will have different memories because they were born over a fourteen-year span of time. The older ones will remember the comfort and stability she brought to them as adolescents during the desperately hard and bitter years of the Depression—how she could make a pot of red beans and a pan of corn bread taste as good as a steak dinner—how she could make the light from a kerosene lamp seem brighter, and the cold winds blowing across the

New Mexico prairie not quite so biting. To be sure, there was heartache enough to share at times, but there was always a mother's quiet and constant love.

And as the five boys grew older, the horseplay and hilarity almost raised the roof. They teased her until she blushed and laughingly scolded. They never missed an opportunity to untie her apron strings in passing. It was not unusual for one of them, fully grown, to sit in her lap while the rest of us enjoyed the show—including Nonnie.

When the grandchildren began to come along, she somehow managed to make all thirteen of them feel as if they were special. And of course, to her, they were. We were privileged to have Nonnie for so many years and privileged that her grandchildren were able to come home to her even as young adults and find healing for their wounds. Again, not so much by her words of wisdom, but by her quiet listening and her indescribable ability to comfort just by being there.

To her children's spouses, she became more mother than mother-in-law, especially when, with the passing of time, they lost their own mothers.

Here Daddy's voice broke, and it took a minute for him to continue.

And when she was old and infirm, she considered them her sons and daughters. But more than that, they were her friends.

So many were her friends, and many of you gathered here today became family for her, especially when she was growing old and her children could not be with her all the time. Often you made your way to the doorstep of the white house trimmed in blue paint and decorated with red geraniums to enjoy a good hot cup of coffee with her. And you found that same indefinable comfort, solace, and strength to go on.

In later years, you made your way to her house to deliver groceries, or to take her where she needed to go, or to make repairs, or do chores around the house. In your turn, you gave *her* comfort and solace and strength to go on.

And go on she did. It is one of the paradoxes of life that old age comes to us at a time when we just don't feel like handling it, but when she had to give up the house she had enjoyed so very much and leave her home town of more than fifty years, she did it with grace and strength, making the difficult adjustment to life in her children's homes.

She has left so many of us with a precious heritage: that there can be love and laughter in the bitterest of times; that there is tremendous power in a meek and quiet spirit; that there is healing both in listening silence and in a gentle word and touch; that *all* things in life can be used to mold us into the gentle benediction her life became.

Thank you so much for being here today to honor her with us.

From somewhere above us, the choir began to sing the old hymn, "Whispering Hope," another favorite of my Nonnie's.

> Soft as the voice of an angel,
>
> Breathing a lesson unheard,
>
> Hope with a gentle persuasion
>
> Whispers her comforting word:
>
> Wait till the darkness is over,
>
> Wait till the tempest is done,
>
> Hope for the sunshine tomorrow,
>
> After the shower is gone.

∽

Going back in memory to that Saturday afternoon in a little church in a dusty West Texas town, I saw a bit more clearly what I *really* wanted to be when I grew up, and I realized the monumental task before me to achieve it. Maybe there was still hope for sunshine tomorrow, though it seemed at the moment the shower would never go away. But, my Nonnie always said it would be so.

I have been reminded of your sincere faith,
which first lived in your grandmother Lois
and in your mother Eunice and,
I am persuaded, now lives in you also.
2 TIMOTHY 1:5

Wormin' My Way
Back to You

The counselor leaned back and lounged in his chair as is the manner of good counselors. Scott and I began our tales of woe, and before long he snapped bolt upright in his chair. Undeterred, we continued unburdening ourselves. He eventually shook his head in wonder and probably broke the cardinal rule of marriage counseling by looking shocked.

"You two really *don't* know how to communicate very well, do you?" he observed.

I, personally, was insulted. I knew *I* could talk a blue streak and Scott had a college degree in communications. Once the guy got his equilibrium back, he helped us see we had a lot of pride to swallow, and we slowly began to nourish our relationship back to health. In the process, we tried several techniques our counselor suggested—some helpful, some hilarious, and some downright humiliating.

I loved the write out your feelings technique. As a writer, I could pen my spouse to the wall any day. Scott began to receive reams of overnight mail from me; I left it waiting in his truck to be reviewed in the morning after an evening's argument. I must say, I had the art of sounding maritally correct down to a science, especially on paper. My defense would resemble a well-prepared legal brief with plenty of melodrama thrown in for good measure. One morning in return for one of my lengthy and brilliant treatises, I found the following note stuck to the coffee pot: "Dear Becky, I hate your shirt. Love, Scott."

With the mirror technique, one partner is to listen actively to the spouse and then repeat back word for word what the spouse just said. On the other hand, role-playing involves pretending one is, for example, the mother of the other while he or she vents old frustrations at the role-player. We found both of these absolutely impossible to carry out with a straight face, but I heartily recommend them for the comic relief they provide.

The help your man meet your needs technique works well for us, and actually, I made this one up all by myself. When I find myself in need of a hug or words of affection, I locate Scott and put my arms around his neck.

Then I say, "You think I'm so sweet and pretty you can hardly keep your eyes off me, don't you?" He can't resist a smile and obediently nods. I am fulfilled and happy. Actually, he reports that my putting words in his mouth causes him to realize he really does *feel* the words. So—I am working on this line next: "Scott, you just love cute, nicely-rounded women. You'd hate to see me lose an ounce, wouldn't you, sweetheart?"

Other exercises and experiences have helped too, but they must wait for my authoritative self-help book, *We're Happily Married and We Haven't Figured out Exactly Why.* Probably it has a lot to do with just getting our minds back on each other again.

All we can say is, we thank the good Lord every day for helping two starry-eyed kids keep their promise to each other.

I can't imagine we would ever take the wonder of a good marriage for granted again. To put it in simple country terms, we had the socks scared off us. I had been awakened out of my sleep-walking state, and I knew I wanted more than anything else in the world for my family to be intact—and not just intact, but as happy as possible. How could I give it my best shot when I was almost always exhausted? On the other hand, how were we going to be a happy family when there was a large financial shortfall every month?

I will never forget the moment I made the "Big Decision."

I had gone to a ladies' retreat with a group from our church and was sitting in the audience listening to a good friend describe her marriage to an alcoholic husband. For years, she put off having children, taking the financial burden of supporting herself and her husband on her own shoulders. Eventually they had a baby and she continued to juggle a full-time career and a family. She stood at the podium, tears standing in her eyes, as she spoke softly.

"I thought there was no way out, that I had no choice but to keep working. But then one day I felt the Lord speaking to me in my heart.

"'What would happen if you just quit? What would happen if you just stepped out in faith and trusted Me to provide?'"

As she spoke, I felt my heart jump. The words, "What if…" echoed in my own mind. Then she finished her story.

"There were some difficult adjustments, and I won't kid you, it has been a financial strain. But when I handed my husband the role of sole provider for the first time in our marriage, his whole attitude changed. Today he is sober and growing in the Lord. He has incredible patience with me. He has become the leader in our home and every day I think, *God, it's a miracle!*

A miracle. What a novel idea. Maybe I could get one of those.

I drove home from the retreat faster than I should have, waded through piles of papers waiting to be graded, stacks of laundry waiting to be folded, and found Scott in the kitchen. He was making sad sandwiches for the kids using bologna with rigor mortis and lettuce with no pulse, slapping the stuff onto bread the texture of croutons.

I took him by both hands, led him to the hammock outside, pulled both of us into it, and announced triumphantly, "I'm quitting work!" He exhaled at length and started to speak, but I was hot on the campaign trail now.

"Look, Scott, our family life can't get any worse than it is right now. We're microwaving underwear to get it dry in time to wear it and eating stuff out of the refrigerator that looks like it needs a shave.

"I'm sending up the white flag, throwing in the towel. This camel's back is broken, this filly won't ride, this heifer won't milk, (deep breath) not gonna do it anymore. How else can I say it?

"I have only so much time and energy to give and when I'm working, I have nothing left for the people I love the most. No one is mindin' the store around here! Whatever the cost, we *have* to find a way to get me home again."

Scott blinked twice and asked, "Is that it?"

"Yep," I answered, bracing for another round.

"Okay," he said.

"*What?*" I said.

"Okay," he repeated slowly. "We need you. To be honest, I'm relieved. And that's a surprise to me, too. We'll find a way to make it."

The stars came out in the sky above the lake and I relaxed against him. In just three more months I could be at home again with my family. It seemed far too good to be true. I checked to see if I might not be glowing in the moonlight. We swung contentedly in the hammock and smooched until Rachel hollered to us from the back door.

"Gabe just lost his baby tooth in his sandwich!"

So do not worry, saying, "What shall we eat?"
or "What shall we drink?" or "What shall we wear?"
For the pagans run after all these things,
and your heavenly Father knows that you need them.
But seek first his kingdom and his righteousness,
and all these things will be given to you as well.
Therefore do not worry about tomorrow,
for tomorrow will worry about itself.
Each day has enough trouble of its own.

MATTHEW 6:31-34

Homeworm Bound

After turning in my letter of resignation stating I would not renew my contract for the following year, I experienced a short period of doubt. Was I a quitter? Did I simply have a short attention span? Was I wasting my college degree? What about the sacrifices my family had made to help me get through college? Would I be able to face being a retired teacher after nine long months of faithful service? What about the students I had come to love? Didn't those children need me?

Proverbs 14:1 provided my reassurance. "The wise woman builds her house, but with her own hands the foolish one tears hers down." Yes, I was making a wise decision. My house was in desperate need of repair and a woman's touch. I would finish out the school year, then I would close that chapter of my life and open up to what the Lord would have me do at home.

Once it was settled, I felt a tremendous sense of relief and much of the pressure was off. The remaining weeks of teaching were some of the most fulfilling as I observed the progress my students had made in their learning. During the week of standardized testing, I explained to the children that they would be answering many questions for the test people.

"I want you to do your very best and color the dot by the sentence you think best answers their questions," I instructed. After the third grueling day of testing, one little boy named Christopher (beautiful blue eyes, lashes a mile long) looked up in disgust.

"The test people sure must be lazy to make a bunch of little kids work this hard to tell them answers to stuff they could find out their selves if they would just go to school."

After the days of testing were over, I thought it would be downhill all the way to the last day of school and retirement. The only remaining hurdle was the innocuously named event called field day.

My students had gone on to the playing field under the supervision of Mrs. Nuefeld, the only parent to show up that day. There they waited with excitement for Mrs. Freeman, femininity personified, to get the athletic contests going.

The first challenge I faced was to transport two ice chests at once across the school parking lot to load into my van with the ultimate goal of unloading the chests at the playing field. One of the ice chests brimmed with iced down soda pops and the second was loaded with water balloons to be used in one of the main events.

Naively, I had assumed I would have plenty of parent helpers, since I had sent heroic Mrs. Nuefeld on ahead with my class to the playing field. Evidently the parents were better acquainted with field day than I. Not a single parent was in sight, and I began to suspect the main event might be about to take place on the school parking lot with Mrs. Freeman being the sole contestant.

I managed to push, heave, and shove until, miraculously, I had one heavy ice chest atop the other on the dolly. But when I began rolling the dolly across the pavement toward my van, it started to weave in spite of my best efforts. Spectators began assembling at the school's office window. I understand from later accounts that a collective gasp ascended when I finally tripped and both ice chest lids flew open, sending fifty cans of pop clattering about over the parking lot and underneath faculty cars. A myriad of brightly colored water balloons bounced and popped among the cans, like kernels of popcorn, making blurping noises as they prematurely spewed forth their contents.

I sat down on the pavement, shoulders shaking like a leaf. The faculty watching from the window decided they were observing a nervous breakdown in progress and immediately dispatched Carl, the school counselor, to my aid. Once Carl determined I was laughing rather than crying, my audience was shocked to see him sit down on the pavement and join in my hysteria. I will have to say, he *is* an effective counselor. With his help, I was able to get on my feet, reload the sodas and the few remaining water balloons back into the ice chests and then, a few minutes later, unload them at the playing field.

I had also to unload a ten-gallon drinking can filled with orange Kool-aid™, and as I waddled from the van to the picnic table, I unwittingly pressed the spigot against my abdomen. By the time I made it to the track, I was not a pretty sight. I had begun the morning wearing a white pantsuit. I arrived at the track wearing brilliant orange Kool-aid.™ To protect myself against a monster Texas sunburn, I donned a sunbonnet in a fetching, neon shade of pink. Even from across the field, the children recognized me immediately.

"It's Mrs. Freeman!" they all cried at once. They ran to meet me and hugged me around the waist and came away with sticky orange faces and arms. "Can we have snow cones now? Huh, please, can we?"

Feeling badly about having left them waiting for so long, I consented, not thinking about setting a limit on the number of syrupy cones they could each consume. Before I realized it, the blankets we were to sit on during breaks were covered with kids and cones. I had a virtual sugar orgy on my hands.

I looked around furtively, wondering how to get control of the situation and immediately noticed the disapproving frowns aimed in my direction from the other teachers. They, of course, had wisely told their children to wait until after lunch for dessert. Forget lunch. I would have been smart if I had held out until after the athletic events.

After endless crabwalks, tricycle races, and sack hops, lunch time arrived. All the other classes organized their picnic areas, with room mothers handing out food, napkins, and drinks in a synchronized rhythm. On our blanket, however, food was the last thing on my students' minds. It was the lunch *sacks* we were interested in, for we had our own unique contest going.

"Shaun has thrown up *seven* times, Mrs. Freeman!" announced Jacoby. "That's the most of anybody!" She held tightly to Shaun's hand as if he were a prize trophy. Amazingly, Shaun was grinning. Though green around the gills, he was obviously proud of his accomplishment.

About this time, Mr. Manley strolled by. He was to be promoted and transferred to another school in the coming year. Running into me on the field in all my kaleidoscope of color caused him to glow with appreciation, as if he had had a stroke of great good fortune.

"Freeman," he said to me with a tinge of sadness I could only assume was sincere, "I'm gonna miss you next year. It's going to be like a dadgum divorce." Then he wiped an imaginary tear from one eye, turned dramatically, and whistled back toward the school building. If he hadn't been such a big man, I would have sworn I saw him skip once or twice.

Mercifully, the last day of school arrived. I scanned the children, trying to store up memories. They would forever be special to me: they were not only my first class, they were possibly my last, at least for a very long time.

My gaze settled on Dustin, my tiny, hyperactive challenge, who amazed me daily with deep and insightful questions by the zillion and just generally drove me crazy. I turned to observe my no-nonsense Chris and was reminded of the day when I had persuaded Scott to dress up as Johnny Appleseed and visit my class, complete with a tin pan cap. I had asked Chris to suggest a place where we "might put Johnny Appleseed" in our crowded room, and he responded dryly, "Why don't you lay him out on the reading table over there? He's been dead two hundred years."

And Jacoby. Would there ever be another Jacoby? Jacoby is a she, the shortest girl in the class, of stocky build, who feared no one. She had fallen in love with sweet, shy, and tall Howard, who was temporarily looking rather goofy while waiting for a front tooth to fall out.

One day, Jacoby and Howard had found two worms on the playground and had adopted them. The two clever children named them—surprise, surprise—Howard and Jacoby. The two worms occupied our science table for weeks, and no two worms were ever loved more dearly, except possibly Gabe's.

I glanced on toward Brian, whose ready smile could light up his entire face, but who often cried just as easily. I had not understood why, until Christmas time when I asked the children to write their wish lists to Santa. Brian wrote for a very long time, then, while my back was turned, stapled his letter closed with about thirty staples.

I was not happy with Brian, because I needed to read over his work before it was sealed, and I told him so. While Brian went on to P.E. class, I pulled out all the staples, grumbling all the while. When I read what he had written, I felt as if I'd taken a blow to the pit of my stomach.

"Deer Santuh," it read, "All I want is my dad to cum bak home. But mom won't let him. If you cood maik mom luv him thats ol I want for Chrismis."

I sat for a minute getting myself together, then sprinted to the gym, stood in the wide doorway, and motioned for Brian to come with me. We marched hand in hand to the teacher's lounge where I let him put quarters in the vending machines until we had candy and pop enough for the both of us. Then I pulled him onto my lap.

"Honey, I'm sorry I fussed at you about the staples. And I'm awful sorry about your daddy being gone." He relaxed against me and I tightened my arms about him. "You know, Santa can't do just everything. But no matter what happens at Christmas, Brian, remember I love you and so does Jesus. And we always will." He buried his head in my neck and cried a bit. We both did. Then we dried our tears and ate candy and drank Coke™, and by the time Brian went back to P.E. class, he was smiling, at least for a while.

I think that, of all my students, Brian and Dustin tugged most at my heartstrings. Providentially, the two little guys had found kindred spirits in one another, both having come from broken homes and both loving to draw pictures better than just about anything in the world. During the following summer I tried to contact Brian but couldn't find him. I hoped he and his mother had moved somewhere to rejoin his dad. But I did locate Dustin, invited him to visit us at the lake, and on a sunny afternoon, I picked him up at his home. His grandmother told me he had gotten up four times during the night to see if it was time to go to my house. As I buckled him in the seat of my van, it was obvious he was ecstatic.

"Miz Freeman," he lisped, "I've had teachers before, but I *never* had one want to take me home!"

On the last day of school when I said goodbye to the children, I told them it had been a wonderful first year for me. (Now that it was over, I was already remembering the best times most.) Christopher of the big blue eyes and long lashes looked astonished.

"You mean this was your first year to teach school? *Man,* Mrs. Freeman, you learned a *lot!*" he declared.

Yes, Christopher, I learned a lot.

I learned that every child is special. I wish I could describe each one. Every one gifted and talented and treasured by their teacher. If any of my students gets to read this book, I want you to know Mrs. Freeman thinks of you and prays for you still. You will always be my first class, the smartest, sweetest group of seven-year-olds in the entire "Great State of Texas" to me.

I also learned that the people who teach our children are absolute heroes if they just keep showing up on Monday and are still on their feet by Friday. I am no longer naive about all that teachers do. I understand the sacrifices, as well as the rewards. So, hug a teacher today. He/she can use it.

Another hard but vital lesson I learned is to realize I have to say "no" at times to good things in order to keep my life in balance and my priorities straight. I loved my students, my amazingly patient principals, and my fellow teachers, but I love my own children and husband even more. And to be honest, I love myself enough to know I need time to be alone in order to be at peace with myself, my family, and my Savior. For me, I had to make a choice.

An excellent wife... smiles at the future...
she looketh well to the ways of her household.
PROVERBS 31:10, 26- 27, NASB
☙

The Nightcrawler Years

It was a shock to realize Zachary had turned thirteen during the winter. Ready or not, we were entering the teenage zone: the stage when an adolescent's brain synapses quit firing while the rest of their body races toward adulthood. I had the feeling I had not made the decision to become a full-time homemaker a month too soon.

More and more often I was finding myself in conflict with Zach over a topic I remember as a source of tension between Mother and David during his teen years. I had sworn I'd be smart enough and strong enough to avoid the conflict, but it was upon me. The topic is, of course, hair.

Picture this: bottom half of head is shaved to the scalp, top half is left to grow at will. He then parts the mop down the middle and lets it fall so that he comes out of the bathroom ready for school looking exactly like Alfalfa from the "Our Gang Comedies," circa 1936. The hair fountains from the part, in palm tree fashion, exactly as boys wore their hair during the Depression. He calls it "cool." I call it a bad hair day.

The topic of hair, however, fell into second place in order of importance recently when Zach lost his temper and took it out on his bedroom wall. This resulted in a dent in the wall and a five hundred dollar medical bill for a broken fist. The call went out. 1-800-MOTHER.

"Was it the knuckle bone directly below the little finger on the right hand?" she inquired.

"Well, yes. How did you know?"

"Because David broke the same bone when he was Zach's age. Only he broke his on someone else's chin. It's called the boxer's fracture. Welcome to the teenage zone, Honey."

"HELP!" was about all I could muster.

"Well, whatever you do, keep your sense of humor. Don't ever stop talking and hugging. Try to keep conflict over non-earth-shattering topics to a minimum. Discipline with less emotional turmoil than I did—but *do* discipline.

"You will blow it on occasion, but just remember, no matter how good a job you do raising the kids, you are still going to raise four little sinners in need of the grace of God."

I hung up the phone feeling somewhat better. I grabbed for pencil and paper. "Let's see now..." I licked the pencil and wrote, "(1) Keep sense of humor. (2) Discipline. (3) Keep huggin' and talkin.' (4) Even if we do it all perfectly, the kids won't turn out that way."

Just then the phone rang, and it was Mother again. "I forgot the most important thing: Pray a lot—with Scott—together. It will make all the difference."

I continued taking mental stock and decided the sense of humor thing shouldn't be all that hard, given my Erma Bombeck vow. I'd been working on that since they were toddlers. Besides, the kids were all developing their own senses of humor, and getting to be a lot of fun in the process.

One morning as we were about to leave the driveway for school, I realized I had forgotten to eat breakfast, so I asked Zachary to run get me a banana.

The next thing I knew he was running toward the house with his arms flattened against his ribs and his head cocked to one side. Then he turned around and ran back to the car in that same peculiar way—without a banana for my breakfast.

"Son! What are you doing?" I demanded. He looked back at me with sincere surprise.

"Didn't you tell me to run like a banana?"

At least Zachary and I were still hugging and talking. I was reminded of a great evening with the kids not long ago when we had watched a James Bond movie together. Bond had narrowly escaped death as he dropped miraculously from a plane onto a yacht in front of a beautiful woman. Then he cooly introduced himself. "Bond. James Bond."

Rachel was supposed to be cleaning her room instead of watching TV, so I tactfully reminded her of it.

"How's your room, Rachel?" I asked.

"Duhty," she answered, doing a perfect imitation of the famous secret agent. "Very duhty."

I laughed but dispatched her to her room while I, feeling a sudden rush of domesticity, dispatched myself to the kitchen to bake a pie. Not owning a pastry cutter, I resorted to cutting the shortening into the flour with two sharp knives. The flashing steel caught Zeke's eye.

"Ah-so," he observed, "Num Chuck Mom."

Zach hitched his stool up to the opposite side of the counter and offered his observation. "Nah," he said, "she's Mother Scissorhands."

Maybe humor *will* help carry us through this wormy stage, however corny it may get. I knew Mother had suffered all our teenage agonies as if they were her own, but I also knew beyond a shadow of a doubt she'd had a lot of laughs during those difficult years. She had kept a big brown envelope for each of us marked, "Becky's Treasures," "David's Treasures," and so forth. Sometimes when we get together, we drag out the envelopes. We usually end up rolling in the floor.

It's easy to track the changes in the notes we wrote to her as we neared, and then entered, the teen years. Rachel's notes are generally matter of fact and to the point. One of my favorites from her first grade year reads, "I love God and Mother." Another school paper reads, "Plants live in deart. Plants need to be waterd some. The end. roten by Rachel Arnold."

By the third grade, her notes became more sophisticated, even manipulative. One afternoon when Mother was out, Rachel took a telephone message. It read, "Momma, I have to go to the Dintest Jan. 10 - 1972. If you *Love me* you'll tell me to stay home."

As she neared junior high age, her notes changed slightly, "Mom, I've been borrowing pencils from my boyfriend cause I'm out. Don't buy me any."

During the school year, Mother felt we ought to eat a standard breakfast of eggs, bacon, toast and juice (this was before she learned about happy DL and lousy DL). I have never been much for breakfast anyway, but none of us liked eggs, and all of us had written notes to Mother about them at one time or another.

Rachel's got right to the point, "I hate eggs, I do!" while mine reflected a certain agony of the soul, "That was all I could eat—I got a stomach ache from them—but they tasted good—but don't give them to me again because I get a stomach ache. Anonomys"

David's egg notes had a man-of-the-world quality about them since they were written after he was in high school. At least three of them dealt with a situation which may reveal that my absent mindedness just might be inherited.

Mother had a tendency to put eggs on to boil and leave home for the day. David had a tendency to drop in from school to eat lunch at home and find the eggs exploded all over the kitchen, the pan dancing bright red on the burner. David would turn off the heat, set the pan in the sink to cool, and nonchalantly write notes like, "Good job, Mom!" or "Well, Mom, I hope you like your eggs hard!" and finally, "Well, Mom, you did it again!"

Both Mother and Daddy went through the phase when they felt we should have some musical training, especially since we all loved music. They thought we would take to lessons like a sick kitten to a warm brick. I made it through two years of piano lessons but refused to play when there was a single person in the house to hear it. Then came voice lessons, and in desperation, I penned another tactful note:

Dear Mother,

I do not like voice lessons. Here are the reasons: (1) I'm tired of quacking; (2) I have not got to sing words and even if I did, she wouldn't like it; (3) she said, 'Be careful, don't strain, I don't want to make your voice any worse than it is'; (4) I worry all week about it and I sweat."

Mother had already told me that she and Daddy agreed each of us had our hardest year in the eighth grade, which of course, became their hardest year with each of us.

"This is the year," she had warned, "when otherwise reasonably nice thirteen-year-olds become carnivorous. They will eat each other alive in their attempts to become part of the in crowd."

I knew why she felt that way. When I was thirteen, I don't know which I was more thankful for; the fact that Jesus saved me from hell or that He saved me from drowning in junior high peer pressure. Sometimes I think they may be one and the same.

On a weekend retreat with my youth group from church, I found the Lord through a simple prayer as I lay on my bunk looking at the stars through my cabin window. The next day I was sure it was my radiance that lit up the morning. Having found a friend in Jesus, I never felt loneliness again, even when on the outskirts of the in crowd.

Sometimes during eighth grade, I would take my Bible and read it in the school bathroom stall to avoid the cliques chattering away with each other in the cafeteria. It sounds pitiful, but it gave me strength and hope and before long, I had an increasing group of good friends I enjoyed all the way through high school.

Several of us began bringing our lunches to school and then at lunch break, we would walk to my house, where we rounded out the lunches or whipped up something for ourselves from the fridge. We giggled and laughed like all high school girls do, but we also shared our hearts and prayed together. We may even have offered a prayer of gratitude that we were not still in junior high. I'm sure Mother did. But then my little brother entered eighth grade purgatory.

One evening during David's eighth grade year, he was supposed to go back to school for rehearsal with a small, elite choral group for which he had been chosen. (Aside from the fact that he had a nice voice, he was the only boy in eighth grade whose voice had sufficiently changed that he could sing a baritone solo.) Mother and Daddy knew he was struggling with feeling shut out of the group, but felt he should be made to participate in the hope he would eventually feel that he belonged. They insisted he go, and he left the house angry and upset. By midnight, he had not returned.

Mother called every friend she knew to call, Daddy drove to every place he could think of that David might possibly be, and then they settled down in the darkened living room to wait for dawn and to pray. I crept from bed and sat up with them, wrapped in a quilt but still trembling as if I were having a chill.

When daylight came, Daddy and I started out again to look for David, first in the nearby woods. I'll never forget the sound of Daddy's voice calling for David, nor the drive to the police station to fill out a missing person's report.

We had already checked with all the hospitals in our area, but while Daddy and I were gone, Mother thought of one more friend of David's they hadn't particularly approved of, and she jumped in her car and drove to his house. She rang the doorbell several times before the sleepy headed boy slowly opened the door.

"Noel," she said, fighting back tears, "is David here?"

He nodded and left the door ajar, and soon David appeared, looking a little defiant, but sad and sheepish as well.

"Davey," Mother said softly, "let's go home." He nodded and they drove home in silence. Mother fixed him some breakfast, keeping an eye on the drive so she could let Daddy know immediately that David was safe. When we arrived, she hurried to meet us with the good news. Daddy ran inside, took David in his arms and his cries of relief echoed through the house.

All of us cried that morning, including David, and it was the last time he ever stayed out all night without permission. In his sophomore year in high school, we were discussing that Rachel was having a hard time in eighth grade, and he shocked us all by declaring, "Man, I *loved* junior high!"

One of several positive things that came out of that awful night was that Mother and Daddy began to set aside Friday evening, when we three kids were all usually out somewhere, to pray for us. They would build a fire in the fireplace and sit on the rug in front of it together and pray for us—for our safety, for our spiritual well-being and for our futures.

Not long after Zach hit the wall, Daddy told me about a visit he had just made to see David and Barb and Tyler in Indiana, where they live in a small bungalow situated on a river. Daddy, David, and Tyler spent the entire morning floating down the river in a boat. Little Tyler, age four, never once mentioned being tired or restless.

Daddy was amazed that David had taught his young son to cast from the boat already, and, somewhere around mid morning, Tyler landed a small fish. His enormous brown eyes danced and his dimpled face almost split open with his smile. As Daddy finished telling me about that morning, his eyes grew misty and his voice had a catch in it.

"I was very aware," he smiled, "that life had come full circle for me, and I had been given the great privilege of watching my son being a great dad to *his* son. Going through those hard teenage years seemed enormously worthwhile."

I'm sure Daddy meant to encourage me with the story. And sure 'nuff, he did.

Sons are a heritage from the Lord,
children a reward from him.
PSALM 127:3
ॐ

Are You a Man
or a Worm?

From the desk where I type, our backyard is in full view, with the lake beyond. Almost the entire half acre is covered with items of metal, wood, or rubber, and Scott assures me every item will eventually become essential. When it does there it will be without cost, because he had the foresight to haul it home.

I have compiled the following inventory, to be sung to the tune of "A Partridge in a Pear Tree."

In our lakeside backyard my husband gave to me,
Twelve pipes a laying,
Eleven Schwinns a swarming,
Ten boards a warping,
Nine puppies barking,
Eight trash cans filling,

Seven cans a rusting,
Six bowls of dogfood,
Five Lawn Mo-wers!
Four fighting kids,
Three gas tanks,
Two buildings, outhouse style,
And a bass boat whose engine has expired!

Given the success of the television show, "Home Improvement," I feel confident I am not the only woman who has a husband in love with backyard junk and most of all, "man" tools.

Today's man is not satisfied with the old "hitting-the-thumb-with-the-hammer" accident. A man of the nineties can now shoot himself to death with a twopenny nail. Scott has observed a contractor securely shish-kabob his thumb to his forefinger while trying to nail a simple board to a simple wall. Ah, progress!

In fact, Scott very nearly lost the ability to father children as the result of an encounter with a "man saw." It happened when he casually walked up behind a buddy who happened to be wielding a circular saw. Seventeen stitches on his upper, inner thigh convinced him to never *casually* approach anyone with a power tool of any kind again. He even gets skittish when I plug in my electric handmixer.

Power hand tools excite almost any man, but real men almost always go on to bigger things. To really get *my* man salivating, it takes *heavy machinery.*

His first introduction to this addiction came with his first job after we were married, where he operated a forklift for a firm which produced medical supplies. It took him hardly any time at all to wedge the forklift between the ceiling above and the concrete floor beneath. He found himself and his machine sitting at a forty-five degree angle for some time. It began to seem like an eternity after the news buzzed over the intercom that the president of the company was touring the building and would be in his area shortly.

One summer while we were vacationing in Florida in a posh resort (thanks to sharing the rent with three families), Scott almost ran himself down with his own van. It was hard not to notice that our old Chevy van seemed a bit out of its league among the Cadillacs, Mercedes, and Jaguars, even before it began to make embarrassing noises. Scott felt compelled to play auto-mechanic-man in full view of all the well-to-do vacationers strolling about in their tennis whites.

In his attempt to repair the U-joints on the vehicle, he jacked the back wheels of the big, heavy, awkward machine onto a curb and crawled underneath. Apparently, it is important to put the emergency brake on when removing the U-joint of a car, because the "park" thing doesn't work once the U-joint is gone.

Scott remembered this when he found himself joyriding across the road, hanging on to the underside of the van for dear life. Thank the Lord, he escaped with only a few road burns on his backside, his macho image only slightly the worse for wear.

He loves man-sized machines, and he comes by it honestly. His father, Jim, rode a huge motorcycle to work for nearly thirty years. Now that Jim is retired, he spends his days in his garage, happily tinkering with his BMW between road rallies.

Scott's grandfather was also a motorcycle man, back in the days when motorcycles were called scooters. Bev, Scott's mom, thinks nothing of driving alone across the country to snow ski for a weekend, and his long, tall brother, Kent, drives a diesel truck with a gooseneck trailer even if he's only going to the local Get-It-Kwik for a loaf of bread. His sister, Laura, can outmaneuver most men driving a tractor, and in the company of her brothers can also blow gaskets, rotate distributors, and re-throttle spark plugs. (I'm pretty sure that's what I've heard them say.)

My side of the family is another matter entirely. I once purchased a Little Tikes™ picnic table in a box, and, in my attempt to assemble it, produced a flat plastic barge which the kids liked even better. Certainly, my father is not one who could be called even remotely handy. He refers to caulk, the builder's best friend, as "gookum pucky," and once managed to gash his head while operating a lawn sprinkler. After thirty-eight years of marriage, Mother keeps a phone number for a repairman whose ad reads, "We fix what your husband fixed." The only other man I know who might be Daddy's equal is our friend, Gary. When working alongside Gary, Scott truly appears to be a mechanical wizard.

Gary watched in awe as Scott miraculously fixed their broken dryer—by plugging it in. He became very nearly transfixed with wonder when Scott unclogged their overflowing commode by using—as a sheer stroke of plumbing genius—a plunger.

When we first met Gary and his wife, Mary, they had just moved to the country from Dallas and bought a lovely older home with acreage. The older couple from whom they bought the house were very sentimental about one particular young tree in the front yard.

"We planted it in memory of a dear relative," they explained reverently. "We'd appreciate it if you'd take good care of it."

Gary, eager to experience rural life to its fullest, purchased a new, bright red riding mower for his acreage. At last the day came for Gary to mount the mower. He thrilled as the engine roared to life, and he slipped it into gear, man and machine moving as one entity. Mary stepped out of their new home just in time to see him flatten the memorial sapling. Struggling to gain control, he backed over it again from the opposite direction. The lawn mower seemed to have a mind of its own.

The next evening, Gary courageously climbed on the mower again. This time Mary sat sipping coffee in the kitchen, a safe distance from Gary and his machine, watching him through the patio door. He seemed to be doing better than the day before. Suddenly, over the rim of her coffee cup, Mary saw headlights coming toward her.

"Surely not," Mary thought. Gary and the monster mower proceeded to hum steadily toward the patio door as she grabbed her coffee and backed up quickly from the table. The lawn mower collided with the door like some toothy creature out of a horror movie and proceeded to eat and digest the screen.

Mary takes no chances these days. When Gary is mowing, children and dogs are not allowed outside. She says he is the only man she knows who needs an air bag on his lawn mower.

On any given Saturday morning, Scott's neighborhood buddies appear from nowhere like June bugs to a back porch light, drawn by the roar of serious mechanical equipment in operation—be it chain saw or Weed Eater.™ Wally, a sweet grandfather of six, is the worst little boy of them all. He sometimes appears at the door asking to borrow a tool or a trailer, but I know he is actually hoping to find Scott fiddling around with some piece of machinery in the backyard. I've decided it's the "man" way of finding out if friends can "come out and play."

Before long, Scott peeks around the corner with his Saturday cup of coffee in hand and Wally by his side, with the eager look in his eyes that says, "Can I go, huh, can I, please, huh, can I?"

What's a wife to say to two grown up little boys? So, I put another pan under the dripping kitchen sink I had thought I might ask Scott to fix and give him the goahead.

During the spring after I had decided to turn in my resignation but while I was still teaching, I was jolted awake at 6:30 A.M. by an earthquake. Or so it seemed. I grabbed my robe and vibrated toward the source of the racket. There sat my husband atop a bulldozer (who knows where he got it?) digging a swimming pool-sized hole in our backyard (who knows why?). As far as I've been able to determine, he dug the hole purely for the fun of it, and thoroughly enjoyed filling it back up again the next day—for the same reason.

I watched Scott from the window as he toiled with the bulldozer in the sun, his muscles rippling with moisture. I felt a fresh surge of attraction for this man, realizing with affection that he looked good, even in sweat. With that flush of tenderness, I went to my leaky kitchen sink and filled a glass with water, then popped in a few ice cubes. I walked down the backdoor steps and waited for Scott to notice my presence and turn off the engine. When all was safe, I lifted the glass in his direction.

"Are we playing with our Tonka Toys™ this morning, sweetheart?" I asked coyly.

He pulled on the brake lever, reached gratefully for the water, wiped his moustache, and grinned. I noted the Tom Selleck lines on each side of his mischievous smile. Muscles, sweat, mischievous smiles—they always lower my resistance.

"Becky?" he said in his most endearing "little boy" voice.

"Yes, Scott?" I answered, trying to appear nonchalant about the huge crater in my yard.

"I like my tractor," he grinned.

This was news?

He released the brake and the engine roared again. Before my very eyes he transformed into a boy of about eight, eyes sparkling with adventure, and "vroomed" his big toy around the sandpile mountain. I couldn't help but enjoy watching him play "Big Guy" because he gets such a kick out of it. It's reassuring to know he can handle (and enjoy) tasks that would overwhelm me. Vital tasks, like, digging really big holes. I'm sure if he'd lived in an earlier time, he would have been a Dan'l Boone.

But in the twentieth century, my kitchen sink is dripping and I need to empty the bucket again. I wonder if it would work if I rented a jackhammer and told Scott he could chisel up the entire driveway in exchange for fixing the sink. Probably not. A leaky faucet is no—vroom, vroom, vroom—"man" job!

So God created man in his own image,
in the image of God he created him;
male and female he created them.
God saw all that he had made, and it was very good.

GENESIS 2:27, 31

Worm Sunny Days Back Home

Right now, I am pinching myself to remind me that this is not a dream. It is summertime and the livin' is easy. Fish are jumpin' all over the lake. I've been sleeping everyday until 10:00 A.M. My house is clean, I have seen that most glorious of sights, the bottom of the laundry basket! I may even become what is called "centered."

My husband, after a year-long diet of corn dogs and popsicles, almost broke down when I served him a hot meal with *three items* on his plate.

"And it's not on a stick!" he blubbered.

Best of all, I am enjoying real *communication* with my children—without yawning. We have even played badminton and gone swimming and whipped up a batch of burnt oatmeal cookies together.

Seriously though, we are in a rather scary place when we consider my not working and what the future holds, such as college tuition for four. I realize I may eventually have to go back to work, at least part-time. If so, I would much prefer to operate out of my home.

Maybe I could be a one woman show for ladies' clubs. I could write the invitations, cater the dinner, give a humorous talk, sing a song or two, maybe even learn to tap dance. Of course, all of this would probably be done with my dress on inside-out and backwards, wearing one red and one black shoe, my hair and forehead dyed plum purple, and an accidental eyebrow pencil mustache. Whatever it takes.

But Scott and I have learned some valuable lessons from my short-lived career. For one, our family is too precious and our time with our children is too short to let them become merely an "add on" to another busy life. Any possibility of outside work will have to allow me the time and energy to keep my family first, worms and all.

I once thought that when all my children were in school, the timing would be perfect for me to have a career outside the home. But I had forgotten how much it meant to me, as a child and as a teenager, to have my mother at home. She was nearly always available to talk, sometimes over cookies and milk and sometimes over dirty dishes if her day had been hectic, but she was *there*. And frankly, I needed her. And frankly, my kids need me right now more than most things money can buy.

As for college degrees, Scott and I managed to get ours by working, scholarships, grants, and government loans. Surely God can provide for our kids just as He provided for us. He's already done some pretty amazing providing, come to think about it.

The scariest thing is realizing Zach is only four years away from being ready for college—leaving home, maybe. Our children are growing up so fast. Lately I've been looking back over the years I had at home with them as preschoolers, and thinking of some of the precious memories I would have missed if I'd gone to college and to work sooner than I did.

"Mom? Look. I made a present for Jesus."

I look up from my reading to see Zachary, age four, holding a small box covered with a wash cloth. I gently lift the cloth and inspect the contents: a small Bible, some rocks, and his prized possession—a fishing lure. The living room grows quiet as the sun filters through the curtains, gilding Zachary's upturned and reverent face. We are standing, so it seems, on hallowed ground.

"I was wondering," he lisps, " does Jesus have a fishin' pole? I'll let Him borrow mine. And does He have a Bible already?" He pushes the box toward me. "Could you put this up high so I can give it to Him when we go to heaven?"

I remember the day Rachel spread her arms as wide as she could manage and exclaimed to her brothers, "God's pinkie is this big!" And the day she bounded to the car from Sunday School with the marvelous news that Jesus had straightened the "cricket" legs of a poor man in the Bible.

"But Mommy," she frowned, "I never saw a man that had bug legs before! Did he have to hop everywhere he went?"

As one might expect, Gabriel had his own burning question about God, asked, not once, but several times. It is that deeply debated theological question of the twentieth century: "Does God have hair in his nose?"

One day, when Gabe sat at the kitchen table happily making roll after roll of "rope" out of Play Doh™, he suddenly looked up as if to say, "Eureka!"

"Momma!" he excitedly blurted, "I figured out how God makes worms!"

Sometimes the task of teaching a child the difference between God and a television super hero or Santa Claus provides another challenge for parents. During one period, I had been concentrating on explaining to Gabriel that God's power is real and that Superman's power is just pretend. I thought my lesson had been well taught and well received. A few days later, Gabe and I came upon a picture of Superman which offered a golden opportunity to check out what he had absorbed.

"We know who has the *real* power, right, little buddy?" I probed.

"Yep," he replied without a moment's hesitation. "Batman!"

As December approached, Gabriel gave me reason for believing there might still be hope for his theological education.

"Momma, I'm gonna ask God instead of Santa Claus for a metal detector," he announced, "cause He's the guy that can make a tree—right?"

By George, I think he's got it! Now for the lesson on "needs" versus "wants."

The incredible thing about childish, oft-distorted prayers is that so many times God will just right out *answer* them. Several years ago, when Zachary was about to turn five, I found him working like a Trojan, pulling weeds from our back yard. He told me God would give him a horse if he would just pull weeds every day. I explained that we only had a backyard the size of a horse's hoof and that God was proud of his work, but please don't expect a *real* horse. Maybe a toy horse. But of course, he would hear none of that. It would have to be a real horse.

To this day I shiver when I remember the afternoon, shortly before Zach's birthday, that a neighbor (who had no idea of Zach's prayer) called quite out of the blue.

"Would you possibly be interested in having a Shetland pony for the boys?" she asked. "We can keep it in our pasture if you could supply the hay."

Be assured, I asked Zach to pray for every conceivable need from then on. Come to think of it, I'd better get him started on his college education.

But one thing I do know. I fully expect one day to see Zachary, Ezekiel, Rachel Praise, and Gabriel, sitting near the feet of Jesus. They will be talking and laughing and perhaps casting for a celestial fish in the River of Life. Off to the side, surrounded by a heavenly glow may be a small yellowed box holding a tiny Bible and a few rocks—minus one fishing lure.

What more important work could I have done in my life than helping them make the choices to get them there?

But his mother treasured all these things in her heart.

LUKE 2:51

AFTERWORD

It is about 6:30 P.M. on a summer Friday evening, and I am sitting at my word processor in still-wet clothes, typing with very shaky hands and an unbelievably grateful heart. I want to get today's events down on paper before I forget them, although I can't imagine how they could possibly ever fade from my memory.

This week began like a lovely dream. As first-time authors, my mother and I suddenly found our manuscript being pursued by not one, but two wonderful Christian publishers at the same time. This, after two years of rejection slips and numerous re-writes, although we had had some close calls and significant encouragement along the way. I felt like an old maid who was suddenly presented with proposals of marriage from Tom Selleck *and* Tom Cruise—a delicious dilemma.

I had spent the day pinching myself to be sure it was real, not simply a euphoric, fog-like movie. As I ran errands about town (as if I were an ordinary mortal), I enjoyed imaginary conversations with the people I met while standing in line at various counters.

"Ahem," I mentally intruded upon several, "you may be unaware of this fact, but you probably should know you are standing in the presence of a soon-to-be-famous author."

Heady stuff. But that was an eternity ago. This afternoon, within five minutes, everything changed.

Happily sitting by the lake reading and lounging in the sun, I kept half an eye on half a dozen kids frolicking in the shallow water. A car pulled into the drive and my friend, Janet, stepped out with her son, fourteen-year-old Clint. She had come to pick up her daughter, Cricket, one of Rachel's best friends. I was delighted to see one of the few people I had not yet told about the book, and I immediately blurted out the morning's events, which had even included a *conference call* from one publisher.

I had in mind to jokingly say, "I'll have my people get in touch with your people and we'll 'do lunch.'" However, before I could offer this nifty line, Zachary verbalized one sentence that shot through me like a bullet, reducing me to complete and instantaneous panic.

"Mom," he said, half-worried, half-joking, "Is Gabe dead?"

"What?" I hollered.

"Well, he was swimming here a while ago. His friend, Jud, is out there in the deep water with a life jacket, but I don't see Gabe."

Sheer terror engulfed me when I saw Gabe's life jacket laying on the bank, telling its own story. He must have taken off his life jacket to practice swimming in the shallow water and (No, please God!) drifted into the deep.

A quick questioning of the seven people present revealed no one had seen him leave the water.

I immediately dived into the water, clothes and all, screaming irrationally to my child, who I had to assume for the moment was somewhere in that murky water. I groped around frantically for a minute or so, and every time I came to the surface, I begged Jud to remember when and where he had last seen Gabe.

"I don't remember," he insisted, "but I don't think Gabe is drownded."

Realizing we were getting nowhere, I ordered all present to form a human chain to comb the water where he had last been seen. Janet was an R.N.—she could perform CPR—if there was still time. Even as she began to untie her shoes, she had presence of mind to send her Clint to Jud's nearby house to check for Gabe and/or call 911. We moved forward, our eyes frantically scanning the water, now murkier than ever as we stirred up the sandy bottom.

In the next moment, the most wonderful sound I believe I've ever heard came from the top of the hill. Clint's adolescent voice rang out like a thousand heavenly angels to this mother's ear.

"He's up here!"

We all splashed to the bank, where my knees went out from under me, and I collapsed on the grassy shore.

"I think I might like to faint now," I managed. Little Jud stood over me with a water gun pointed in my direction, his expression a curious mixture of compassion and impatience.

"I *told* ya I didn't think he was drownded," he said flatly.

Gabe had been playing in Jud's backyard, without the faintest notion that anything unusual had been going on at the water's edge. I desperately wanted to run to my son and hug him to me, but my knees were still jelly. Finally, I found my pulse and trudged up the hill to Jud's house, my clothes dripping puddles around me. I found Gabriel fascinated with Jud's new puppy, and he waved me to come stroke the black bundle of fur. Walking past the pup, I went straight to Gabe, too weak to scold. I held him in my arms and absorbed him with my eyes. Then I held him and looked at him some more, and I thought what a marvelous child he was and how deeply I loved having his grimy little arms around my neck.

When the blood began to flow at a normal rate through my veins again, I reluctantly left Gabe to play with Jud as we had previously planned. I drove the short distance back to our cabin and found Scott outside mowing the lawn. He was blissfully unaware of all that had transpired. When he saw me, he stopped the mower and, anticipating the big news of the day to be from editors, walked toward me with open arms.

"Well," he beamed, "are we going to be published?"

"Yeah, yeah," I brushed aside his question and fell into his arms, the tears finally coming in a rush. "We're going to be published. But did you know we have the most precious five-year-old boy in the world? And he's *alive!*"

It is now 11:30 P.M., about four hours since I wrote that last sentence and I am now warm and dry. It's unusually quiet in the house, considering we have seven children sleeping here. This summer has been one continual come-and-go party. I never know which of my kids will grace us with their presence at breakfast. But here in the living room, with a dim light shining from over the kitchen sink, Gabriel lies serenely asleep on the couch. He is still in his cut-offs, with no shirt. One arm lies above his dark head in relaxed abandonment.

He had planned to spend the night with Jud, but Jud's mother brought him home a couple of hours after the drowning incident because he had developed a headache. When they arrived, Scott and I had elbowed each other all the way to the front door, each wanting to be the first to receive our son into our arms. Scott beat me to him, and to the aspirin bottle for his headache, and to the rocking chair to rock him, but we took turns kissing Gabe's cheeks and arguing over who loved him most. He fell asleep between us, loving all the attention. Scott laid him on the couch where I now watch him sleeping. Before going off to bed, Scott said in a teasing whisper, "Don't let him drown again. I like him."

I can still feel a physical ache around my heart at the memory of the afternoon down by our beloved lake—the agony of searching for Gabriel's body, knowing that seconds count, the look on his brothers' and sister's faces as they feared the worst for their little brother—and the sudden awareness of the incredible fragility of life.

I probably will never be angry with any of my children again. At least, not for several days. At the moment, I could eat each one of them with a spoon. (For the uninitiated, this is actually a term of endearment in the South.) Earlier, Janice called to check on me and to make sure I was up to having seven children spend the night.

"You bet!" I said without hesitation. "I just *love* children. I'm looking forward to having a houseful of them tonight."

Perspective. I had prayed this week that God would continually remind me of what is truly important. Throughout the week, the children have been locked out of my room for hours at a time while I had "important business" to conduct by phone. There were editors with whom I needed to negotiate, and thoughts about how to market the book (the book that tells parents how important it is to cherish time with their children). I had been generally spacey—out to lunch. At one point Gabe had lost all patience and pulled on the leg of my shorts.

"Have your feet come down to the ground yet?" he demanded jealously.

I picked up the phone for the fiftieth time that week, frowned and shook my head to quiet him. As he walked sulkily out the door, I heard him groan.

"I wish this wasn't a special day any more," he muttered.

It has been the best of days and the worst of days, a dickens of a day, so to speak; a wonderful book contract offer, combined with what seemed like a brush with the death of my child. I feel as if I have been on a roller coaster ride that left me more than a little woozy. I agree with Gabe. I am ready for this special day to be over.

Dear Lord,

Please don't put me through any more "drownding experiences." I *get* it. I really do. Without my husband and my children, worldly accomplishments would be meaningless. Thank You for Scott, Zach, Zeke, Rachel, and Gabriel.

As for being an author, I know You will keep me humble. That is a fairly easy job for You, as I usually take the fall before the pride goeth too far. And maybe this is the beginning of the provision for our family I have been praying for.

Use me as I strive to be honest about who I am: a flawed human being who is completely loved, accepted and forgiven by the King of kings, who somehow delights in calling Himself my friend. As my friend, You have tasted my tears. As my friend, You have shared and inspired my laughter.

May those who read this book come away blessed and refreshed and aware that no matter how messed up we are (and somehow everyone secretly seems to think they are more messed up than everyone else), You are absolutely wild about us. And You want me—us—to know joy even when life hands us a worm, or a bucket of them.

And by the way, in case I haven't mentioned it before, thank You. *Thank You* for Scott, Zach, Zeke, Rachel, and Gabriel. I am so glad they're all home tonight, safely tucked in bed. And that they are breathing nicely. (Okay, so I checked.) I'm still just a little nervous, that's all.

In Jesus' name, Amen.

Now unto him
who is able to do exceedingly abundantly
above all that we ask or think,
according to the power that worketh in us.

EPHESIANS 3:20, KJV

Marriage
911

With love, to Scott—
for still wanting to grow up with me.

Contents

∾

Acknowledgments

W ho would have thought she would have taken me seri- ously? I was definitely writing with tongue (or should I say *pen?*) planted firmly in cheek. But here was my editor, Vicki Crumpton, on the other end of the phone, and she sounded serious.

"Becky," she said, "how about giving me a proposal for that authoritative/marriage self-help book? You know, the one you mentioned in *Worms in My Tea*—the one called *Our Marriage Is Better and We Still Haven't Figured Out Exactly Why.*"

"Well," I laughed, "first of all, you know I was just joking around. And second, I'm anything but authoritative. I'm not even *that* great at helping myself. I still need lots of people supporting me."

"Exactly—that's why I think *you* should write this. It would be fun."

I decided not to ask, "For whom?" I was both thrilled and terrified. The truth? I still am.

As things moved along we decided it might be best to choose a less complicated title. Little did any of us realize how compli- . cated it would be to come up with a less complicated title. I only know that at one time we were all ready to call this book, *We Can't Think of a Good Title, So You Make One Up*. Vicki came to the rescue with her brainstorm, *Marriage 911*, just in the nick of time. I love it.

So a special thank you, Vicki, Colyer Robison, and Greg Webster—and all my other friends and team players at Broadman & Holman—for helping to pull it off. It hasn't always been easy, but with you guys, it's always been a hoot.

There's another special lady to whom I owe a heartful of thanks for helping to make this book a reality.

I must admit, however, that I didn't completely pull this off alone. You see, the manuscript was complete, but something was missing—some pieces to the puzzle were out of place. So a week before my deadline, I flew home to my mother's writing nest and chirped, "Help!" With the skill of a plastic surgeon, she knew right away exactly where to nip and where to tuck. She has a gift for this, pure and simple.

So even though this was not a co-written project, fans of my mother (Ruthie Arnold) will still find pieces of her tucked into scenes—places where she spiced up a passage, or put pieces in more logical order, or cleaned out excess words. She continues to help me grow in this difficult, glorious, nebulous craft called writing, just as she continues to help me grow in this difficult, glorious, nebulous thing called life. On both accounts I'm learning from the best. So thank you, Mother. I love you more than I can say. (And I will help you clean out the garage next week—I promise!)

To Mary Rusch, my dear friend—We've been through it all, haven't we? How grateful I am for your insightful critique, your constant encouragement, and your never-ending sense of fun.

To Melissa Gantt—You came into my life just when I needed a friend. Thanks for your cheerleading and wonderful input.

To Dean Dykstra—Thank you for offering to read this manuscript and for the honest, excellent suggestions. I took them to heart and I believe it made a tremendous difference in the final product.

To Mike Hyatt—thanks for your assistance with the business end of this project so I could have more freedom to concentrate on the fun part.

And last, but not least, to my precious, precious husband, Scott—We each take our share of ribbing in these pages, but you've always had the wonderful ability to *laugh* at "us." Our souls, sometimes, are laid bare in these pages—but you've always had the wonderful ability to be open about "us." You didn't leave me alone on some writing limb; you shared in the process and helped make this book better reflect some of who we really are. And as peculiar as our "us-ness" is, I love it.

So thank you, My Love, for being there.

∾

Pull yerself up a chair
and set a spell

We're on vacation now, at probably my most favorite place in the whole world—the Florida Coastline. I've had the exquisite pleasure of two hours alone on the beach. Alone, that is, except for my icy cold fruit drink, a gentle ocean breeze, the faint echo of waves splashing the shore, a pen, and a notebook. What more could a body ask for? Maybe a good book. Maybe a good friend. Yeah, that's it. A good friend.

Since there is the possibility that you and I might become friends by the time we finish this book, may I invite you to curl up and get comfy? And don't forget to pour yourself a cup of soothing hot tea or rich coffee.

For the bulk of our time together, shall we toss around the topic of marriage? After all, that is what the title on the cover portends. But before I get too personal, I'd like to preface what is to come with a few pre-book thoughts.

I've agonized over exactly what to say, how to put into words what Scott and I have discovered and are learning daily. Marriage is complicated because people are complicated. Some of us couples do seem a bit more befuddled than others, I must admit. If there were a simple formula for success, believe me, we'd have found it by now. I've certainly done my research. All I know is that our marriage is better now than it has ever been, but I'm still hard-pressed to say exactly why. Perhaps in the process of writing, as is so often the case for me, I'll begin to see it all more clearly.

At this point, all I've got are these fragments floating around in my head of what has worked for us—but I think they are significant fragments. And though our relationship is for the most part good and solid, there are days when I've moaned, "Oh, shoot. I don't know how to make a relationship work. Who do I think I am to write a book about marriage anyway?"

I can relate to Erma Bombeck's conclusion in her latest book, *A Marriage Made in Heaven or Too Tired for an Affair.* She wrote, "I wanted to end this book with a wise and wonderful statement on how marriages work. I don't have a clue."[1]

But at my lowest points, just before I pick up the phone to call the publisher to inform them that I am not the right person for this project after all, Scott gently reminds me, "Becky, this isn't supposed to be a how-to book on marriage."

Oh, yeah, I think to myself, *That's right!* and I relax.

It's only our story—and not even the whole story because I can't possibly write everything. There are things between my husband and me that are held sacred and private. And some incidents are forgiven and forgotten and never to be dug up again, even for the sake of an intriguing book. Still, our marriage never seems lacking in plenty of material we can share.

Scott also frequently issues another reminder. "Becky, you've got to write this book in the genre where our marriage, for the most part, belongs—on the humor shelf." I frown, but I must admit he's absolutely right.

Since neither Scott nor I appear to have a shred of hope of being nominated for sainthood, I will be sharing with you the selected few fragments we have been able—by the grace of

God—to apply now and then. I have no formulas for you, no miracles or surefire twelve-step programs between these pages. Instead, I'll offer glimpses into a real-life marriage in the works. Perhaps you will come away saying, "Whew. At least we aren't as crazy as that couple. Things are better in my relationship than I thought!" Or you may say, "Well, how about that? We aren't the only couple in America whose relationship sometimes feels like a roller coaster out of control."

But remember, I'm taking the risk of being vulnerable here by opening the curtain on scenes from selected "Days of Our Lives." So will you read with a kind heart, please? In turn, I'm praying as I write that my words might touch some husband or wife, that our stories might be used to encourage some couple hanging on by a thread to "hangeth thou in there," as Kay Arthur is fond of saying. At the very least, I hope we both might come to the end of this book saying, "A good time was had by all."

And if, by chance, I happen to touch your heart, I'll be keeping the Italian Cappuccino fresh and hot for our next visit together.

Becky Freeman
Destin, Florida

Romance, window dressing, and pickled pigs' feet

I am not, by any stretch of the imagination, what you would call a naturally wild and wanton woman. But I'd been married fifteen years, and I felt our marriage needed a little—spice.

It all began with a romantic suggestion I gleaned from a book titled *Light His Fire*. The author, Ellen Kriedman, suggests that wives use their ingenuity to come up with imaginative ways to have fun seducing their mate. The book assured me that, done properly, this technique should fire up the I-feel-a-chill-in-the-air times most couples experience at some point in their relationship.

Nothing new here, really. Ever since the days when perky Mrs. Marabel Morgan first suggested we Christian women greet our husbands at the door dressed in plastic wrap and/or an apron, we wives have spent a couple of decades trying to outdo the Total Woman. Personally, I have come to the conclusion that such efforts leave me feeling more like a Totaled Woman. Not that I hadn't given wild and creative tactics my best shot, mind you.

One night as I stepped out of the shower wrapped in a towel, I spied the lights of Scott's pickup in the driveway of our home. Our closest neighbors were raccoons and possums, so I didn't worry about the undraped window overlooking the drive. Suddenly I could almost hear Dr. Kriedman whispering in my ear.

Why not? After all, you're married to the guy. Be playful! Be sexy! Have some fun with your man!

So I dropped the towel and stood there in front of the window wearing nothing but my best seductive smile. As it happened, Scott was not alone. This night he had with him our good friend Gary, husband of my dear friend Mary. As the two men walked casually toward the house (I learned later), Scott glanced toward the window, returned for a second to his conversation with Gary, and then jerked his head back toward the window, his eyes wide, his mouth agape. He then alternated between trying to divert Gary's eyes from our bedroom window and gesturing frantically for me to run for cover.

Lamentably, though it is easy to see *into* a lighted home from the dark, it is quite difficult for the one standing inside the house to see *out* into the dark. Because of this phenomenon, I imagined Scott must surely be whooping it up out there in the night air. I even thought I heard him egging me on with playful wolf whistles. Later I would discover the "whistles" were actually high-pitched sounds made by Scott's vocal chords desperately searching for the natural range of his voice. In any case, I simply responded to what I had assumed was my husband's enthusiastic reaction.

Finally, having safely escorted Gary into the kitchen, Scott breathed a sigh of relief and began to relax. Observing that nothing could undo the damage that had already been done, my husband nonchalantly poked his head into the bedroom.

"Hi, Hon," he said casually, "Gary's with me."

My screams, I'm sure, awakened every possum and raccoon in nearby trees. I thought I would die. My thoughts were a frenzy. *I've* just flashed my best friend's husband! It doesn't get any worse than this. Of all the stupid antics . . . this absolutely tops the list! I vowed to avoid Gary for the rest of my life. I couldn't possibly face him again without dissolving into a puddle of shame and embarrassment.

The next morning, Mary, Gary's wife, called bright and early. "Becky," she said brightly, "Gary asked me to deliver a message to you." Switching to a deep French accent she went on, "He says to tell you 'Becky, jou look mahvahlous.'"

When the laughter finally began to clear on her end of the line, Mary added, "And, hey, I just want you to know, since I've been feeling a bit under the weather lately, this probably *made* his week."

Because they both had a great sense of humor, we all recovered fairly quickly. With time and understanding, I am now able to hold a normal conversation with Gary without benefit of a paper bag over my head.

The Window Story has already made its way through our small town, down grocery store aisles, across neighborhood fences, into most of our fellow parishioners' ears between services, and is probably being translated into several foreign languages. My best friends, and even my husband, love to tell it at appropriate gatherings when conversation drops to a lull.

After that little escapade, one would assume I would have laid to rest any impulse to do something wild and crazy and romantic for at least awhile. One would assume.

Then one evening, feeling rather amorous, I stepped out of the bathtub and noticed a large, yellow, transparent bag hanging over the towel rack—a bag that had been used to cover Scott's dry-cleaned shirts. Viewing all that plastic, I thought I heard voices again. This time it was the Total Woman speaking.

If at first you don't succeed, try, try, again.

Inspired, I draped the mustard-colored wrap around my torso, ingeniously holding it together with a couple of bobby pins I found in the sink. Slinking toward the bedroom where my husband was reclining with a good book, I opened the door with a flourish. He continued to read, so I loudly cleared my throat. He finally glanced up, shook his head as if to clear it, frowned in bewilderment, and scratched his chin. Not quite the reaction I had anticipated. It got worse.

"What have you done to yourself now?" Scott asked sincerely. "You've made your entire body look like one of those supermarket meat trays of pickled pigs' feet!"

I wasn't as crushed as you might expect from that verbal blow to my ego. I had to admit, a last-minute glance in the bathroom mirror had filled me with a few serious doubts. I had gone into this mission knowing its outcome was chancy, at best. But I was no longer in a wild and crazy romantic state of mind, either. As to my pork-minded husband's chances for an evening of love, I have just one thing to say—"That little piggy had none."

The following Fourth of July, this little piggy went to market to shop for the outdoor barbeque we were planning. And guess what I found? A meat tray full of pigs' feet covered with plastic wrap. A wicked smile spread across my face, and I instantly knew what cut of meat my husband would be having for dinner. Did I laugh as I thought of Scott sitting down to a plateful of hog hooves? All the way home.

A few months later on a morning before I took our kids to school, I printed out a copy of the above story, hoping to proofread it later over a cup of coffee. Once my offspring had been safely deposited, I wheeled into the local convenience store and got my caffeine fix in a paper cup. I went back to my car, settled into the front seat, and picked up the loose manuscript pages I'd brought with me. When I turned to the beginning of the last page, I blinked and read the first lines again: "The whole team was up for the homecoming game. I believe we really played our best. . . ."

Then it hit me. This meant that Zachary had taken his report to school with the last page of my chapter stapled to his homework assignment. His amended report would now read: "The homecoming game was a great disappointment. We all realize that we must overcome our loss if we are to be up for the next game. But I was no longer in a wild and crazy romantic state of mind. . . ."

I threw down the papers, squealed out of the parking lot, and raced to the principal's office where I explained the situation as well as a situation like this can be explained. I might add that Zach's principal, Mr. Stahmer, is a sight to behold. He's at least seven feet tall and just as impressively broad, exactly what seventh through ninth grade boys need in a junior high school administrator. His mere size can be intimidating, even for a *grown-up* who's lost her homework. He was kind—not completely understanding, but kind.

Together we walked up and down halls and searched football fields for signs of Zachary, hoping to catch him before he turned in the fateful paper. Finally, Mr. Stahmer stopped in front of a classroom door and peeked inside.

"He's in here, Mrs. Freeman."

"Oh, good," I replied hopefully, "Maybe we can catch him before he goes to his English class. What class is this?"

"English," he said.

"Ooops," I said.

At that point Mr. Stahmer pushed open the door and asked the teacher if Zachary Freeman had, by any chance, turned in his homework.

Yes, he had. From my position in the hallway outside the door (I had no desire to enter and face my son), I heard the ruffle of papers and the sounds of a teacher chuckling. Soon Zach appeared at the door, red-faced and frantically trying to unstaple my "contribution" to his assignment. He was brief and to the point, though thankfully he is gifted with a sense of humor.

"Mom . . . only you . . . No, don't explain it. Just take it and go home . . . yeah, *now* would be good."

Sometimes I think I was put on this planet to make more messes and embarrassing mistakes than anybody else so that the rest of the world—having met in me the absolute Champion of the Awkward Moment—can press on feeling infinitely better about themselves.

We laugh a lot as a family; it's simply a matter of survival. We've found there are few shortcomings that can't be helped by a healthy dose of humor. And so far—whether it's intentional or not—I'm seeing to it that everyone gets their daily spoonful around here.

A cheerful heart is good medicine.

PROVERBS 17:22

∽

T W O

Peculiarity breeds content

D o you really—I mean *really*—think so?" I asked my husband sincerely.

"Oh, Becky, *everybody* thinks so," Scott stated unequivocally.

So what was the subject of our discussion? It was my husband's opinion—and, according to him, the rest of the world's
opinion—that I am a *peculiar* person.

It's not all that bad to be labeled "peculiar," really. Webster
defines peculiarity as "something that belongs to only one
person, thing, class, people; a distinguishing feature." I rather
like that definition. *Unique* has a nicer ring to it, but *peculiar*
will do just fine.

One of my most distinguishing features of late is my
fingernails. You see—oh how can I explain this? I have none.
There. I've admitted it. And I don't mean that they are short
or bitten down to the nub. I mean, for the most part, they are
nonexistent.

It all started when we went to the Christian Booksellers
Convention in Denver, Colorado, last summer. Our publicist

told my mother and me to be prepared to sign nearly two hundred copies of our book *Worms in My Tea*. "Wow!" I shouted over the phone, "Do you really think that many people will want to get copies of our book?"

"Oh sure," she answered. "We're giving them away."

Well, even if it was a freebie-give-away deal, the event still fell under the category of a "booksigning." And if my hands would be on display for two hundred bookstore managers, I intended to make memorable encounters. I would begin by having my own nubby nails professionally covered up with the most beautiful fakes I could afford. Thus innocently began a vicious cycle I am still coping with six months later.

From the day I walked into the beauty salon, I should have seen the handwriting on the wall. When the manicurist kept insisting that I relax, stating that I was one of the most tense manicures she'd ever sanded, I should have politely taken my leave. Instead, I courageously squeezed back tears and nodded toward the patch of blood oozing from my index finger directly beneath where Attila the Beautician's file was flying back and forth at warp speed. But I have to admit that as soon as the swelling and bruises subsided (on my fingers, not the manicurist), my new set of acrylic nails indeed looked gorgeous.

By the time I arrived in Denver, I found myself using copious gestures when given the opportunity (yes, even making opportunities) for the sheer pleasure of waving my new nails around. Pointing was a great deal of fun. So was scratching Scott's neck. It wasn't until I was asked to sign an actual book that I realized there was going to be more to owning fingernails of length than I had bargained for. I came at the page, pen in hand, from a variety of angles. However, with my newly extended appendages, I may as well have been writing with a large pogo stick. My signature would not have passed preschool penmanship.

After signing the one hundredth book, I began to experience some success by squeezing the pen tightly between my knuckles. But my fingers eventually grew numb in that position, and I'm afraid it finally began to affect my thinking processes. Originally, my desire had been to come up with catchy individual greetings above my signature like "Wormly Yours," "Love, Laughter, and Joy," or "May you find laughter in all your worms." I preferred that no two messages be exactly alike. After the hundred and fiftieth book, my mind began to wander, and I found myself writing odd salutations from bits of hymns I'd sung in childhood. I vaguely remember signing one book, "All Glory, Laud, and Honor, Becky Freeman." I know the recipient of that copy is still shaking her head wondering exactly what message I was trying to convey. I have no idea, but it was certainly heartfelt.

Scott took this new change in my hands' personality in stride, until one night when he was trying to get to sleep and heard me crunching away on what he assumed was a bag of tortilla chips.

"Becky," he moaned, "cut it out. What are you eating at this time of night anyway?"

"My fake fingernails," I answered matter of factly, "Want a bite?"

I have never had a problem with nail-biting in my entire life. At least not until I acquired the artificial variety. Suddenly nail-biting took on an almost gourmet flavor. I've chewed off acrylic nails, gel nails, and plastic nails. All delicious. The problem is that with each set of nails I bite off, my natural nails also peel off one layer at a time. My real nails now look as though my hands have been through a meat grinder, so I'm forced to cover them up when I go out in public. Now do you understand the vicious cycle I've begun?

To save money on my nail addiction, I've learned to apply them myself. Another benefit of do-it-yourself nails is that I can avoid the bloodletting at the beauty salon. The drawback is the danger inherent in allowing a peculiar person, such as myself, to run around freely armed with a large bottle of Super Nail Glue.

Just the other day, I was trying to glue on a nail while I was driving to a luncheon for professional writers in Dallas. Have to look sharp when we're among professionals, now don't we? To make a long story short, I spilled the glue inside the plastic trash can/drink holder that sits between the front seats of my station wagon. Why I did it I still don't know, but instinctively I crammed my hand into the spilled glue and when I brought it back up, the plastic trash can/drink holder was now a permanent appendage on the end of my arm. I thought to myself, *This simply won't do. Can't very well walk into Steak and Ale with a trash can attached to one's right hand!*

While maneuvering the steering wheel with my knees, I used my one unattached hand to peel off the plastic device. The pain was intense, but I kept myself from screaming aloud by using my old Lamaze childbirth breathing technique. However, when I looked at my hand, I almost let out a screech anyway. Tiny bits of trash—old cookie crumbs and pieces of gum wrapper—were super-glued to my fingers. Luckily, I had a file handy to sand the stuff off, and I sailed into the meeting exuding professionalism.

So you can see why my husband (and a few other people) has come to believe I am peculiar. I have to admit, since becoming a "real author," my life seems to be combing new depths of peculiarity. One moment I feel saucy and intelligent, ready to conquer the world—like Diane Sawyer. The next minute I am unpinning a dry cleaning label from my dress while approaching the podium to speak—suddenly, Minnie Pearl again.

This past year, I have been privileged to meet incredible people, and, at moments, I've even been treated as a near-celebrity. But 98 percent of the time I'm a housewife who lives in a cabin in the boonies with a husband, four kids, two dogs, a bathroom that needs scrubbing, and a frozen chicken that needs thawing. At this moment, I'm typing at my computer wearing hot pink sweatpants, a pink and white striped flannel shirt, a red robe, and socks that don't match. Zach and Zeke, my teenage sons, are watching the television, which is about five feet away from my wall-less "office." Gabriel, our eight-year-old, is wrestling a sleep-over buddy in the back bedroom at top volume. My ten-year-old daughter, Rachel, just walked up, leaned on my shoulder, and informed me that she might throw up any minute now. (She's been home with a virus today.)

Many people think that the circumstances under which I create these chapters might fall under the category of *Peculiar*. (Rachel just returned for more attention, stopping to pinch my upper lip and inform me that I have a mole growing there with a hair sticking out of it. Children certainly know how to keep one humble.)

So even though sophisticated people and agencies occasionally telephone our home/office/school/zoo now—the kind that link their last names with an "&" (i.e., Barnes & Noble, Broadman & Holman, etc.) instead of their first names with an "n" (i.e., Jim Bob 'n' Ida Lou)—I haven't even bothered to change the message on our answering machine to try to make us appear more businesslike. I mean, who do I think I could fool anyway? Executives and neighbors are all greeted by the identical message, delivered with as much Southern hospitality as I can dish out: "Hello, you've reached the home of the Freeman Family and other wildlife." I side with Popeye the Sailorman on this point—"I am what I am."

And what does Scott think of all this? He shakes his head in wonder at what has transpired these past months and pretends he has serious doubts about me and my grandiose adventures—at least in public. But my husband is always the first one I want to see after an exciting bit of news or an interesting encounter or an unusual experience or a new idea. Why? Because, in truth, no one—not one soul on the face of this earth—has shown as much pride and joy at the fact that I am a peculiar woman as has my own husband. He's consistently my best friend and cheerleader, even when my ideas seem hare-brained to everyone else.

Just the other day Scott and I took a walk together down our country road, holding hands. "Becky," he continued on a subject we discuss often, "you are *so* weird. I never met a person in my whole life as strange as you are. But you do intrigue me. When I come home I don't know whether you are going to tell me you've got another book contract, or that you've run over the neighbor's mailbox, or that you tried to sterilize all our tooth-brushes and ended up boiling them into one big plastic glob. I've got to stay around just to see what happens next."

Yes, we've finally accepted the fact that our love is a many-peculiared thing, but it took us awhile to embrace it.

And the LORD hath chosen thee
to be a peculiar people unto himself.

DEUTERONOMY 14:2, KJV

∾

THREE

Cut him some slack
so he can go fish!

Would it surprise you to know I was a bride at age seventeen, and Scott, an eighteen-year-old groom? "How on earth did that happen?" you may be asking. Believe it or not, if it had been in frontier days, we might have married even sooner.

When we met in our youth group at church, I was thirteen, Scott was fourteen. It would be two more years before we would be considered boyfriend and girlfriend, but that most intimate of all acts between a man and a woman happened right away—we *talked*.

We were returning home from a trip to Mexico with a bus full of kids from a youth mission trip (probably returning from a lecture warning against getting married too young). It was nighttime and Scott and I converged, sitting on the floor near the rear of the old bus, with hours ahead of us to talk and get acquainted. Because I didn't have big brothers or much experience with boys in general, I always felt awkward making conversation with guys. Not so with Scott. It was effortless. And we didn't discuss weather or sports or school, either. We talked of God and the meaning of life. We shared our ideas about love, our secret hopes and dreams for the future.

Even at age fourteen, Scott had an uncanny way of skipping over preliminaries and getting right to the heart of people. At that moment he became the first real boy I considered a friend. Not a boyfriend, mind you, but a friend who just happened to be male.

It was impossible for me to picture being anything but a buddy to Scott at that point in time. I was too relaxed around him. Too able to be myself. There were no nervous jitters or butterflies, so this couldn't possibly lead to anything romantic, I had reasoned. Even stranger, now that I look back on it, Scott was the best-looking guy at church. His reputation for being the Champion Hayride Kisser was known far and wide—the girls were falling all over themselves to get his attention. I can't believe I didn't join the herd right away, but years later Scott told me he had prayed a prayer that night on the bus.

"Lord, please give me a wife like Becky. And until You do, I'm not going to date another girl." True to his vow, Scott put his lips on hold for The Right Woman. For two years during the ages when most boys go after girls with unprecedented frenzy, Scott patiently bided his time. It eventually paid off.

At the end of those two years, he and I went on another mission trip, this time to Guatemala and El Salvador. By the time we said good-bye to our summer adventure, we were hopelessly in love. And was I ever thrilled to be the recipient of those famous kisses! I still am, but like everybody else who has ever married, or who will ever marry in the future, we had no idea what we were getting into. All the premarital counseling in the world can't prepare us for the reality of sharing life with another person at very close range. I guess it was inevitable that we would make most of the mistakes it is possible to make. One of the first had to do with getting tangled up in a fishing line—The Invisible Marriage Fishing Line.

You haven't heard of it? Well, then I'm going to let you in on a little secret: When couples get married they are tied together by an invisible fishing line. From that moment on, their goal is to keep the line pulled just so—not giving it too much slack but not pulling it too taut, either. When there is excessive slack, the two of them get all tangled up and in each other's way constantly. The fancy term psychologists use for such situations is *becoming enmeshed.* On the other hand, when the line is pulled too taut, the husband and wife become so independent that the line can easily break under the strain—and there's nothing left binding them together anymore. The professional word for this stage is *polarization*—where one partner is basically running toward the North Pole while the other flies due South.

Keeping the tension in the line in balance requires paying attention and constantly checking the drag. If a couple becomes fairly adept at keeping the fishing line just right, they may actually hit the stage of Balanced Relational Health termed *interdependence.* I wish someone had explained this invisible fishing line to me during premarital counseling. Maybe they did, and our ears were stopped up with youthful infatuation.

Just two months after I turned seventeen, I graduated early from high school, married Scott, and went straight from my parent's home to my husband's duplex. So I never had an opportunity to be a woman of independence. If there is one thing I regret about marrying at age seventeen, it is that I never experienced college dorms, or having my own apartment, or having a time in my life that I could look back on and call my own. I have no "single days" on which to reminisce. I went directly from being someone's daughter to being someone's wife. As a result, I clung to Scott, wanting him to fulfill all my identity needs—and nearly choked him to death in the process.

If, for example, Scott were five minutes late coming home from work and I happened to hear a siren in the distance, I would be sobbing at a neighbor's door in an instant—convinced my young husband had been fatally injured on his motorcycle.

When he did come through the door, I was so overjoyed to see him upright and breathing that I would often run and jump into his arms, wrapping my legs around his waist and nearly knocking the breath out of him like an overly enthusiastic golden retriever.

To Scott, my arms around his neck probably began to feel more like vise grips. Fortunately, with the passage of time, my fears eased. Within five years we also had two young sons to help occupy my overactive imagination. But there was one pivotal experience we still refer to as "The Time Becky Decided, Once and for All, to Give Scott Some Slack."

The saga began one summer afternoon when Scott came home from a hot day of roofing and announced that he and his partner were going to take off for a little rest and relaxation. They planned to ride their motorcycles to Arkansas to do some trout fishing.

All I could visualize at that moment was Scott's body lying mangled on a highway or floating facedown in some mountain stream. I put my twenty-two-year-old foot down. I would not allow it, I said. He said he did not need my permission, nor had he asked for it. For three days I cried and begged him not to go, but he would not be moved. The morning he walked out the door and resolutely mounted his motorcycle, I sat down cross-legged on the shag carpet in our living room, holding a baby and a toddler close to my chest, and sobbed as if their father had already been pronounced dead.

Somehow I managed to survive the rest of the day. But I distinctly remember eating at Taco Muncho and looking wistfully out the big picture window, over the top of a burrito and my babies' heads. Just then a young guy on a motorcycle drove into view, and waves of grief hit me again. I gathered up the kids and barely made it out the door and into the car before I collapsed into tears again.

Finally, it dawned on me that I could not spend the next 120 hours bawling. My eyes had swelled nearly shut and I was making the kids miserable. I would have to do something constructive to take my mind off Scott's lifeless body on the highway and streams of Arkansas.

So I planned some outings. I had a couple of friends and their wee ones over for lunch. By the fourth day of Scott's absence, I was beginning to have a pretty good time. Then I went to visit my parents at their home across town. As I was sitting at their kitchen table munching on chips and laughing at something cute little Zachary had just said, Mother suggested the kids and I drive with them to Sweetwater to see my grandmother, Nonnie. It was starting to sound fun, and I was grateful for another diversion. Then the phone rang. It was Scott.

He was having a terrific time. However, unbeknownst to me, he was suffering from a belated guilt trip. So he offered a plan he thought would ease his conscience and make me happy at the same time.

"Hey, Becky," he said on the other end of the line, "I've got a great idea. How about you pack up the boys and take a bus up here and join us? It's really pretty country."

In my mind, I was thinking, *Gee, I'm just about to adjust to the idea of being a single mom for a week. Actually, I'm even starting to have fun. I was looking forward to going to Sweetwater too. But Scott must be missing us terribly to ask me to take such a long bus trip, with a two-year-old and a baby, to meet him. Poor, lonely thing! How could I possibly turn him down in his hour of need?*

In the space of a few hours I was boarding a bus with a baby on each hip. But with each turn of the giant wheels and every fresh whiff of diesel fuel, I knew I'd made a terrible mistake. If Baby Zeke wasn't wet or dirty or crying or nursing, Toddler Zachary was spitting or biting or whining. Seventeen agonizing and sleepless hours later, we dismounted into a tiny, filthy bus station somewhere in the hills of Arkansas. It was four o'clock in the morning. Now I was spitting, biting, and whining.

When Scott and his buddy, Randy, showed up at the station, we were faced with a dilemma. How would we drive from the station to the cabin? Motorcycles were our only form of affordable, available transportation. I know it was soooooo stupid and soooooo dangerous and I could still kick myself for it, but all of us ended up riding to the camp on Scott's motorcycle. By zipping Baby Zeke in Scott's leather jacket and placing little Zachary between Scott's back and my stomach, we could all fit on one Honda. I was suddenly a motorcycle mama in every sense of the word, but I was far from proud of the fact.

When we arrived at the cabin, there was more cause for concern. First of all, the cabin consisted of one big room with two beds, a kitchenette in the corner, and a bathroom—it would have to house me, Scott, our two boys, and Randy. When I checked the small refrigerator, it contained nothing but a cool box of worms and a few canned drinks. And there was precious little money left in the food budget after Scott paid for my luxurious bus trip. I could tell right off the bat it was going to be a real challenge for me to be a happy camper.

While the guys went trout fishing, I walked across the dirt road to a questionable looking Bait & Beer shop carrying the baby in my backpack and holding my toddler by the hand. There I purchased a loaf of bread, two dozen eggs, butter, and milk. For breakfast we had French toast, for lunch we had toast and eggs, and for dinner I served fried egg sandwiches. The same menu was duplicated the next day, only I reversed the order for variety.

But it wasn't until night fell that the real nightmare began. It was awkward enough to be sleeping in the same room with Scott's business partner, but I could deal with that. The worst part was that Randy snored. And from his bunk only five feet away from us, I could tell immediately that this was not just your average snore. Oh, no. Randy had a snore to be reckoned with—it would have registered at least a 7.5 on the Richter scale.

I woke Scott a couple of times and begged him to go over to Randy's bed and give him a good hard shake. He finally did, and there was blessed relief for all of ten seconds. Then with the force of a seagoing foghorn, Randy's sinuses geared up again—this time with a vengeance. I got out of my bed, took my pillow and blanket into the bathroom, and stuffed my ears with torn-up pieces of toilet tissue. The foghorn continued to blare, even through the closed door and with water running in the sink. I finally cried myself to sleep in an empty bathtub with towels and pillows stacked over my head.

After a few days of this "blissful" vacation, Scott wearily helped me and the kids board the big bus toward home. The seventeen-hour trip back home gave me plenty of time to ponder the absurdity of this situation. When the trauma finally came to an end, and all of us made it safely back home, I kissed my shag carpeting. I had learned my lesson and was more than ready to let go some slack on the Marriage Fishing Line.

Since then, I've made a concerted attempt to look happy—almost gleeful—when Scott goes off on one of his "guy trips." The last thing I want to do is make him feel bad about getting away for a little free time. I simply don't have the strength to pay for any more guilt trips.

Scott, on the other hand, never seemed to struggle as much with giving me space. For the most part, he has always been delighted to let me spread my wings and try new experiences. Besides, when I'm gone it gives him and the kids a chance to bond—and eat pizza in the living room without getting yelled at.

I remember returning home last spring after attending a three-day writers conference. I walked into the living room, expecting to be greeted by hugs and kisses and choruses of "We missed you!" Instead, Scott and the kids sat entranced by some television show. I cleared my throat and began telling them how I was going to be speaking in front of important people soon and how impressed they should be to claim me as their wife and mother.

No one batted an eyelash. Just yak, yak, yak about a football game or something.

"But don't worry," I continued my soliloquy, "even with fame and fortune knocking at my door I'll always keep you, Dear Family, first in my heart."

"That's nice, Dear," Scott commented as he wrestled Zachary for the remote control. Seeing such callous disregard in the presence of greatness, I could contain myself no longer. Walking directly through the mass of tangled bodies on the living room floor, I positioned myself in front of the television.

"I AM QUEEN!" I announced at the top of my lungs.

From Scott's horizontal position on the floor he hollered in my general direction, "Hey, Your Highness, get me a Dr. Pepper, will you?" The fishing line pulled me to earth with a jerk. (However, be assured Scott got his own Dr. Pepper.)

Isn't that the way it always goes? Married people are constantly playing at this game of marital checks and balances, of adjusting the drag on each other's lines. And couples seem to be constantly shifting roles to help balance out the other.

One may say, "Here—have some free time—grow and stretch—enjoy!"

But then he senses something has gone too far, so he adjusts the drag and pulls in some of the slack. "Hey—wait a minute, you're getting too far away."

Then, perhaps, he realizes he jerked the line *too* hard and hurt feelings in the process. Another adjustment is needed. "Oh, I'm sorry. I didn't mean to *burst* your balloon—just *deflate* it a little. Let me give you a hug. I *am* really proud of your accomplishment."

In time, more tugging is felt on the line and he responds enthusiastically but with a gentle warning. "Need some more space, you say? Go for it—fly away for a new adventure! But don't forget where your home and heart are, OK?"

Mother says that being married is like taking on a Siamese twin for life. In most things we do, that other person has to be considered. Marriage is often the school to which God sends us in order to learn what it means to be less than totally centered in ourselves—to begin to give consideration to the needs and desires of another, and then in widening circles, many others. But at the same time, we need time alone—to pursue our own dreams or to get together with our own friends.

And so it goes. Push and pull. "Let me go!" "Wait—hold me close!" The line stretches and loosens in a perpetual dance of adjustment. Once in awhile, between "too taut" and "too much slack," we experience brief moments of Balanced Relational Health. Most of the time, however, we're busy flopping around in stages of Unbalanced Relational Lopsidedness. Still, I prefer to deal with tangles and stretched-out lines than to live a life of total autonomy. I understand that autonomy is very poor company on a cold night.

*He said, "Let me go . . . . If I have found favor in your eyes,
let me get away to see my brothers."*

1 SAMUEL 20:29

∾

Showdown at the hoedown

Under normal circumstances my husband can gracefully tolerate any number of my faults. I can back over multiple mailboxes, get stuck in ditches, leave my purse in out-of-town restaurants, and forget to mail important checks, yet all is quickly forgiven.

But in our earlier married life there was one thing my husband had never been able to tolerate, not even for a second, and that was for me to be in a negative mood. His attitude was, "Get over it and get over it yesterday." Here was an area in our marriage where I had come to feel *I* wasn't being given any slack in the ol' fishing line—no leeway to express even one moment of plain old everyday grumpiness. Once every month we added my drop in hormones to Scott's lack of tolerance, and we had an explosion just waiting to happen. Unfortunately, one time happened to coincide with my birthday.

Scott and I were driving to Dallas to meet my parents at a country-western family steak house, The Trail Dust, to celebrate. The Trail Dust had long been a family favorite; it had a wonderful band and was one of the few wholesome places where we could go to two-step, waltz, or Cotton-Eyed-Joe. Mother and Daddy were getting to be quite the fancy country-western dancers and we had always enjoyed each others' company, so we were looking forward to the evening out with them.

As we were driving, I mulled over the variety of special occasions we'd celebrated at this ranch house over the years—Scott's graduation from college, numerous birthdays, and a couple of anniversaries. Then, however, I recalled a couple of special celebrations that had been a little hard on my ego. On my thirtieth birthday, for example, the band leader had coerced me into coming up to the front, donning a white cowboy hat, and galloping around the dance floor on a stick horse while the packed-out restaurant sang "Happy Birthday to You." Now, isn't that special? I'd been stuck in one of those classic unavoidable dilemmas. If I declined to trot around the floor like an overgrown child on a stick horse, I would have looked like a spoilsport. If I accepted the invitation, I would look like an idiot. Better to be an Idiot than a Party Pooper, so I pranced proudly with my head held high and my dignity still somewhat intact.

But there had been yet another celebration dinner at the Trail Dust I remembered that had pretty much stripped me of any remaining vestiges of pride. That evening, Scott and I had been seated across the table from some rather dignified young men from our church—one was an engineer, the other a physician. To this day I don't know how it happened because I had certainly not been drinking anything stronger than root beer, but as I was debating a serious point, I became airborne and somehow fell straight back in my chair and onto the floor. There I sat in my ladder-back chair, staring at the *ceiling* instead of across the table at the two young men.

Of course, I was wearing a dress. Of course, I landed with my boots sticking straight up in the air. As nonchalantly as he might have reached for a fallen set of keys, Scott scooped me up and, without a word, set me back in the upright position. Didn't lose a beat. Just propped me up like a rag doll and went right on with his meal and conversation. The two gentlemen, as I recall, sat poised with forks in midair, blinking as if to be sure of what they had just seen.

As we drove toward my birthday celebration, I recalled these past events and felt suddenly uneasy about another Trail Dust celebration. As Scott and I neared the halfway point on the highway to the familiar steak house, my general uneasiness turned to strong irritation coupled with a sudden high-dosage bolt of low self-esteem, and things went downhill from there.

"So why don't you like my dress, Scott?" I began.

"I didn't say I didn't like your dress!"

"Well, you didn't say you *did*, either. And you didn't say I looked pretty tonight. You always tell me I look ravishing when we go out. What is it? Do I look heavy? Are you embarrassed to have me as your partner?"

"I'm not going to have this conversation, Becky."

"You are talking to me, so you *are* having this conversation."

Silence followed for the next thirty minutes. I guessed maybe we *weren't* having this conversation after all. When we pulled into the restaurant parking lot, I could stand it no longer.

"I can't believe you ruined my birthday dinner by refusing to tell me I look ravishing!"

Then I flounced out of the truck, slammed the door hard enough to loosen every tooth in his head, and marched into the steak house. I was pretty sure Scott would follow me, even though my behavior was not all that ravishing. After all, it was my birthday and we were meeting my parents, for goodness sake. But did I mention that my husband has a wee stubborn streak?

I walked into the restaurant and glanced back over my shoulder, expecting to see a properly penitent husband. There was a huge empty space instead. So I made up a plausible excuse to tell my parents. I told them that Scott had probably gone to get some gas and would be right back, all the while inwardly hoping that what I said would turn out to be the truth. I kept a sharp eye peeled for him—even praying that he would walk through those swinging doors any minute and the standoff would be over. But no sign of my tall husband graced the entry. After about twenty minutes I ran out of excuses. We were into a standoff to rival the one at the O.K. Corral. But no longer up to a shoot-out, I began to cry into my iced tea.

Not knowing what else to do, Daddy asked me if I would like to dance, and I managed to nod. So I "Waltzed Across Texas" in my father's arms while the tears poured down my cheeks over the fact that my birthday dinner had been ruined, my husband was behaving like a stubborn mule sitting out in the parking lot, and, most of all, I was not ravishing tonight.

Finally, I told my parents that Scott and I had had a little tiff on the way to the restaurant. They both managed to feign surprise and registered the appropriate sympathy for me. Then I told them that if they would excuse me I had to go out to the parking lot to apologize to my hard-headed, insensitive husband.

I found Scott sitting in the truck, his hard head resting against the steering wheel. As soon as I opened the door, Scott took a good look at my tear-stained face. "Becky," he said grimly, "what time of the month is it?"

How *like* a man—so totally irrational!

"It's my birthday. That's what time of the month it is. Did you know that it is my *birthday?* How can you stand me up on my *birthday?* And in front of my *parents!*"

"Becky, I'm sorry," he said, shaking his head as if to clear it. "I just don't know what to *do* with you. You're like a different person when you hit a certain time of the month. You hate yourself. And you try your best to pick a fight with me. And it works every time! You've got to do *something!*"

I felt tremendous relief that he wasn't going to leave me stranded there and began to hope the evening could be salvaged.

I even toyed with the remote possibility he might be a tiny bit right.

"Well," I said, sniffing and trying to smile, "I'll make you a deal. I'll see a doctor soon if you'll come inside and do the Cotton-Eyed-Joe with me."

When we walked back inside the restaurant and to our table arm in arm, Mother shook her head and grinned.

"You know, you two are a lot of trouble—but you're never more trouble than you're worth. Let's eat!"

We made it through the evening, even managed to have a good time. Once as I waltzed in my husband's arms, he stopped and whispered something in my ear that I desperately needed to hear.

"Miss Becky, you look ravishing tonight."

The end of a matter is better than its beginning,
and patience is better than pride.

ECCLESIASTES 7:8

∾

F   I   V   E

Hot-blooded heartthrobs
on slow boil

I wish I could say that that one waltz fixed everything that was
haywire in our marriage. But the truth is, the showdowns
kept coming with alarming regularity.

I've often compared Scott and myself to a hot-blooded Italian
couple. Now, I *look* the part. Italian or Spanish either one, they're
both supposed to be hot-blooded, aren't they? I look like the
type you might expect to find dancing on a table in a cantina
with a pair of castanets clicking.

Scott, on the other hand, looks like the all-American
guy—tall, lanky but broad shouldered, wheat-colored hair,
square jawed. The kind of good-looking guy that could make a
woman salivate, present company included.

Who knows what made us spark with so much anger? I guess
it's the same thing that made us passionate about each other
when things were good. We're just two very *intense* people. Plus,
we *were* teenagers when we married, and in many ways, I think
we got locked into a pattern of relating to each other like a couple
of kids.

Scott and I were good, well-mannered children. We were each considered easy-going and agreeable. Maybe we were just saving up our tempers all those years for the day we could get married and go berserk.

So what, exactly, had we two "crazy kids" been arguing about all this time? Probably the same things every couple fights about. Perhaps our conflicts *were* a bit more—shall we say—theatrical, but the subject matter is fairly universal.

After having been married for three years, we began the classic struggle of starting a family. Baby Arrives. Man Watches Lover Turn into Mother. Man Misses Wife. Woman Feels Pulled in Two. Baby Drains Available Energy Needed for Couple to Do Anything about It. Just when Life Gets under Control, the Home Pregnancy Test Turns Blue Again.

Then we fought about how to raise the little tykes—how to discipline, how old they should be before being punished, and when discipline should be administered. How much attention they should have, how long they should be allowed to cry at bedtime, and how much our lives should revolve around them.

Every now and again when Scott and I see a young couple with babies and toddlers, we each have the overpowering urge to cry. We so empathize with that difficult, wonderful, exhausting, precious, draining time of life. As our kids have grown older, these conflicts have abated, but the Preschool Decade certainly took its toll.

We have each been jealous of the other's work, the kids, attractive coworkers of the opposite sex, *un*attractive coworkers of the opposite sex, time-demanding projects, good causes, television, engrossing books, church activities, best friends, rutabagas—well, maybe not rutabagas. Whatever was perceived as having more value in the eyes of our mate than ourselves left us open for feeling neglected. Our insecurities screamed, "Pay attention to me!"

We fought often over finances: bouncing the checking account; scraping the bottom of the piggy bank for kids' lunch money; bouncing the checking account; having to ask the chief wage earner for money (which always leaves the "askee" feeling like a needy child); bouncing the checking account; having to "sweat it out" over bills, needs for our children, grocery money, doctor appointments, and the ability to keep our thoroughly used cars on the road; bouncing the checking account; wondering if it is better for a mother to work and help out with financial tension or to scrimp by so she can stay home with kids; and finally, in case I haven't mentioned it yet, bouncing the checking account.

Even now, on Paying Bills Night when Scott sinks into a chair with envelopes waiting to be stuffed with money we don't have, a dark, ominous cloud settles over the entire house. Instinctively, the kids and I begin walking on tiptoe. We find ourselves gently touching each other on the shoulder as we pass in the hall like survivors of some past crises. Sometimes we whisper soothing words of comfort to each other: "It's almost over now. Daddy's nose isn't flaring as wide as it was a few minutes ago."

We both have struggled with periods of low self-esteem. Here's an example of a typical anger-producing conversation when the female of a relationship is suffering from a drop in self-confidence.

"Honey," she begins, "am I getting too fat, or do you think these jeans are shrinking?"

"The jeans look the same size to me."

"Then find some other skinny girl to squeeze into them. There's no way I'm going out looking like a giant rump roast tonight!"

And here's a conversation where the male of our species is experiencing a period of diminished self-esteem. Notice the man exhibiting the male tendency to lean toward defensiveness.

"How was your day, Sweetheart?" he begins.

"Oh, fine. I bought groceries, fed the kids, and the house is clean. I *am* a little tired though. I'm looking forward to a good night's rest."

"Oh, sure. Why don't you just *save* the big rejection speech and say, 'Not tonight, Dear!'"

Do any of these scenarios sound familiar? The only common cause of discord we haven't experienced is "a lack of communication." We may be communicating in loud, obnoxious, staccato voices, but we are rarely at a loss for words. Our love is intense. Our anger is intense. Our communication is intense. We are just your plain old everyday, average, amazingly intense couple. And that is why we were ready to call it quits one day, and the next morning we were committed to live together in passionate union for all eternity. Understand? No? Well, you're in good company. Neither do we. It just is.

But if there gets to be *too* many conflicts—no matter what the source—it is easy to wake up one day and find oneself in the danger zone. I had no idea how close we were.

What causes fights and quarrels among you? Don't they come from your desires that battle within you? You want something but don't get it.

JAMES 4:1–2

If I hear that song again, I'll scream!

I couldn't breathe. I couldn't think. The world was tilted on edge and sliding into blackness. Somehow I made my way through the haze of chattering children in the school cafeteria and into the teacher's lounge. There, my red-rimmed eyes met those of Laticia's, a fellow teacher. She immediately understood my need for help and put her arm around my shoulders. She carefully led me to an empty hall where I collapsed in sobs.

Laticia is a tiny woman with beautiful, creamy, coffee-colored skin, and she has a fiery strength about her. Right now, I needed her strength. I had none left of my own.

"What is it, Becky?" she gently asked when my tears began to subside. "What's the matter?"

"Oh, Laticia, it's over. My marriage is over! I just talked to Scott on the phone, and he sounded so cold, so distant. He said he's made his decision. He can't stand to watch us hurt each other any more. He wants a divorce, and he says there's nothing I can do to change his mind."

Usually talkative, Laticia was quiet, letting me pour out my pain.

"He's right, you know," I continued. "Our relationship has been one exhausting experience after another. It's up and down and back and forth. One moment we're at each other's throats, the next we're madly in love. But after these last few months we're like pieces of elastic that have been stretched one too many times. We're worn out. We just don't have it in us to keep bouncing back. It's like walking around nitroglycerin, never knowing what might set off the next explosion. Is this any way to live? Oh, God, what am I going to do? How will we tell our children? Is this really going to happen to *us?*"

I felt as though my chest had been ripped open and my heart pulled out. It physically ached. I had never felt such a relentless wrenching. *Lord, I can't take this pain.* Then I remembered my class. I had to go and get my twenty first-graders from the playground, take them back to my room, and teach them math. *How can I have a nervous breakdown in the middle of a school day? In five more minutes I have to add two-digit numbers together in front of a class of seven-year-olds. I have to calm down. Good teachers don't fall apart in front of the children. We're professionals. But today, oh dear God, I'm a child.*

Laticia was one step ahead of me.

"Listen to me, Becky. Get your kids, and then bring them into my classroom. They can watch a movie with my class this afternoon. You take what time you need to pull yourself together. Then we need to talk."

My first-graders and I knew each other well at this point in the year. I loved them, and they loved me back, as children are so easily prone to do. After bringing them in from recess, I led the little guys and gals back to my classroom. Then I sat down on my reading stool, tissue in hand, and managed, between sniffs, to talk to them.

"Kids, you know how some days you have to come to school—but you are hurting inside because you've had a disagreement with Mom or Dad that morning?" They all nodded in sympathy. "Sometimes you even cry. Well, Mrs. Freeman is having some of those hurt feelings, and I need you to be especially kind today. In a minute I'm going to take you to the class next door and let you watch a movie so I can take a few minutes to rest and feel better."

As they filed out the door one by one, each of my students said, "We love you, Mrs. Freeman" or "I hope you feel better." Children's arms reached out to pat and hug, to comfort the "professional." Their open tenderness helped.

I dropped off the children at Laticia's door, thanking this mentor-teacher for her kindness. As I walked away, I thought, *She's a good friend, but she can't possibly understand any of this. I see the way she and her husband love each other. The way he picks her up at 4:00 sharp on Wednesdays for their "date night." The flowers he sends, the beautiful clothes he buys for her. Weekend get-a-ways. The romantic ways they talk about one another. If only . . .* but it was useless to waste wishes on what could never be.

I went back to my empty classroom, turned out the lights, lay my head on my desk, and wept again. It seemed the tears would never stop, and like one of my first-graders, I wondered where bodies store all that salt water. My mind drifted over the years with Scott. I loved him. I knew he loved me. How, then, had it come to this?

We'd had the most romantic of courtships. We'd never had a single disagreement; we were Romeo and Juliet, lovers for all time and eternity. Sure, we had been just seventeen and eighteen years old when we got married, but we came from good families. We were involved in a solid church and had received the blessing and emotional support of friends and family. And we were both mature for our ages. Everybody said so.

However, not long after the honeymoon we began to realize, with a sense of impending doom, that we were actually living with someone other than the person we had signed up to marry. In spite of the feeling that there had been some mix-up, we still loved each other—maybe even too intensely. Perhaps it was that desperate desire we both had to love and be loved that seemed to increase the intensity of the pain we experienced when we went through periods of disillusionment and perceived rejection. In recent months, those feelings of rejection and anger had almost drowned out all feelings of love.

After years of clumsily walking on eggshells, it was time to face the facts. Our marriage was turning us into scrambled omelets. Divorce, the unthinkable, had gradually become the object of our daydreams. Logic told us that throwing in the towel might cover up some of the mess we were making of each other's lives.

How else could we end the vicious cycle? For seventeen years we seemed doomed to play the same old groove in the same old record. It had sounded like a bad country song, hummed slow and sad, with a "poor me" twang. I could write the lyrics myself.

I start talkin' and a bawlin'
He packs his bags and starts a walkin'
While I'm cryin' in my tea cup
He's sleepin' in the pickup.
Three nights of bein' alone
We miss each other to the bone,
We've got the headache, heartache,
This-is-all-that-I-can-take blues.

Finally tired of feeling smug
Someone reaches for a hug.
Passion lingers for a while
But there's fear behind the smile,
'Cause the song's about to end
Another battle's 'round the bend.
We've got the headache, heartache,
This-is-all-that-I-can-take blues.

And so now it had come to this. Anything—*anything*—but continue to play that same record.

I heard the door open and Laticia entered the room, inter-rupting my tears and my thoughts. She sat down and looked at me seriously with her big, black eyes before she measured her words carefully.

"Becky, think hard before you give up on your marriage. You've got to fight for your relationship. Charles and I have survived much worse than you and Scott."

It was a startling challenge, one I hadn't expected. My eyes flew open.

"What? But . . . but . . . you and Charles are so . . . together!"

"It hasn't always been that way. We've hurt each other terribly."

I could tell by the intensity in her voice that she meant *horribly* terribly. A faint glimmer of hope lit the dark corners of my mind.

"What did you do?" I asked, dabbing at the edges of my eyes.

"First, we got some counseling. We still go to group sessions. You and Scott probably need outside help. It's like you've both been involved in a bad wreck. When it is this bad, it's time to call an ambulance—a paramedic. Neither of you has the strength to help the other right now. Get help. I promise you, there is such a thing as starting over. But you've got to fight for it."

Fight? I felt whipped already—bone weary. I'd think about her words later. I was just too tired to make important decisions right now.

That evening, I dragged myself through the door of our home, completely drained. Scott would not be coming home tonight, and I didn't really want him to, not the way things were. I preferred to have a quiet supper with the kids and go to bed early, and alone, rather than face another battle. But in another way, I did miss him. I missed the times when we had managed to dodge the minefield and, between battles, had found each other's warm embrace. If only, if *only* . . .

After I put the children to bed, I lay staring into the darkness. I thought of how Scott and I were each capable of being two different people. I felt lonely for a *part* of who Scott was, but not for the other part of him—the part I'd talked to on the phone today. I could manage without that robot-like stranger.

I finally fell asleep with that odd mixture of emotions playing in my head. I dreamed of talking with the Scott who was my old friend about this awful, impossible situation with Scott, my husband who wanted out of our marriage. He had been my best friend since I was fifteen years old. We'd grown up together. Who would I talk to now about this hole that had been left in my heart? I wanted my sixteen-year-old-friend-Scott to magically appear and help me cope with losing my thirty-three-year-old-husband-Scott.

I slept fitfully and woke after the dream. Lying there, I thought of Zachary, Ezekiel, Rachel Praise, and Gabriel. I knew my husband would be thinking of our children tonight too. He loved them so and was a wonderful father. It would be killing him, as it was me now, to think that our own pain would harm their innocent lives. I wondered also, if my husband was lying awake somewhere in the darkness out there missing the "kinder, gentler" part of me.

And though I didn't feel it then, I know it now. There was a Shepherd moving in the blackness, guiding our paths, and keeping watch in our darkest night.

"I will care for My sheep
and will deliver them from all the places
to which they were scattered on a cloudy and gloomy day."
EZEKIEL 34:12, NASB

SEVEN

Does "as long as you both shall live" mean a lifetime guarantee?

The digital clock bleeped 6:00 A.M. The state of our marriage reminded me of the state of Alaska—expansive and cold. Especially when I contemplated the large empty spot beside my pillow that morning.

Like an earthquake victim, I longed to be able to trust solid ground—all those foundations on which I had always been able to depend. But the terra was no longer firma. If my marriage was failing, what about everything else I believed in? *Does God care about us? Is He even out there at all?* It was as if the tidy box containing all I had known and believed was shaken of its contents. And what, if anything, would I be able to put back into my box of beliefs?

I've since learned that having your box tipped over is always frightening, but it usually happens to everyone at some time. Often it is the only way to clean out the junk, making way for fresh beginnings. Eventually what goes back into the box is yours and yours alone. No hand-me-down belief systems or other people's treasures.

Rolling over toward the nightstand, I flipped on the radio—hungry for the sound of a human voice, even if it had to come from a small, black box. The "Let's Get Up and at 'Em" hosts were talking about the weather forecast and arguing about some obscure bill floating around in Congress. Then, with total disregard for my personal crisis, the perky morning DJs began cracking perky morning jokes.

Didn't everyone know that life as we'd known it had come to a complete halt? I thought to myself, *A newscaster—a Walter Cronkite-type—should be breaking in any minute now to announce, "This bulletin just in: Scott and Becky Freeman, adorable couple and parents of four remarkable children, are on the verge of marital collapse! A National State of Emergency has officially been declared."*

Instead, those Good Morning morons were droning on about cumulous cloud formations as if nothing else of significance had happened yesterday! Incredible! As I wondered how the rest of society could continue their trivial little lives in the midst of Our Relationship Trauma, I could almost hear Scott's voice, teasing me: "Just because you've always been able to charm the hair off a bullfrog, you assume the world revolves around *you*, Darlin'. Someday you might be in for a surprise."

Well, as Gomer Pyle used to say, "Sur-PRISE, sur-PRISE, sur-PRISE." *Someday* had arrived with a bang. It was painfully obvious the world didn't take its daily spin with me as its permanent axis.

So here I was, in the middle of the worst personal crisis of my life, the sun still rising routinely in my eastern window. The numbers on the clock still clicking ever onward. Radio personalities still trying to get laughs before 10:00 A.M. Even under the best of circumstances—in peacetime—I've always thought it was in bad taste for people to try to be amusing in the morning.

In desperate need of comfort, I shut off the radio and reached for the Bible on the nightstand. At that point, I knew my situation warranted using the most theologically advanced method of gleaning insight from the Word of God. So I closed my eyes, opened my Bible, and randomly stuck my finger on a verse. Honestly, I was too hurt and confused for a system that might have required more effort.

It always amazes me that God graciously chooses to meet me at my point of need, however pitiful my efforts to reach Him. The Shepherd comes after His lost, disoriented sheep when He hears their bleating, no matter how faint or weak their cries.

As my stomach turned in knots over whether or not my husband would—or should—come home, my eyes rested on Proverbs 27:8: "Like a bird that wanders from her nest, so is a man who wanders from his home" (NASB).

At that instant the churning in my belly stopped. The Good Shepherd was clearly showing me that my husband, no matter what he said in anger and frustration, had wandered from his nest. Furthermore, as a bird longs to get back to her young, my husband, at this very moment, was missing his home—his family. Even, perhaps, *me.* My prayerful response to that deep revelation was, "Dear Lord, Scott is feeling just as lost and alone and miserable as I am. Oh, *good!*"

Since the world had not blown up, I still had to get dressed and ready for work. My four children also had to be prodded, breakfasted, and delivered to the bus stop. Somehow, I struggled through the next two days. Other than letting me know where he'd be staying, there was no other communication. During those days, I stumbled from being courageous, positive, and self-assured; to angry, resentful, and fed up; to blubbering like a vulnerable little girl. On the second day of Scott's absence as I was driving home from teaching school, I thought again of what Laticia had said earlier.

"You and Scott will have to fight for your marriage. It's hard, especially at first. But you have to decide if your love is worth the effort."

I cried again—half talking to myself, half in prayer. "*Is* it worth it, Lord? Wouldn't it be better to bow out gracefully now, rather than risk doing any more damage?"

Not wanting to think, I reached for the radio dial and turned it on. A song by Michael Martin Murphy filled the air. I'd always loved the melody, but this time the words held even greater impact.

> "Right in their hands is a dying romance
> and they're not even trying to keep it alive.
>
> What's the glory of living?
> Doesn't anybody ever stay together anymore?
> And if nothing ever lasts forever—tell me,
> What's forever for?"[1]

The words struck like an arrow in the core of my heart. Forever. I always thought true love would last forever. My mind drifted back to an altar, a seventeen-year-old girl draped in white lace, an eighteen-year-old boy decked out in a white tuxedo with tails—and a vow.

But, we were just babies. We didn't really know what we were saying! I continued to argue with myself.

Yes, Becky, you didn't know all the pain marriage would entail. But you were fully aware of the promise you were making to that young man before family, friends, and God Almighty. You knew forever meant a fair amount of time. It was a promise you really intended to keep. A vow!

I had no rebuttal for that round. As a matter of fact, I could remember exactly what I had said to my bridegroom on June 27, 1976, because I'd composed the words myself: "*Scott, I promise to be your faithful wife until one of us lays the other in the waiting arms of the Savior or until we meet Him in the air together.*"

People always said I had a way with words. And I'd certainly left no room for misunderstanding with *those vows,* had I? No "if" or "but" clauses. Not a loophole—other than Rapture or death—in sight.

Standing there, on the brink of the Canyon of Divorce, reality dawned. Aside from the fact that we had promised, of our own free will, to be faithful to one another, I also began to think of the practical implications of an honest-to-goodness divorce. I thought of the loneliness, of starting over, of dreams dashed, financial stresses, our families torn apart, friends hurt, but most of all, our children caught between the two parents they loved.

Scott and I were living through the "for worse" part of the marriage deal. But what reason for separating could we offer our children that would make any sense? And what sort of lesson would we be teaching them about how to handle problems that would come up in their future relationships? They knew things were tense between their daddy and me, but at the time they had no idea that Scott's absence was more than a business trip. Oh, how I wanted to keep from hurting them!

We can't give up. Not yet. If for nothing else than for the sake of Zachary, Ezekiel, Rachel, and Gabriel.

I twisted the simple gold band around my finger. Those of you who have read our "falling in love" story from *Worms in My Tea and Other Mixed Blessings* may remember the significance of my wedding band. Scott had originally given it to me while we were on a mission trip to Guatemala as a gesture of friendship and budding love. He was sixteen years old at the time; I was fifteen. He'd used the last of his money—twelve dollars—to buy the tiny, rose gold ring. I knew, even then, that if I ever married this guy, the twelve-dollar ring would be the only wedding band I would ever want. I took it off and looked inside at the Scripture reference, Jeremiah 24:6–7—a verse I'd claimed for myself and for Scott at the beginning of our dating relationship.

Maybe there's hope. God keeps His promises much better than we do.

The phone rang, breaking my contemplation. It was Scott, his voice soft and tired. He wanted to take the kids out to dinner.

Said he missed them. Swallowing hard, I asked, "So, how are you feeling about their mother these days?"

"I don't know. I guess I'm just tired of hurting her. Becky, I just want to set you free to find somebody who'll make you happy. I don't know if I can be the kind of guy you need. I'm not a Joe Have-It-All-Together Christian in a three-piece suit."

"If I'd wanted Joe Christian in a three-piece suit, I would have married him. You're the only man I've ever wanted, Scott."

"I can be ornery, and I'll probably always be a sort of rebel."

"I can be frustrating, and I'll probably always be something of a basket case."

"No wonder we've made such a happy couple."

"Oh, Scott. What are we going to do with us?"

"I just don't know if I have it in me to take another run at it, Becky."

"I know. I know. But I've checked the Official Marriage Rules, and they don't seem to allow for throwing in the towel."

"Yeah, but we've broken so many Marriage Rules that I don't know whether there are too many of them left to worry about."

"So you're saying you want to give up?"

"No, I don't want to give up. Everything I've loved and worked for is tied up with you and the kids and our home."

"So you're saying you want to try again?"

"No, I don't want to try again either. I'm afraid we'll end up making the same old mistakes over and over again."

"So you're saying . . . "

"So I'm saying I don't know what to do." Scott paused, and when he spoke again there was a quiver in his voice, "But I sure could use a friend right now."

The line grew quiet. So much silence after such violent storms. I felt the hotness of familiar tears welling up in my eyes. There he was again. My sixteen-year-old best friend inside my thirty-three-year-old ornery husband. How could I bear to lose this?

When I found my voice, I answered. "Me too. I miss you. Come on home."

"I'll be there in about twenty minutes."

I hung up the phone and ran to the bathroom. I had less than half an hour to get casually knock-'em-dead gorgeous. My husband was coming in for a landing at the family nest. At least, it was a start.

"For I will set My eyes on them for good, and I will bring them again to this land; and I will build them up and not overthrow them, and I will plant them and not pluck them up. And I will give them a heart to know Me, for I am the LORD; and they will be My people, and I will be their God, for they will return to Me with their whole heart."

JEREMIAH 24:6–7, NASB

The ruckus ain't worth the reward anymore

I have to admit it. Six feet of boots, blue jeans, and denim shirt looked pretty good to me as Scott slowly walked into the house, gently closing the front door behind him. I suppose, after a couple of lonely days and nights, I didn't look too shabby to him either.

Wordless, he took my hand, led me to the bedroom, sat down in the old green rocker, and pulled me to his lap. I nestled my face next to his in that warm spot just under his ear and wrapped my arms around his neck. For a long time we held each other in that position and just rocked and wept. How could we love each other this much and be so miserable at the same time?

I finally let out one of those Grand Finale shuddering sniffs that always follow momentous crying spells, and then I found my voice.

"Scott, I heard something on the radio today that nearly broke me up. Have you ever heard the song, 'What's Forever For?'"

Scott wrinkled his forehead.

"What station did you hear it on?" he asked.

I gave him the call letters then added, "I think it's a brand new station."

Scott shook his head. "What time did you hear it?"

"It was on the way home from school. I guess about 4:45. A few hours before you called tonight. Why?"

"Because I heard the same song at the same time on the same radio station and it had the same effect on me."

"*Somebody* must be trying to tell us something," I whispered.

"Yeah, but what is it?"

"He is saying you're going to have to rock with me a looooong time, Baby."

"All right," he agreed, "but under one condition."

"What's that?"

"You've gotta switch sides. My right leg's gone numb."

With that touch of humor and the meeting of smiles, we began making up the way we always make up after a big fight. Since this conflict had been what they call a real "humdinger" here in Texas—and such a traumatic thing as "divorce" had been seriously taken into consideration—the making up period was extended accordingly. We both called in sick and spent the entire next day at home.

Well, we *were* sick! Before we took the day off our heads had hurt, our eyes had been swollen and red, and our stomachs had been twisted into painful knots. But it is amazing what staying home and resting will do for a body.

As an aside, when the kids are home we've worked out a secret code for letting them know Mom and Dad would like to be left undisturbed for awhile. Scott tells them, "Your momma and I are worn out. We need to take a little nap. Don't even think about knockin' on our bedroom door unless there's a fire. Even then, make sure the fire is bigger than a breadbox."

The little ones are gullible enough, but the teenage boys have been known to give their father an exaggerated wink and say,

"Suuuure, Dad." I think we need to come up with something a bit more creative than taking a *nap*. But what? Conducting a secret investigation? Developing photographs?

During Open House at Gabe's school last fall, the children had been asked to draw pictures of their daddies. The fathers were to guess which picture was drawn by their own child. It took Scott all of two seconds to find his. Gabe had drawn a man lying on a bed, snoring. The caption read, "My Daddy likes to take LOTS of naps."

As much as physical affection helps, rebounding from a big blowup is a lot like getting over a stomach virus. The patient is tender for awhile, even after the retching is over and the healing has begun. As we began the process of talking about what to do about our volatile relationship, we both agreed on one point: We were getting too old for this. Sure, the passion was always great after a good knock-down-drag-out, but the rewards just weren't worth the agony to either of us anymore.

One evening, not long after the fight, I settled down in my personal library—a hot bathtub full of bubbles—to read my Bible. Once again my eyes settled on a verse that seemed made-to-order for us: "If you keep on biting and devouring each other, watch out or you will be destroyed by each other" (Gal. 5:15).

The words carried the weight of a plea from that Someone who cared deeply about the two of us—the same Someone who had fixed it so that we both heard that "Forever" song at the same time on the same day. The warning was simple: If we continued this pattern, we would eventually eat each other alive. I had a sudden macabre vision of Scott and me taking angry bites out of the other until nothing was left but a pitiful pile of bones.

Something happened in that bathtub full of bubbles that marked the end of an era for me. I realized we were going to have to make some significant changes if we were to survive intact as a couple. And if we were not going to sink or jump ship, we needed to find a way to get the boat turned around.

Look also at ships: although they are so large and are driven by fierce winds, they are turned by a very small rudder wherever the pilot desires.

JAMES 3:4, NKJV

❧

Is there stop 'n' go counseling for couples on the run?

As Scott and I walked down the thick, carpeted hallway toward the mahogany door marked "Licensed Family Therapists," I fought the urge to run. As people strolled by, I wanted to stop and offer them a word of explanation.

My feelings reminded me of the time I was about seven years old and I could not yet ride my bicycle without training wheels. Desperate to cover my handicap to any window-peeking neighbors, I rode up and down the sidewalk loudly declaring, "I know how to ride this bicycle *without* these training wheels! It's just that my Daddy doesn't know how to take them *off!*"

In much the same way I wanted to shout, "Look, we really don't belong in this psychiatric building! My Sweetie and I are just dropping by for a 1:00 appointment—more like a *visit* really—to tie up a few loose ends. Everything is completely under control. No need to call any white-coated men with straitjackets. It is true that some people do refer to me as a 'fruit cake,' but it is just a little joke."

Instead, I managed a weak smile and put my hand in Scott's for reassurance.

After having talked it over, Scott and I had decided to take Laticia's advice and seek outside assistance. After numerous phone calls to a variety of counselors, one significant psychological truth was already beginning to emerge. This business of getting marriage counseling was going to cost us big bucks. A one-hour session would cost about eighty dollars. And this was supposed to be *good* compared to the prices for mental health in the big city.

I was confident of one thing: Scott and I would have to be fast learners and the therapist a speed talker if we were going to fix our marital problems before we went broke. There could be no whiling away of precious seconds in the therapist's office with idle chitchat. As a matter of fact, I would have preferred the doctors simply tell us what we needed to do to live "happily ever after" in one easy session—and stick any follow-up instructions in a pizza box "to go." Unfortunately, there was no listing under Drive-Through Counseling Services; no Therapy to Go; and most of all, no One-Hour Cure or It's Free.

As Scott leaned against the heavy door to the waiting room, we could hear the strains of savage-beast-calming music pouring from the soothing, omnipresent stereo. I walked in with my head held high, giving the other patients in the waiting room my most impressively sane smile. Then I sank into the pale blue velvet chair beside my husband, took out my notes, and mentally rehearsed what I would tell the therapist.

My imaginary conversation was interrupted by the heart-stopping announcement, "Mr. and Mrs. Freeman, the doctor is ready to see you."

I noted with relief that our therapist was dressed casually—dress slacks, plaid shirt, no tie. He had a kind smile and relaxed demeanor, putting us quickly at ease. As he shook our hands and greeted us pleasantly, most of my apprehension dissipated. However, I did have to keep myself in check as we followed the doctor toward his office. I wanted to blurt out, "Move it, Doc. The clock's a-ticking and, at least in this case, talk ain't cheap!"

As soon as the door to the private office closed behind us, I took charge, planning to move things right along. Talking like an auctioneer, I quickly gave the counselor a verbal synopsis of our problems. Then I let him know I'd be happy to give him summarized notes on any other information he might need in the future.

There was a two-second pause before the counselor answered back. That pause, as you know, represented another nickel—down the drain. I wondered if we could all simply agree to dismiss repetitive phrases, nervous ticks, and prolonged periods of breathing for this one pricey hour. We had a lot of information to exchange if all our problems were to be solved by two o'clock.

Scott and I began our tales of woe, and the counselor eventually shook his head in wonder and probably broke the cardinal rule of marriage counseling by looking shocked.

"You two really don't know how to communicate very well, do you?" he observed.

I was insulted. I knew I could talk a blue streak and Scott had a college degree in communications.

Next, the counselor walked over to a chalkboard on the wall. In the first $20.53 of this session, he gave us a great piece of generic advice. He drew a line down the middle of the board. On one side he wrote the word, *Reacting*. On the other side of the line he wrote the word, *Responding*.

"Scott and Becky, " he coached, "one of your goals here will be to move from the reacting to the responding side of the board." That sounded easy enough. Like a game, perhaps. In the next $15.86 of our time together, it became apparent that we were dealing with issues slightly more complicated than Tiddly-Winks. At this point Scott leaned over and coarsely whispered in my ear.

"Becky, you're embarrassing me. Stop snapping your fingers and saying 'Cut to the chase.'"

I tried to relax, but it was hard not to think of the amount of milk and cereal and ground beef I could buy for *eighty bucks!* I had to remind myself of the fact that we were here to learn. Soon, however, I did begin to wonder when we'd get to the part where the counselor would put Scott in his place and tell him he'd better shape up if he was going to keep the love of a charming, fast-thinking woman like myself.

Instead the therapist turned to my husband and began asking him several questions—how was he feeling, what changes had taken place in his life, what were his expectations of marriage. After $18.46 more of this sort of dialogue I thought, *Well, what am I? Chopped liver?*

But as Scott continued to share, I gradually began to *hear.* I even began to *understand*—how I had knowingly at times, but mostly unknowingly, hurt him. When my turn came to express some of the pain I had also experienced, it was with an immediate sense of relief. Why? Because I could also see that Scott was listening—*really listening*—to my concerns.

Considering the shape we were in, I honestly doubt we would ever have been able to see each other's side of our problems without the help of an official go-between. Incredible perspective can be gained from having a wise, neutral third party involved when the web gets too tangled for two.

In the counseling process, we would eventually learn a variety of techniques for improving communication—some helpful, some hilarious, and some downright humiliating. My absolute favorite is a technique I actually invented myself. I'm pleased to announce that I'm still using it with excellent results. As a matter of fact, this very afternoon I received a letter from a young mother of three whose husband is in the Air Force, serving in Saudi Arabia. She asked permission to borrow this technique to try on her husband when he hits American soil. I thought the device might bear repeating here since it seems to be on the cutting edge of therapeutic advancement. I call it the "Help Your Man Meet Your Needs Technique," and this is how it works:

Whenever I find myself in need of a hug or words of affection, I locate Scott and put my arms around his neck.

Then I say, "You think I'm so sweet and pretty you can hardly keep your eyes off me, don't you?" He can't resist a smile and obediently nods. I am fulfilled and happy. Actually, he reports that my putting words in his mouth causes him to realize he really does feel the words. So I am working on this line next: "Scott, you just love cute, nicely-rounded women. You'd hate to see me lose an ounce, wouldn't you, Sweetheart?"

Even with the good advice we'd received on our first day, I am sorry to report that we were unable to tie up all the "loose ends" of our marriage in one easy lesson. Scott and I would be back at the counselor's office several more times that spring. And I must also admit that all the sessions did not end as warmly as the first. Once we both walked out of the building and raced toward our separate cars. Then, with tires squealing and rubber burning, we each pulled out of the parking lot as fast as we could drive—in opposite directions. Maturity under pressure has never been one of our strong points.

Another time, Scott went to a session without me. Once, I also went alone. On yet another occasion, we both left the counselor's office hurting so badly that he insisted on a morning-after follow-up session just to make sure we each made it through the night. There was no way to avoid some pain. As I've said, it hurts to get our boxes tipped over—to clean out all the junk inside a relationship. It hurts to get the needle on our records bumped out of familiar grooves. And the intermediate sounds aren't always pleasant either. At least not until the needle finally settles onto some new bands of beautiful music. Because of this experience, I've come to a new understanding of a passage from Hosea that has always bothered me: "Come, let us return to the LORD. He has torn us to pieces but he will heal us; he has injured us but he will bind up our wounds" (Hosea 6:1).

Why would God intentionally wound those He loved? Was it some kind of cruel game? The more I come to know the Wonderful Counselor, the more I realize that there are times when He has to break us down in order to heal us. And as I read the entire story of Hosea, it is obvious that God takes no joy in the tearing-down process. Like a surgeon who must cut in order to heal, God occasionally has to make painful incisions in our hearts that will eventually allow us to live life more fully and with greater joy and freedom than we ever imagined.

As I finish this chapter, it is dark and quiet. The only light in the house comes from my computer screen. Kids are tucked in bed. Scott's on his way home from a visit with his folks. All is well. So well, in fact, that my cup—and my eyes—runneth over with gratitude.

If by chance there is a man or a woman reading these pages whose marriage is out of control, may I stop here for a moment—right here in the middle of this page—and encourage you as Laticia and her husband encouraged us? Perhaps you may be led to a counselor, a pastor, a book or a tape, or a wise and trusted friend. But begin to look, as you pray—there *are* great sources available for aching relationships.

It is ironic that we human beings are trained for almost every conceivable skill in life, but most of us are never really taught the dynamics of human interaction. And there's a lot to learn. If two people have the desire to make a marriage work and are willing to combine action with that desire, a good relationship is possible. Not perfect—but good. If Scott and I hadn't made the long walk down that hall, pushed open the mahogany door labeled "Licensed Family Therapists," and sacrificed some hefty grocery money, we might not be happily crunching our corn-flakes in unison today.

One of the most poignant quotes I've ever read about the process of giving and receiving help comes from the book *When a Leader Falls.* The book is thoughtfully written by two friends of mine, Deb Frazier and Jan Winebrenner, and is published by Bethany House. They wrote:

> We all like being the one who is able to give, who has all the answers and has everything under control . . . . But God doesn't allow any of us the comfort of such a role indefinitely. We need Him, and we need one another. We all are destined to do time on the bottom of some heap. At any given moment there exists within the body those who need assistance and those who can provide it and the players are constantly changing.[1]

Scott and I have been on the bottom of a few heaps. And hopefully, we'll help pull a couple of fellow travelers up off the bottom of theirs along the way. No one has it all together, but I'm convinced that is exactly why we need each other. Life has its way of forcing us to take turns. No one is immune to struggles and trials. But when the Lord has granted us hope and healing, it's a joy and privilege to comfort others in their time of need.

If only you could be here tonight when my husband comes in the door—if you could see the friendship, the love, the spark between us now. How we'll hold each other close and talk into the night even though we know we need to get to sleep. And if you could have seen the mess we had made of our marriage only a few short years ago, you would appreciate what God, our Good Shepherd, has done.

Perhaps I love picturing Christ as my personal Shepherd because I have always found my greatest comfort in the Twenty-third Psalm: It seems to have a universal application to every conceivable human ache. I wonder how many millions of frightened men, women, and children have been wrapped, like a cozy warm quilt, in David's comforting words?

Often the Shepherd led me through the dark valley with the light of His Word. Other times it was through the spoken and written counsel of wise men and women who'd already trudged through this sort of darkness and could now help others navigate rocky terrain. Because of where Scott and I have been, the green pastures we are enjoying tonight are incredibly precious to me. Not that we've completely "arrived," by any means. The chapters to come will make that more than clear. And there will probably be some more dark valleys to cross when we will feel hurt, lost, and confused again. But as we cry for help, I now know—deep in my soul—He will *always* find us and He will *always* lead us home. That's what our Shepherd is for.

Because the Lord is my Shepherd, I have everything I need! He lets me rest in the meadow grass and leads me beside the quiet streams . . . . Even when walking through the dark valley of death I will not be afraid, for you are close beside me, guarding, guiding all the way.

PSALM 23:1–2, 4, TLB

T E N

After I walked a mile in his shoes, his feet didn't smell so bad

Shortly after we had called 911 to rescue our marriage, we went to Florida for vacation. We had five days with nothing to do but lie on the white, sandy beaches by the majestic ocean, bask in the sun, swim, and eat. Scott, especially, needed it.

He had taken an extra job remodeling a house so our family could enjoy this quality time together. We'd even graduated from marriage counseling. Then "why come" (as my kids used to say) were my husband and I not speaking to each other—again?

Scott had been gone so much before we left for this trip that by the time we had crammed the last beach umbrella and floatie into the van and settled into the front seats for the trip, I was looking over at a man who seemed more like a stranger. Was any vacation worth the amount of time we had spent apart these weeks? Could any trip, no matter how exciting, be worth watching my poor husband drag his aching, exhausted body home night after night while the kids asked me, "Do you think we'll ever get to see Daddy standing up with his eyes open again?"

I begged Scott to give it up—we'd stay home, go to Six Flags over Texas and stay in a local hotel this year. But my husband's brown eyes could see nothing but deep blue. Captain Scott *would* take his family to the sea. Come you-know-what or high water. Both possibilities now loomed imminent.

Driving sixteen hours with four kids in a fully packed, loudly reverberating van was not particularly conducive to meaningful dialogue. Scott and I managed to be on our best behavior—at least at the outset of the trip. Our small talk consisted of the usual polite conversation starters.

"How was your day, Honey?"

"Great. And yours? Hey, do you think it might be fun to let the children stop and play at the next rest area? Maybe we could even have a little family picnic?"

So far, so good. But somewhere between Louisiana and Mississippi, our courteous parley began to suffer somewhat.

"What do you mean you're tired of driving, Becky? You haven't even left the off ramp yet!!"

"Would you rather I ruin our whole vacation because I fell asleep at the wheel?!?"

Somewhere between Alabama and Florida we began reserving communication for only the most basic of human needs—and then it was a rather sketchy pantomime affair played out with grunts, scowls, and shrugs. The back end of the van, loaded with four wide-awake and cranky kids, was on the verge of mutiny. Captain Scott's crew was about to sink before we even hit water.

We survived the van voyage only a little worse for wear. And now here I was on the vacation of our dreams. Unfortunately, it had fallen my lot to entertain my own sad and miserable self on this lonely stretch of beach. Scott had long since walked with the kids farther down shore to take them fishing. As a matter of fact, my family was now fishing as *far away* from my resting place as possible while still technically remaining in the same state.

I sighed audibly and pulled out the reading material I had stuffed into my beach bag. Then I stretched out on a towel, preparing to dive into, and hopefully to lose myself in, the paperback I'd retrieved. I looked at the cover and moaned. The letters that stared back at me tauntingly declared: *What Men Really Want* by Herb Goldberg. *Great*, I thought, *just what I'm dying to know.* My initial reaction was, *What am I supposed to get out of this?* But then I remembered the reason the book was in my possession in the first place.

My friend Kathy had given me the book. Her husband, Greg, had given it to her on the occasion of their separation, hoping Kathy might understand that so many of his behaviors were just typical of most men. If she had understood, he thought, maybe she wouldn't have expected so much. Maybe she wouldn't be filing for divorce. Maybe he wouldn't be coming home to an empty, quiet apartment and dying inside with loneliness. Sadly, Kathy was beyond trying—the marriage was over. Still for some reason, she thought *I* might get something out of this book, so she tucked it in my hand before I left.

I sat reading that horrible book in the Florida sun for two days, forcing myself to swallow the bitter pill of learning how a "traditional" man thinks and functions. I often argued out loud with the author.

"Who do you think you are? What's a woman supposed to do? Just suppress all her needs and give 100 percent to the man?!"

However, about halfway through the book, my defenses started to drop and I began to *listen* to what I was reading, praying for an understanding spirit. It was one of those significant turning points, at which I look back and say profoundly, "That was a *Significant* Turning Point."

I realized, and finally came to the point of accepting, the different ways men and women react to each other. I'd probably heard them before at one of those "Ten Ways to Merry Matrimony" seminars, but this time I understood.

First of all, it finally dawned on me that men do not respond to tears and hurt feelings as many women would expect. When most men see a Ball of Female Emotions rolling in their direction they tend to have one of two responses: duck or brace for impact. When their distraught wives come at them, arms flung out for a reassuring embrace, tears flying in all directions like one of those backyard Water Wiggles gone mad, the natural male response is fight or flight. It took seventeen years for me to accept this, and it happened that day on the beach.

In addition, I discovered that men are physically *made* to handle conflict that way. In one study, scientists hooked men and women up to some wires that would test their responses during a confrontation. Now, I suspect men and women the world over have fantasized about hooking each other up to electrical wires during fights, but under scientific control, the results were amazing.

The study showed that a man's emotions were much more intense during a conflict than those of a woman. In other words, a man's boiling point came when the woman was still on a slow simmer. To avoid lashing out and boiling over, the man shuts down. Meanwhile, the woman is still wanting to duke this thing out and has the intense desire to continue fighting until a resolution can be found or until she at least gets a reassuring hug. (Which, if the truth were told, is usually the resolution she is seeking in the first place.)

"So *that's* it!" I said aloud there on the beach, feeling a strange sense of relief.

As a member of the gentler sex, all I knew was that the best way for a person to gain *my* sympathy was to cry. I also knew instinctively what to do to help a friend in pain. I'd put my arms around the poor girl and let her cry it out. Then I'd sympathize with the victim's pitiful plight and let her talk until she felt better or until we finished the cheesecake.

When Scott and I were newly married, the day came when he inevitably hurt my feelings. I, a product of centuries of genteel Southern breeding, grabbed my hanky and turned on my body's automatic estrogen-propelled sprinkler system. I do declare, my gentleman husband's response just nearly gave me the vapors. I was *completely* dumbfounded that my hero didn't respond with pats and hugs and "I'm sorrys." I couldn't believe he could be so callous and cold. Not a *sliver* of cheesecake did he offer to console my aching heart.

Using female logic, I came to one conclusion: I must not be communicating with enough *intensity.* So I cranked up the volume and increased the melodrama. Same response. Scott would take a hike or brace for a fight. Each year I added a more spectacular technique to try to gain Scott's affection. I'm too proud to admit some of them, but let me just say we've replaced a few dishes and patched a few nicks in the walls as a result of those failed experiments.

Again, it was the same song, zillionth verse: Fight or Flight. Finally, I hit on an astounding gem of truth. "More of the same is not going to do the trick," I told myself. "You can cry for sympathy for the next forty years, Becky, and you can bet your darlin' dentures that your old wrinkled-up husband will be leaving just as fast as he can get his wheel-chair out the door."

That's when I discovered the second Amazing Secret: The best thing I can do to break up a stalemate in an argument is usually the *exact opposite* of what I naturally feel like doing. When I feel like launching into a screaming rage, that's my clue to stay especially calm and collected. At this point I need to use all the powers of the Holy Spirit available to me to respond with dignity and decorum. Of course, when this happens, it's truly miraculous. (It's not in my makeup to be naturally dignified or decorumed.) If I have an overpowering urge to fight it out "right here, right now, to the finish," that's my signal to take a walk and cool off instead.

"Isn't that denial?" you may ask. "Stuffing your feelings that need to be released?" Glad you asked.

I don't think so. It's less about pretending natural emotions don't exist and more about self-control and redirecting. Proverbs 29:11 kept coming back to my mind in those days: "A fool gives full vent to his anger." Even psychologists are beginning to question the wisdom of "letting all your inward anger out." If this practice is carried on for too long, they are finding it actually increases rather than decreases violent feelings. I'm no psychologist; I just want results, and this approach seems to work much better for me.

Still, there's the problem of what to do with my jumbled emotions and pain when Scott has managed, either intentionally or unintentionally, to temporarily break my heart. Mind you, I still have my crying spell if I'm up to it. After all, it's my pity party. But I usually host it alone now and ask the Lord to be my Comforter. I may get together with a trusted friend who lets me cry on her shoulder and is known to keep rich dessert in her kitchen. When I'm quite finished, I dry my tears and get on with doing something I love doing until the timing is right, both of our tempers have cooled, and we're ready to take a first stab at reconciling.

Notice I say "first" stab. Usually it takes more than one attempt, but I know now to just keep waiting and gingerly testing the waters before one of us attempts the final, once-and-for-all "making-up talk." If Scott's still angry, I'm learning to just leave it alone and get busy doing something else I enjoy instead. Maybe I'll go for a cup of coffee and browse at a bookstore, have lunch with the girls, take a walk in the woods, or go to the mall for some intensive shopping therapy. Anything but mull and stew!

On one occasion I took the kids and checked into a motel for the day. Had a ball. It got me away from the scene of the crime so that I wouldn't lose my dignity or say things I regretted. Now at those times of conflict, I still have a little ache in my stomach. It reminds me that all is not well between me and the man I love. I miss the sauce—the "gravy," if you will—of romantic feelings. But better to deal with the pain constructively and wait patiently for the right timing than to blow pieces of each other's emotions all over the place. That way there's less mess to forgive when all is calm on the homefront again.

I can't tell you what a difference this change in attitude made almost immediately. That day in Florida I put the book down, and since I'd already used up the first forty-eight hours of my vacation going about in sackcloth and ashes, I decided I might as well enjoy all that I could salvage of the rest of it. A full day had not passed before Scott noticed I was actually having a good time without him. Since it was totally out of character for me to act "normal" when I've been upset, it got his attention—and attracted him like a bee to honey.

One night toward the end of the week, Scott and I walked hand in hand on the beach and had a long talk. He asked about my sudden change of heart, and I told him I was finished with falling to pieces trying to gain his attention. I could see the visible relief on his face as he heaved a sigh. Then I told him I forgave him for being a man. I could see visible signs of confusion on his face.

"Huh?" he began.

But before he could say anything, I added a P. S. "Scott, I just want you to know that when I'm having an emotional day or you've hurt my feelings and you don't want to deal with it, I have to have some way to cope. I'm trying to look to God to supply the love I need, but I may need to talk with a friend. I may need to get away from the house. I may need a Gold Card."

He started to protest, but then, from a sidewalk cafe in the distance, we heard the strains of the classic beach song "Boardwalk." I smiled up into my husband's handsome face, and even in the moonlight I could see his eyes sparkle mischievously. Without a word, he grabbed me by the waist and twirled me around with expert ease before landing me back in a romantic dip and planting one of those *Gone with the Wind* kisses on my lips. As you can see, making up is one of our fortes. We've had a lot of practice. Of course, music and stars and waves didn't hurt the mood either.

All the work and late hours Scott had put in to get us to this moment by the sea with these brilliant stars overhead seemed suddenly worthwhile. I melted deeper into my sea-lovin' husband's arms, savoring the night wind, moonlight, and seagulls' call. Closing my eyes, I pondered our rocky, weird relationship.

Scott and I may never understand fully how the opposite sex really thinks, I decided. *But right now*—as I rested my head on my Captain's chest and squeezed him close—*I couldn't care less. Right here, for at least tonight, I'm gonna get smothered in gravy.*

In quietness and in confidence shall be your strength.

ISAIAH 30:15, KJV

∾

Send an sos
for pms—asap!

When Gabriel was in first grade, he came home from school complaining about the behavior of a certain little boy who sat in the desk next to him.

"Mom," he moaned, "this is the whiniest kid I ever saw. I mean, *nobody* can do anything to make him happy! All he does is gripe, gripe, gripe—*all day long!* Really, he's got the worst case of PMS I've ever *seen* in a kid."

Obviously, Gabriel had learned that whatever PMS meant, it was bad news, but he didn't quite have all the details worked out. I struggled to keep a straight face and informed Gabriel that boys do not get PMS. Later I happened upon an entry in Gabe's journal, apparently written after he had had a battle with his big brother, Zachary. It read: "I jest had sum thing ownlee girls have. PMS WITH ZACHARY FREEMAN!"

Poor kid, now I had him worried about his sexual identity, so his father decided it was time for a man-to-man talk.

"Son," he told him, "don't worry about trying to understand women or PMS. I'm thirty-six years old and I'm more confused than ever. I've learned one thing after living with your mother and working in an office with fifty-two women. When you see a woman coming toward you who says she's having 'one of those days,' get ready to duck, run, or hand her a fistful of Kleenex."

Even the teenagers in our house are skittish at certain times of the month. During one particularly stress-filled, premenstrual week, I did not get the help I felt I needed to bring the groceries in from the car, so of course, as I hauled a gallon jug of milk from the car, I threw it against the wall of the entry hall like most mothers do. Boy, did I regret *that* little burst of temper. A few weeks later, I was again bringing in the groceries and I asked the boys to get up and help me unload the car. Zeke started to complain, but just in time, Zach—older and wiser—intervened.

"Hey, Zeke, better jump up and salute. Mom's standing near dairy products."

We laugh about PMS because laughing is at least one way to cope with it.

I had finally recognized a pattern in my life that *had* to be related to PMS. For two or three days of each month, my whole world seemed to turn black. I could think of no reason during those days to put one foot in front of the other. All of life seemed bleak. Only a few days before, my family seemed charming and lovable. Suddenly they turned into hideous imbeciles. I found myself fighting the urge to growl and bite! And what mental image did I conjure up of myself during this week? A fat, ugly one.

When Scott and I really thought about our up-and-down relationship over the years, we finally began to realize that we usually had a fairly big blowup about once a month. I don't know—call it genius—but after seventeen years we began to wonder if there might be a correlation between the angry fights and the flux of my hormones. Well, what do you know? There was. As a matter of fact, we could set our watches to the times when it would be best to run, duck, or hide the dairy products.

I now wonder how many of our revolving conflicts were due to a drop in estrogen rather than a drop in communication? It was so hard for me to believe that part of our problems might be related to premenstrual syndrome that I strongly denied it for years. How I hated the thought of being patronized simply for being a woman with a hormonal cycle!

Our conversations often reminded me of a scene from the sitcom *Cheers*, when the articulate and emotional Diane vehemently explodes at Sam.

"I hate you with the white hot heat of a thousand suns!"

Sam calmly responds to her furious statement with a sing-song version of "Somebody's crank-y."

That sort of response from Scott was about as effective as throwing Texas chili on a fire to try to extinguish the flames. But to his everlasting credit, he was the first to entertain the thought that hormones might be affecting my attitude. It had first dawned on Scott the night of our birthday shoot-out at the Trail Dust. At that point he learned to do what all successful husbands eventually learn to do. He consciously chose to not take my moods so personally, at least not before checking the calendar. In the bouts that followed before I got around to seeing a gynecologist, I insisted there were substantial reasons for my anger, but he kept his resolve. After a few more months of denial, I began to think about the possibility that PMS was a real problem and it had greatly affected our relationship.

Two days later I was sitting alone in my doctor's examining room, tissue in hand, crying over a picture in a magazine. It was a fuzzy portrait of a mother nursing her newborn infant. *Oh, that's so sweet. I remember how precious my babies were. Now I'm all out of babies. I'll never hold a newborn of my own again.* I flipped the page and saw a recipe for a chocolate Easter bunny cake. Fresh sobs began to flow as I remembered the bunny cake my mother had baked for my fifth birthday. *I loved that cake!* On the opposite side of the page was an ad for Charmin toilet paper. *Oh, how Nonnie used to love Charmin toilet paper. And*

Dove soap too. I miss her so much! It was all too much. And just then, my gynecologist rounded the corner and glanced at my tears and tissue.

"Let me guess," she said, stroking her chin. "Hormones acting up a bit these days?" Over the top of my tissue my red eyes blinked affirmatively. Once inside her office, we discussed all the options available for coping with PMS.

"Becky," she gently informed me, "after about age thirty—and especially after having had multiple children—premenstrual syndrome often becomes more pronounced. "

"Well," I deadpanned, "in my situation PMS is pronounced like a four-letter word."

She smiled. "There are some things you can do. A change in diet may help. You probably ought to cut out caffeine and chocolate."

"Life without *coffee* and *chocolate?*" I asked. I had not realized how serious my condition was!

I noticed the doctor ease away from me ever so slightly. She also moved a large hypodermic needle out of my reach before she continued. "Another medical alternative is to take a non-addictive mild antidepressant—only on the days when PMS is acting up. Also, a good multivitamin with lots of B6 and calcium would be advisable."

"I can go for that," I sighed.

Today my entire family would like to line up and applaud this doctor. Even though I only take the prescription about three days a month, it has made a tremendous difference. I don't really know how to describe the change, except to say that instead of screaming and throwing jugs of milk, I might only raise my voice slightly and twist the lid on the jug more tightly than usual. I now deal with a controllable irritation instead of a tidal wave.

I found another huge help in a book by Jean Lush called *Emotional Phases of a Woman's Life.* I especially appreciated her candor when she talked about her own experience with PMS. "I was horrified to think that someone would uncover my terrible dark secret. How could I ever manage to live a life of service to God when, for three or four days out of the month, I turned into a monster? Eventually I learned that I was not a freak of nature, as I had suspected. For years I thought I was somehow different, perhaps even crazy. I'd look around at other women, and they would seem to have themselves all together."[1]

What a relief to know someone else had battled the same feelings! Though Scott is not a great reader of self-help books—especially about women—he did read the first few chapters in *Emotional Phases of a Woman's Life*. It was enormously helpful for him—especially the part where Mrs. Lush describes a typical woman in a typical monthly cycle. He thought he was reading my autobiography.

Two other approaches have been especially helpful to us. Women who suffer from PMS should prepare for the Big Event by keeping the calendar as free from stress as possible. I call it cocooning. For those dreadful one or two days out of the month, I allow myself to lie back, wrap up in a blanket, and take long naps if I feel like it. My hot baths are longer, my walks more leisurely. Rather than tackle the deep books I usually enjoy, I may read mindless magazine fluff and watch a lighthearted comedy. I simply don't expect much out of myself, and my family has been kind enough to do the same.

In addition, Scott has taken a slightly more "parental approach," and at times it works fairly well. When I am displaying some "missed-nap" grumpiness, Scott has learned to simply take me gently in his arms. Sometimes he will even lead me by the hand to the bedroom and, even while I'm protesting, stretch me out on the bed, cover me with a comforter, kiss my furrowed brow, and walk calmly away, shutting the door firmly behind him.

Then he barricades it for three days.

A couple of months ago, my sister Rachel called from Virginia Beach. I could immediately tell she was fighting back tears.

"Becky," she began, "this is a hard phone call for me to make, but Mom said you'd understand. I think I'm losing it! In the parking lot today at the mall, a van was waiting for my parking place. I was trying to get Trevor buckled in his car seat and they started *honking* at me. Suddenly, I was absolutely *livid!* About five mafia-type guys unloaded from the van, but at that point, I didn't care if they *were* the mafia. I wagged my finger at them and roared, 'You boys need to learn some manners!'

"When I finally got home and calmed down, I realized that I could have put Trevor and myself in a dangerous situation just because of my temper. It scared me to death."

I had to laugh at the picture of my "very together" sister shaking her finger at some rough, gang member-types and telling them to mind their manners. "So what time of the month is it?" I inquired. Care to guess what her answer was?

I overnighted her a copy of Jean Lush's book and the phone number of a couple of information lines and warned her to avoid carrying any dairy products for the time being. (By the way, if you're having a real emergency, and that cup of yogurt is about to be airborne, PMS Access is 1-800-222-4PMS and PMS Relief is 916-888-7677.)

Last night we talked again. She'd been to the doctor and was also finding many of her worst symptoms alleviated. She had found a natural herbal remedy, along with high potency vitamin and mineral tablets of calcium, magnesium, and a multiple B. They seem to work well for her. It made me feel wonderful to know that I might have been able to pass on some help and encouragement to my sister. She's so often done the same for me in other areas. We talked about how many of our women friends also struggle with serious bouts of monthly tension.

So I'd like to dedicate this chapter to my sister and all you fellow sisters out there who are searching for and trying new ways to cope with PMS in your lives and in your marriages. My prayers are with you. (Scott says *his* prayers are with your *husbands.*)

As a matter of fact, why don't we all go to the fridge right now, grab a large jug of milk, take off the lid, and raise it in a toast. Here's to us, the Survivors of the Hormone Onslaught! Now take a swig right out of the jug (go ahead, the kids aren't looking). Let's all say "Ahhhh . . . " while we wipe the mustache from our upper lips with the back of our hands in triumph. Finally, I think we should pat ourselves on the back for having the amazing self-control not to throw the container against the wall. We women need to take small victories whenever we can find them.

"I have told you these things, so that in me you may have peace. In this world you will have trouble. But take heart! I have overcome the world."

JOHN 16:33

❧

It's a guy thing

In addition to responding to conflict differently, I've noticed one or two other basic differences between the male and the female of our species. For the better part of seven years, I carried at least one child in my womb. The experience gifted me with stretch marks down to my ankles. I clean up after their stomach viruses, await their beck and call for chauffeur services, listen sympathetically to their stories, and soothe their hurt feelings. You can often find me, bleary-eyed and martyr-like, typing their book reports after 11:00 P.M. Even so, they rarely seem to notice my sacrifices. I've been taking an informal inventory this week, and here is a sampling of the comments I've received from my children concerning my few *flaws*—flaws which they seem intent upon magnifying.

1. "MOM! This is a ditch, not a driveway! You are *nuts!*"

2. "You mean even after I left a note scotch-taped to your nightgown last night you *still* forgot to put those jeans in the dryer?! Now I have to wear the ones with a *hole* in the leg?!???"

3. "The battery's dead in the smoke alarm again, Mom. I guess after you burn *three* cobblers in a row, it takes its toll on the ol' Energizers."

(Yeah, but one of those cobblers bubbled up and burned into the shape of Jimmy Durante's nose, and we even saved it to show the neighbors. Not just every old mom burns food with flair.)

To be fair, I also received a few hugs and dutiful pecks on the cheek at bedtime, even a couple of "thank-yous" thrown in for good measure. But I'd truly love for someone to explain why the *father* of my children can simply walk into the house, put down his briefcase, grunt "Hi kids—howyadoing," and all four offspring nearly hyperventilate trying to be the first to get close to him. They are crazy about this man, and all he has to do is stroll into a room and breathe. It's been a phenomenon I've enjoyed observing as I mull over the things that keep me loving this man to whom I am married.

To my way of thinking, this whole masculine phenomenon is sort of a throwback from old Clint Eastwood movies. I'm sure we all remember how much effort Eastwood put into his intimate relationships (at least his pre-*Bridges of Madison County* days. As I recall, Clint spent—on average—one hundred and ten minutes of a two-hour movie chasing bad guys, stopping only briefly to sneer into the camera. He didn't give a thought to his girlfriend all day long, much less contemplate giving her a call to let her know he might be running a little late. Yet when he finished allowing his quota of criminals to "make his day," he simply sauntered into a scene, gave a pitiful excuse for a wink—which was more like a wince, really—and waited for his leggy Insignificant Other to fall helplessly into his arms. And amazingly, she did it! What's the deal?!?

Scott tells me it's "A Guy Thing"—the masculine *mystique* that attracts women and children to a man with magnetic, invisible charm. Although I admit there must be something to that theory, there are a few other "Guy Things" that don't exactly ooze with "mystiquey," magnetic charm.

Just out of curiosity, have you ever noticed how a man orders food at a fast-food drive-through window? First of all, I've come to believe that the mere sound of a masculine voice causes the ordering equipment to suffer a nervous breakdown, thereafter eliminating all possibilities for meaningful communication. Add to that the fact that men have an innate desire to be *cute* while placing their order through the drive-through micro-phone. It's as if they believe the invisible mike on the plastic menu screen is actually connected to a standup comedy stage somewhere in the recesses of the restaurant. But when their cute antics backfire, men are surprisingly offended. Here's an example of a conversation between my man and a typical fast-food machine.

"Hello, welcome to Royal Burger. Can I help you please?"

"I don't know. Can you?"

"May I take your order now, sir?"

"Well, of course you *may*. But should you do it today or tomorrow? That is the question."

(Long period of silence. Scott winks at me as if to say, "Watch me have a little fun with this character.")

"Did you say 'cut the mayo and hold the tomato,' sir?" the voice continues, and by the sound of it, I get the feeling he's handled wanna-be comedians before.

This is where the waiter turns to a fellow employee and winks as if to say, "Watch me have some fun with this jerk."

And Scott, still thinking he is in control, persists. "Cut the mayo on what? I haven't ordered yet!"

"Do you want fries with that?"

"Wait a minute! With that *what?*"

"Will that be a small, medium, large, or jumbo super saver, sir?"

"WAIT, WAIT, WAIT!" Scott now is babbling. "I'm not talking to a stupid machine anymore. Hey, look—I can see the *real you* from here if you'll take a peek out of your little window! Well, you can just read my lips: Hasta la vista, baby! I'm outta of here!" As we peel away with tires screeching, we can hear the invisible waiter droning patiently through the speaker.

"Yes, sir. Do you want some fries with that, sir?"

I've got to hand it to them. They don't call them fast-food employees for nothing. Those kids are pretty quick on the draw.

There's yet another "Guy Thing" that puzzles me. Why is it that grown men, who would shudder at the thought of going off to war, will risk their lives to avoid admitting they need help on a home improvement project? Currently, my husband is building a huge, two-story shell over our small cabin—by himself. It is turning out to be very much like a Hollywood stage front, actually. To people driving by, it looks as though we live in a large home like the one owned by June and Ward Cleaver. Inside, however, the original small cabin still stands, with our family running about like six hamsters in a five-gallon aquarium.

A couple of weeks ago, Scott decided to caulk the upper corner of the gable end on our new roof. Now, I might mention that the peak on this outer roof is twenty-eight feet above ground. Unfortunately, Scott's scaffolding was just shy of allowing him to reach the peak, so he decided to take his caulk gun in hand and jump for it. Obviously, this was a *Man-Made Decision.*

The Man managed to leap high enough to grasp the top corner of the roof with his left hand, the caulk gun ready to fire in his right. Glancing down, he quickly discovered he was no longer hanging *above* the scaffolding, but had swung out away from the house and several feet away from the scaffold. In other words, Scott was dangling twenty-eight feet above the ground, holding on for dear life by one hand. Of course, we can all be thankful he had a caulk gun in his other hand for that special, added sense of security.

No one was home that afternoon except Scott and Gabe, our youngest and smallest son, so calling for help was not an option. I later learned that my husband made a flying leap back to safety, achieving a one-point landing on a small two-by-four board which, happily, lay across a section of rickety scaffolding. Thank God for those years Scott had spent in gymnastics in his younger days! It goes without saying that I often pray for angels to watch diligently over my husband—especially when he's doing one of his "Guy Things."

For He will give His angels charge concerning you,
to guard you in all your ways.

PSALM 91:II, NASB

∾

Letting the tides
of forgiveness wash away
old pain

The other day I talked with my editor, and she told me of a frightening new trend in marriage counseling. The new theory is that marriage is so often doomed to failure that it is better to simply look at a first wedding as a stepping-stone, a practice ground for the next marriage. In other words, you make all the mistakes on the first relationship and then walk away—leaving a junk heap of ruined love—and start fresh with someone else. (What if we held this theory with our firstborn children???)

I thought about this new approach and then I answered, "Vicki, you know, the sad part in all of this is that the same starting-over approach can take place within the original marriage instead. At several strategic points, Scott and I basically reintroduced ourselves, shook hands, and began again."

The only hitch in starting over within the original relationship is this: What do we do with this junk heap of mistakes we've made? We have to find a way to deal with all of the grudges that accumulate over the years. How tempting it sounds at times to walk away from it all and fall into the arms of someone new who doesn't know I look like a small underground animal in the mornings. But eventually, I know I'd discover the "new and improved husband" would have a few obnoxious surprises for me too. Maybe he'd pick his toenails and belch while he watched television. I don't know what form it would take, but I know enough about human nature to know it would be *something*.

Unless people plan to spend their lives starting over with new relationships when the old one wears out, the junk will eventually have to be faced and periodically swept out. And actually, that is a great definition of forgiveness—sweeping the old junk off the porch and starting anew.

Easier said than done, I know. There were some things that Scott had done and said that cut so deep, that seemed so unfair and hurtful, that I thought at the time I would never get over them. (And I'm sure the reverse is true for him.) But even if we are wronged unjustly, God asks us to forgive just as He has forgiven us. Ouch. And if God were to weigh the scales with me, I'd come up pitifully short. That's why I need more than everyday grace. I need the *amazing* brand. And it's that same amazing grace and forgiveness our loved ones need from us. I'll be the first to admit we are talking about a supernatural phenomenon here. There's no way we can forgive others without His Spirit working in us.

It also helped me to understand that holding a grudge hurts no one but myself. All the psychology books say that grudges physically inhibit the production of seratonin, a chemical essential for a sense of well-being. Listen, I need all of *that* stuff God designed to come my way. I don't want to stand in the way of a natural, sense-of-well-being chemical invading my body, especially while I'm working on the delicate task of improving relationships.

The process of letting go of anger and applying forgiveness is rarely accomplished overnight, although that does happen on occasion. Forgiveness, for me, was a gradual process. It was much like cleaning away a grimy old film from a pane of glass. As the glass became clear, I could see more and more of the goodness in our relationship. I wrote the following poem in a journal describing some of the feelings I had during the letting-go process.

> Oh, now I remember Our Love
> Sometimes it comes in gentle waves
> Tugging at the lonely beach
> Which was
> For a time
> My heart
> Now and again, monumental whitecaps
> Spill onto shore
> Flowing back to sea
> With the debris
> Of antique hurt
> Yes, I remember Our Love.

BECKY FREEMAN © 1991

I seem to continue dipping back into the sea for metaphors that paint living portraits of love's inner workings. At least I'm in good company. For ages, poets and writers have been drawn to the ocean as they struggle to describe the majestic, strong, unpredictable, cleansing, soothing, healing qualities of love. I especially like this oceanfront view of forgiveness.

I have to admit it was scary to let go of some of my old broken shells of hurt and let them ride out with the waves. They had taken time to collect, to arrange in order from tiny sand-dollar hurts to major conch-shell pains. Perhaps I was struggling to save the old shells in case I needed them for some future "Show and Tell." However, I am reminded of Marlene Dietrich's words: "Once a woman has forgiven her man, she must not reheat his sins for breakfast." Letting go means *letting go.*

And letting go, without grasping for old grievances again, is what we eventually did. As Scott and I rode out with the new tide of love and forgiveness, I must confess that the adventure of sailing in the wide open sea made that isolated beach full of shattered shells seem dull indeed. But I can't say it was easy, especially at first.

As I realized how difficult it was for us to do the necessary "letting go"—the slate-cleaning, broom-sweeping, tide-washing sort of forgiveness it takes to hold a marriage together—I noticed something else taking place on the side. I began to view through more understanding eyes of compassion my close friends whose marriages had floundered.

"For I will forgive . . . and will remember their sins no more." This is what the LORD says . . . who stirs up the sea so that its waves roar.

JEREMIAH 31:34–35

❧

Divorce busters
anonymous

Some of my best friends are divorced. Actually, all of my best friends are divorced. Well, that's an exaggeration. But I *have* had the painful experience of watching three of my best friends' marriages crumble. I'm talking best, best, best friends—deeply committed Christian friends. I know it's selfish of me to whine when it is my *friends* who have really done the suffering, but whine I must. Friends of the "splitting-up victims" are oft-ignored casualties. At least it's been true with me, because in most cases I felt as if my own heart was pulled in two. And it hurt.

If there had been a recovery group for Friends of Couple Friends Who Suddenly Aren't Couples Anymore, I'd have been first in line on at least three occasions. And now that the specter of divorce had brushed so frighteningly close to us, I thought of our divorced friends more often, and with a lot more empathy.

The other day at lunch I asked a group of married gals, "How did you feel the first time you found out a close friend was getting a divorce?" I expected to hear them say, "Devastated."

Or, "Afraid for them. But afraid for us, too. Because if it could happen to *them,* who's to say it couldn't happen to us?" Or perhaps, "I wanted to console them, but I didn't know which one to comfort without appearing to be taking sides."

The answers I got instead were surprising:

"I never really knew anyone very well who was going through a divorce."

"Oh, I felt bad. But I never thought for a second it could happen to us."

"We grew distant from our divorcing friends. We didn't stay in touch because—you know, they were *single* again. I didn't think they really wanted to hang out with married couples anymore."

I shook my head in disbelief. It was pretty awkward admitting to this group of happily married women that most of my closest friends eventually ended up in a court of law with divorce attorneys arguing over their assets. After that tiny confession, I doubted I'd be getting deluged with "best friend" applications. I know things do have a tendency to crash and break around me sometimes, but I promise—I cross my heart—I didn't have anything to do with all the marriage fallouts. If anything, I waged valiant one-woman campaigns for "sticking it out"—even when I was struggling in my own relationship.

The divorce of Couple Number One was by far the greatest shock. They were our best friends—the couple we'd sit around with, stay up late and talk with, and eat pizza out of a box on the coffee table with. They'd often have us over, along with other friends, to sing and strum guitars and eat chocolate chip cookie bars. And nearly always we'd tease about the ups and downs of being newly married. But we all knew we'd make it, for heaven's sake. We were Christians. And we all knew, for Christians especially, marriage is *forever,* and even if it wasn't the *greatest* at the *moment,* it would always get better around the next bend.

A couple of years went by, and we watched with joy as our friends became parents of a baby boy, and they loved that little guy so much.

Then, late one Sunday afternoon, we were visiting in their brand new home after supper. We all sipped coffee, laughed at their cute little guy playing in the corner, and oohed and ahhed over our newest baby boy sleeping in my arms. I looked up and smiled at our friends. She was leaning on his knee and his arm was around her shoulder.

"I think we're finally growing up," he announced, "We're going to make it." The evening sun cast a rosy glow through the window and onto the carpet, and all was well.

Two weeks later they were separated. He did not know there had been a lot of pain hiding behind her smile that Sunday afternoon. He tried to hide what had happened as long as he could from his "Christian" friends because Christians don't get divorced. When we found out, we phoned him right away.

"Come on over. Come now. You are our friend, our very best friend, and we love you. We'll order the pizza."

So he came, and none of us turned out to be very hungry after all. But our very best friend lay back on our couch and he talked and he cried and he hurt. And we talked with him and we cried with him and we hurt so bad that I thought all our hearts would break. He thanked us for still being his friend. We knew that no matter what happened next, we would always love this man. And though we were angry and confused, we knew we would always love her, too, for somewhere out there she was also hurting. Yes, the First Divorce was probably the hardest of all.

Amazingly, God has His own way of weaving broken threads into tapestries with the passage of time—tapestries made stronger and, in some ways, even more beautiful by the addition of those delicate, fragile, pain-filled strands. So it has been with our friends. A couple of years later our friend married a wonderful woman, and we loved her and unanimously adopted her right away. And now we get together and drink coffee, and talk 'til dawn, and eat pizza off boxes on dining room tables. And we are Best Couple Friends.

Couple Number Two's marriage died a slower, more predictable death. The wife had been friends with Scott since grade school—the proverbial girl next door. My husband has always had good taste in women, and I liked her immediately. Her husband was charming, with a deep voice and a wonderful sense of humor—but he almost never hugged his wife or told her he loved her. She was lonely almost as soon as they said, "I do." When she and I found ourselves pregnant at the same time, we became fast friends. The first time we got together for lunch, we ended up praying that God would heal what was wrong in her troubled marriage.

Housekeeping was never her forte. I love that in a person. And she smiled and laughed out loud a lot. Another ten points. I could tease her about always having only three things in the refrigerator to eat—bologna, Velveeta cheese, and red Kool-Aid—and she'd laugh it off as she asked if I wanted mayo or mustard on my bologna and cheese. I have to admit she could whip up a pretty mean sandwich and somehow it always tasted delicious at her house. Probably because she served it with lots of juicy talk and laughter—along with the bottomless glasses of Kool-Aid.

And then, her husband walked out. She was in agony, but she is a strong woman and her faith grew even stronger. After a few months she prayed him back home, and they had two happy years and one more child together. But then, he walked into the living room and told her she had gained too much weight from the last pregnancy and he couldn't find a clean sock. That was all he could take, and he walked out the door again—this time for good.

But this time she could not bring herself to pray for him to come back home, only to be hurt again. God gave her peace in letting him go. He married an old girlfriend soon after their divorce. And my girlfriend, well, she did what she always did best. She bloomed where she was planted. She made lemonade out of lemons. She smiled and laughed through her tears.

And even though a survey said it would be more likely to be killed by a terrorist than to marry after the age of thirty, she found a man. Not just any man. One who had never been married. One who was handsome and loved children and was involved in a good church and who had been waiting and praying for a woman who could laugh out loud and make great bologna and cheese sandwiches. God wove another tapestry out of yet another tangled mess.

In Couple Two, divorce had come through the door un-wanted—and yet by the time it finally arrived, there was almost a sense of relief that the long, pain-filled cycle was over. I didn't hurt as badly or for as long as I did for the first couple, where I loved both parties equally and it all came as such a surprise.

But the Third Divorce has been a real doozey—for everyone, but especially for me. For one thing, I was a Marriage Counsel-ing Graduate, and things were better for us, so I felt qualified to save my friends' marriages. For some time now Couple Number Three has appeared to be nicely on their way to Divorce Recovery. I, unfortunately, am still finding myself wiping away an occasional tear.

If you've read my past books, you might understand why this couple's breakup has been particularly tough for me. Number Three is so hard because it involved our good friends Gary and Mary. THE Mary of *Worms in My Tea*, the best friend/beauty operator that dyed my forehead purple and whose bright blue quote is blazoned on the back of our book announcing, "Becky, you have to find time to write a book, even if you do have the dirtiest floor in America."

And this divorce involved THE Gary of the Riding Lawn-mower—the one who backed over the precious memorial sap-ling and went on to devour the screen door. Yes, and they are also one and the same Gary and Mary of the Window Story from this very book.

I'm so sorry to have to break the news like this, but Mary says I just can't go on writing about her and Gary as if they are married since they've been separated and/or divorced for nearly two years now—unless I'm going to start writing romantic *fiction,* that is.

I can almost joke about it now, but if ever there was a serious crusader out to save somebody else's marriage it was *moi,* with Gary and Mary as my projects. I just could not accept the fact that they couldn't work things out. Theirs appeared to be one of those easy-to-fix cases—no heinous sins, no knock-down-drag-outs. (Of course, marriage counselors say they'd rather work with angry, passionate couples than those who have no flame left to fan. Let's put it this way, Smokey the Bear would have been proud of Gary and Mary!)

I prayed and I empathized and consoled Mary for awhile, thinking this decision was a case of temporary insanity. When it came to actually signing the papers, I thought surely the shock of finality would bring them to their respective senses. Instead, their resolve to end the marriage grew more firm every day.

OK, I thought, *So you guys want to play hardball. Well, let's try some reason and common sense on for size.* I bought the book *Divorce Busting* and studied how to become a certified Divorce Buster Representative. I photocopied pages and memorized lines and even hand-delivered underlined copies of Top Ten Reasons Not to Go and Do a Stupid Thing Like Getting a Divorce for Pete's Sake for both parties to read at their leisure. Still no change.

As the court date drew near, I was getting more desperate. I thought about calling the governor to see if she could grant a stay in the execution of a good friend's marriage. Instead, I stopped by the church one summer afternoon, walked into the pastor's office, and made an announcement.

"Listen. This is getting serious. Gary and Mary think they are getting a divorce, and I'm sorry, but we just can't allow this to happen. I need heavy-duty prayer to stop it. So could you pray with me, please?" My pastor is a kind man. He graciously bowed his head and prayed with me. Though he probably knew I was up against something out of my control, I think he also knew that I was not yet ready to concede the possibility of defeat. Then I found two more ladies whom I felt were closer to God than I was, and I asked them to join me in a powerful where-two-or-more-are-gathered-together-in-My-name prayer.

The divorce date approached with unrelenting speed. There was no sign of letup. There was no alternative but to get tough. I finally lost it, yelling at Mary in frustration one night. Then I wrote her a long letter spelling out the scriptural error of her ways. I let her know I was putting into practice what I felt at the time was a painful, but necessary, last resort: I would be pulling away from our friendship altogether—hoping against hope that without my "enabling" support, she'd be struck by The Light, see the error of her ways, and ta-duumm, she and Gary would fall hopelessly in love with each other again and live happily ever after. God could make it happen. He hates divorce. He could do the impossible for my friends just as He had done the impossible for us. After all, didn't He see me wearing myself out to be His special little helper on this case?

For months, Mary and I stopped talking. On the day of her divorce, I did drive to her house, left her a Coke (we often brought each other Cokes for a treat) and a note telling her that I cared and I was sorry she was going through this day of pain and that I would always be her friend. But we were not on the same wavelength anymore. And we remained distant for many more months.

During that time, God began unraveling some important truths for me. First of all, I have no control over other people's lives. Some things are simply out of my hands. One day I was reading the biblical story of the paralytic. You know, the one where the friends cut a hole in the roof to give their buddy a chance to get close to Jesus, so that he might be healed. Suddenly, a phrase struck me right between the eyes. Luke wrote that the man's friends dropped him "right in front of Jesus" (Luke 5:19).

And I knew God was telling me, "Becky, that's what you must learn to do. Other people's problems are not yours to fix. You are a little Mothering Fixer-Upper by nature. But sometimes the only thing you can do for Mary, or anyone else for that matter, is give them to Me. Drop them right in front of Me. I'm the One who does the healing and I'll do it in My way, in My time. Remember?" So in my mind, I plunked Mary and Gary down the hole in the roof, right in front of Jesus. And amazingly, He's doing just fine with them, and all without my assistance.

Second, I realized that all that time I spent obsessing over Gary and Mary's breakup had drained my own family of energy. I was also neglecting other friends, so I redirected my focus toward reviving other friendships. I have to admit, angry as I was, I still missed Mary. She's always been amazingly accepting of me and my faults. I could tell her anything and know she'd never think less of me. She's forgiving. She's got a wonderful wit. She's a great conversationalist. She's the type of friend that's hard to replace. I missed a lot of things about being buddies.

Today, thanks to the Master Weaver, our friendship is on the mend, and I think it is even stronger for having gone through the fire. We are both still learning a lot, as individuals and as friends. For me, it's been about accepting the things I am powerless to change, about accepting people as they are, and then learning to extend a hand in grace rather than in judgment. It was painful for me to accept helplessness—the fact that there was nothing I could do to prevent one of my closest friends from taking a path that might lead her into even deeper pain. But Outcomes are God's department. And who am I to throw the first stone? We all fall short, all of us make messes of areas of our lives. We are all in need of grace.

Though Scott and I never made it to a divorce court, we both toyed with the idea. I've read countless articles on "How to Have a Marriage that Lasts Forever." Tucked into each one is usually a personal testimony about the mutual, steadfast avoiding of the word *divorce*. Testimonies like—

"Sure, we had our problems through the years, but we never, never, never uttered the word *divorce*. Murder, yes. Divorce, never. And that's why we've been able to stay happily married since dinosaurs roamed the earth."

I wish I could honestly say this was also true for us. I wish that the word *divorce* had never played dangerously about our heads or made its debut out of our mouths. I'm in wholehearted agreement with the theory that divorce is an escape hatch best left "off-limits." Unfortunately, we did tangle with the idea and got into some pretty major snarls as a result.

It was as if subconsciously we thought, *Well, if other couples that we know really well can get a divorce and survive, who's to say we wouldn't be better off?* Gradually, almost imperceptibly at first, that sort of thinking began to take seed. Then at times of great frustration, the seed burst forth and the possibility of divorce leaked into our thoughts and eventually burst out in the heat of anger. Once fired, the damage done was serious.

But in light of all of our frailties, I'd like to dedicate this chapter on the subject of divorce to anyone who has failed their marriage in any way. Whether you once failed in a marriage that is still alive and well today, or whether you failed in a marriage that did not survive the battle. Whether you were an initiator of the breakup, or whether you were the one who tried to hang on but just couldn't find a way to hold it together. Whether you have uttered the word *divorce* aloud, or just fantasized about it once or twice in the privacy of your own thoughts. Everyone I have ever talked with has messed up *big time* at some time in a relationship. So welcome to the human race.

There's one last thing I'd like to share before closing, with permission from an old friend. Remember the first wife of Couple Number One—the one that disappeared from our lives that beautiful Sunday afternoon? It had been fourteen years since we'd communicated. This year I found myself wishing I could reconnect personally with her—to put a sense of closure on old scars. So I wrote her a letter and I asked her to forgive me for not reaching out earlier. I told her that I still thought of her and cared about her. She wrote me back a book—twenty-six heartfelt pages. In part, here is what she had to say:

Dear Becky,

First let me say, to you and your precious family, including your mom and dad, how very sorry I am for any pain that I caused and for walking out with no explanation.

Oh, guys, how I wish I could give you an explanation for our divorce—we both were lacking in communication skills and (as I learned in counseling right before I filed for divorce) missed each other's intentions and hearts for a long period of time. The vast chasm between us just seemed impossible to fill, especially since I did not believe that my God practically cared and could work in the situation. We were both *very* defensive and hurt, (could not hear each other) and I felt *so* alone. For some reason I could not accept myself because I could not handle the situation. I didn't trust others, and I hated myself—believing that I was defective and no one could help someone like me.

Let me just say, divorce is not God's way, and I could never choose it again. I say that not on my own strength, but on the power of the Spirit who lives inside of me.

Your conclusion that God can "take even the mistakes in our lives and weave them into a tapestry of beauty" is so true. I have married again—a wonderful man who is a friend, a companion, and the godly head of our home. Our son is growing tall and strong in the Lord, and we've been blessed with another daughter. He has led me through darkness and into His life and light, and I love Him for it.

And by the way, I now go by my middle name. I found out it means "One of Grace."

Her letter not only healed old scars; it was an incredible lift to my spirit. After all these years, God's grace has indeed made something beautiful out of all our weak and broken threads.

All in His way. All in His time.

> When finally tangled webs we leave
> Oh, what practiced Hands can weave!
>
> BECKY FREEMAN © 1995

"For I'm going to do a brand new thing.
See, I have already begun!"

ISAIAH 43:19, TLB

∾

Enjoy the local breakfasts and bed

R emember how I introduced this book? The part where I talked about wanting to share fragments of truth—ideas and actions—that have helped us improve our marriage? Well, it is now time to share one of the most significant fragments—a secret to unbridled bliss, if you will, that has revolutionized our relationship. A couple may increase their chances of experiencing this bliss—without any bridles whatsoever—by at least 78 percent if they will simply incorporate two suggestions (according to a recent galloping poll*). Actually, if these ideas really begin to catch on, we may eliminate divorce worldwide.

The big secret? Go out to breakfast together once or twice a week in a smoke-filled, bacon-sizzlin', small-town cafe. (Preferably, it should be located on a farm-to-market road next to a feed and ranch supply store.) And on at least one of those

---

* The 78 percent statistic was taken from a broad-based random survey based on my broad-based random imagination.

mornings it is important to go back home, while the kids are at school or at Mother's Day Out, and go back to bed together. And I don't mean to catch up on some "zzzz's." That's all there is to it. Busy couples just need to get away to a little more Breakfast and Bed.

Winston Churchill is said to have stated, "My wife and I tried two or three times in the last forty years to have breakfast together, but it was so disagreeable we had to stop."[1] Poor Winston. He should have come to me for advice first. He probably just did it all wrong. One has to follow important guidelines when breakfasting with a mate who is not, by nature, a morning person.

First, let's discuss the prerequisite of dining at old, cafe-type establishments. I know some of you big-city folk are already protesting. But I'm sorry; sharing a French croissant and sipping orange cappuccinos at La Madeliene's just won't cut the mustard if you are really serious about bliss. Drive an hour through traffic if you must, but get thee and thy betrothed unto the boonies. And don't stop until thou smellest pork on the grill and strong coffee at brew. If thou art greeted by a friendly, plain-faced waitress asking, "Whutkinah git you folks this mornin'?" thou hast surely uncovered a royal treasure.

Why *breakfast*, one may ask? What about meeting for a leisurely lunch or an elegant dinner? Those meals have particular lures of their own, I must agree, but I'm inclined to believe that mornings have special pressures of their own. And cooking a meal at that hour is way beyond the reaches of my imagination, however active it may appear.

Once I did offer to cook breakfast for my husband, but he would hear none of it. I had said, "Honey, I'm going to whip you up a little breakfast surprise with everything I have left in the refrigerator—Jimmy Dean sausage, fresh cranberries, and Actifed syrup." It took Scott no time at all to let me know that he wouldn't have his little woman slaving over a hot stove in the morning for all the cough syrup in China. Isn't he a prize?

But why insist on savoring this morning meal at a laid-back, old-fashioned *coffee shop?* Because in my opinion women do not need the added stress of having to doll themselves up before noon to go out to a fancy restaurant. Think about it, ladies. If you slip on a pair of faded jeans, a sweat shirt with a smiley face on it from 1974, tennis shoes with matching shoestrings, and slap on a bare smidgen of lipstick before walking through the door of a country cafe, I can almost guarantee you are going to be the most gorgeous woman in the joint. This is your chance to shine with the most minimal of effort.

Second, breakfast out in a simple cafe is an affordable habit. Even young couples on strict budgets can afford most items from the "Breakfast Specials." My personal favorite is home-made biscuits with gravy on the side for a mere buck fifty, or sometimes I'll go for a scrumptious breakfast burrito with hot sauce for a paltry ninety-five cents. Talk about a bargain. I always order a Coke *and* a cup of coffee because I like the taste of the Coke and the *smell* of the coffee. When meals are this cheap, you can afford to indulge in a few luxuries.

Another benefit you simply will not find in a la-de-da restaurant is what we country folk term *local color.* I mean, why pay for entertainment when it is sitting right there on a county road next to the feed and ranch supply store? As my dad says, "This is the kind of place where you can see some real characters."

My preference, as far as characters are concerned, is round tables full of lined-faced old-timers wearing overalls and baseball caps. Sometimes they wear wire-framed glasses, and they often have a chaw of tobacco tucked away in their front pocket. Like apparitions from days gone by, they have little on their morning agendas but sipping bottomless cups of coffee and shooting endless breezes.

In contrast, as soon as we are finished eating, Scott and I usually check our watches and discuss our busy schedules for the day. But many times, a quick glance over at the "What's Your

Hurry?" round table will make us think twice about getting up. By their mere presence, the old-timers make our bodies want to shift into slow gear. So quite often, we'll take a deep sigh instead, maybe even put our feet up on a nearby chair. It's a clincher that we are going to "set a spell" when Scott lifts his cup to the sweet-talking waitress and answers her standard inquiry with, "Sure. Fill 'er up one more time."

In my opinion, old-timers at coffee shops should be honored as the last genuine examples of American relaxation in a group setting. Once their generation is gone, we may never see it again. In this country-style, laid-back, coffee-serving atmosphere they help create, Cafe-Style Therapy begins to take place. Many a sore subject in our marriage has been successfully worked out over a checkered tablecloth in a wooden booth. And it's nearly impossible to get angry over controversial subjects when George Strait, Doug Stone, and Vince Gill are twanging out their ballads from a radio in the kitchen.

In this warm atmosphere, Scott and I are forced to talk in soft, pleasant tones to each other. As a result, we are almost always reluctant to end the conversation. A few times we've talked our way right through the breakfast bunch, past the mid-morning stragglers, and on into the time when the waitress writes the lunch specials on the chalkboard—all without realizing how much time has actually passed.

As I have stated plainly, I still do not like getting up early. But the idea of going out to eat will tantalize me out from under the covers most of the time. And the experience of having enjoyed a laid-back meal—of having had unhurried time with my husband—is usually enough to tantalize me back under the covers when we get home. This morning, as a matter of fact, Scott asked me if I wanted to come with him to get a bite of breakfast.

"Sure," I whispered sleepily. Then I added teasingly as I yawned and stretched, "And maybe then we can come back here for dessert."

Before taking off for the cafe, we still had to get the kids ready for school. As I was making up the bed in our bedroom, Gabriel poked his head around the corner. "Hey, Mom," he said, "how come Daddy's in such a good mood this morning?"

"What do you mean, Honey?"

"Well, he's whistling and singing and telling silly jokes out here in the kitchen."

"Hmmm," I answered, "I think he's just excited about getting to go out to breakfast with li'l ol' me, Sugar Pie."

Scott rounded the corner just in time to hear my explanation and then gave me an exaggerated wink along with a grin that melted me like—like butter on a stack of fresh hotcakes.

So there you have it—the quick and easy secret to continued marital bliss: Linger for breakfast at an old-time cafe and give your partner a round-trip ticket back home for dessert. If only these mom-and-pop restaurants would stay open on stress-producing holidays, Scott and I might remain in a state of married bliss from here to eternity.

If an outing to the local Breakfast and Bed is not your cup of java, I hope you will find a way to spend some time alone together on a regular basis doing something you both are crazy about doing. Particularly in the years of raising a family, it's the best system I know for "romancing the home."

Go, eat your food with gladness, and drink . . . with a joyful heart. . . . Enjoy life with your wife, whom you love.
ECCLESIASTES 9:7, 9
☙

"Good mornin', Mary Sunshine! Please go back to bed"

I realize by this point that I've spent a good deal of time sharing the unusual penchant Scott and I have for long, meaningful, uplifting conversations. You are entitled to ask, "But exactly what sort of things are said in those intriguing little chats?" So I thought it might be well to invite you to eavesdrop on an actual conversation with my husband that started last night and continued upon rising this morning—sort of a real-life example of how effective communication takes place in a home.

Please keep in mind that Scott is a natural born philosopher. I've even begun to think of our small lake as my husband's own Walden Pond. Most of the time it is here that he works and walks and weaves his intriguing form of logic for the entertainment of family and passersby.

Last night I was in the kitchen when I overheard Scott discuss a news item with Zach and Zeke, who as teenagers are recognizing that the world they inhabit can be hard to figure out at times. A tragedy had occurred in a nearby town—apparently a pastor had killed his wife and then had taken his own life by jumping from a bridge.

"Dad," Zeke asked, "what made him *do* that?"

I braced for Scott's answer, hoping against hope he might say something like, "Well, Son, we just don't know. But there are a few people in this world who just snap under pressure."

But no, he looked my impressionable son straight in the eye and said, "Boys, it's time you realized that everybody's crazy."

Now, I'm delighted that Zach and Zeke adore their father, but I don't want them to get the wild idea that every person they see, including themselves, are candidates for the funny farm. So I jumped into the conversation and begged to differ.

"Scott, not *everybody* is crazy. That's ridiculous."

"*You* are crazy."

"I know, but that's not the point. The *whole human race* isn't crazy."

"Yes it is."

"Where do you get that idea?"

"Romans 3:23 says that 'All have sinned and fall short of the glory of God.'"

"Your point?"

"That means everybody's crazy. Some people *do* accept God's grace. But, even so, we're still all crazy as Betsy Bugs." I decided to drop the conversation before I turned the wooden spoon I was holding into a lethal weapon or got the urge to go jump off a bridge myself.

That night, Scott turned in early, but I stayed up late reading and writing. Young mothers are always faced with the dilemma: How can I possibly go to bed and waste all this peaceful solitude *sleeping?!* So by the time I crawled into bed, I glanced at the clock and saw it beamed 2:00 A.M. through the darkness. *I might be dead on my feet all day tomorrow,* I thought to myself, *but it was worth it!*

Seconds later it seemed, some large, male lunatic woke me up by throwing the covers off my snuggled-up body. "Get up,

Miss Peeky" he shouted cheerfully (Scott likes to call me that). "Get up!" He hovered over my face, bouncing on the bed like a friendly puppy while my heart struggled to get up to a semblance of a regular beat. "Your daughter needs you to make her an egg!"

It is a burden to be married to a Morning Person.

"She knows how to make an egg!" I hollered back. "And my name is not Miss Peeky! And don't wake me up like that again, either. It's rude and unthoughtful and that light's giving me a headache!"

Undaunted, Scott smiled happily and began to chant, "Peek-y is crank-y, Peek-y is crank-y."

For the sake of my children, I managed to pull myself out of the bed and into an upright position. Opening my eyes was not an option at the moment, but I felt my way toward the kitchen where a distinct sulfurous odor filled the air. Following the smell and heat, I found Rachel pouring what looked like little yellow erasers into a bowl. I managed to bring one corner of my mouth up and into a semi-smile and lean against the oven. With this support, I found the strength to offer my assistance.

"Do you need help, Honey? Those scrambled eggs look a little tough."

"No," Rachel answered brightly, "I'm doing fine. And by the way, that's a fried egg."

I've trained my children well. Where food is concerned, they have very low expectations and will eat just about anything edible served at any degree of doneness.

I turned my attention to Zeke. "Zeekle, Honey, do you want me to help you with your eggs?"

He gave me the once-over and in his new boy/man voice ordered, "Mom, go sit down on the couch. I cook my own eggs all the time."

At that moment Scott came whistling out of the shower, wrapped in a towel. He walked over to the couch where I was still trying to pry open one eyelid with my fingers and planted a kiss on my cheek.

"See how nice it is when you get up and help the children?" he said merrily. "Why don't *you* drive them to the bus stop today?"

Oh, please, not that. No, no, no. That would mean I would have to put on a pair of pants and get both legs in the right holes too! But Scott was determined that I needed to do this. When all the kids were loaded into the station wagon and had nearly strangled each other over frontseat privileges, I collapsed into the driver's seat and started the engine. Mr. Morning Man was now watering the flowers in the front yard and playfully squirting my car window with the hose. He waved at me with a silly grin plastered on his face until I was completely out of the driveway. I thought grimly to myself, *He looks like Laurel from one of those old Laurel and Hardy movies.*

The second I reached the stop sign, all the kids piled out and headed across the street to wait for the bus. Though I was still fighting fatigue, I remembered to wave at them and even blew kisses in their direction from across the road where I was parked. Suddenly Rachel stopped, turned, and jogged back across the street to tell me something. *Isn't that sweet?* I thought. *She probably wants to tell me she loves me and enjoyed my getting up with her this morning.* Instead, my daughter began pleading with me through the side window.

"Please *go away*, Mother. The bus is almost here and the kids might see you." I glanced in the mirror at my uncombed hair and unmade face and immediately saw her point.

When I pulled into the driveway back home, Scott was no longer in sight. I walked to the front door and leaned against it hoping against hope someone with the strength to open it would happen along. In a few seconds, Scott opened the door and I fell into his arms. He responded to me in precisely the way I would have hoped, probably because I was comatose and noncombative. He patted my back and spoke soothingly.

"Poooooor Peeeeky," he crooned. "You have such a hard time with morning. I'll tell you what. I'll do most of the mornings from now on. It'll be my special time with the kids. My contribution to the family."

Did I say my husband looked like Laurel? No, no, I meant he looked like an incredibly handsome Hercules with the Nobel-prize winning compassion of Mother Teresa. As he led me to a chair and brought me a cup of coffee, I wept in gratitude all over his shirt sleeve.

He wanted to renew our theological discussion from the night before. He seems to especially enjoy morning conversations with me. I think it's because he knows he has an unfair advantage. He talked of all of the people in the Bible who God had used even though they had "messed up real bad." This was to substantiate last evening's point that everybody's crazy. I might have been down for the count, but I was not totally out. With what strength I could muster, I raised my head from the kitchen counter.

"Not Joseph," I manage to squeak. "Joseph always did the right thing. And Daniel too."

Scott laughed and pinched my cheeks. "You're so cute." Then he imitated my squeaky voice—"Not Joseph. And *not* my Daddy!"

I ignored his teasing and, gathering more strength, sat up on the bar stool to my full height. "That's right. And not my kids. *They* won't mess up and be crazy."

He grinned and poured himself another cup of coffee. "Becky, we work well together. You think our children are going to be perfect, and I think they're going to mess up. Either way, they've got a parent who believes in them."

This is a weird way to raise kids, I mused, and slumped back to my head-on-the-counter position. Scott interrupted my thoughts by slamming his hand on the counter, bringing me upright once again.

"Oh, shoot!" he moaned. "We missed Earl Pitt's radio spot! He's starting a 'Save the Ugly Vegetable Society.' He's all up in arms about hard-hearted vegetarians cutting the eyes out of innocent potatoes and brutally chopping off the heads of cabbages."

This is the sort of deep, meaningful conversation we are capable of having before 8:00 A.M.—one topic always flowing smoothly into the next. I was reminded of George Eliot's immortal words: "O, the comfort, the inexpressible comfort of feeling safe with a person, having neither to weigh thoughts nor measure words, but pouring them all right out just as they are, chaff and grain together."[1]

This conversation was classic chaff, but it was cozy in a way, this mindless chitchat. So many women complain, "My husband never talks to me!" So I consider myself lucky. But even so, it was apparent that someone needed to throw a little "grain" into the mixture of this chitchat and see if it couldn't be raised to a little higher level. So I took the bull by the horns and changed the subject to one of deeper significance. I told Scott about the Oprah Winfrey show I had seen the day before.

It was a "Sleepless in Seattle" episode where they matched a widower with a date. I told him how much the widowers missed their first wives and how much they had loved each other and how you never knew when one of us could be gone. The enormity of it hit me, and I wiped a tear from my eye. Scott came over to my chair, leaned down, and kissed me passionately. (That is really love considering the way I looked and the fact that my teeth hadn't yet encountered a toothbrush.) Then he said something else that was odd but, in its own way, touching.

"Peeky," he said, "for somebody I can't stand, I certainly am crazy about you." My eyes gazed deeply into his.

"I know," I replied in earnest. "I feel exactly the same way about you." Then I asked him the same question I ask him nearly every day. It's almost become a ritual.

"We love each other so much, don't we?" He answered as he always does.

"Yes, we love each other so much." Just before Scott left for work, he tossed me one last bit of philosophical cud to chew. "What we have got here, Becky, is a dioclassical relationship."

I blinked at that one, but it was like him. He's always inventing words. When we were courting he would take me on nature walks and pretend to be some sort of naturalist—making up scientific-sounding names for the plant life along the trail. They sounded so authentic and believable that I was actually fooled for a while. I believe it was the "paleoedible chlorophillia endometriosis" that finally clued me in.

Scott bulldozes his way through the minefield of psychology and its jargon in much the same way. Standing in the doorway, he expounded one last word on his new theory before bidding me farewell.

"A dioclassical relationship is one in which two people who are totally opposite—who irritate each other constantly—each grow to find the other completely irresistible."

With that explanation, he gave me a quick good-bye kiss and darted out the front door. I glanced sleepily at the clock. I was due for a radio interview in half an hour to publicize *Worms in My Tea,* and I realized I must somehow get coherent. I couldn't remember where the broadcast was from, but I hoped it was from the city of Seattle. I wondered how the Sleepless in Seattle people would feel about an interview with Tired in Texas. I'd like to tell those heartbroken widowers and widows not to be too particular about marrying the perfect mate next time around. After all, there's even love to be found for two dioclassical crazy people. As long as they master the art of effective, meaningful communication.

And he informed me, and talked with me, and said . . .
"I have now come forth to give you skill to understand. . . .
for you are greatly beloved."
DANIEL 9:22–23, NKJV
∾

Advice from a pro

This past September I opened my mailbox and found an envelope. It had a fragile appearance, the edges slightly yellowed. The letter inside had obviously been typed on an old manual typewriter, deepening my impression that I was holding something timeless and special in my hand. The return address read "A. Gordon" of Savannah, Georgia.

Arthur Gordon had written a book, *A Touch of Wonder*, over twenty years ago. It has turned out to be one of my all-time favorites. The title caught my eye as I was browsing in an offbeat bookstore, and it was one of those books that came to me at just the right moment to fill just the right spot. His affirmative way of viewing life lifted my spirits when the going was tough. It also made me doubly thankful when the going was good.

Since I had been so moved by his book, I determined to find him and tell him so in a letter.

Even though Mr. Gordon had written more than ninety articles for *Reader's Digest*, no one I talked to at the magazine had heard from him since 1988. However, I eventually located an editor at *Guideposts* magazine who agreed to steer my letter to the proper hands. While waiting for a reply, I dug for more interesting tidbits about Mr. Gordon and his life.

I discovered Arthur Gordon has intriguing Southern roots. He hails from Savannah, Georgia, and is the nephew of Juliette Gordon Low, world-famous founder of Girl Scouts. The memories he records of his feisty aunt are priceless. He was educated at Yale and then went on to Oxford as a Rhodes scholar. He fought in the United States Air Force as a lieutenant colonel during the Second World War, receiving both the Air Medal and the Legion of Merit.

But to me, one of the most interesting of Gordon's experiences was the day he spent in the little village of Burwash, England, with Rudyard Kipling. Yes, *the* Rudyard Kipling—author of *The Jungle Book* and the immortal collection of *Just So Stories*. Mr. Gordon was a young man just starting his career; Kipling was sixty-nine and in ill health. Gordon had been offered a secure teaching job back home in America, but his dream was to become a writer. He hoped this meeting with Kipling, one of the world's greatest writers, might provide some direction for his own life's work. The two men ended up talking at length while sitting in a boat in the middle of a fish pond. So deep were they in conversation that Gordon never got around to asking for that direction, but without his asking, and in the course of conversation, he received his answer.

"Do the things you really want to do," Kipling told him. "Don't wait for circumstances to be exactly right. You'll find that they never are."[1]

With those words ringing in his head, young Mr. Gordon went home to America, turned down the teaching post, and got to work on his dream of writing. And one day that young man would go on to write a book about Wonder.

"Lord of all things," it begins, "whose wondrous gifts to man include the shining symbols knowns as words, grant that I may use their mighty power only for good."

Today that man is in the winter of his life. And I, fairly new at this business of crafting "shining symbols," am finding encouragement and example in the words he wrote many years ago.

In my letter to him I had asked, gingerly, a personal favor. Would he share some personal reflections for those whose marriages might be going through "a rough patch," as the British say? He graciously answered my request in the letter condensed below.

Dear Becky,

Many thanks for your nice note and the kind words about ATOW. If you're a writer yourself, you know that admiration is the fuel we run on. So an unexpected gallon or so does help.

Marriages in trouble. I have noticed that when the going gets really rough the partners tend to demonize each other, see nothing good, only the bad. Result is, mutual appreciation dies and there's nothing to cushion the shock in quarrels or recriminations. If the combatants would make an effort to recall one or two things they used to admire in their partner and force themselves to say so, however grudgingly, it might save the marriage. See the last sentence or two in the chapter in ATOW called "How Wonderful You Are." Maybe you can make something of all this.

How many t's in combatant, I wonder. One is probably enough.

Good luck with your new book project. I envy you your energy!

Best regards,

AG

Smiling, I made myself a cup of gourmet coffee and returned to my chair, this time with my dog-eared copy of *A Touch of Wonder*. I opened the chapter Mr. Gordon had mentioned and remembered at once it had been a favorite.

"To be manifestly loved," I had underlined, "to be openly admired are human needs as basic as breathing. Why, then, wanting them so much ourselves, do we deny them so often to others? Why indeed?"

Great question, an answer for which I am still mute. There is no reason, with any solid legs to stand on, for human beings to withhold their admiration from each other. After all, it isn't as if by hoarding our words of praise we are keeping anything of value for ourselves.

At that point, I made an important decision—one I'd been contemplating for some time. I would do all I could do in my remaining years to focus on the *best*—not only in my husband, but in all of life. And when I came across something wonderful—especially in my loved ones—I determined to openly share my admiration.

Do not withhold good from those who deserve it, when it is in your power to act.

PROVERBS 3:27

Looking for gold with
rose-colored glasses

Perhaps a pair of rose-colored glasses should be issued to couples a year after the honeymoon as a reminder to accentuate the positive.

Gary Paulsen is a sensitive, award-winning writer of young adult fiction. In his book *Clabbered Dirt, Sweet Grass* he compares the grain pouring out of a threshing machine to gold: "Rich, pouring, a river of gold as grand as the cream that comes from the separator is the wheat or barley or oats, and the dust and noise and itching and red eyes are forgotten in that river of richness."[1]

In an interview with *Writer's Digest* magazine in July of 1994, Gary Paulsen comments on this use of "perception" as a writer's device, but as I read his comments I saw a much broader application. He used life on the farm as an example.

> If you turn it just slightly, a lot of the stuff on the farm would be ugly. But if you dwelled on that and looked at it from that angle, it would ruin the book, the beauty that you're trying to see. So what you do is you hold up each thing and you say,

I wish to write about working with the threshing machine and threshing grain—which I've done and know how hard it is, and I know the dangers of it, with that *?!#! belt humming right next to your face. But if I wrote that sense of it, it would change what I was trying to say. And so I looked for the beauty in the wheat: the gold coming out of the threshing machine, that rich grain that just runs and is the most incredible thing. I chose the perception, the view I took of the diamond . . . . I just decided from what angle to look at them.[2]

The correlation is painfully obvious, is it not? The lazy, obvious way to view others is to focus on the "threshing machine belts" in their personalities. Unfortunately it doesn't take long, at this angle, to "demonize" the loved ones we used to admire—as Mr. Gordon's letter had warned. It takes a conscious decision to "choose the perception," perhaps even squinting at times, to see the gold in those we love. And if we, as husbands and wives, could find a way to do that consistently, I'm convinced we'd wind up with a marriage that "just runs and is the most incredible thing." Such small determinations, such vital differences. A small rudder turns 'round an enormous ship.

As to changing one's point of view, some of the best advice I've heard for couples who are stuck in a miserable cycle is this: Stop It. Fix It. Do It Now.

If a good marriage is something we really "want to do," we can't wait around for better times, more money, less stress, or the other person to change. We've got to determine now, today, *we* are going to go for the gold.

And so it is with all of life, really. A few years ago, I realized it only *made sense* to concentrate on the good—the river of gold—whenever I had a choice in the matter. After all, the negative pushes its way into our lives like an annoying houseguest—every day. But the positives—like gold—take more effort to glean. I determined to do whatever it takes to make the changes in myself that could lead to a rocking-chair-love-affair marriage.

Thankfully along the way, Scott independently came to a similar conclusion. Knowing now that I am helpless to control another human being, I am supremely thankful that Scott has chosen "us." And not just "us," but he wants the best possible, growing-old-happy-together "us" too. My husband has made it perfectly clear that he is in this relationship for the long haul. Good times and bad. Sickness and health. Holidays and Blah Days. Crazy About Each Other and Ready to Strangle One Another. Commitment is a *gift*, freely given—one I could never demand, but one I cherish as no other.

Also out of that turning point—that realization that the "gold" in life is worth the effort to find—came a poem summing up my Philosophy of Life. On the days when my life lines up with the words of this poem, I find a tremendous peace and sense of good.

No, I Won't Take Off My Rose-Colored Glasses

It only makes sense to fill my mind with the Goodness of God
to leave the hard questions in His Hand
to trust He sees the Big Picture, when I don't

To fill my ears with music that soars—and honors love

To fill my mind with Scripture, great books, vivid poetry—
courageous, joyful, dancing words

To fill my eyes with the smiles of children,
and watercolor sunsets

To fill my senses with the sound of my Love's voice,
and the touch of his skin

To spend time with those who have been seasoned
with warmth and wisdom—who've walked a long time with
the Friend of Friends

To fill these walls with laughter splashing over,
so that our home beckons, "Come and join!"

If I don't, the World will surely fill the empty spaces in my head
With unrelenting news of violence, hate and destruction—
and when I'm worn to the ground in Despair
how can I help those who need me most?
If my cup is not full of Light—
What will I have to share
with those who cry out in their Darkness?

No, I won't take off these Rose-Colored Glasses,
I work too hard to keep them on

BECKY FREEMAN © 1994

It is amazing how much better life looks with some rose-colored shades. Gold begins popping up all over the place.

To be held in living esteem is better than gold.

PROVERBS 22:1, TLB

Holidays on ice

I love this day. It is the third day of January, my sister Rachel's birthday. Come to think of it, I believe it's her big "3-0." While this is great cause for celebration, I must admit, there is an even greater one. In addition to being Rachel's birthday, today is also the most thrilling of all the holidays for millions of stay-at-home moms. It is the day *after* Christmas vacation—the day kids go back to school and husbands go back to work. This is the day life gets back to normal. Yes, I *love* this day.

My poor children, however, looked as if they were marching off to the guillotine when I rounded them up for the school-bound carpool. I hoped they wouldn't notice the spring in my own step, so uncharacteristic of me at an early hour. Scott was faring no better than the kids. He looked at me with sad, puppy-dog eyes.

"Which tie looks best on me," he asked, "in case I decide to hang myself with it instead of facing rush-hour traffic again?"

I gave him my best sympathetic hug, but I had to work hard at suppressing the smile twitching at the corners of my lips. I couldn't help it—this was to be the first day in weeks that I would find myself alone—*alone at last!!!* My feeble attempt to control my excitement faltered as Scott apparently read my mind. He walked out the front door and turned for a parting shot.

"It seems to me the *least* you could do is quit humming the 'Hallelujah Chorus' under your breath."

For some years now, I have fought the creeping awareness that the holidays make the old, everyday variety of stress seem like a trip to the beach. For me, taking down the Christmas tree and the festive feeling that goes with it far exceeds the "sounding joy" of putting it up. Scott and I are finally ready to admit that we are hopelessly holiday impaired. If there is a twelve-step program for cranky-on-special-occasion-aholics, please let me know. We are at the end of our merry ropes.

I would have preferred to write this chapter as if I were looking in on some past problem that we used to have and could report that now everything is just peachy at our house from Thanksgiving through New Year's Day. But this particular area of our marriage remains a giant puzzle. We simply don't handle holidays well. Or any special occasion. And the hitch is, holidays seem to appear every year with relentless regularity.

It is hard to confess this because so much joy and warmth and *specialness* is supposed to begin bubbling up around Thanksgiving, Christmas, Valentine's, and other days of that ilk. Unfortunately for us, Groundhog Day, St. Patrick's Day, and—for heaven's sake—even Daylight Saving's Day can cause Scott and me to evolve into walking nervous ticks. You name the holiday, we've blown it to smithereens.

In our first year of marriage, Scott was such a bundle of nerves about his newlywed Valentine's Day performance that he signed his romantic card to me using his first *and* last name. It read, "To my darling Sweetheart. I will always love you. Sincerely, Scott Freeman."

Ironically, we are fairly jolly souls on regular days. We only turn into jerks on days when we are *expected* to be jolly. The added pressure pushes us over the edge when it is imperative for all to be calm and all to be bright.

So it should have been no surprise that this year—like most years—Scott and I found ourselves fighting to keep the Grinch within from stealing Christmas from all of us. Occasionally, we actually won the battle. But far too often we let the Grinches and the Scrooges in our personalities have the upper hand. It didn't help that I began this Christmas vacation with my stress level already set at low simmer. Even as I was writing a chapter for this book, it became painfully obvious that I was suffering from a severe case of burnout. How did I come to this revelation? Let me back up to the Monday before school let out for the holidays.

As I was trying to decide whether to go Christmas shopping, put up a tree, write Christmas cards, finish my chapter, clean the house, get dressed, or bake goodies for the kids' class parties, the phone rang. It was the principal of the kids' school.

"Mrs. Freeman," she said in a clipped voice, "could you come in today? There is something I'd like you to see."

"I'll be there in fifteen minutes," I answered before grabbing my purse and heading out the door. I had a strange feeling that the something she'd like me to see was going to be something I didn't particularly *want* to see. But if I had to see something I didn't want to see today, I wanted to get it over with as soon as possible.

I arrived at the school and walked down the hall toward the office. At one point I had to step over two school backpacks lying on the floor. Numerous papers had obviously made their way out of the backpacks and onto the surrounding floor. As I stepped over them to reach the office doors I thought, *Somebody ought to pick this stuff up. This sort of mess could be a real safety hazard.*

I walked into the office and was immediately greeted by the well-groomed and equally well-tailored principal. We shook hands and exchanged pleasantries as she steered me out of the office and back toward the spot where the two backpacks lay unfurled. On second examination, I realized the backpacks looked rather familiar. As a matter of fact, I was beginning to believe they might be the ones belonging to my two oldest sons. The principal got right to the point.

"Do you recognize these bags, Mrs. Freeman?"

"Should I have an attorney present before I answer that question?"

"No. Actually, I know to whom they belong. But do you know *why* they are here?"

"No." I was running out of clever responses.

"Well, they are here because out of the *entire* elementary school, there were only *two children* who had to dump their backpacks in order to find their permission slips for the field trip today. Would you like to guess who those two children were?"

I shook my head in the negative, but that didn't stop her from telling me.

"Zach and Zeke have had *two weeks* to get their permission slips turned in, so it is not as if we sprang this on them yesterday."

"But I signed those slips a week ago!" I protested. At this point, her control was beginning to slide and her eyes had a mild look of hysteria to them.

"Oh, no doubt. But your boys forgot to turn them *in!* So this morning, while an entire busload of students waited to depart for "The Nutcracker," your sons sat cross-legged in this hall, frantically searching their backpacks for their permission slips! Luckily, they found them. If they had not, I assure you they would not be seeing the ballet today."

"I'm so sorry. They do seem to have trouble getting organized."

Gathering her remaining wits about her, the principal continued in a more professional tone of voice. "Well, I am going to have to ask you to help them get a grip on this thing over the holiday break. They are the sweetest boys, but if you could see the insides of their desks you wouldn't believe it."

"Oh, I might. But I guess I am partly to blame. I've always had a problem getting my act together too."

We talked a few more minutes. But just as I was pledging to be more diligent about helping the boys get ordered, I happened to glance at my reflection in the office window. Even in the faint outline of the glass, it was easy to see that something was bobbing atop my head. *What is that?* I thought. Reaching up, I pulled one bright pink curler out of my bangs. I smiled up weakly at the principal.

Slowly, desperately, she shook her head as if to say, "What's the use?"

Weakened in spirit from being called to the principal's office, I eventually experienced that horrible phenomenon commonly referred to as Writer's Block. It is not subtle either, this infamous Writer's Block. It lands upon its victims' heads with a resounding thud. The first indication something was awry came to me as I was rereading the opening I had written for a new chapter.

So here we are in the middle of this book. Ta-duuuummmm!

I'd sure like some fudge. With lots of nuts.

I wonder why they make those Styrofoam packing thingies look like big white peanuts?

The End.

At that point I should have turned off the computer, put on an apron, and whipped up batches of burnt cookies. That always seems to lift my spirits. You know, the fragrance in the air, the joyous buzzing of the smoke alarm. But this time, I was beyond a quick sugar-and-smoke-alarm fix. Instead, I took to bed and made a list of fifteen people whom I felt I had disappointed or let down in some way. I do not recommend this as a Christmas tradition. I cried for the better part of the day, and thus primed the pump to respond at the slightest provocation for the rest of the season.

My daughter, Rachel, the one who is sometimes gifted with a heavenly wisdom beyond her years, crawled into bed with me and put her arms around me.

"Momma," she said matter-of-factly, "you can cry today all you want to and you can feel sorry for yourself for just *today*. But tomorrow you have to knock it off and get up and put some makeup on. Because to tell the truth, you look like roadkill."

I graciously accepted her offer and hosted the most pitiful of semi-private pity parties known to women. For one day only, I promised her and myself. OK, I must admit there was quite a bit of residual sniffing still going on the next day. But at least I managed to get my sad self out of bed the next morning.

At first Scott tried to play the comforter. That role doesn't suit my husband longer than about three hours. It wasn't long before his "sympathizer batteries" ran out and he said something snippy to me and I said something ugly back to him and then he shouted at me.

"How could you act like this during Christmas vacation?"

"How can *you* be so insensitive during the most holy of holidays?" I railed back at him.

A couple of days later we were still, shall we say, not up to par. But we loaded the kids in the station wagon anyway and set off for my parents' house to celebrate an Arnold Christmas— one week early. Mother and Daddy would be going to Virginia to spend Christmas with my sister, Rachel, and her little family, so we had planned an early family celebration.

On the way there, the engine on our panel wagon must have picked up on the mood inside the car, and it began to overheat. We pulled over and parked under a bridge where Scott used a bottle he found on the ground to scoop up questionable looking water from nearby puddles to pour on the steaming radiator. The kids were fascinated by the bottle, and I told them I thought this would be a really good time to play the Quiet Game. Through my open window, I could hear Scott muttering to himself.

"Is it not humiliating enough to be the only couple driving a station wagon with wood-grain panels on the sides? Oh, no! Now strangers are getting a chance to see me and my family parked under a bridge while I forage for used bottles."

He was finally able to resuscitate the car and coax it back home where we reloaded the six of us into Scott's mini-pickup truck. By the time we reached my parent's house, I walked through their front door a few steps behind the kids, smiled a big plastic smile, and bravely said, "Merry Chriswaaahhhh!. . ." Then for the first time in years, I collapsed sobbing into my mother's arms.

Mother swept me into a back bedroom and into the hug I needed.

"Honey," she said as she handed me a Kleenex, "I've been wondering when this was going to happen."

"You have?" I asked, gulping back tears. I had fancied myself a strong and independent woman, but here I was at my mommie's house, blubbering like a child again. I hated losing control, but at the same time—after all that had been building up inside—it was a relief to let it all out. I spewed and sputtered like our overheated car for several minutes. When I finally began to cool down, Mother gently unstuck my hair from the side of my teary face and pushed it back so we could see each other. She looked like she was underwater.

"Look at what you've taken on this year, Honey. Our first book has only been out a few months with a second one due out this spring, and you're already writing a third one on your own! And every time I talk to you, you've got new ideas for other projects that keep your mind going on constant fast forward. On top of that, this is the first year you've started to speak in public. Add financial stress to this new 'career' and a marriage that you value, four kids who need you, housekeeping duties, cherished relationships to keep up with . . ."

"And I'm blowing it in every category, Mother," I wailed. "What am I going to do?"

"For starters, you need a break. *Nobody* can do it all! A lot of the pressure you're feeling may be coming from your own mind. Recently I discovered something about myself that surprised me. I am, in many ways, a perfectionist. I care so much about what other people think of me that the stress of wanting to please had started to effect me physically." She paused, and I thought, *Gee, even fifty-something, mature women deal with this?*

"I also think," she continued, "that everybody talks to themselves in one way or another, all day long, and sometimes that self-talk can turn into self-condemnation. Lots of times we think others are upset with us when they really aren't. I'm having to learn to retrain my thoughts. I read somewhere that the "default mode" of the human mind is negative. It comes naturally. So we have to purposely direct our minds to think positive thoughts about ourselves, and about others. That only comes supernaturally."

"But, Mother! I'm giving speeches on how to have wonder and joy in life! With all I know to be true, why am I so down right now?"

"Because you need to hear someone tell you the same things you tell others. We all need to hear a genuine human being say to us personally, 'Be kind to yourself.' Becky, you're exhausted. You've just overdone it. Take it easy and be gentle with yourself for awhile. Let the Lord show you what really is essential and how to do it."

When the chips are down, my mother knows how to give comfort like no one else I've ever known. As she has admitted to herself, she isn't perfect. But even when I was a child, I always thought her ability to empathize was a special gift. Her mother before her, my Nonnie, had the same uncanny knack for knowing exactly what to say to soothe frazzled minds.

In those few minutes, bathed in the warmth of my mother's understanding and compassion, I began to feel life and strength slowly flowing back into my wilted mind and body. My thoughts turned to Christ, who left His peaceful home to "beam down" to our world—to have His fresh-born senses invaded by noise and rush and aches and pains. But somehow He knew the secret of keeping The Peace—be it in a noisy animal stall, a storm-tossed boat, or in the midst of pressing crowds on special holidays.

Like the shepherds and wise men of old, I was suddenly filled with a sense of urgency. I wanted to gather up my family and go find this Christ Child, this Prince of Peace. Wouldn't it be lovely to simply be still and worship quietly, for even a few moments, at His side?

Scott and I had one week before the Real Christmas Day to find out if the holiday impaired might begin the process of becoming holy repaired.

"Come to me, all you who are weary and burdened,
and I will give you rest.
Take my yoke upon you and learn from me,
for I am gentle and humble in heart,
and you will find rest for your souls.
For my yoke is easy and my burden is light."

MATTHEW 11:28–30

ॐ

Scott finally quacks up

I turned over in bed one morning a couple of days before December 25th, opened one sleepy eye, and glanced at my husband snoring happily on his pillow beside me. Something was different about him. I opened my eyes wider and moved closer for another look.

Then I reached toward Scott's face thinking, *Is that thing what I think it is?* It was. For some odd reason my husband's upper lip had ballooned during the night and now completely draped over his bottom lip. I was on the emotional mend, but apparently the holiday stress had begun to have a most unusual effect on him.

"Wake up, Scott!" I shouted. "I think you're turning into a duck!"

As you can well imagine, Scott sat as straight up in the bed as he could, considering the added weight of his lip, and gingerly patted it. Dropping it over the side of the bed, he looked into the mirror at what appeared to be a large, fleshy beak. Then she turned pitifully back to me.

"It's finawy happened," he managed to say. "I'm awergic to Chwistmas. And pwobabwy my wife too." He sat staring into space trying to adjust to new realities for another minute or two, and then his morbid gaze happened to fall upon a book I had just purchased on the subject of joy. He grabbed the paperback and stared at me, his eyes tormented with suspicion. The title? *Talking to Ducks.*

We made it through the morning, and at noon I offered to fix him some soup, but he said he wasn't sure he could get a spoon through his lips.

"Oh, come on, Honey," I coaxed. "Try to eat a little. It'll be duck soup." I flopped on the bed with convulsions of laughter. He didn't seem to find that helpful.

We never found out exactly what had caused his deformity, but we were enormously grateful it turned out to be temporary. After that crisis had subsided, we were faced with yet another problem. For the first time, Scott and I would be spending Christmas Eve at home with just the six of us. We've always spent Christmas Eve with Grannie Ruthie and PawPaw George or Grandma and Grandpa Freeman where we were aided in bringing good cheer by a number of cousins. From the moment we dropped the Home Alone bomb, our kids were nervous wrecks.

It was a painful struggle for them—wrestling with the whole concept of trusting *us,* their own parents, with the enormity of staging Christmas Eve. I did realize that my children hated the artificial—but authentic-looking—Christmas tree I put up every year. And sure, I've accidentally burned the arms and legs off more than my share of gingerbread men. But it was truly a blow to our egos to realize that our children didn't believe their mother and father had the maturity, or wherewithal, to conduct a major holiday event without more responsible adult supervision around.

We set out to prove them wrong. We'd show them we could handle a family holiday with the biggest and best of grown-ups. I'd turned over a new leaf last week at Mother's. We'd do something rich with sentiment, a time they would never forget. We'd take them to the mall.

This was not just any mall. This was the Galleria Mall in downtown Dallas, where there was skating, huge Christmas trees, caroling in the background, gorgeous decorations, and hot cappuccinos beckoning from sidewalk cafes! It was, I must say, a stroke of genius. All that atmosphere, and I didn't have to do a lick of work. Just in the nick of time, Grandma and Grandpa Freeman blessed us with a surprise visit at the skating rink. Christmas Eve was saved!

Back home, Scott and I shared the Nativity story by the light of the tree, held hands in a circle as we prayed with the children, and then later served egg nog with nutmeg on top. I had even bought a card table so we could play table games just like a real Norman Rockwell family. What do you think about that? Not too shabby for a couple of Christmas Eve Scroo—er, green-horns, I'd say. Maybe there's hope.

Christmas morning, though, was a little shakier. There were a few hurt feelings and tense moments over who got what and who didn't and episodes of "Mom always loved you best!" But for the holiday impaired-in-recovery, it's not easy to be gleeful two days in a row.

With this dilemma in mind, Scott and I have been mulling over the subject of New Year's resolutions. After all, just two days ago we tossed out the old calendar and brought in the new with its fresh pages promising new starts. I must confess that my standard New Year's resolution is to not make any New Year's resolutions. It's always too depressing when I break them. This year, however, we've decided to attempt a resolution or two. What can it hurt?

First of all, we would like to try lowering our "special occasion" expectations. Second, we want to work at minimizing the level of stress in our lives. Last night as we were lying in bed Scott made a profound declaration that is already helping me feel more relaxed.

"Becky," he said, "I think we have both decided we want a good marriage. And a long one. We've got a lot tied up in this deal. For all these years you've been the one who reads the books and tries to figure out what to do to make our relationship better. I think I'd like to give it a shot. I'll even make it one of my New Year's resolutions. I think I'll just read a few books and see if I can figure this marriage stuff out for myself, and then I'll let you know what we need to do."

I loved it but had to laugh. "So does this mean I'm fired from being the Head Relationship Figurer Outer?"

"Yep."

In a strange way, I'm finding the new arrangement a big relief. Trying to understand how to make our complicated, intense relationship work smoothly has certainly left me exhausted—and more confused than ever. I was more than happy to give Scott a "go" at it.

Whatever transpires, this should be an interesting new year. Glancing again at the new calendar, I see we are facing another holiday test very soon. In twelve short days, it will be—the birthday of Dr. Martin Luther King Jr.

Just thinking about Dr. King and his timeless speech made me realize that I, too, have a dream—a dream that a husband and a wife will walk hand in hand into one holiday after another with peace and joy and love and harmony in our hearts.

Next New Year's Eve, perhaps Scott and I will be able to gaze happily into each other's eyes, share an intimate kiss at midnight, and look back on nothing but warm and happy memories of the Christmas vacation when we learned a full year's worth about living. If so, rather than singing the familiar chorus of Auld Lang Syne, our children just might hear us singing triumphantly, "We made it at last! We made it at last! Thank God Almighty, we made it at last!"

Love . . . . Always . . . hopes.

1 CORINTHIANS 13:6–7

ॐ

319

Tucking good stuff in *each other's* mailbox too

For some strange reason, Spring has decided to give the South a special preview this week. Though our calendars plainly state that it is early January, balmy breezes are winding their way from the open backdoor to my desk. Just last week, we had snow and ice. Today it is eighty degrees, and I'm wearing a ponytail and shorts! Last night, as Scott and I lay in bed, he opened a window and, believe it or not, a *mosquito* flew in. A mosquito in the middle of winter!

And this morning I had an interesting off-season visitor to my bedroom. Others might have screamed; I simply stared him down until he slunk away. I'll admit he wasn't all that threatening. Most green lizards are harmless, but at the very least, this one had guts, lying there basking in the heat of my electric rollers. This particular lizard was an anole, cousin to the chameleon. They have long been son Gabriel's favorite warm weather toy. Outside on a maple leaf, they are a brilliant shade of green. But once Gabriel gets them in his warm little hand, the gorgeous color fades to a nondescript, ugly brown.

As I took a "spring" stroll this January morning, I thought about how much we human beings are like the temperamental little anole. How easily we absorb the atmosphere around us into ourselves. Scott and I, both being cut of ultrasensitive cloth, are particularly vulnerable to outside input. Our emotions fluctuate like crazy Texas weather according to what we happen to be hearing, seeing, and learning all around us.

Because of that, I'm getting picky, picky, picky these days about what I allow to come in and around my head. For the most part, Americans have the privilege of choosing what we hear, read, and see. It is my desire to make the most of that freedom by actively seeking out Good Stuff. Interestingly, I've found that when I do happen upon something wonderful—an uplifting book, an intriguing verse of Scripture, a funny tape, an interesting article, a beautiful piece of music—I almost always end up sharing parts of it with Scott. And he does the same for me.

It occurred to me this morning, that this tradition of sharing the Good Stuff with each other has become a gentle way of looking out for one another—a mutual feeding of the other's soul. Speaking of food, when I've been served a luscious dessert, my automatic response is to offer my husband a bite. I want him to experience the same deliciousness I'm enjoying. And so it is with life.

Part of my reason for sharing Good Stuff with Scott is selfish, I must admit. It's my attempt to try to drown out, or at least balance out, all the negative junk the media slings his way. Whether we realize it or not, we are both subconsciously affected by the Bad Stuff Out There (hereafter referred to as BSOT).

For example, I hate it when we watch a television show or a video where the female lead turns out to be a lying sneak. For the next few days, Scott will look at me suspiciously as if he's wondering what evil is lurking up my so-called innocent sleeve. As for me, I may have a frightfully realistic dream that my husband is involved with another woman—as a result of seeing a movie with a similar plot. No matter how much Scott assures me of his faithfulness, there's a little part of me that is unreasonably *furious* with him for a couple of days. If exposed to enough BSOT, even human beings start turning an ugly, nondescript shade of brown.

On the other hand, inspirational movies or books or experiences can have a profound "greening-up" influence. Scott and I were deeply moved by the movie version of *Shadowlands*, the poignant love story of C. S. Lewis and Joy Davidman. Having been reminded of the brevity of life, we held each other closer in the night.

At the end of a long day, when the busyness of the house begins to quiet, one of the moments Scott and I look forward to the most is the exchanging of our mental mailboxes.

How was your day? Wait 'til you hear this! Guess what I learned how to do today? What do you think about . . .

I look forward to these times, much as I look forward to opening the morning mail. You never know what might be in the box. And, like mail, it is so much more fun when there's some Good Stuff in there. There's nothing more discouraging than endless deliveries of overdue bills and "friendly reminders" for dental checkups. We want interesting chatty news from each other. Funny anecdotes are always nice. Words of thanks and verbal "cards" of encouragement are also appreciated. And love notes are a perpetual favorite.

Herein lies the secret of keeping Married-for-Life Conversations a brilliant anole-green pleasure, rather than an ugly anole-brown bore. To have interesting marriages, we must show our selves interesting. As individuals, we can't stop growing, stretching, and learning.

Every day other "letters" crowd Scott's "mailbox." Lots of it, pardon my French, is a bunch of BSOT. Therefore, I want mine to stand out. I want to be the juicy, attention-getting one. I purposefully try to notice the Good Stuff Out There (GSOT)—uplifting items of interest—and when the time is right, I tuck some of it in my husband's box. And I look forward to the surprises he brings home to me too.

Sometimes, however, it can be pretty risky to arm a loved one with certain new and interesting bits of information, even if you are pretty sure it falls into the category of GSOT. I'll never forget the grenade I accidentally tucked in Scott's mailbox a few months back . . .

You are a letter . . . written not with ink
but with the Spirit . . . on tablets of human hearts.

2 CORINTHIANS 3:3

Just please—I beg of you—don't bore me!

After having been so "greened-up" by the movie *Shadowlands*, I decided to follow up by reading the book. All the while I was reading about this unlikely pair of lovebirds, I found myself tucking away favorite quotes and passages in my Scott-Would-Get-a-Kick-Out-of-This-Too mental file. When I read that C. S. Lewis and his intellectual companions often held their deepest theological discussions over mugs of beer in local English pubs, I chuckled aloud. I kept trying to imagine professors at a nearby seminary popping 'round for an after-class chat over a brew at a local pub. And I knew Scott would appreciate this historical tidbit about the esteemed author of *Mere Christianity*. My husband's always questioning traditional, Americanized approaches to Christianity. Actually he loves to question untraditional, un-Americanized approaches to Christianity too. He just basically loves to question any and all approaches to everything.

Just as I surmised, Scott did enjoy the morsel of Lewis trivia. Unfortunately, the next time we went to church, our Sunday

School class took up a serious debate on whether Jesus turned the water into real or benign grape juice wine. Scott always makes me nervous when controversial subjects are under discussion, but I was even more nervous when I realized I had just handed him a potential bomb with the tidbit about Lewis. It was unlikely he would be able to keep himself from pulling the pin.

Needless to say, sitting next to Scott during the Pseudo Wine vs. the Real McCoy Wine Discussion was about as much fun as taking a little swim at a shark convention with a nasty cut. Just before I slapped my hand over his mouth, I vaguely remember hearing my husband say, "Well, if you ask me, what we all need right now is a good beer to help everybody calm down."

The next time I go to a Sunday School class with my husband, I want a sign to wear around my neck that says, "The opinions expressed by the man sitting next to me are not necessarily those of his wife. Actually, you can't be sure they are actually his own either. He just likes to keep things interesting."

Right now Scott is reading a book that compares marriage to the art of deep-sea fishing, and he is marking passages he wants me to read later. I'm reading James Herriot's latest book and getting a tremendous kick out of this country vet from Yorkshire. Every so often I have to stop to read a passage aloud for Scott's entertainment—using my best Cockney accent. We both listen to talk radio fairly often, so there's always the latest political hot topic to discuss. I never know whether Scott's going to come home sounding like Rush Limbaugh or a Bleeding Heart Liberal.

What am I trying to say? After all these years together, we continue to value what is in each other's noggin. And because the world is full of new things to learn and share, how could we ever get bored with one another? Hate one another, maybe. Disagree with one another? Oh, yeah. But become bored with each other? Unthinkable.

When I went back to college to complete my degree a few years ago, I can remember saying to Scott, "I'm all right with a professor who doesn't believe *anything* that I believe in—even if he challenges all my treasured values. At least he provokes my thinking. I'll even take a professor who is rude and obnoxious. But I can't *stand* a professor who stands up there and bores me to tears! I want to scream, 'Do SOMETHING! Say ANYTHING! But please, please, please don't *bore* me one more second or I will *explode* right here in this chair!' " Perhaps those same feelings apply to marriages.

Sometimes I tease Scott by telling him my life would have been so much easier if I had just married a boring couch potato. I've wondered what it would be like to live with a low maintenance guy who only needs a remote and a bag of potato chips to make him a happy camper. Scott is always looking for more—more excitement, new experiences, more intensity in our love. Quiet evenings at home are not his cup of tea. He likes to *go*.

Many evenings all I want is a hot bath, a quilt, and a good book. On the other hand, Scott is jumping up and down by the front door like a Chihuahua who's ready to go outside and play. More than once I've thought, *If only I had one of those little tranquilizer guns, I could just shoot him and put both of us out of our misery.*

But the real truth is, I'd much rather be dealing with a man who has an overly rapid heartbeat than one who is brain dead on the couch. At least I'm not bored.

For if I were, as you know, I might just explode in my chair.

An idle soul shall suffer hunger.

PROVERBS 19:15, KJV

∾

The brain is a pretty swift aphrodisiac

This past summer, there was a fascinating article in *Life* magazine entitled "Brain Calisthenics." The article basically says that scientists have discovered that when people learn something new—even in their old age—their brain cells begin to branch wildly. This makes it easier for the synapses to fire and the entire brain to function better. It's like boosting the power in a computer.

The researchers also say the best brain exercise is to learn something unfamiliar. A mathematician might take up painting. An artsy, creative person might learn a computer skill. And the new area should require periods of focused attention.

So there's some news about how to keep our gray matter healthy. Now what does keeping our brain in good shape have to do with love? Interesting that you should ask. While I'm in this scientific mode, let's examine another theory that should help make the connection.

In his wonderful book *The Romance Factor*, Alan McGinnis points to another piece of intriguing research in his chapter entitled "Creating the Conditions for Ecstasy." He lists nine "triggers" scientists have found that will often precipitate feelings of joy, wonder, even ecstasy. By incorporating some of these triggers into our lives and our relationships, McGinnis believes we can live on a higher plane. Not only will we be more joyful as individuals, but also we will bring richness to our marriages. Some of the triggers include Music and Art, Natural Scenery, Play and Rhythmic Movement, Beauty, Sexual Love, Creative Work, and Religion. Another of those triggers is the Discovery of New Knowledge. Therein lies the answer to the question, "What does keeping our brains in good shape have to do with love?"

When our minds are growing—discovering new knowledge—we have more to bring to our relationships. It triggers new ideas to talk about, we become more interesting to be around, and we develop a more curious nature. We want to know our mate's opinion on a variety of issues, which makes them feel esteemed. We are not bored, so we are not boring. We also become more physically attracted to one another. An intriguing mind is a powerful aphrodisiac. The most successful mistresses have known this secret for ages. (So I've read.)

I realize as I write this that some people must be thinking, *Why is this classic "dumb brunette" writing about keeping intellectually fit?* Well, they have a point. But there is a difference between *absent*mindedness and *simple*mindedness. You see, my mind is not simple; it is just absent. Wait a minute, that doesn't sound quite right.

Anyway, I may be lacking in common sense, I may not remember to pull the cookies out of the oven on time, and I may find myself in circumstances to rival those of Lucille Ball's. None of that means I'm not smart. I was a member of the National Honor Society, even if I occasionally went to class with my dress on wrongside out.

There are several ways I keep the old gray matter moving while I'm doing intellectually stimulating things like moving the laundry from the washer to the dryer.

For one thing, I order lots of cassette tapes. I've attended at least twenty "seminars" while folding clothes or loading the dishwasher or taking a walk—seminars on marriage and family relationships, how to write and get published, self-esteem, in-depth Bible studies, public speaking, etc. You name the subject—somebody's taped a seminar and made a buck on it. Oh yes, I almost forgot! I also took a course on how to increase your memory. Can't remember the name of the course, but it was highly effective.

With so many books on cassette, I am also a much better driver. Now I can drive and "read" by listening to a cassette instead of driving and reading with the book on the steering wheel. The kids seem more relaxed.

There's also a wealth of learning available at local colleges. For mothers who dream of getting their degree someday, it may be possible to get a start on that dream sooner than they think. When my three oldest children were in school, I went back to college to finish my degree. Gabriel went to Mother's Day Out two days a week, so I used that time to go to class, and in three years I had a diploma. I loved college. I loved being around university kids. I loved the smell of new text-books. I loved eating at the campus cafeteria and discussing new ideas and test scores and degree plans over coffee. I loved the whole enchilada.

The first time I went to college I was only seventeen and a newlywed. Scott and I had arranged to take all our classes together. We enjoyed the experience for the most part, but we were always irritated by one person in particular. It was the "old lady" student. You know the type. She was the woman in orange polyester who always sat on the front row and asked the professor a thousand annoying questions. She was always bucking for additional homework and destroying the curve for the rest of the class. However, when I went back to school at age thirty, I found *I* had turned into that "old lady." And I discovered another amazing fact—old ladies have a lot more fun with higher education. I also found out I looked pretty nifty in orange polyester.

Many churches have wonderful classes—with Bible studies that go beyond filling in one-word blanks. I've thoroughly enjoyed taking a couple of Precepts developed by Kay Arthur, and I understand that Bible Study Fellowship is also a wonderful source for those wanting to go into a deeper study of Scripture. Few things are as exciting as discovering a new truth or a significant correlation in Scripture—especially when you have to dig for it and know you'll get to share it with other women.

Meeting new people and getting together with old friends is another way to stretch the old brain and bring fresh news home to one's mate. When someone asks me what I miss most about my year of teaching, I always answer, "Lunch and recess." I loved the lunchtime workroom chats with my peers and I loved the relaxed playground chats with my little students. I think I learned more at lunch and recess than I did teaching in the classroom.

Now that I'm at home writing, I especially depend on my friends to keep me from feeling like a recluse and climbing the walls. Once a week, I meet with a few of my best friends for lunch—women my age whom I've known for several years. Then once a month, I meet with two local women writers whom I consider good friends. But they are also mentor-types. They're older, wiser, and much further along in their relationship with God than I am. And they both like chocolate. I believe, as a matter of fact, that a woman's spiritual maturity is in direct proportion to her affinity for chocolate. We are fast becoming an *incredibly* mature group.

A few months ago I began driving to Dallas to a once-a-month meeting of crazy, eclectic professional writers. Yes, you must be either crazy or eclectic or both to join. In this group are a couple of romance writers, a best-selling spy novelist, journalists and columnists for major newspapers, children's authors, screenwriters, computer nerd freelancers—and me. I am the token Naive Christian Humorist. With this crew there is always something exciting in the hopper—from big New York book contracts, to movies, to exciting publicity campaigns. I always feel like a kid with her mouth hanging open; I can't wait to get home and share the "buzz" with Scott.

Aristotle said, "To learn is a natural pleasure." I couldn't agree more. It's my goal for us to keep up with those brain calisthenics through the years. Unlike physical exercise, I actually find brain building kind of fun. I'm hoping by the time we are one hundred or so—even if our bodies have gone completely to pot—our inquiring old minds will still want to know. By then we'll need all the aphrodisiacs we can get.

To these four young men God gave knowledge and understanding of all kinds of literature and learning.

DANIEL 1:17

ᴏᴠ

Love my kids,
and I'm yours too

I once cross-stitched a sampler with the well-known saying, "The greatest gift a father can give his children is to love their mother." I might add that the reverse is also true: "The greatest gift a husband can give his wife is to love her children."

One evening not long ago, my husband stayed home with the children while I went to the grocery store. Shopping for a family of six when four of them are male takes a while, so it was late when I got home. When I walked back into the house, all was dark and unusually quiet. After setting down a bag of groceries, I tiptoed into the bedroom, lighted by the soft glow of the moon sifting through the window. Scott was lying there, his hands folded behind his head, staring at the ceiling. He seemed so pensive I immediately thought something was bothering him.

"Hey," I said softly and sat down on the bed beside him. "What's the matter?"

"Aw, I was just thinking about my daughter," he grinned sheepishly. "And how much I love her."

Evidently it had been a very good evening. "What happened with Rachel tonight?" I asked.

"Well," he sighed and searched for words to convey what he was feeling. "I had built a fire outside to burn some excess wood, and the telephone rang. It turned out to be a tough discussion with someone and I was upset. So I went outside to unwind by the fire, and, before long, our little girl came out of the house and snuggled by my side.

"'Dad,' she told me, 'you look like you could use a hug.'" He paused briefly and breathed a contented sigh.

"She's my little sweetheart, you know."

"I know," I smiled as I rubbed the back of my husband's neck. "And I hope she always will be."

The next evening Scott came home from work and found me asleep on the couch. He woke me by tickling my nose with a long-stemmed red rose. Before I could properly gush over it, Rachel strolled in from her room, beaming from ear to ear. Her strawberry-blonde curls boing-yoinging happily as she plopped down on the sofa beside me. In her small, slender hands she held a lavender basket of fresh daisies and pink carnations. Tucked into the arrangement was a card in Scott's handwriting.

"Thanks for the hug," it read.

Rachel's brown eyes twinkled, and she smiled triumphantly in my direction. "You just got *one* flower. Daddy gave *me* a whole basket!"

I'd say that little girl has got it made. I speak from experience. I am thirty-five years old and still a daddy's girl. But Lord help the first boy who asks Scott Freeman's daughter out on a date . . .

A couple of nights ago our family watched *Father of the Bride* on television. At the beginning, Rachel was sitting across the room from her dad. By the time it got to the scene where Steve Martin and his daughter play a final game of basketball together on the eve of the big wedding, Rachel was curled up under her daddy's arm. I don't know which of them wiped away the most tears. I do know I wouldn't take a million dollars for the memory of them snuggled together like that.

While Scott has his little daughter wrapped around his pinkie, he has Zach attached to Pointer, Zeke on the Ring Man, with Gabe holding onto Thumbkin. Last weekend, I watched Zeke help his father work on our house. Zeke voluntarily stays by his dad's side for hours most weekends, fetching and hauling and hammering and whatever it is that guys do to build a house together. Hardly a word passes between them—which is just the way they like it. Peace, quiet, good hard work with one's own hands—this is the stuff those two live for. Two peace lovers in a pod.

Later that same evening Rachel and I were eating a snack supper at the kitchen counter when Zach burst through the front door dressed in a camouflage suit, smelling of musty woods and crisp fall air. His dad followed close behind wearing a mischievous grin, which should have alerted us but didn't. Suddenly, the "boys" pulled a dead duck out their game bag and laid him with a flourish on the table in front of us. Rachel screamed and gagged appropriately, which I'm sure is what they were after. My snack didn't look so appealing after that, but it was worth it to watch Zach and Scott having so much fun together.

Then there's Gabriel. Age eight. All boy. The day after Thanksgiving, he asked his dad to bring the Christmas ornaments down from the attic. As fathers tend to do when asked to rummage through high, dark storage places on their day off, Scott brushed off Gabe's question, mumbling something about waiting a week or so. Not long after, I found Gabe quietly crying in a corner.

"What's the problem, Gabe?" I asked.

"Mom," he said earnestly, wiping away a tear, "I just want to *see* the ornaments. I'll put them away as soon as I look at them. I just want to see some *Christmas* today!"

What's a mother to do? I found Scott as quickly as I could and explained the gravity of the situation—that our son had to have a little Christmas right this very minute. Scott climbed up in the housetop, click, click, click. And down he came bearing gifts—a huge old popcorn can filled with Christmas treasures.

Gabe's lashes were still wet as he beamed up heartfelt gratitude to his father, the hero of the hour. Not to worry about me. It's my joy and privilege to stay behind the scenes in thankless anonymity.

Gabe's heart so overflowed with gratitude that he went to work right away making Scott's Christmas present. He tore a huge piece of cardboard off an old box and set about drawing a scene of his dad fishing. On the end of the crayon-drawn pole he pasted a real string and a real hook. Then came the inscription.

Dear Dad,

I Love you more than fish Love worms. I will never forget this christmost.

Love, Gabe

I loved seeing my child share open admiration for his daddy—even more than fish love worms.

The glory of children is their father.
PROVERBS 17:6, NKJV
ॐ

TWENTY-FIVE

Insecurity and other irresistible qualities

I am a secure woman. I think. Oh, I don't know. Maybe not. But sometimes I wonder if other people think I think I am as secure as I think I think I am.

I guess I still have a few insecurities about the issue of my own security.

Today, for instance, I was feeling less than my best. I had a hard day. I was overwhelmed, discouraged, blue—and feeling very insecure. One thought kept coming to my mind: *I want my husband. I want to be held in his arms and hear him say everything is going to be just fine. I want to hear him say that I am not a failure.* Scott has become a physical and emotional refuge for me—a safe place where I can be engulfed by his loving arms and shielded from the world.

When he got home tonight, after holding me tight, he took my hand and led me outside. We walked about a mile, under the stars, and he let me talk until I felt better. Then he told me everything was going to be fine and that I was not even close to being a failure.

Is there any emotion more common than the feeling of insecurity? It is so easy—terribly easy—to be shaken from the treetops of self-assuredness. It's amusing really, how all our fine accomplishments can fade into nothingness with the slightest embarrassment or someone's casual hint that we might not be meeting the standard.

In 1868 Dostoevsky wrote, "If you happen to have a wart on your nose or forehead, you cannot help imagining that no one in the world has anything else to do but stare at your wart, laugh at it and condemn you for it, even though you have discovered America."[1] How easily do the mighty fall under the ax of imagined criticism.

One moment I believe I am all grown up, filled with the wisdom of the ages, with talent to spare. The next I am back in junior high, wondering if I'm ever going to be cool enough to fit in with the popular crowd.

Even the invincible Mark Twain appeared to be confused on the subject of self-doubt versus self-confidence. Once, with head and pen held high, he wrote, "A man cannot be comfortable without his own approval."[2] Of course that was in an essay written for the public. Nearly thirty years later, in the privacy of his notebook, he wrote, "We are offended and resent it when people do not respect us; and yet no man, deep down in the privacy of his heart, has any considerable respect for himself."[3] Maybe with the passing of years Mark Twain simply grew more comfortable—more secure, shall we say—with admitting his own insecurities.

Hey—wouldn't it be ironic if the sign of a truly secure person is his ability to admit his insecurity? Actually, there's a potential "immortal quote" in that question: "A man's security is in direct proportion to his ability to admit his insecurities"—a wise and profound statement by Becky Freeman. Perhaps it could even be cross-stitched.

In a good marriage, the partners are *always* sensitive to each other's insecurities. In *somebody's* good marriage anyway. Rather than poking fun at each other's foibles, they consistently reassure each other of their individual worth. We're trying to improve our average on this particular Good Marriage Test, and, actually, I think we are beginning to get fairly high marks.

I've had more than a few personal experiences over the past few years that have left me feeling somewhat insecure, including one or two booksignings.

I am crazy about bookstores, but I'm more than a little nervous about booksignings. If there is a nice group of friendly faces lined up at the table, it is hard to beat a booksigning for an afternoon delight. However, if nobody comes, it's about as much fun as being the last one picked for a baseball team in P.E. class.

You see, most of today's busy customers in large bookstores want to be left alone. Book browsing is a quiet, private affair and I, of all people, understand this. Who needs the pressure of a not-so-well-known author hawking her book in the middle of the store? But oh, the agony of being the mid- to unfamous author in the center of the store sitting behind a draped table, with a pen and a stack of one's books—and still being completely ignored. I've discovered people will walk twenty feet out of their way to avoid making eye contact with me in this situation. After a long, lonely stretch, I once thought about holding up a sign reading, "Will Autograph Books for Food."

Mother and I once spent three hours in a bookstore where no one bought our book except the owner of the store, who finally took pity on us. Eventually, however, a couple of friendly women walked though the front door and straight up to our table. It seemed obvious by their smiles and faces that they recognized who we were.

"Hey, Mother," I whispered, "here come some live ones." After exchanging the warmest of greetings and names of each other's grandchildren, the ladies politely asked if Mother and I could point them to the location of the reference materials.

Was I ever ready to be hugged when I got home. But I'm not the only partner in this marriage who suffers from occasional spells of insecurity. Scott also has his bad days . . .

It all began a couple of weeks ago when Gabriel came home from his Cub Scout meeting toting a little box containing a rectangular block of wood, two axles, and four plastic wheels. Little did I realize the momentous significance of that box. But as soon as Gabe showed the wooden block to his oldest brother, Zachary, I knew this was one of life's Big Deals.

As Zachary tenderly stroked the rectangle of wood, a faraway look came to his eyes.

"Gabe," he said wistfully, "you are in for the most special time of your life. I remember my first pinewood derby. Dad and I spent hours together sawing and sanding and painting my car. And I had the fastest car at the race. It was one of the best days of my life. Grandma even still has Daddy and Uncle Kent's first pinewood derbys from when they were little boys. It's the ultimate father/son experience." (Yes, my fifteen-year-old really talks this way at times. Even though he makes rude noises and standard fifteen-year-old obnoxious comments, he can also be surprisingly sentimental and eloquent.)

When Scott came home from work that evening, Gabe solemnly walked up to him. He was holding the piece of pine with both hands as if it were the Holy Grail and laid it in Scott's outstretched arms. I watched in fascination as Scott's eyes misted over. "Ah, Gabriel, my son. We have a race for which to prepare, do we not?"

For the next ten days, every evening was filled with pinewood strategy sessions. I could always tell Gabriel's whereabouts because I could hear the "shissh, shissh, shissh" of sandpaper smoothing the car to perfection. A shiny coat of black paint, a red pinstripe, and a fire motif completed the hot rod of pine. After drilling a few strategically placed holes and filling them with buckshot, the father/son drivers were ready.

On race day, Scott and Gabe dashed off early to get some graphite for the wheels. The rest of us—Zach, Zeke, Rachel, and I—joined them a little later.

When we walked into the rented fire station hall, I saw thirty little boys lining the walls, each holding a homemade hot rod in their sweaty little palms. Behind each Cub Scout was a father holding his son's shoulders with his sweaty big palms. The dads were all trying—with some difficulty—to look especially casual and nonchalant. But I knew, as did every other Cub's mother, that this was not only a testing ground for little boys' cars. The men were on trial for their fatherly racing know-how, intelligence, and influence. Successful Dadhood was on the line.

Gabe started out with supreme confidence. Even after his spiffy looking car lost the first race. Even after he lost the second race. But by the time he lost the fifth and sixth races, it was obvious that our little Cub was the owner of the Slowest Pine in the Woods. He was not only feeling insecure, he was also in the bathroom in tears. By that time, Mother Lioness was swallowing lumps in her throat. And Father Lion had joined his son in the bathroom. After comforting his Cub, Scott dried Gabe's tears and managed to get him back out on the race floor to help root for his teammates still left in the running.

Two hours later, we were back home and Gabe had recovered. As a matter of fact, a buddy came home with him and they were happily racing and comparing their cars in the back room. But my husband sat quietly on the kitchen bar stool, slumped over the counter, gazing blankly at the rain drizzling down the windowpane.

I handed him a warm cup of coffee and slid silently onto the stool next to him. He looked up at me with basset hound eyes, insecurity seeping from every pore.

"I lost the race," he said brokenly.

"Oh, Honey," I consoled, "you and Gabe had the *coolest* car."

"We lost the race. I let my son down."

"But your car *looked* the fastest."

"We lost *all* the races, Becky. Not just one or two of them. We lost *all* the races."

"I'm so sorry, Scott. What can I do to help?"

He stuck out his bottom lip. "Well," he sighed, "could I just have a hug?"

I was happy to oblige.

"Do you feel better now?" I asked as I gently pulled away.

"Well, yeah," Scott nodded, still looking pitiful. "But . . . um . . . I might need a kiss too."

"Oh," I smiled, kissing his forehead. "And is there anything else I can do for you?"

He was pouring it on thick now. Make-believe sniffs. Big exaggerated frown. But his hands massaging my back betrayed his sad performance. Father Lion was feeling his masculinity coming back again—and what was a lioness to do but respond to him in his hour of need.

When nobody comes to our party or we lose the Big Race, we need to be held—we need some refuge. From our experience, may I offer this helpful "freebie" tip? A tad of pitiful insecurity at just the right moment, and played in just the right way, could work to your advantage. Never forget that famous quote by that immortally insecure woman: "A man's security is directly proportionate to his ability to admit his insecurities."

What woman can resist a pitiful, playful, insecure, secure man with a touch of little boy-cub in him?

For You have been a strength . . . to the needy in his distress, a refuge from the storm, a shade from the heat.

ISAIAH 25:4, NKJV

∾

Look, I never promised you a thornless rose garden

(Or did I? I can't seem to remember . . .)

Am I losing my mind? Or does every mother of four seriously think she is getting Alzheimer's? This afternoon I received two phone calls that left me worried about myself again.

One was from Colyer, the competent publicist at Broadman, calling about an interview for the month of April. "This will be just before you leave for Phoenix, right?" Colyer asked.

"Right. Sure . . . Phoenix?" *Phoenix, Arizona?*

"Yes, I believe you've been booked for nearly a year to speak there."

"Oh, I see the problem," I explained. "I probably wrote the info down somewhere before I got this year's calendar. There were only a couple of things I needed to remember to put on the new calendar, so I'm sure I stuck them somewhere in the back of the old calendar and just threw it away when I tossed away the old year. Don't you think?"

Colyer was unruffled, as always. "Becky, I can always tell people that you really are the person you come across to be in your books," she said.

A few hours later, a lady named Ann called. All the time we were exchanging chitchat I was thinking to myself, *Ann . . . Ann. . . who is Ann?*

"I just thought I'd better call to make sure everything's on for next Thursday," Ann was saying.

"Yes," I stalled, "that's always a good idea. Can't be too careful." I cleared my throat and ventured, "Now, what is it that we have *'on'* for next Thursday?"

"You are speaking to our Garden Club."

"I am?"

"Yes, we've had you booked since last fall."

"Oh, well, *there's* the problem. You see, I threw away last year's calendar and I didn't have a "this year's" calendar last year, so the problem is that I didn't write it down on something I haven't thrown away yet. Does that make sense?"

She said she would understand as long as I showed up at the Garden Club next week with something witty and wonderful to say that would take up at least thirty minutes of the meeting.

Now my head is spinning because I'm overwhelmed. I'm already behind this week on my writing, and my deadline's looming large on the horizon. Why am I behind schedule? I had to go out to lunch with two sets of friends two days in a row because I believe in keeping relationships in good repair. And then, of course, this morning Zeke had a toothache, so I had to take him to the dentist, and on the way home we saw a used Blazer for sale. Since Zeke is totally embarrassed by the fact that I'm the only mother in the world who drives a Buick station wagon, we had to go for a quick test drive. I really liked that zippy little Blazer. Since it was eight years old I thought I could squeeze it into my budget. As soon as I got home I had to call the bankers and check interest rates on a used-car loan.

By the time I'd finished chatting with the bankers about the book I'm behind on writing, I'd lost so much actual writing time that I ended up negotiating one of those Desperate

Mother bargains with Zeke. If he would promise to clean the kitchen so I could catch up on the manuscript, I'd let him stay home from school the rest of the afternoon. He snapped up the offer. Just as I was about to settle down in front of the computer and get down to some serious business, the phone rang again. This time it was Zachary calling from the high school nurse's office.

"Mom, could you come get me? My stomach hurts and my head aches."

This time I turned into Selfish Corporate-Sounding Mother.

"Zachary, this is not a good time for me. Can we please reschedule this? Let's see, I have an opening for a kid with cold and flu symptoms next Tuesday. How would that work for you?"

"No, Mom! I'm doubled up with cramps."

"How doubled up? Are you just bending-over-slightly-and-whining doubled up or curled-up-in-a-ball-and-moaning doubled up?"

"Mom, I'm dying here! I'm lying in the nurse's office, writhing in agony on the floor!"

"Yes, I know, Son. But I'm really behind on my writing, and I've just been reminded of the fact that I have to go to Phoenix—you know, the one in Arizona—and now I've got to come up with a little talk for a Garden Club I also forgot about and—hey, guess what?—I'm in the middle of buying a car all by myself without even your daddy helping me. So, if there is any chance you are faking this sickness at all, I think it would be a very good idea for you to confess now."

"Mom, I'm going to call 1-800-CHILD-NEGLECT if you don't come get me right this minute!"

"Okay, but you'd better look really green around the gills when I get there," I said, dropping the phone in its cradle.

As long as I wasn't going to be winning any Mother of the Year awards anyway, I threw caution to the wind tonight and called in all favors from my husband with whom I've had a two-day "spat" a-brewing.

"Oh, dear, forgiving husband," I said sweetly over the phone, "It seems as though I've gotten myself in a wee bit of a bind today, and I thought I should just call you and let you know my head is about to burst from the stress. Is there any chance that you might come home early and take three healthy children and one slightly green teenager to the movies tonight?"

"OK," he agreed, "but you owe me one. Hey, wait a m-inute—I thought we were fighting."

"We are. But this just shows you what a desperate woman I am. Look, in a couple of days when we make up for all the things you did wrong, I'll be really, really nice about it. I'll never forget this favor—ever—if you will remind me. But you might want to write it down on my 'this-year's' calendar, just in case."

Bless him. My husband is, at this very minute, hauling our kids to see *Little Women*—a movie I'm sure all he-man types have been dying to see for some time now. Anyway, I'm thankful. He came, he took, I con-curred. And I now have an entire evening to ponder all the things I've forgotten.

Where *do* the remembering-impaired go for help? This can be a serious condition—with disastrous consequences. I con-fessed the enormity of my problem to a group of friends last week.

"Oh, come on, Becky," they said in cheerful unison, "it's not *that* bad."

They knew me well, but I could see I would have to produce some evidence.

"Look, you guys, I forgot my purse a couple of weeks ago on my way to an appearance on 'Good Morning Texas!' It was my first time to be on "TV" and I was frantic. I had to ask Scott to meet me on the road with my purse at 5:30 A.M."

"Well, that's pretty bad," they agreed, "but we've all done things like that. It's not as if you've ever forgotten a *child* or something!"

There followed a deafening silence. All eyes were upon me, waiting for me to join in the chorus of "Yeah . . . at least I've never done anything as horrible as *that!*" Finally, one brave soul asked, "Becky, you never really forgot one of your own *children?*"

"Well . . ." I stammered around for an excuse, "I hadn't had him very long! I'd just given birth to him a few days earlier, and I wasn't used to having four kids yet. I was having problems keeping count with the three I already owned. Anyway, we went to a frozen yogurt place and ordered cones. Zach, Zeke, and Rachel were sitting across from me, their sticky elbows upon the table, happily licking their treats. Out of the blue, three-year-old Rachel had a thought.

"'Hey, Mom, why can't we bring the baby in the store?'

"My eyes flew open, and I jumped from my seat in the yogurt shop to the parking lot in one incredible leap. Thank the Lord, Baby Gaby was safe—and sound asleep."

When the expressions of disbelief died down, I finished the sordid story.

"For months afterwards the kids kept reminding me, 'Remember you have *four* of us, Mom.'"

Now I know that many people, besides myself, have trouble remembering names. Sometimes I will be telling Scott about one of our *own children* and I'll say something like, "You wouldn't believe what—oh, shoot, what's the name of that kid? He's second to the oldest, and it rhymes with 'meek' . . . yes, thank you . . . you're right, it's Zeke. Well, you wouldn't believe what Zeke said the other day . . ."

Yesterday I suffered a most embarrassing moment. I was having lunch with two friends, Fran and Gracie. I've known these women for nearly two years now and meet with them monthly. Over a cup of coffee, Fran began relating a terrible personal tragedy of gigantic proportions. I was deeply moved and gazed into Fran's eyes with great compassion.

"Oh, *Gracie,*" I sighed. "I'm so sorry."

Gracie, sitting across from me, observed all this and gently said, "Becky, honey, I'm sure you *are* deeply sorry. But *I'm* Gracie—that's *Fran* you're talking to there."

At that point, all three of us laid our heads down on the table and laughed 'til we nearly cried. It just goes to show you that critically forgetful people are still capable of bringing joy to others—in their own way.

As I contemplate all the things I've forgotten, it is amazing I've ever been able to accomplish anything. Writing with Mother was always disconcerting because I kept forgetting where I put our latest chapters. Interviews have been another challenge. Early one morning last fall, the phone rang and I reached over to answer it. A deep voice on the other end was making an announcement: "And here, on the air with me today is one of the authors of *Worms in My Tea*—Becky Freeman! Well, Becky, how *are* you this morning?"

"Um . . . actually . . . I'm a little fuzzy . . . ," I managed as I worked to clear the morning frogs out of my throat. Yes, I'd forgotten the radio interview.

I've whispered quiet thanks time and again for the fact that my books have played up the fact that I am absentminded—it's considered a humorous device. That way, the mistakes and flub-ups I continue to make in the public eye are all a part of the character. It's a pretty good arrangement. What if I had written a how-to-be-together-like-me book?

Maybe my "forgetfulness issue" is simply destined to be a permanent thorn in my side. Right now, in some movie theater with four kids spilling popcorn all over him, Scott probably sees my little problems as a thorn in his side, too. But herein lies another lesson in marriage.

(Now all I have to do is remember what it is.)

Oh, yes—the lesson is that when we marry someone, our "thorny problems" also affect them. To me, a true "thorn" is a fault with which one seems to be permanently afflicted—no matter how many organizers one buys and promptly loses. But I must admit it does seem a shame that my innocent bystander spouse is often "stuck," if you will, with the fallout from my prickly thorns.

However, I've noticed something. It seems to me that most wise, old, happily married couples have resigned themselves to accepting a few of each other's sticky habits and personality traits. Either they've accepted the "thorns," or they've decided to downplay their seriousness in light of their loved one's other more rosy qualities.

I will probably always battle my "thorn of forgetfulness" to some extent, no matter how hard I work to compensate. And Scott will always battle a few of his thorny old faults too—though I can't seem to recall exactly what they are right now. See—there is a positive side to forgetfulness.

Oh, wait. I just remembered one of his faults. He crunches and slurps his cereal in a most irritating way. I've instructed him time and time again about correct cereal-eating etiquette, but—to no avail. I thought about not allowing him to eat a bowl of cereal again, but then I decided I would just have to deal with it. So when he gets out the box of cereal, I go take a bath and turn the water on "high" so I can't hear the "crunch, crunch, slurp—crunch, crunch, slurp."

My concluding advice? Stop and smell the roses whenever you can 'cause, honey, you're gonna need to remember how pretty they were and how good they smelled when you come across each other's thorns.

And when I forget my own advice, somebody please feel free to remind me.

"Can a woman forget her nursing child . . . ? Surely they may forget, yet I will not forget you. See, I have inscribed you on the palms of My hands."

ISAIAH 49:15–16, NKJV

I still "have it"

Can we talk? We've hung around together for several pages now. I think we can be honest with each other. I have a rather personal question: Does anyone else out there ever wonder whether or not you still "have it"? Not, of course, that you'd ever want to *use* it. But let's suppose something happened to your better half, and after a few years of grieving and loneliness, you absolutely had no choice but to go out there and reel in another mate—do you think you'd still have what it takes to get him on board?

In our heart of hearts, I think most married folk secretly ask themselves this question on occasion—especially when our own marriages seem lackluster. It often seems to surface when we reach our mid-thirties or early forties—the classic "mid-life" syndrome, I suppose. Well, I've reached my mid-thirties and, just for the record, it's nice to know—I mean I am absolutely *certain*—that I still "have it." I could still snatch another male in record time if I should find myself suddenly alone. The only problem is that my "catch of the day" would be over the age of seventy. With this select population of men, I am a hands-down winner.

In all fairness, I probably owe my ability to attract men-living-on-social-security-and-creamed-spinach to my mother. Her affinity for cafeterias has been well documented, but did I ever mention the fact that she had a "boyfriend" in every Luby's cafeteria? And she's been none too discreet about it either. I remember one conversation in particular between my parents.

"George," Mother began, trying not to look pleased, "it happened again. At the cafeteria. A nice, older gentlemen just couldn't keep his eyes off me. Then he followed me to the cash register and asked me if I was married."

"Ruthie, Ruthie, Ruthie. If I've told you once, I've told you a hundred times—quit batting your eyelashes at the senior citizens."

"I know George, I just can't help smiling at these men. They look so—lonesome. I think what they really like about me is my hair. Not many women wear their hair long and in a bun anymore. I probably remind them of their mothers. Yes, I think that's it. They like my bun."

Daddy slowly lowered his newspaper and raised his eye-brows. "Without a doubt," he agreed.

Even when they moved 1,500 miles away to Virginia, it only took my mom about two weeks to find a new, aged admirer at the local cafeteria. It was uncanny.

Now I'm the same age my mother was when she began giving old men heart palpitations as she floated by, and I'm discovering I am my mother's daughter for sure. For I, too, am now attracting elderly men at every turn. I don't think it is my hair, either—for though it is long, it isn't bunned.

I just know I have it with these old guys, but what exactly is this mysterious "it"? I'd like to think that it is my friendly smile or my rather "voluptuous" figure. (I've heard that many men from previous generations preferred their woman with a little more meat on their bones. Ah, the good old days.) Yet there is something about this that worries me. These graying men may think they are going to have to lower their standards of perfection if they—at their age—are going to catch the eye of a younger woman. So what if, when I walk by, they are actually thinking something like, "Now there goes a little chickadee even *I*, at age ninety-seven with no teeth, might have a chance with. I doubt she could do any better considering her mid-thirties condition and all."

I think I'll just not worry about it. When a woman gets to be my age and is trying to make peace with her own older, wider, more wrinkled "body model," she takes all compliments at face value. A compliment is a compliment, and I need all I can gather at this stage of the game.

Now I haven't frequented cafeterias quite as often as Mother, so for me this phenomena started with older fellows who worked behind counters. I'd be friendly to them as they counted out change, and before I knew it they were hooked. If I didn't come into the store for a week, they'd act crushed—as if I weren't showing enough interest in our relationship. Running in for milk and bread or a roll of duct tape became complicated.

Away from home, I ran into similar problems. On a late night trip home from Houston, Scott stopped at a burger place so I could run in, get a cup of coffee, and go to the restroom. I was wearing a peasant blouse and a Mexican-style skirt, but keep in mind that I had also been asleep in the car up until that point. This meant I had smeared my eyeliner, drooled off my lipstick, and my hair was packed into a large, flat pancake shape.

But as I walked in, I noticed immediately that there was an older gentleman working behind the counter. He looked to be in his mid-eighties. I ordered a cup of coffee, trying to cover my morning breath as I gave him my order. He asked me if I knew what an attractive woman I was. (I checked his eyes for signs of cataracts.) After an interesting parley, he finally handed me my coffee—with plenty of cream and sugar, if-you-know-what-I-mean.

As I turned to leave, the charmer asked me where I was going. I told him my family was waiting in the car. He gave me an exaggerated "don't leave me now" look before signing off with a wrinkled wink. I hated to snag his heart like that and then leave town, but when you've got it, you've got it. And in situations like this, what's a woman with a lot of "it" to do?

As exciting as my over-the-counter encounters have been, they've been nothing compared to the delightful conversations I've had with elderly men in bookstores. First of all, I should explain that my idea of paradise would be to be snowed in for a week in one of those huge bookstores that serve gourmet coffee and cheesecake. If I have a free afternoon in the big city, you can find me browsing through aisles with an armload of books and a silly grin on my face. And often, I end up running into elderly men who seem to be browsing for a younger woman with an armload of books and a silly grin on her face.

My favorite encounter was with an elegant, white-haired, bearded gentleman. He was slim, tall, and impeccably dressed—starched white shirt, plaid suspenders, red silk tie, and tweed dress slacks—like a distinguished old professor out of an English novel. As I was scanning the "relationship" section of the store, the elderly man approached with twinkling eyes and a charming smile. He was holding a piece of paper tightly in his hands. He looked from me to the paper to the shelves and back to me again before finally gathering the courage to clear his throat. As I glanced in his direction he made a slight bow and ventured, "Excuse me, madam, but do you think these books are listed by the title or by the author?"

I was pretty sure he knew the answer to the question, but I replied in my most sweetest and most helpful tone, "I believe they are listed by author."

"Oh . . . well that won't help me much . . . I only have the title here with me."

He held out a slip of paper for me to read. The book he was looking for was called something like *Say It Right the First Time.* I was curious. I hadn't imagined, at his age, that communication would be a problem. I was intrigued by his desire to improve himself. Then I remembered his dilemma.

"Sir, if you tell the lady at the front desk the name of the book, she can look up the author and location for you on her computer."

"Oh," he stammered, obviously not in any hurry to head toward the front desk, "You've been most helpful . . . most kind. Um . . . my name is Manning. May I ask yours?" As he extended his hand, I put mine out for a shake, which turned out to be more of a gentle squeeze. I thought for a moment he might bring my fingers to his lips for a kiss. Blinking myself back to the question at hand, I answered:

"I'm Becky." (I was careful not to give him my last name in case he fell hopelessly in love with me and might try to look me up later. I learned all about Stranger Safety when I taught first grade.)

"Well, Ms. Becky, tell me what book you are looking for so I may return the favor and help you." *(So he did know his way around the store—just as I thought!)*

"Well, actually, I'm doing some research for a book I'm writing on marriage."

"Oh, my! You mean to tell me you're an author! How lovely! And I must say, I've always been *fascinated* by the male/female relationship."

"Is that so?" I asked, flattered by his enthusiastic response.

"Oh, yes. I've taught anthropology and have studied the primates for years—I've especially enjoyed comparing their mating habits to those of Homo sapiens. You know, in the wild, female gorillas always seek out the strongest, most handsome male. Several females, one powerful male. Stimulus, response. Same thing with people, you know."

Hmmm. I wonder if this old fellow fancies himself Top Gorilla, I thought to myself.

"Well, yes," I answered, wondering all the while what in the world I was doing discussing the mating habits of gorillas with an elegant old chap in the middle of a bookstore. However, ending up in odd places is a pattern with me, so I plunged on.

"Manning, I have to take issue with you on one point. I believe there is something that makes human beings uniquely different from the animal world. For humans, between stimulus and response, I believe there is *choice*."

Manning smiled and said, "Interesting theory. You've obviously given this some thought. Tell me now, what advice would you give a babbling old man on how to grow up?"

"I think I'd tell him, 'Don't be in too much of a hurry.'"

"I like that. I've always said it is important to have a childlike, downright *indecent* curiosity about life. I find the world a fascinating place in which to live, full of fascinating people—like you, for instance."

I wisely avoided asking him what other "indecent things" he might be curious about and steered our discussion in the direction of home and family. He had lived in France, England, Wales, and Scotland. I should see the marvelous libraries of Europe someday, he said. I found out he was married—for twenty-four years, in fact. "That's a pretty long marriage," I commented, hoping to gather some encouraging advice for this book, perhaps. It was not to be. "Yes," he answered, "Unfortunately the first one lasted even longer than this one."

After a few more minutes of conversation, I glanced at my watch. Manning's face fell, and I felt sorry for hurting his feelings with my "I'm-in-a-hurry" gesture. But he spoke softly, allowing me a graceful exit.

"I see that you are thinking about taking your leave. But I must tell you, Ms. Becky, I'm truly sorry to have this conversation come to an end. It has been positively marvelous making your acquaintance." After shaking hands good-bye, I walked out the door, smiling to myself.

It surprised me to find my heart fluttering like a school girl—if only for a split second. Not only did I still have it, but this seventy-plus man *absolutely* still had it. Charm is charm at any age. Flattery works wonders, transcending generations. If I were his wife, I don't believe I'd let this debonair bookworm wander unaccompanied down aisles of large bookstores.

Scott has never begrudged me my gentlemen admirers. The way I see it, Scott is actually a very lucky man. He can rest assured that no matter how old he gets, or how senile he becomes, he will always be Top Gorilla as far as I'm concerned. How do I know? He's got charm, and he's got his following of cute little old lady admirers. If this mutual admiration of senior citizens holds steady, the older we become, the more attractive we will be to one another. We've got a lot to look forward to in our Golden Years, and I'm ever so glad we're headed that way together.

> *They shall still bear fruit in old age;*
> *They shall be fresh and flourishing.*
>
> PSALM 92:14, NKJV

cv

A little slapstick livens up dull days

Just when I think my life is growing dull and I'm running out of material, something seems to fall in my lap from out of nowhere.

It's a laid-back Sunday evening. Or at least it was. The family seemed content and all of them looked happily occupied. Some were sprawled on the living room couch watching a movie, one was soaking in the bathtub, another reading a book. So I thought I'd sneak off for a few minutes to work on this manuscript.

Suddenly, the body of a large man fell against the door, knocking it open as he collapsed at my feet. I recognized him as my husband. He had contracted into a fetal position, holding both legs against his chest. As I helped him to the couch, he winced, and through his clinched teeth I understood him to say, "You'll never believe what I did."

"Oh? What makes you think I wouldn't believe it, Baby?"

I cautiously untied his shoes and helped him out of his jeans. At this point he began to see the humor in the situation. He was laughing and moaning at the same time. I could see a large scratch across one thigh—and whatever it was that had given him the scratch had also torn through his jeans in the process. On the other leg, a large goose egg was already beginning to swell on his right kneecap. It hurt to look at it. I ran into the kitchen for ice and asked Zeke to help me move his dad into the living room, where I gave him a couple of pills for his pain.

Once we were able to assess my husband's wounds and had determined nothing was broken, I asked for details. "So would you like to talk about it now?"

"Well, it's really embarrassing," he said.

I thought of all the dangerous situations my husband had put himself into as he worked on our house every weekend—wiring high-voltage electrical circuits, lifting heavy beams, operating circular saws from lofty perches, and of course, hanging from the rafters by one hand with a caulk gun in the other. I thought to myself, *Nothing my husband did to injure himself would surprise me.*

I was wrong.

"Come on, Scott," I probed, "I promise I won't yell at you. What did you do this time? Were you trying to move that table saw without asking for help? Did you fall between the beams? Did the truck trailer collapse on you? What?"

He grinned sheepishly. "Remember that metal workbench I moved from the neighbor's house to our backyard today? Let's just say that while I was running around in the dark, I found it."

"Should I ask *why* you were running outside in the dark?"

"Maybe that wouldn't be such a good idea."

"Come on, I can't stand the suspense. Tell me."

"Well, you know how our septic system has been overloaded with all the rain we've been having? So, I thought I'd be frugal and go outside behind a tree in the dark and . . . well, you know. I'd just finished two large glasses of iced tea, so I guess I was in a hurry to get to the woods. That's when I ran into the workbench and turned a flip into the night air."

So collapsed was I with laughter that I laid my head on Scott's shoulder and wiped the tears away. He was in the same condition, though every time he laughed it also brought on a moan.

"So, Scott," I gasped, "what you are trying to tell me is that you nearly broke both legs trying to . . . "

"Yes. Are you satisfied now?"

"Yes. I am. I really am. Scott?"

"What?"

"Can I use this?"

"What do you mean?"

"Can I write about it?"

"Becky, you're like a vulture circling weakened prey. Every time anybody does anything stupid, there you are, like Lois Lane, with her pad and pencil. Am I nothing but *material* to you?" But even as he said it he was laughing, so I felt pretty sure I was close to getting the go-ahead.

"Oh, Scott, you know I love you with all my heart and I am so sorry you are in pain. But how could you question my motives? Didn't I just give you my very own pain medication a few minutes ago?"

"What pain medication? I thought you gave me some Tylenol."

"Well, we're out of Tylenol. So I gave you some of my Midol PMS multi-symptom relief pills."

"What??? You gave me *girl* pills!?"

"See how cranky you are? You needed those pills. You'll feel much better in a few minutes."

"What do those things do?"

"Well, they keep you from fussing at those who love you."

"Is that so? And how?"

"They make you go to sleep and render you incapable of communication."

"Hmmm . . . Well, I *am* feeling kind of drowsy." His eyelids began to droop.

I waited a few more minutes before I spoke again.

"So it's okay with you, Honey, after you drift off to sleep and everything, if I go back out to my office and write about this?"

"Um . . . what? . . . I 'm so tired . . . whatev . . . "

"I'll take that as a 'yes,'" I said, and dashed for the computer.

As deadlines approach I find myself sounding more and more like an ambulance chaser, but I just can't help myself. As long as bad things happen, we might as well make the best of them and put it to good use. Right? Grist for the mill and all?

It's now the morning after the "accident." I rolled over in bed about 6:30 A.M. and woke my husband from his peaceful slumber by seductively wrapping my leg around his swollen knee. Honestly—I forgot! Once he stopped shrieking, he managed to get dressed for work. As he hobbled around in his pitiful condition, I asked him, "So, Scott, what are you going to tell the gals at work this morning about how you got your limp?"

"I'll say it was a skiing accident. Or maybe I got sideswiped by a truck. Which story do you think sounds more manly? "

"Well, don't worry," I answered, batting my eyelashes, "your little secret is safe with me."

"Suuure it is. I'll proofread the chapter tonight."

I love a man with a limp and a great sense of humor. One who doesn't take himself too seriously. One who is generous with potential humorous material. And who thinks I am witty too. As they say, "If you don't have a good sense of humor, get one."

I couldn't agree more. We could never have survived without the gifts laughter brings to our relationship. It is a diffuser, a stress-reliever, and a unifier.

Not long ago, Scott and I were lying in bed watching a scene from a romantic comedy. We both got so tickled we had to hang on to each other to keep from falling off the bed. We hadn't laughed that hard in months—it was one of those front-teeth-sticking-out, tear-wiping, side-aching sort of laughing spells. It felt especially good to be sharing it together.

Elizabeth Cody Newenhuyse, one of my all-time favorite writers, interviewed several couples for her book *Strong Marriages, Secret Questions*. She concluded, "The healthiest couples I interviewed were those who punctuated their remarks with wisecracks, understood each other's humor and frequently dissolved into laughter. Because life is funny . . . . It is also a powerful, and underrated, bonding agent."[1]

Life *is* funny. And unbelievably, it is getting even funnier at my poor husband's expense. It is now the *day after* "The Day after the Accident." A few hours ago, as I was putting my makeup on in the bathroom, the body of a large man fell against the bathroom door, knocking it open as he fell to the floor. Guess who? Same song, second verse. He was once again holding his knee and curled up in the fetal position.

"Oh, Scott," I said as I helped him sit up. "What have you done now?"

"Well, it's embarrassing," he moaned, gingerly examining his wound.

"It's broad daylight, please tell me you weren't looking for a tree . . . "

"No, no, no. It wasn't that bad. This time, I just whacked my leg with a two-by-four."

"Hold on a second, don't say another word. You hop in the tub and soak your knee while I run get a pad and pencil."

I was back in a flash.

"OK, Scott. Now tell me again what happened, and don't leave out any details."

"Well, there's not much to tell, really. I was trying to get the porch post aligned, so I picked up a two-by-four and gave the post a few hard whacks. Only on one of the back swings I whacked my sore leg."

My husband seems to be stuck in a painful slapstick comedy routine. And here he was, *literally*, slapping himself with a stick.

I am truly sorry he's in pain, but you have to admit, he's been entertaining.

Somedays it's really a lot of fun to be married.

*I delight in weaknesses, in insults, in persecutions,
in difficulties.*

2 CORINTHIANS 12:10

Love me tender
and get away with just about
anything

Men should know that women sometimes get together and play a game called "Let's Compare Husbands." It's a lot like poker. And, as with face cards, not all hubbys' personality traits have equal value. According to the rule book, having the correct combinations is also important. I've played a few rounds myself and have had some pretty stiff competition, but usually I'm assured of having at least one ace in the hole. This is the way it goes.

"All right, girls," Player Number One says, "I'm holding a man who picks up his own socks and knows how to whip up a box of macaroni and cheese by himself."

"Wow," replies Player Number Two. "That's going to be a hard pair to beat. But I'll raise you. My husband can unstop a backed-up commode and doesn't mind changing the cat box."

"Oh, you're kidding!" says Three. "You've got a man with a strong stomach? All I've got is a regular paycheck coming in, a great father to the kids, and no snoring at night."

"Well, ladies," I say as I lay down my cards with a flourish. "Read 'em and weep. I've got a husband who's stubborn, knows how to say just the wrong thing at just the wrong time, and has the patience of a gnat. But when he's good, he's very, very good. He is tender. He is playful. And girls, I'm sorry to have to tell you this, but—he's also Romantic with a capital R."

"Oh, pooh!" the rest agree. "Becky wins again. It's not fair when she's always holding the King of Hearts."

I may be *slightly* overstating the case, but I haven't yet met a woman who wouldn't trade neatness and steadiness for a man who enjoys candlelight dinners, interesting conversations, and romantic waltzes.

I know there are many men out there who think Romantic equals Softness which, in turn, equals Big Sissy. Most of these men, unfortunately, are dateless, divorced, or sleeping on the couch. Take it from me, the surest way to a woman's heart is the most direct route—go straight for the heart.

Scott's natural ability to bring out the heart—the real depth—in people is one of the most attractive and, I think, romantic of his qualities. As hard as it is for us to control our tempers when things get out of hand, there is no way we can break off this relationship. There are too many topics we still haven't discussed into the ground.

Not long ago, our oldest son Zachary looked at me very seriously and said, "Mom, Dad is deeper than anybody I know. He's, like, deeper than the deepest well."

And Zeke, our second born, is so much like Scott it is almost spooky. Both of them have rather soft voices and a slightly hesitant way of speaking, but don't let that fool you. Not long ago, Zeke and I were talking in the kitchen. He was perched on a bar stool and I was actually *cooking*.

"Mom," he said in his newly husky voice, "I have all these deep, meaningful thoughts. But it is hard for me to say them. I don't have a way with words like you and Zachary. But I have all these really important thoughts." He paused for a second and then added softly, "Dad understands."

Both our boys have told me they love the way their father treats them—like real people with profound minds and interesting ideas, not like dumb little kids. A man who can make *teenage boys* feel significant and intelligent and respected as individuals has a gift.

Then there is music. A woman can tell a world about a man simply by finding out what sort of music he likes and how he responds to it. When it comes to music, Scott's affinity for soulful romance is off the charts. Listen to "When a Man Loves a Woman" and you've got my husband pegged. He's the type of man who will turn up a sexy song on the radio in his truck (parked in our driveway) and come running into the house to pull me outside so we can dance together under the stars. Especially if there is a full moon. The same is true for me. I've pulled Scott out from under a car where he was working just to two-step to a love song in broad daylight—even while he was covered with grease.

Little hard to hold on to him, but we manage.

When I think of romance and tenderness in our relationship, I also think of the countless little things that add to our love. The way we fit together when we lie in each others' arms at night. We call it "spooning." Then there is the way we sometimes talk to each other like little kids just because it's fun. When Scott completes a special project on the house, he might come take my hand and in a boyish voice urge, "Come see my big roof!" After being out on the lake, he might come up to the back porch and holler, "Hey, Miss Peeky! Come see my big fish!"

There's something else I find romantic about my man. I know, down deep, my husband believes in me, and he would fight to the death to defend my honor. He's been tested a time or two, as a matter of fact, and no woman could ask for a more gallant hero. He is, and has always been, my best fan. When I sang for him the first time, he loved it.

"It's a gift from God, Becky," he coached. "Let 'er rip!" Ditto for my early attempts at writing and speaking.

And I must ask, how many men would allow their wives to write and speak about their personal, private lives—letting her poke fun at their crazy relationship for all the world to see? A secure man. A good sport. A man who trusts me to write with openness and humor, without guile.

As a matter of fact, he graciously reads my work while allowing me to stare at him, taking note of every twitch, every minuscule response. By some miracle, he is able to completely tune out the fact that my face is five inches away from his. He just pencils his critique as if I am invisible. Then he always tells me the truth—where the manuscript made him want to laugh, where it touched him, where he had no idea what on earth I was trying to say. One of his most common markings is R. T.—for rabbit trail. He thinks I tend to wander off the beaten path too often and forget where I'm headed. Once the writing project is a wrap, I can always count on one thing: He will be prouder of me than any other human being on the face of the earth.

I like this man. Very much.

I like the perpetual conversation we have going. I like the little nuances of familiarity—baby talk, pet names, pet phrases. The mutual fan club. The meals we've shared—from greasy cafes to candlelit romantic restaurants. And perhaps, most of all, I've enjoyed the slow dances to beautiful music under the stars.

One of the most tender and touching stories of real-life married romance I've read is Madeleine L'Engle's book *Two-Part Invention: The Story of a Marriage.*

It is good, I think, for young couples to read and hear the stories of other long and romantic marriages. It puts a larger perspective on minor irritants we struggle with every day.

Ms. L'Engle is the famed Newberry Award winning author of *A Wrinkle in Time.* She was married to Hugh Franklin, whom some of you may remember as the handsome and distinguished actor who played Dr. Charles Tyler on the television show "All

My Children" for years. After forty years of a loving, intimate marriage, Hugh developed a terminal form of cancer. A lump still forms in my throat when I read Madeleine's account of holding her dying husband to her breast in his hospital bed as he took his last breath. She was unable for several moments to release her embrace. Then she turned to the doctor and spoke at last.

"It is hard to let go beloved flesh," she said.

Madeleine closes her autobiography with a beautiful line from a poem by Conrad Aiken, a poem Hugh had read to her some forty years earlier on the night he proposed marriage:

Music I heard with you was more than music, and bread I broke with you was more than bread.[1]

I cannot read those words without thinking of Scott, and I cannot think long on them without tears coming to my eyes. For one day I, too, may have to "let go beloved flesh." And when I do, it will be my husband's tender, romantic presence that I will surely miss the most. The presence that can make even everyday "bread and music" extraordinary.

"My beloved is . . . outstanding among ten thousand. His mouth is full of sweetness. And he is wholly desirable. This is my beloved and this, my friend.

SONG OF SOLOMON 5:10, 16, NASB

∾

I know you love me,
but do you *like* me?

I remember having a conversation with my mother when I was in my early teens. We were discussing one of Mother's friends—let's call her Mona—and the trouble she was having with her daughter—let's call her Jessie—who happened to be growing up into something of a snit, making life miserable for everyone around her.

"I know Mona loves Jessie," Mother sighed, "but sadly, I don't think she's ever really *liked* her very much."

It was the first time it occurred to me that parents, though obligated to love their children, might actually have a child whom they struggle to like. The thought made me uneasy.

"Well, Mother, " I questioned tentatively, "you like me, don't you?"

She laughed and gave me a hug. "I am absolutely crazy about you! You're one of the most fun things in my life, as a matter of fact. I get a kick out of you, Kid."

Whew, was I relieved. The conversation demonstrates, however, the importance of knowing we're not only loved but we're *liked for who we are*. And we human beings never seem to outgrow the need for such affirmation.

Now and again over the years, I've found myself not only asking that question of my mom and other people, but also of God. In truth, I think everyone comes to this point in life, probably many times. Sure, God loves me. The Bible makes that plain. But, does He like me? I mean, does He like *me?* And the answer found to that most basic of human questions colors every other relationship, especially the closest ones. Take the relationship with mates, for example.

If we believe God is just waiting to catch us in a mistake, we are more likely to judge our mates when they blow it. If we think God simply tolerates us, we may resign ourselves to merely "putting up with" our spouses. But if we could only *believe,* really believe, that God actually is delighted with us, that we are His adopted sons and daughters who bring Him joy even in the midst of our imperfections—that He *likes* us—wow! We could be free to really live. We could accept others and see through their faults and love them anyway.

I've been mulling over the whole biblical panorama lately and have asked myself, "Taking the whole lump of Scripture together, what is God's main, number one, heart's desire in it all?" I've come to some serious conclusions. Seriously. I have deep spiritual thoughts, you know, and a longing to understand the big picture. So, can I share with you what I'm "putting back in my box" these days? It has to do with the importance of believing we are liked by God and how that belief affects marriage and other relationships. First of all, I've come to believe that God's Plan A—what He wanted from the beginning—was simple, and somewhat surprising.

In the beginning of it all, God created the heavens and the earth, but His heart—ah, His *heart*—He poured into a plot of ground called Eden. He wasn't coerced into the idea; this was something He *wanted* to do. Then having done such a fine job with creation, He created a man and a woman to walk and talk with Him, companions He could love and *enjoy* in the cool of the day in this setting of astounding beauty. Adam and Eve, in turn, loved and enjoyed Him right back. God not only saw that it was good; He saw it was *very good.* In other words, He not only loved His children; He liked them—had fun with them, if you will. Plan A was, to borrow a popular phrase, the way things ought to be.

All through the Bible, from Genesis through Revelation, it is my belief that God's highest and best is still Plan A. All that happens in between is to get us back to the essence of the original plan, the plan that involved being not only a part of God's creation but His intimate friends. I heard Phillip Yancey, in a recent talk to our writers group, refer to this as "God's passionate pursuit of man." God Almighty, King of the universe, *wants* to be our friend. He not only loves the world; He *likes* having a relationship with us mortals, for some reason. (I still have a hard time comprehending that part, but what a great, wild thought!)

I will admit that *love* is the foundation for relationships, through good times and bad, but *like* is the stuff of joy and fun—and I really want both! As an example, I trust my husband will always love me, and that's great. However, lots of people have relatives they love but don't necessarily like. A friend of mine told me the other day, "Listen, Beck I love my in-laws, but to tell you the truth, it wouldn't hurt my feelings if I never saw them again." Who wants to be loved like that—only long distance?

If I'm honest with myself, what really gives me goose bumps is to feel I am liked by my husband, that he enjoys my company, that I double his pleasure when I am around. Who can resist a person who makes you feel liked? One of the highs of being married, actually, is falling in *like.* One of the highs of being a Christian, actually, is falling in like with God. We have to believe first, however, He wants to be our Friend and enjoys our company.

That's why Jesus came. He is our hope for getting back to Plan A. Interestingly, Jesus amplified the Father's desire for friendship with us. "Greater love has no one than this, that he

lay down his life for his friends . . ." I no longer call you servants,
. . . . Instead, I have called you friends" (John 15:13, 15). Soon
after He spoke those words, He lived them. He walked up a long
dusty road, with a heavy cross full of splinters upon His bleeding
back, and gave His life for me, His friend.

Then early one Sabbath, in the cool of the day, Christ
appeared to Mary, whose poor heart was breaking in two. Mary
didn't recognize Him at first—at least not until He said one
word that made her soul dance again. He simply spoke her
name.

"Mary."

At the sound of her name coming from Her master's lips, she
knew she had found her Friend again. Jesus continued to offer
more tangible proofs that He *wanted* to walk, talk, and sup with
those whose feet are sculpted of clay. The first thing He told
Mary to do was to tell His "brothers" the good news of His
return, not His backstabbing, cowardly, so-called buddies who
betrayed him in less time than it takes a rooster to crow. He
called the disciples His *brothers*—first "servants," then "friends,"
and then "brothers!" The Son joined the Father in the passionate
pursuit of intimacy with man.

The next thing we know, Jesus was on a beach, cooking up
a surprise breakfast for His old fishing buddies. As He called out
the familiar, "Why don't you cast your nets on the other side?"
the scene grew comical, fairly bursting with joy. Peter , hearing
the voice of His Savior and Friend, could hardly jump out of
the boat fast enough, swimming madly toward shore and, I'm
sure, toward a bear hug to end all bear hugs. Later Jesus found
a couple of guys heading to Emmaus and casually joined them
in their walk, chatting about Scriptures, and going home with
them for supper. Note how *human*, how *friendly* were His first
encounters back on earth.

In all this, did He not make it all too clear that He doesn't
want to love us from *afar?* He went out of His way to hang
around a while just to let His friends know that no matter how

they had blown it, He still liked them, enjoyed their company, and accepted them "up close and personal." If any questions remained about God's deep desire to pursue a friendship/love with us, Jesus removed all doubt in the garden of Gethsemene, and finally, in His resurrection.

In his tender and honest book, *Shame and Grace,* Lewis B. Smedes writes, "Grace is seen . . . full face in the story of Jesus. As I read the gospels, I am entranced by the simple and spontaneous way He accepted people heavy laden by their sense of being unacceptable."[1]

I've begun to notice that whenever I'm having the hardest time accepting my husband and kids—when I judge every move they make and become a demanding perfectionist—it's because *I* am drifting away from the simple truth that God accepts me as I am. Subtly, I'd started thinking again of Him as a menacing Being, waiting in the wings to catch me when I mess up. Only when I am filled with the assurance that He not only loves and forgives me but likes me as well—warts and all—do I find myself able to relax and enjoy my fallible self and family.

Malcolm Smith uses a wonderful analogy in his teaching series "Relationships that Last." In paraphrase, he says; "We all have a sucking, gnawing need to be loved and approved of by someone. The problem is, we're all going around like ticks trying to suck blood out of each other, but it can't be done because there's no dog! Human beings will never find their complete sense of love or identity in another human being. We need something other than ourselves—drawing on the love of God until we are immersed in the assurance that we are loved, we are loved, we are loved."

I would add only one postscript: Also we are liked, we are liked, we are *liked.* As hard as it is to believe, by the Creator of the universe. The trickle-down effect of accepting that fact is amazing.

Because people who are filled up—who believe they are loved *and* liked by God—are not only less threatening, they make

much better friends and marriage partners than hungry ol'
nervous ticks.

The Lord *your God is with you, . . . He will take great
delight in you, he will quiet you with his love, he will
rejoice over you with singing.*

Zephaniah 3:17

∾

For all good gifts
around us

Remember "The Cosby Show" episode where Clair, mother of five, finally acquired a room to call her own? She spent the entire day alone in her newly remodeled room, stretching out on the fresh carpet, dancing with abandonment to music coming from her boom box, stopping only once—to order "room service" from her husband. Downstairs the children were dumbfounded. What in the world could Mom be doing up there all by herself? Wasn't she getting bored or lonely? My bet is that every mother smiled when she heard those questions.

What mother of multiple children hasn't dreamed of a room of her own behind a locked door? Something besides the bathroom. And during the preschool years even a chance at privacy in the bathroom is pretty iffy. I have been known to lock myself in the car on a Sunday afternoon, leaving the kids to their daddy, in order to read the newspaper.

But I have come to the end of that. It is over. Finished. Today is a Red Letter Day for me. At this very moment, I am working at a desk in my very own, brand new office. I have already rolled around on the new carpet. And it is as wonderful as I've always dreamed it would be.

So today I want to pause and thank the man who made all this possible: A Craftsman Extraordinaire—my talented husband. He built my beautiful room all by himself. From the fresh white paint, to the natural wood-framed picture window, to the ponderosa pine wainscoting, to the deep green marbled wallpaper with its rosy border, to the plush champagne-colored carpet, to the bright fluorescent lighting above my head. Every nail, every brush stroke, every jot and every tittle was done by my husband.

Actually, this is more than just a Red Letter Day for me. It has been a Red Letter Week. Remember the supercool Blazer that Zeke and I took a spin in? Believe it or not, I found an even cooler, "superer" sport utility truck parked in my driveway this week. A red rose was stuck in the steering wheel.

After Scott peeled me off his neck, he said he thought I'd probably gotten all the humiliating material I could squeeze out of the old panel station wagon, and now he wanted me to ride around town with my head held high when I plow down mailboxes and run into ditches.

I spent the entire next day tearing around country roads, stopping only long enough to phone Scott to ask if he had any long errands he'd like me to run. I told him I basically planned to *live* in my supercool sport utility vehicle for the rest of my life. It is *such* a relief to finally be cool.

And that's not even all the new stuff I got this week. I know it sounds like we must have just hit the jackpot, but, honestly, everything just seemed to come together at one time. It's been like Christmas in February for me.

Anyway, after nearly nineteen years of marriage, I received my first piece of truck-delivered furniture. Last November, I walked into a real furniture store and ordered a couch outright. I even picked out the fabric—a homey, rich, red plaid. But it felt so weird—like I was my mother, or a normal, settled grown-up or something.

All of our furniture has been either Early Marriage (out of some relative's garage) or Wal-mart pressboard and laminate specials—until my couch showed up at the door last week, that is. It's a name brand, too. La-Z-Boy. I love the sound of that. I like telling my friends, "Oh, that piece? Yes, it's new. A La-Z-Boy, don't you know?"

The seats on both ends of my couch actually *recline!* And the cushion in the middle flops down, turning itself into a handy snack table, though I've threatened to flatten any member of my family who dares to eat an actual snack there. There is also a nifty secret drawer where the family can store the remote control, magazines, books, and, more than likely, forbidden snacks they'll be trying to hide when I walk unexpectedly into the room.

I owe special thanks to my husband who could have easily whined about my spending money on a couch when it probably should have gone toward boards and sheetrock and tar paper or some other ugly but expensive things that we really need. You see, the entire family is very much looking forward to the day when we can tear down the walls of our cabin within a house and the six of us gerbils can all expand.

This week has been a remarkable week in the life of the Freemans. After so many years of barely making ends meet, we have realized that for the first time in our marriage we can actually breathe when we balance the income against the outgo. All that we have done without and worked so hard to build is beginning to take shape. We are becoming The Mama and The Papa and looking forward to the days when we will be The Grandma and The Grandpa. When we stand in our yard and gaze up at the house we are building together, and see the lake beyond, and realize the memories we already have of this place—our home—we don't even bother to wipe the tears from our eyes. And how do you thank God for genuine miracles?

And today, on this Red Letter Day of my life, the main thought that keeps running through my mind is, *What if we had quit too soon? Oh God, what if I had missed this?*

Every good and perfect gift is from above, coming down from the Father.

JAMES 1:17

∾

THIRTY-TWO

Real-life vows for Bubba

Well, the latest news around here is that Bubba is fixin' to get hitched. And he's young, so Melissa, his mothering boss, is concerned.

First, I should introduce Melissa. She is a new friend—a gift from God to me in these boonies. She and her husband, Mike, have just moved into our neck of the woods and are operating this cute, country "village market" down the road. Melissa and I laughed the other day at how quickly we've become "kindred spirits and bosom friends." Melissa loves to read, talk about books and relationships, and laugh. She hates housecleaning, loves gourmet coffee and frozen yogurt, and worries about her weight. Not only that, but she and Mike have two charming, funny kids—Joshua and Sarah—who are terrific playmates for my kids. (That's JOSHUA GANTT and SARAH GANTT—who threw mortal fits to have their names in this book. Will that work, guys?) Anyway, Melissa read about me in my first book before we ever met, and she told me she knew right away we would relate. She was right.

But back to Bubba. Melissa is not unsympathetic to Bubba and his fiancée's desires. She and Mike, like Scott and I, met at church as preteens and married as teenagers. But she'd like to give Bubba a more realistic picture of what day-to-day marriage is like when you marry young.

Bubba is eighteen, as cute as cowboys come, and head-over-boots in love. He and his intended plan to be married right after her high-school graduation. Then they would like to go straight from the chapel to Happily Ever After. But Scott and I, and Melissa and Mike—all partakers of early marriage—know all too well that "happily ever after" only happens in fairy tales. "Happily here and there," maybe. Or "More happily than not," perhaps. But nobody, except Cinderella and Sleeping Beauty, gets Happily Ever After every day. So as a favor, Melissa asked me to add a chapter to this book so she can give it to Bubba before he ties the knot. She wanted me to write some *real* wedding vows. In other words, what's the real scoop behind the "I do's"?

So, Bubba, here's my best shot. For convenience's sake, I will use Scott and me as the sample bride and groom in this demonstration.

I, Scott, take thee, Becky, to be my lawfully wedded wife. . .

To have—That is, when you don't have a headache or aren't too tired from chasing kids all day or staying up all night with a baby. Since quantity and quality ebb and flow, I'll try to go with the flow and not whine with the ebb. And I'll try to remember that sometimes the sexiest thing a man can do for a woman is talk to her and listen to what she is trying to say.

And to hold—Even when you come toward me crying like a Water Wiggle gone mad and everything in me screams, "Run fast—in the opposite direction!" Because no matter what is wrong, I know, most of the time, that what you really want and need is to be held.

Being faithful only unto you—This means I will never, ever see or touch any other woman's naked body up close and personal. (Not ever? Whew, this is a toughie.) You will be it for me. The end of the line. But that's OK, because one real woman is all that I'll ever need. And I'll remember that to light your fire I've got to strike the match early in the day with tender touches and romantic talk.

In sickness—I'll do my best to be helpful and sympathetic, even when you have the kind of sickness involving vomiting and other disgusting unmentionables. I'll bring you a cool rag and tell you, "I'm sorry you feel so bad," in a sympathizing tone of voice. Until I get the hang of it, I'll call your mom and ask what I should do with you.

And in health—It may be somewhat of a challenge to stay healthy when you are first learning to cook—and everything is either burnt to a crisp or comes attached to a stick. But I can always run out for a salad. So I'll pretend I love burnt corn dogs and popsicle dinners because I care about your feelings more than food.

For richer—Realistically, we are going to be looking at a ten-to-twenty-year wait on this one—especially if we are going to put each other through college. But it will probably be even more years if at least one of us doesn't get a degree. In the meantime, we can dream together, can't we?

For poorer—This may mean sharing-a-small-cheeseburger-with-no-soft-drink-at-McDonald's poor. It could very well mean Ramen-noodle-soup-for-three-days-in-a-row poor. Perhaps even Salvation-Army-Clothing-Store poor. And we can't run up credit cards or go home crying to Momma and Daddy for more money every time the going gets tough. Together, we'll find a way to make it. But to be honest, we can probably expect to fight a lot about money on the way—especially when things are tight.

In good times—We'll have a lot of these if we can just remember how to play and have fun together after we are "responsible married adults." We'll need to get away for mini-vacations when the stress builds up—even if it is just going for a walk under the stars. And these good times will be so sweet we will forget about the rest of the world and its problems, at least for a while. I'll do my part in keeping it good by looking for the best in you and downplaying your faults. And I'll keep growing and stretching and learning myself because I want to help you do the same.

And in bad—Even when I wake up next to you one morning and you have no make-up on and your thighs look as though they've had hail damage, I will remember it's you I love and not the package outside. And when I think I don't love you any more because all the feeling has disappeared, I won't panic. I'll expect these times will come—and I'll stick it out and do everything it takes to keep us together until the feelings come back again. This includes going for "help" if neither of us knows what to do. (A marriage counselor? OK, for us, I'll do it.)

To love—To tell you "I love you" every single day because women have a very short memory in this category. And to remember that "Gee, you are more beautiful to me now than you've ever been" is equal to at least three "I love you's." Sharing a private joke or a knowing wink across a crowded room may be worth ten "I love you's." And "I'm sorry" and "I forgive you" are equal to at least a hundred.

And to cherish—I'll remember that you need to be treated as a piece of rare china. This means I won't get out of the pickup, walk toward the house, look back to see you still sitting there waiting, and say, "What's the matter, Babe, your arm broken? Can't get the door open?"

From this day forward—That means from now to Eternity. Forever. To commit to something like Eternity I will need supernatural strength. Because no human being can ever fulfill all the needs of my heart, not even you, I will remember I'm always loved by Someone. When you turn your back to me in the night, I will hang in there because I know I'm accepted by a Savior who never fails me. And when I act like a jerk, and I fail at loving you, remember His love will never fail you either. And with the Lord guiding us, there can always be fresh starts.

'Til death do us part—This means the only way I will ever leave you is if one of us dies from sickness or is killed by a tragic accident. Unless one of those two things occurs, we won't separate. I will never walk out and leave you a note telling you to "Get an attorney. It's over." This is the most binding contract we will ever make, and even though we are young, we both know that forever is a really, really long time. Someday we'll get old. And I want to be rocking next to you, holding love-weathered hands. Sweethearts, forever and always.

Well, Bubba, that about sums up what I took an entire book to write—at least from the man's point of view. You are young and in love, and I envy you a little. But not *too* much. Because I *really* like what I have—nearly twenty years after I married my eighteen-year-old groom. Just wait until you're middle-aged and know each other's faults and have weathered some major storms—and are still crazy in love. All I can say is that nothing we have ever worked to keep has been as well worth saving.

"This is it!" Adam exclaimed. "She is part of my own bone and flesh! Her name is 'woman' because she was taken out of a man." This explains why a man leaves his father and mother and is joined to his wife in such a way that the two become one person.

Genesis 2:23–24, TLB

❧

Back to the beach

We are on vacation again, and once again, I've had the exquisite pleasure of two hours alone. Alone, that is, except for my icy cold fruit drink, a gentle ocean breeze, the echo of waves splashing the shore, a pen and notebook, and—this time—the company of my old favorite book, Arthur Gordon's *A Touch of Wonder*. More and more I feel this writer and I are soul mates. I suspect we are both easily reduced to sentimental mush—and I have the feeling there aren't many of us around anymore. At the close of almost every chapter, I find myself inwardly shouting, *"I know! I feel that, too!"*

(By the way, in praise of "mushies," Golda Meir once said, "I have always felt sorry for people afraid of feeling, of sentimentality, who are unable to weep with their whole heart. Because those who do not know how to weep do not know how to laugh either."[1] I think she may be on to something.)

Anyway, I wonder if I might share with you a scene from this Sentimental Journey—this "fall in love with life" book? I'm dying to share it with someone, and the only other living thing nearby is a crab-looking critter preoccupied with catching the first wave out of here.

In the scene, Gordon is standing on a spot where the emerald ocean meets the glistening beach. He is lovingly, achingly watching his daughter—dressed in flowing white, barefoot and carrying a bouquet of sea oats—as she and her intended prepare to say their wedding vows. But before the "Will you's?" and "I do's" and "So be it's," the minister admonishes the young couple to pay careful attention to the laws of love.

"Real love," the minister says, "is caring as much about the welfare and happiness of your marriage partner as about your own. Real love is not total absorption in each other; it is looking outward in the same direction—together."

"All true," the author/father-of-the-bride thinks to himself. But as the seasoned father reflects upon his own marriage, his thoughts take a gut-wrenchingly honest turn.

"But you can't learn it from hearing it. You have to learn it by living it, and even then no one but a saint can apply more than fragments of it to his own marriage or his own life. All we can do, even the best of us, is try. And even then, the trying is hard."[2]

I read those words, and as I look out over the top of my tucked-up knees, I notice the seascape has already changed since last I glanced up. The sun has busied itself painting ripe nectarine strokes across the dunes. A white spray of gossiping seagulls vie for prey at ocean's edge, and a huge ship has lumbered into view. But as always, the waves are still lapping up the sand in their timeless rhythmic dance. The steady beat, the in and out of the tide, makes me think of the twenty years I've known the man who is my husband—years filled with reaching-outs, loving words, and tender touches.

"You have to learn it by living it."

Years full of failed attempts to communicate and clashes of anger, coupled with the eventual, inevitable determination to pick up the pieces and try again.

"And even then, the trying is hard."

I think of all the books I've read and the sermons and seminars I've heard on "How to Have a Happy Marriage." Always I close the books and walk away from these sorts of talks with the gnawing feeling that the well-intentioned authors and speakers must have it doubly hard. There *must* be times when the "experts"—the counselors, Ph.Ds, and esteemed seminary graduates—have to deliver their "ten principles of merry matrimony" on the heels of a heated exchange with their own beloved spouses. As for myself, there have been days over the past few months when I have sat down to write in praise of marriage, even as I swallowed lumps in my throat over a squabble Scott and I were having at the time. I still struggle to put into practice the joyous convictions in my heart. After all, we are so very human when it comes to carrying out the laws of love, especially the First-Corinthians-Thirteen-Agape type of love.

"No one but a saint can apply more than fragments of it to his own marriage or his own life."

And that, my friend, is the no-punches-pulled, most unadulterated truth about the inner workings of a marriage I've ever come across. With all the ups and downs and problems and failures, how have Scott and I made it thus far? I've written an entire book on the subject now, and still I haven't figured out exactly why or how. Some things—like our crazy, peculiar brand of love—are impossible to explain. They just are.

There are three things that are too amazing for me, four that I do not understand: the way of an eagle in the sky, the way of a snake on a rock, the way of a ship on the high seas, and the way of a man with a maiden.

PROVERBS 30:18–19

ᪿ

Note from a peculiar husband
on the subject
of his peculiar wife

For the better part of six months, Becky has been handing me chapters from this book to read at what seemed like every turn—under my nose while shaving, beside my morning coffee, on my pillow before I lay down at night—she even read one aloud as I was taking a shower. Some of the chapters made me laugh, some made me cry, some made me glad she didn't write everything she *could* have written.

But there was one chapter in this book that stood out because it showed the "Best of Becky." That was her chapter on looking at life from the most positive perspective—believing the best of God, of other people, of life in general. She is the only person I know who has faced her own failures and inadequacies and has experienced disappointment and hurt from other people, and yet she continues to brush herself off, get up, and try again to "go for the gold." I am honored and awed to be married to this lady.

One day a man named Richard passed my wife on the street. She only smiled and said, "Hello," to him. But he followed

Becky into a restaurant to tell her something that just about sums her up for me too. He said, "Ma'am, I just never met a woman quite like you."

Me either, Richard. Me either.

Notes

Introduction

1. Erma Bombeck, *A Marriage Made in Heaven or Too Tired for an Affair* (New York: Harper Collins, 1993), 256.

Chapter 7

1. Rafe VanHoy, "What's Forever For?" © 1978 Sony Tree Publishing Co., Inc.; all rights administered by Sony Music Publishing, 8 Music Square West, Nashville, TN 37203; all rights reserved and used by permission.

Chapter 9

1. Deb Frazier and Jan Winebrenner, *When a Leader Falls* (Minneapolis, Minn.: Bethany House, 1994).

Chapter 11

1. Jean Lush with Patricia H. Rushford, *Emotional Phases of a Woman's Life* (Tarrytown, N.Y.: Fleming H. Revell, 1987).

Chapter 15

1. Winston Churchill quoted in Alan Loy McGinnis's *The Romance Factor* (San Francisco: Harper & Row, 1982), 126.

Chapter 16

1. George Eliot, *Middle March* (1872), available from Signet of Penguin Books, New York.

Chapter 17

1. Arthur Gordon, *A Touch of Wonder,* "Interview with an Immortal" (New York: Fleming H. Revell, 1974), 63–68.

Chapter 18

1. Gary Paulsen, *Clabbered Dirt, Sweet Grass* (San Diego: Harcourt Brace & Co., 1992).

2. Interview with Gary Paulsen, *Writer's Digest,* July 1994.

Chapter 25

1. Fyodor Mikhailovich Dostoevsky, *The Idiot* (1868), quoted in *The International Thesaurus of Quotations,* Rhoda Thomas Tripp, compiler (New York: Harper & Row, 1987).

2. Mark Twain, *Notebook* (1935), *Thesaurus of Quotations*

3. Twain, *What Is a Man?* (1906) *Thesaurus of Quotations,.*

Chapter 28

1. Elizabeth Cody Newenhuyse, *Strong Marriages, Secret Questions* (Batavia, Ill.: Lion Publishing, 1987), 158.

Chapter 29

1. Madeleine L'Engle, *Two-Part Invention: The Story of a Marriage* (New York: Harper & Row, 1988), 232.

Chapter 30

1. Lewis B. Smedes, *Shame and Grace* (New York: Harper San Francisco & Zondervan Publishing House, 1993), 131.

Chapter 33

1. Quoted in Alan Loy McGinnis, *The Friendship Factor* (Minneapolis, Minn.: Augsburg Press, 1979).

2. Gordon, *A Touch of Wonder,* "Wedding by the Sea," 19–23.

∾

Still Lickin' the Spoon

And Other Confessions *of a* Grown-Up Kid

For My Family of Origin
Daddy, for teaching me to listen to the rain.
Mother, for making everything all better.
My brother, David, for showing me how to chill and be real.
My sister, Rachel, for reaching out to all of us
with her child-heart.
The child I was, am, and ever hope to be
is grateful, indeed, to be growing in this family.
I love you all.

෨

Contents

Acknowledgments

B revity is not my strong suit when it comes to thanking the
dozens of people who help create and produce a book. So
many faces float in front of my mind, and each of them makes
me smile for different reasons.

Thank you to my husband, Scott, for freeing me to write and
grow, for good-naturedly taking the kids out for pizza as deadlines loomed close, and especially for loving me even when I'm
more obnoxiously *childish* than charmingly *childlike*. You are,
pure and simple, my hero.

Thank you, Zachary, Ezekiel, Rachel Praise, and Gabriel.
You've not only been wonderful sports letting Mom tell your
stories; you've risen to the level of shameless hams. Bless you, my
children! Because I get to be your mom, I will always be rich.

Ruthie Arnold is not only an incredible mother but also my
teacher. Thank you for passing on to me the gift of laughter and
the love of words. And, Daddy, I always remember your praise,
always your love. If you ever criticized me—even once—I
cannot recall it. Thank you both, for giving me roots and the
reassurance that my wings really would hold me up.

Hugs and thank-yous to Lori Smith, Marilyn Deuell, Mary Johnson, Melissa Gantt, Gracie Malone, Fran Sandin, Tina Jacobson, and, finally, Deborah Morris and the Round Table. Because you, my friends, regularly invite me to come outside and play, I do not go stark raving mad or climb the walls of isolation.

To Bob Briner, friend and mentor, for opening my eyes to the most effective ways to share God's love. Bless you for the encouragement you've brought to so many—from famous artists, athletes, and executives to a little-known gal from the boonies of East Texas. Because of your inspiration, hundreds are lighting candles rather than shouting at the darkness.

Thank you, Mike Hyatt, for being an advisor on this project and a friend in this life.

Finally, to my Broadman family. I do not say this lightly: Broadman & Holman is more than a publishing company. This is a family of fun and caring people who also happen to be top-notch at what they do for a living. Warm-hearted thanks to:

- Vicki Crumpton, my editor and friend. You are that rare combination in a person: one who is able to give on-target critique coupled with generous praise, both at the same time.

- Colyer Robison, for being the most cheerful and encouraging publicist on the planet. (Has anybody *ever* seen Colyer so much as frown?)

- Greg Webster, for being ever-serene in the midst of all life's storms—publishing and otherwise. You and your wife, Nancy, are "Young at Heart" personified—how blessed are your six children!

- Bucky Rosenbaum, for listening and for your prayer on a difficult day. (By the way, I couldn't write about Winnie the Pooh without thinking of you.)

- Trish Morrison, Rene Holt, Susan Linklater, and Becky Yates for taking me in from the cold on my first all-by-myself-out-of-state trips—and into your hearts and homes. You've gone far and above the call of PR duty and have crossed over, permanently I'm afraid, into the realm of Buddy-dom.

So many more names I'd love to mention from the B & H family. But it would take a whole chapter to thank each of you for your warmth (both in person and over the phone), your enthusiasm for our books, and for the behind-the-scenes work you put into helping these words ultimately reach someone's heart. Please know that you are much appreciated.

To the readers of my books. It is a high honor when anyone takes time out of a busy life to attend to someone else's thoughts. Thank you for letting me share with you. It is your input and feedback that continue to give me assurance that I am not alone in this lovely, loony thing called life.

And finally, to Abba, my Father. I cry with joy that I am Your child!

Can't I Just Grow Up to Be a Kid?

Eight-year-old Gabe hugged his side of the car as I swerved to avoid a tree and almost hit a mailbox in the process. Backing my station wagon out of the driveway is still not my forte.

Our original wagon, the Titanic, which some of you may remember from *Worms in My Tea*, eventually sank—much to our teenagers' delight. For three lovely months thereafter, I drove an almost-new, quite sporty Ford Explorer. Two small fender benders and a smashing encounter with a Winnebago, however, put me back in the driver's seat of our current nerd-mobile.

My husband, Scott, believes it is fate. Or God's wrath. Or a twisted joke. There he is, a red sport truck hunk, coupled with a station wagon woman. Even the car's "wood-grain" panels are in reality sun-faded contact paper. To add insult to Scott's injury, it also droops down in back, like a toddler's overloaded diaper. Our older children—Zach, Zeke, and Rachel—appropriately nicknamed this car, Sag. But, as Gabe will tell you, "It's real, whole name is Sag, the Tragic Wagon."

The one blessing of driving a station wagon is that there is plenty of metal around me and my kids—and folks can see me coming from afar in time to swerve out of my path.

"Mom?" Gabe asked, grabbing for the books flying off the seat as I rounded a corner on three and a half wheels.

"Uh, huh," I answered, absently pushing all the wrong buttons as I searched in vain for the radio knob. I knew I was only half listening to my child, but I simply can't listen to children *and* operate heavy machinery at the same time. Groping for the radio, I activated the cigarette lighter. *Well, that'll sure come in handy,* I thought, *if I take up smoking in the next ten minutes.* The next button I pressed turned on the windshield wipers. *Wrong again. Not a cloud in sight, and here I am driving down the highway with the wipers waving, "Alert: the driver of this car is clueless!"* The next knob sent a stream of water up the front of the windshield. *Well, maybe it's a good thing those wipers are in motion after all.* By this time, with my windshield and dashboard in full swing, I could not remember what it was I'd been searching for in the first place. So I flipped on the radio, hoping the music would eventually jar my memory.

That's when I heard Gabe's voice again, seeping into my consciousness.

"MOMMM!" he was now shouting as he waved a paper napkin back and forth in front of my face. Then, carefully enunciating his every word, as if I were hard of hearing or spoke a foreign language, he said, "Mom. Are-you-pay-ing *at-ten-tion?*"

"Yes, Gabe. You can lower the flag. What is it?"

"I was thinking."

"Uh-huh?"

"I was thinking how you are really smart in math and how you write really good books and stuff."

"Well, thank you, Sweetheart."

"But, Mom," he stopped there, a look of concern wrinkling his brow. He glanced up at the wipers, which were, at this point, methodically smearing hazy twin rainbows of grime across the windshield. Then, turning his eyes back to me, he finished his proclamation. "Did you *know* that you have *no sense at all?*"

There was no animosity in his statement, no trace of sarcasm. He'd just been observing a typical "Mom scenario" and out popped a logical conclusion, the cut-and-dried truth. He felt he should warn me—for my own safety, I suppose—that my mind, however seemingly intact, should not *ever* be counted on to provide a shred of common, useful sense.

Now I've known about this mental deficit for a long time. Many others have gently hinted as much throughout the years. But I'd never heard it stated with such blunt accuracy: "Sure, you are smart, Mom, but you have *no sense at all.*" Like the classic tale of the emperor and his new clothes, a child will openly declare what everyone else dances around.

Art Linkletter once said, "I can say, after a lifetime of interviewing, that the two best subjects are children under ten and folks over seventy. Both groups say exactly what's on their minds without regard for the consequences: the kids don't know what they are saying; the old people don't care!"[1] But, perhaps Oliver Wendell Holmes best summed it up when he wrote, "Pretty much all the honest truth-telling in the world is done by children." The lesson is this: If you ever really want the flat-out truth, visit an elementary school or a retirement villa. Ready or not, they'll let you have it.

A few days after Gabe's honest evaluation of my mental state, I was wracking my "senseless" brain trying to think up a title for this book. So I turned to our resident eight-year-old for advice. After all, Gabriel had been the source of inspiration for the title of my first book the day he gifted me with a writhing nightcrawler in my glass of iced tea. The title worked amazingly well, too, drawing attention to the cover until the stories inside had a chance to grab hearts. *Why mess with a good system?* I thought.

I found Gabriel lounging around on the living room floor, his feet propped up on the couch cushions above him. He says this position makes the blood heat up his head. Taking advantage of his warmed-up noggin, I asked him the million-dollar question.

"Hey, Gaber-Doodle (his nickname du jour), what do you think I should call my next book?"

Like a trained psychiatrist, he answered my question with another question.

"Well, what do you want the title to make people do?"

Honestly? I thought. I looked around at the furniture with its frayed upholstery and our one-bathroomed, in-process home for our family of six. Then I mentally calculated the balance of my checking account.

"To tell you the truth, Gabe, I want people to like this book so much that they'll buy lots and lots of copies. And I hope when they read the stories inside, they will smile and remember that sometimes it's good for grown-ups to act more like kids."

It took him all of two seconds to come up with an answer.

"OK, Mom, you should call it, *Buy This Book, It's Really Good.*"

I laughed. It was an isn't-that-cute sort of chuckle tossed out as I strolled by and patted my son on the head. But I couldn't get Gabe's title out of my mind. *Buy This Book, It's Really Good. Buy This Book, It's Really Good.* I had to admit it had a certain charm in its unbridled honesty. It also reflected my personal goal in writing this book: to see the world from a more honest, child-like perspective.

I knew I wanted the chapter titles to be phrases and questions kids might say. Why not the title too? Interestingly, childhood questions are often the questions I'm *still* asking as an adult. Inside childlike declarations and singsong sayings lies a surprising abundance of wisdom.

Gabe's idea held on as the working title for this book until the time came to set it in stone. That's when it dawned on us that *Buy This Book, It's Really Good,* though catchy, didn't really describe the book's contents. And secondly, I kept having nightmares of some disgruntled reviewer (with no literary taste, of course) changing the title to *Borrow This Book, It's So-So.* But now we were back to the drawing board.

One evening as I was scraping a bowl of chocolate icing and sampling a taste from the spoon, a feeling of nostalgia swept over me. For a fleeting moment, I could almost see myself as a child, barely tall enough to peek over the kitchen counter, hurrying to ask Mother if I could lick the spoon before my brother or sister beat me to it. *What's great about being a grown-up,* I thought, *is that I'm still lickin' the spoon—only I can do it whenever I want, without waiting my turn.* As it turns out, there was a title buried underneath that spoon full of chocolate, and it's decorating the book that you hold.

Aren't we all really kids anyway, dressed-up in disguise? As I quickly approach the Big 4-0, I'm more determined than ever to brighten up, loosen up, and live it up in whatever time I have left on this earth. Who better to observe than children to find out how it's done? Forget the *Seven Habits of Highly Effective People;* bring on the *Habits of Highly Effective Preschoolers!* A gathering of grown-ups was told long ago, by the wisest Teacher of all, that they were simply going to have to behave more like children. "For such," He declared, "is the kingdom of heaven" (Matt. 19:14).

I am a storyteller—more artist than teacher, painting parables better than expounding principles—so there will be no lists of lessons or numbered habits. Instead, as an artist draws a butterfly or a mouse or some such symbol into every painting, it is my intent to draw into every story an imprint of your own child-hood remembered or a present bouncing-around-my-living-room child. Or perhaps, even more often, it will be a glimpse of the children we still are inside. And through the telling of simple stories, I hope lessons will subtly appear and fall where they may into hearts that are hungry for the touch of a child.

If you had a wonderful childhood, perhaps these stories might sprinkle some forgotten joy or trigger a poignant memory into your grown-up days. If your childhood was anything but won-derful (in retrospect, was anyone's perfect?), this book is written especially for you. As the saying goes, "It is *never* too late to have a happy childhood." Most of us have spent a lifetime growing up. How'd you like to join me for a bit of *growing down?*

A little child will lead them.
ISAIAH 11:6

Can I Hold the Baby
One More Time?

Tonight I participated in a scientific experiment. It's something I've not done in nine or ten years, though there was a time when I frequently gathered the necessary drugstore supplies and waited—with hands wringing or pressed together in prayer—for the bathroom/lab results.

Tonight I took a pregnancy test.

I took the test even though my husband, Scott, has had the big No More Babies Surgery (the granddaddy of *all* baby-stopping surgeries to hear him tell the tale). It also goes without saying that I haven't had a clandestine affair or anything. Besides the fact that I am committed to my husband, I signed a publishing contract stating that my services could be dismissed should I fall into "moral turpitude." (Sounds like paint thinner to me, but I think it's some sort of legal term meaning, "Please don't embarrass us unless, that is, you can write it up as family entertainment." I'm pretty sure that a clandestine affair would be considered a tad turpitudish.) Anyway, I was late, and when a woman is late she knows that sometimes, occasionally, the impossible happens.

In case you're holding your breath, the rabbit didn't die. The criss didn't cross. Nothing, and nobody, turned blue. I am still a "me," and not an "us." Looks as though Zach, Zeke, Rachel, and Gabe will be our "quiver complete"—with no surprise arrows being flung our way.

I didn't cry, of course, because the possibility of being called "Mommy" again had been ridiculous from the start. Imagine a woman in her late thirties with three teens and a third grader sitting up nights in a rocking chair cradling the well-diapered bottom of a newborn, patting a cloud-soft nightie draped over tiny shoulders, baby's breath gently tickling her neck . . .

OK, OK, I'll admit it. I've always been a sucker for babies. When I was about seven years old, a beautiful dark-haired woman at our church gave birth to a beautiful dark-haired baby girl. As soon as I spied the mother and baby in the church nursery, I began praying that someday, somehow, I'd get to sit next to them in a pew. "And please, God," I'd add, "let it be before the baby grows up and gets too big for a first grader like me to hold."

Then one glorious morning, it happened. The young mother sat down, holding the priceless bundle of mysterious sweetness, *right next to me.* I was beside myself, immediately plotting—as only a seven-year-old can—how I might take advantage of this once-in-a-lifetime opportunity.

If I can just scooch over close enough I might could, real real gently, touch that soft little baby's head. And if I can make my face look sort of sad and wishing, the lady might say to me, "Would you like to hold my baby, Becky? After all you're getting to be such a big girl! Why, I can tell just by looking at your face, you're going to make a real good mommy someday." Yep, that's what she'll probably say. If I look at her just right.

Unfortunately, as hard as I twisted my face with all angst and earnestness, the new mother didn't "read" my facial expressions. I'd have to *verbalize* my longings—a terrifying thought. I was so shy; I rarely spoke to grown-ups other than my parents unless they first spoke to me. However, when it comes to a chance at holding a real live baby, a little girl's gotta do what a little girl's gotta do. The last chorus of "Now the Day Is Over" droned to an end as I mentally rehearsed my speech and gathered up my courage. The congregation stirred to leave. The men jingled their keys; the women adjusted their gloves and pillbox hats. I cleared my throat, and it all spilled out in one breathless plea.

"Could I please hold your pretty baby girl for just one minute if I promise-cross-my-heart-hope-to-die I won't drop her?"

Thankfully, the mother must have seen the courage it took for a bashful child to blurt out such a heartfelt request. Before I knew it I was holding a real live baby right in the middle of church where everyone could see what a big girl I was. And I knew the entire congregation would be whispering, "Look at that Becky Arnold—what a good little mother she's going to make someday. Do you see how tender she is with that new baby?"

The real baby girl turned out to be much heavier than I'd imagined. Until that moment I'd only rocked two other babies—my stuffed Baby Thumbelina, and my stiff-jointed plastic doll that drank *and wet* orange Kool-Aid. After the minute had passed, my small arm began to quiver from the weight of the baby's soft-hard head. Still, I loved the warm, breathing, squirmy feel of this *live* baby doll. When the mother reached for her child, I relinquished my treasure with great reluctance. I had just been given a glimpse of "mommy heaven."

It was only surpassed, years later, by the intensity of holding *my own* real live babies. I didn't know I possessed such a fierce protectiveness until I heard my first child cry. Though I was weakened from a long labor, I would have wrestled a samurai to get to my newborn son and quiet his fears.

My beautiful babies . . . where did they all go? I look into the eyes of my children now—all of them stretching toward puberty or young adulthood—and search for signs of the helpless infants and chubby toddlers they once were. Here and there I catch an occasional glimpse—a lisped word, a mischievous glance, a gentle pat on my shoulder. Does every mother harbor a secret wish that she could bring back her newborns for just an hour or so?

Like Emily, from Thornton Wilder's play *Our Town*, I sometimes wonder, "Do any human beings ever realize life while they live it—every, every minute? Oh, what I think when I see my youngsters growing up, the precious moments of childhood racing by. How can I squeeze every last second of fun, excitement, and sweetness out of those strange little creatures who are ours for so short a time?" On a wall above my childrens' crib, I hung a cross-stitched poem, reminding me to squeeze the joy out of these fleeting years.

> Dishes and dusting can wait till tomorrow
> For babies grow up, we've learned to our sorrow
> So quiet down cobwebs, and dust go to sleep
> I'm rocking my baby and babies don't keep.
> ANONYMOUS
> ❧

Thanks to this poem's insistent message, the housework waited for most of ten years. (Perhaps that is why Scott periodically asked if he could replace it with the quote, "Cleanliness is next to godliness.") But I cuddled and rocked my babies until their feet dragged the floor.

Honestly, now that I've failed the pregnancy test, I'm relieved to be passing up all the pain that comes with an impending birth—swollen ankles, morning sickness, contractions, dirty diapers, confinement, car seats, potty training, runny noses, and every mother's favorite plague, impetigo. As I've stated from the beginning, it would be preposterous for me to cry—at this stage of the game—over not getting a positive mark on my test.

However, if the crisses had crossed, or the dot had turned blue, I'd have found some way to cope with all the childbearing "downers." Most likely, I'd have dreamed of a well-padded baby's bottom, cloud-soft nighties, and feathery breaths tickling my neck. Even at my age, I might have made a good little mother—just once more.

Oh pooh. Where's a tissue when you need one?

From the lips of children and infants you have ordained praise.
PSALM 8:2
❧

This chapter is dedicated, with love,
to Rachel and Grace Webster.
Welcome to the world, little ones!

Do I Glow in the Dark?

S cott and I have finally done it. We've graduated from pre-school. Well, actually, it is our *children* who have graduated from preschool. We, more accurately, have officially completed all required labs in Preschool Parenting. Funny, this new stage. As I've already admitted, there is a certain melancholy sadness in bidding farewell to the childbearing, toddler-chasing years. But have I mentioned the waves of euphoria that also come with this time of transition?

There is something akin to giddiness in knowing that never again will it be *my* candy-crazed toddler having the temper tantrum at the grocery checkout. Not only that, but Scott and I are now free to spoil other people's children with nary a thought to the consequences. We get to be like fairy godparents to our young nephews and neighborhood children—perpetual nice guys. There are three little preschoolers down the street whose standard greeting to us is, "Do you have a treat for me today?" Scott almost always has a stick of gum or a piece of candy ready for such occasions. If only real parenting were as easy as handing out goodies.

When our son, Zachary (now sixteen), was about eighteen months old, my Aunt Hazel came for a visit. Before long Zach started in with some well-timed whining and foot stomping around the vicinity of Aunt Hazel's knees. Her automatic response to his fit of passion was to kiss him on the forehead and place two gooey cookies in his dimpled hands. I started to give her that don't-spoil-him look, but before I could say anything Hazel slapped her hand on the counter and matter-of-factly said, "Becky, how would you like my advice on raising children?"

"Sure," I replied, eager for any help I could glean at this stage of the game.

"OK, here it is: Give them everything they want; don't ever say no."

I smiled as I raised my eyebrows. "Is this the method you used to raise your son?"

"Of course not. It's my advice on how you should raise my great-nephew."

Now that I'm an auntie myself, I'm free to adopt Aunt Hazel's childrearing advice—to be used only with other people's children, of course. Take, for example, my nephew, Tyler.

First of all, I should explain that Tyler glows. There is no other word to appropriately describe this child phenomenon. By "glowing" I mean when this kid smiles, he smiles all over. The grin that starts at the corners of his mouth spreads out like ripples of water to his dimpled cheeks, moving upward to his eyebrows, causing them to pop up and down with excitement, the lights dancing in his eyes below. Giggles flow freely, not only from his mouth, but seemingly from every joint in his body.

Tyler is also very small for his age. Though he is six years old, he has the tiny build of a child of about four—giving him an almost elf-like aura. I'm always picking my nephew up, without thinking, and loving on him as I would a toddler. When I first saw him last summer, I ran to hug him and then lifted him off the floor in a huge bear hug. He was polite. He even managed to give his crazy Aunt Becky an obligatory pat on the back. But I was startled when I heard his very grown-up voice over my shoulder insisting, "Aunt Becky, I'd like you to put me down now. I was about to go work on the computer."

This spring Tyler came to visit his Uncle Scott and Aunt Becky and all his country cousins at our lakeside home while his daddy, my brother David, went fishing in our area. His mother, Barbara, who is a wonderfully organized mother, had to stay home in Indiana. Before Tyler's visit, she called to brief me on his routine.

"Becky," she said, as always, distinctly enunciating her words, "Tyler usually goes to bed at 8:00 P.M., and it is very important that he do some school work while he is there so he won't get behind on his studies. I'll pack a fresh change of clothes and underwear for every day—you know how picky he is about staying clean. He knows how to brush and floss his own teeth, of course. And he really shouldn't have too much sugar or junk food because it tends to make him hyper."

Barb, please forgive me. I must confess that it only took one week under my watchful care for your son to go completely to pot. Somehow we never got around to the homework. I have no recollection of the toothbrush, though I think we did try using the floss for fishing line. And don't even ask me about the condition of his underwear. The only thing I'm sure that Tyler changed was his affinity for staying neat and clean. But we did manage to have some big-time fun.

For days on end, Tyler fished to his heart's content down at our lake pier (Tyler's "heart's content" averages about eight hours of casting and catching a day). When it comes to fishing, he is his daddy's own son. I remember when David was about Tyler's age, he dug a huge hole in our suburban backyard and filled it with water from the hydrant. There he sat, for hours, certain that at any minute he'd snag a whopper. (I'm sure our mother thought the hole in the backyard was well worth a few days of peace and quiet.) Our local paper even snapped a picture of David fishing at a nearby pond. He was holding three cane poles at once in his small clasped hands.

During most of Tyler's stay with us, he only set his pole down long enough to call up to the house for fresh rations of peanut butter and jelly sandwiches. Oh, and he'd yell for a jacket when the sun began to fade and the evening air took on a chill.

If Barb had seen her son at the end of a typical day at our home, I don't know if she'd ever let him come back. (She tells me she'd rather not know.) Basically, Tyler turned into a grimy ball of worm slime with fragrant splashes of perch and crappie lingering about his hands. However, Tyler could never get dirty or smelly enough to cover his glow. And so, when he flashed his big grin and asked me to take him to the store for fresh minnows, I rarely, if ever, said no.

On the way home from such a trip to Gantt's minnow/deli/convenience store, I happened to glance in my rearview mirror toward the back of the station wagon. There sat Tyler, all aglow, a chicken leg in one hand and a lollipop in the other. He was contentedly alternating fists with bites and licks. It was awfully cute, but I was soon lecturing myself.

Now Becky, you are spoiling this child just because he's your nephew and he happens to be adorable. You've got to quit being such a gullible old softy. What will you tell Barb? That he ate balanced meals because he always had food of equal weight in both hands?

Late one evening, shortly thereafter, I realized things were totally out of control. Wandering into the kitchen I found Tyler perched on a stool behind the counter. He was obviously a kid on a mission. He'd taken two half-gallons of Blue Bell ice cream out of the freezer and positioned one on either side of himself. (If you don't know about Blue Bell, just ask any transplanted Texans in your area and watch their eyes glaze over.) The lids were off both cartons, and Tyler held a spoon in each hand, poised for action. I started to protest, but then he looked up at me with a grin that glowed as big as a Fourth of July sky.

"Man, I love this place!" he declared. "I've had ice cream for supper two nights in a row now."

OK, I know it's awful. But I can't help it. I just can't find it in my heart to say no to a child who's about to glow. Besides, it was only one week out of a year; how much harm can one little week of nonstop sugar and worm dirt do to a kid?

This fall, David and Barb allowed Tyler to come for one more visit. As they were making preparations for this second trip out, Barb called ahead. She was as nice as she could be, but I could tell she was still struggling to recover from Tyler's last visit with us.

"Hi, Becky," she said, "just wanted to go over Tyler's routine. Again." (How can I blame her? She must have been thinking, *Let's try this once more—with* feeling.)

"Oh, Barb," I apologized, "I'm sorry we got Tyler so off schedule last time. You know how crazy things get around here. By the way, did you get the package I mailed after he left?"

"Yes," she answered with measured calmness, "and I really do appreciate you mailing Tyler's homework back. I understand you finally found his workbook in the back of your station wagon under the minnow bucket. Actually, that's sort of what I was calling about. Since we are taking Tyler out of school for the week, do you think you could encourage him to actually *write* something on the worksheets this time? Fill in some blanks, underline a sentence, circle something? I don't care if he stays clean. I can even handle digging the worm dirt out of his pockets when he gets back home. And a week without flossing won't cause his teeth to rot out. But if he can just do some homework this time—all I ask is *the homework*."

As I tried to give Barb my most reassuring response, I heard Tyler in the background yell, "Tell Aunt Becky to be ready to whip out the Blue Bell when I get there!"

What can I say? I rushed right out for a carton of Vanilla Bean and one of Cookies and Cream.

When Tyler arrived at our house this time, he felt easily at home, settling into a routine right away. (In other words, he didn't open his suitcase for the first two days.) One afternoon, when it was raining too hard to fish, Tyler sat and watched a Power Robo Something cartoon on TV. In response to the action on the television, he abruptly yelled out, "Awesome!"

"What's awesome?" I quizzed from the kitchen.

"Nothing," came the serious voice, followed by a heavy sigh from the living room, "I'm sorry, you're too old to understand."

Well, perhaps he is right. (I believe Oscar Wilde once said, "I am not young enough to know everything.") But this much I do understand: Tyler most definitely has the upper hand in our relationship. Even his insults seem cute to me these days.

Toward evening that same day, my glowing but exhausted nephew crawled up in my arms and fell asleep on my lap. When David walked in the door to take his son back home, I looked down at Tyler's sleeping form and then back up at David. On reflex, a little-girl question tumbled out of my mouth: "Can I keep him?" David chuckled, strolled over to stroke his son's hair, looked at me gently, and shook his head no. It was a painful good-bye.

But good news! I am going to see Tyler again soon. This time we'll meet in Virginia where the whole clan is gathering at my sister's for Christmas. I'll have her adorable four-year-old, Trevor, to spoil too. I only have one problem. How am I going to transport two half-gallons of Blue Bell ice cream on the airplane?

What am I thinking? If I'm considering going to these lengths to spoil my nephews, can you imagine me as a *grandma* someday? I wonder if there is a continuing ed course called, "How to Say No to Children Who Glow."

As I was pondering Tyler's glowing charm and my tendency to give in to anything he wants, I came across an intriguing quote by Winston Churchill. Churchill was one of history's *ultimate* charmers, and I believe I might have some insight into his ability to wrap the free world around his chubby little finger. One day he seriously intoned, "We are all worms." And then with childlike confidence and a gleam in his eye he added, "But I do believe that I am a glowworm."

In life, especially as we grow older, we are faced with two choices. Either we can let ourselves go, or we can find ways to glow. Why not go for the glow? I've noticed that people are more patient with the weaknesses of those who grin and giggle and enjoy life to the hilt. Whether this fact of life is fair or not, admittedly, could be argued. But take it from Tyler and Winston: The truth of the matter is, "people who glow rarely get told no." And when it comes to getting vital needs met—like finagling second helpings of Cookies and Cream—one must resort to any means available.

Those who are wise will shine.
DANIEL 12:3
ع

THREE

'Cause It's Fun

E arly one morning this fall, Zeke—our fourteen-year-old—
slunk in from the back door and gingerly made his way
toward the kitchen. He was dripping wet and fully clothed. I
raised my eyebrows in a silent question as Zeke shook his head
and began to chuckle softly to himself. He weakly gathered up
the hem of his soggy shirt and wrung some water into the
kitchen sink in a futile effort to halt the puddling around him.
Then he turned around and looked me full in the face, as if to
be sure of my undivided attention. "Mom," he sighed, "you're
not gonna believe what Gabe's done this time."

Gabe is the quintessential "unique" little brother. He is and
has always been his own person—what some might even call an
odd duck. And speaking of ducks, it was literally an unusual-
looking duck that started Zeke on this morning adventure, leaving him drenched, shall we say, with fresh "Gabe news" to
report.

"Mom, I was sitting out on the dock this morning when I
noticed something funny-looking out on the lake. It looked like
a wounded duck caught in a trotline. So I jumped in and swam

toward the bird to see if there was anything I could do to help the poor thing. When I swam out for a closer look, my 'wounded duck' turned out to be nothing but an old piece of Styrofoam with a pencil stuck in it. And on the pencil there was a flag with a message in little-kid handwriting: 'Hi. This is Gabe. I just made this for the fun of it.'"

Just for the fun of it. Now there's classic "kid reasoning" for you. How often do we grown-ups do something off-the-wall or spontaneous just for the sheer, unvarnished fun of it? Probably not often enough. Kids, however, are masters at this.

I ran into a friend of mine, Angie, a couple of years ago. She'd just finished reading *Worms in My Tea* and was bursting with a story to tell me about her young son, Carson, who sounds as though he could be Gabriel's clone.

She said that one afternoon Carson found an earthworm on the back porch and began begging her to come see it right away. But Angie was busy vacuuming, so she explained to Carson that she'd come out in a little while.

"Becky," Angie reported, her eyes wide, "you will not believe what I saw when I finally came out to the porch. Carson had been *slinging* that worm around and around like a lariat rope over his head the entire time I'd been vacuuming."

"Oh, no!"

"Oh, yes! And did you know that earthworms *stretch?* I swear that worm was between a foot and eighteen inches long by the time I got to it."

"What did Carson say when you asked him why he did it?"

"He told me, 'Mom, I just thought it would be fun to sling a worm.'"

See what I mean? Grown-ups don't think like this. We see some worms, and what do we do with them? The bravest of us might dig them up and use them for fishing bait. But kids, like Gabe and Carson, are so much more creative. They think, *Why not let a worm take a swim in a glass of tea? Or better yet, try slinging one?*

The year I taught first grade was a perpetual eye-opener for me in terms of understanding kids' theories on fun—from stuffing wads of Play-Doh in their ears, to karate-chopping pencils into tiny pieces, to cutting designer shapes into their clothing. I'll never forget the afternoon, right in the middle of teaching a lesson, when one little boy abruptly dove out of his desk and landed on the floor at my feet. Later, as we sat in the office together, he innocently explained to the principal, "I sort of thought it would be fun to see how far I could jump out of my seat."

On another occasion, a shy little student walked up to my desk, opened her mouth wide, and silently pointed to a button she'd stuck to the roof of her mouth. Neither I nor the school nurse could dislodge it—the suction between her soft palate and the metal button was *that* strong. Her mother ended up transporting her child to the doctor's office to have it removed! The next day, when I asked the girl why she'd stuck the thing up there in the first place, her answer was predictable. "I don't know, Mrs. Fweeman, I just thought it would be fun."

As much as I do admire children's penchants for having fun, I realize, as an adult, I must temper my impulses. After all, I don't want to be sitting in a doctor's office with a button stuck on the roof of my mouth or forced to explain a wad of Play-Doh lodged in my ear. Though I've often fantasized about it, I cannot dive out of my seat and onto the floor every time I'm bored with a speaker's presentation. Sometimes I think the adult pendulum swings too far to the "let's behave" side, and we completely forget what it's like to have good, wholesome fun for fun's sake.

In an effort to bring more fun into my life I recently purchased a book called *Ten Fun Things to Do before You Die*.[2] It was written—believe it or not—by a Catholic nun, Karol A. Jackowski. This sister seems like a pretty fun nun (why do I keep envisioning Whoopi Goldberg?), the sort I'd love to meet for coffee and conversation. After forty-two years of living, Sister Jackowski declares she's found four ways to "have more fun than anyone else."

The first piece of advice she gives is to find fun people. Apparently, this is not an easy trick. Sister Karol writes, "One of the hardest things to find in life is fun people. Far too few appear and seemingly fewer survive adulthood." Suggested things to watch for on a search for fun people are: "good storytelling, perfect timing, interesting work, a good appetite, unusual sense of humor, fresh insight, and a brave daring life."

Advice nugget number two is, "Forget about yourself around other people. Not to do so is . . . just plain rude." I like this one; it's a good reminder for a self-centered person such as myself. Mother and I laughed the other day about how we sometimes feel burdened to *entertain* other people whenever we are in group situations—as if it is our obligation to provide the floor show or something. Not necessary, Karol says. "A good general rule is to think about yourself when you're by yourself, and in the presence of others, think and ask about them."

Third, she writes, "Be a Fun Person." To do this you must first make yourself interesting, and then be on the watch for opportunities that have the potential for great fun. Opportunities like "Clyde Peeling's Reptile Farm off the Pennsylvania Turnpike, any Dairy Queen, and, yes, boring meetings."

There *are* limits to fun, but not many. The fourth piece of advice from the Fun Nun is, "If it looks like fun and doesn't break the Ten Commandments, do it." Sounds like a good rule of thumb to me.

On a recent country getaway with a group of women from my church, I found myself gravitating toward one woman in particular. Right from the start Terry exhibited all the signs of being a fun person. In the course of conversation, we discovered Terry had traveled down the Amazon, been lost in South America, and had barely escaped a guerrilla's spray of machine gunfire. She'd also been a full-fledged hippie—her barefoot wedding taking place in a field of flowers. And though Terry has grown into a respectable Bible study leader, she's not finished being daring and interesting. Before the night was out, she handed each of us a drinking straw and with great gusto announced, "I am going to teach you all a new skill—one you can use to totally amaze and impress your kids, or even strangers in a restaurant."

Then, with all the dignity she could muster, Terry placed one end of the straw in her mouth and secured the other end, very carefully, into her armpit. Then she blew. For a few seconds we all sat motionless—stunned at the disgusting noises arising from the crevice in Terry's arm, and grateful we were not in a public place. But within seconds, we all began scrambling like crazy for our own straws to try the trick ourselves. Before I indulged, however, I mentally went over the Ten Commandments. When I could not find a deeply spiritual reason to abstain, I went ahead and blew for all I was worth. I only wish my teenage sons could have seen me in such top form. They would have been so proud. For reasons I cannot begin to explain, it was one of the most spontaneous, fun evenings I've ever had with a group of women.

Besides having fun with straws, we grown-ups could probably take a clue from fun-loving children and simply go outside and play more often. Like the poem said—"Dishes and dusting can wait till tomorrow"—they will still be their dirty old selves tomorrow, waiting for you to tackle them when you are in a better frame of mind. (I know, I've stretched that poem for all it's worth. Now that the babies are grown-up, I'm desperate for a new guilt-cleansing rhyme.)

I love the story from the Gospels where Jesus told Martha, Mary's compulsive-cleaning sister, to "chill out, leave the dishes alone, and come sit a spell with Me." (This is, by the way, my own very loose translation.) Why? He wanted Martha to get in on the conversation while she had a chance. After all, it wasn't every day that Jesus would be stopping by. The dishes could wait. Special opportunities, however, may not. How about this for an updated rhyme? "If you always wait 'til chores are done, you'll never, ever have any fun."

One sunny spring afternoon I had planned to stay home and be a good wife, maybe even cook a Sunday dinner, do the laundry, and read the paper. But then I had not just one, but *two* girlfriends call and ask me to go out to play. What could I do? I told Scott it was obviously the will of God that I go.

So I ended up in Dallas, soaking up sun on a quilt with my two friends. We were each eating a smoked ear of corn on the cob that was dripping with butter and covered with sour cream and bacon bits (to die for). Between stuffing ourselves and gabbing, we also watched magnificent, brightly colored hot-air balloons take off, one after another. With corn between my teeth and sour cream around my mouth, I grinned at my friends and slowly drawled, "I don't know about you guys, but I think this beats bleaching socks."

That Sunday afternoon, my family ended up eating sandwiches and cleaning up after themselves. What they didn't finish, I completed the next day. But what my husband and children *did* get out of the deal was a wife and mother who came home smiling and refreshed and happy to be alive. They agreed it was a pretty good trade-off.

So I say, sail that Styrofoam boat! Get that dusty kite out of the closet and fly it on a warm spring day. Ride a hot-air balloon, eat greasy fair food, blow silly noises through straws! Just do something each day on which you can look back and say, "I did that for the sheer, simple, childlike fun of it."

Eric Liddell, the Olympic runner from the movie *Chariots of Fire,* said some wonderful life-affirming words when questioned by his sister about his spiritual priorities. "Jenny, God . . . made me fast. And when I run, I feel His pleasure." Is it possible that we, too, might better "feel His pleasure" as we seize the moments God gives us full of pure, *unadult*-erated fun?

God . . . richly provides us with everything
for our enjoyment.

1 TIMOTHY 6:17

422

Let's Play Dress-Up!

I 've always believed in allowing people—including little people—the freedom to dress in ways that express their own personalities. Perhaps this explains why, a few years back, one visiting youngster asked me if he could "wear his shirt inside out and backwards like Zach and Zeke always do."

I, myself, have always worn originals. (At least people have always told me, "Becky, that outfit looks very *original.*") This has not been easy for my husband to accept, because he cares about blending in with society's norms when it comes to public attire. As one might guess by now, blending in with the crowd has never been top priority with me.

When Scott and I were newlyweds, all of eighteen and nineteen years old, my husband insisted we always walk, rather than drive, to our classes at the college campus located about a mile from our home. On chilly winter mornings, dressing for warmth, rather than for success, was my goal. My priorities made Scott more than a little nervous.

As I roved through the house, tossing layer after layer of whatever laundry was handy upon my shivering form, Scott would beg, "Becky . . . wait . . . *please* not the wool socks on your hands!"

"We've been through this a hundred times," I'd reply, digging through his sock drawer. "My hands get numb when they're cold and only your wool socks keep them warm enough."

"OK. Put footwear on your hands if you must, but that red bandanna you've been tying around the outside of your coat hood—*that* has to go."

"Scott, I need to keep my hood tied in close to my ears or the wind gets in there and makes them pound and hurt."

"Parading down the street with my bride dressed like a walking garage sale makes my *heart* pound and hurt."

"Ever since I was a little girl, I've dressed in layers to keep warm. My parents always thought it was cute—sort of a waif-ragamuffin effect. Anyway, I refuse to freeze my dirastecrutus for the sake of fashion."

"Just tell me one thing. When do you suppose you will be growing out of this rags and muffin phase? Listen, Becky, we all have to wave our good-byes to Puff the Magic Dragon, put away our pirate costumes, and move on from Hona-Lee." He stopped his lecture for a second, then scratched his head. "And what, pray tell, is a *dirastecrutus?*"

"I have no idea. But my mother always warned us never to let it freeze," I raised one eyebrow in warning, "and who knows what evil might befall you if it does?"

And so the conversation would end. Usually, we'd compromise. I'd wear the socks and bandanna, and Scott would walk a block in front of me, pretending not to know who I was. Little did I know that years later I'd get a small taste of what Scott had been feeling when my lastborn child insisted on dressing himself and parading the results in public. Unfortunately, I did not have the option of forcing my three-year-old to walk a block in front of me, pretending not to be his mother.

My youngest child, as you also may have already guessed, is— well, *different.* As soon as Gabriel was old enough to have a say in the matter, he refused to wear jeans and shirts like the other kids. Wearing them inside out and backwards wasn't even an appealing option to him.

It started out innocently enough. First, he began wearing the standard Superman cape. Just a portable plastic cape adorned with an iron-on *S*. No big deal except for the fact that he wore it every waking—and sleeping—moment. And it didn't take long for Gabe to move on to greater things. Batman came next, and his Batman cape of choice turned out to be my black half-slip secured around his neck by a large, pink diaper pin. (Wouldn't psychologists have a heyday analyzing that?) Eventually, the sight of my personal lingerie on display stopped bothering me, though it continued to cause Gabe's older siblings great fits of public humiliation.

It is important to remember these costumes were worn constantly, everywhere that Gabe went, twenty-four hours a day, for weeks at a time. To ask Gabe to go out the door without his costume would be like someone asking that you or me take a downtown stroll in nothing but our socks and underwear. Gabe's costumes *were* his identity: preschool power clothes. Without them—oh horrors—someone might mistake Gabe for a mild-mannered, average Clark Kent-type preschooler and not recognize him for the incredible, zowie-wow superhero he knew himself to be.

In October, things really began to get out of hand. Even I, who've always been proud of the fact that I'm a free spirit when it comes to matters of dress—not to mention immune to most forms of embarrassment—began to grow self-conscious when I left the house with my son. This, too, began innocently enough.

Several weeks before Gabe's fourth birthday, he commenced begging for a real fireman's costume.

"And Momma," Gabe insisted, "I don't want one of those sissy Halloween fireman suits. I want *real* fireman rubber boots and a *real* fireman coat and a *real* red fireman's hat. And 'specially I want a gas mask."

Silly me. I obliged. Oh boy, did I oblige. It was a cinch to find a tall pair of rubber boots. After much slicker-searching, I happened upon a bright yellow one—heavy-duty rubber with a hood. I even found a large plastic hatchet in a discount bin. The perfect red hat was ripe for the picking at a local toy store; it made a piercing siren noise when its button was pressed. (Within two hours, the siren's batteries mysteriously disappeared. Who in the world could have done that?)

But the coup de grâce—a sheer stroke of creative genius—was the "gas mask," which was actually one of those bright orange pollen masks that allergy sufferers wear when they mow the lawn. (My husband, by the way, is an allergy sufferer. But being the fashion-conscious guy that he is, he would rather be buried alive in grass clippings and found unconscious from a sneezing attack than chance being seen in public wearing one of these "nerd" masks.)

As you might imagine, the costume was a smashing success. For weeks that turned into months, Gabe wore the entire fireman ensemble—complete with gas mask—everywhere we went. Rain or shine. Cool weather or unseasonable heat wave. Gabe took his fireman duties seriously and stood ready to douse a fire or rescue someone from a burning building at the slightest sound of a smoke alarm. (Since our smoke alarm doubles as our dinner bell, he had quite a bit of practice.) I even have a much-prized picture of Gabriel at the mall, sitting on Santa's knee, dressed in his full fire-fighting regalia. Poor Santa had trouble understanding what my son wanted for Christmas, however, since Gabe refused to talk to the jolly ol' saint without his mask secured firmly over his mouth.

I don't remember what Santa actually gave Gabe for Christmas that year, but I do recall that my friend, Mary, gave Gabriel his best-loved present of the season. It was a long, polyester trench coat and a matching hat in a brilliant shade of yellow. From that day until Easter, Gabriel was Dick Tracy. I was so grateful to see my son's mouth ungraced by orange plastic and disposable filters, I welcomed Detective Tracy with open arms.

Today Gabe's growing up—and he has, surprisingly, adopted his daddy's taste in clothing preferences. Very aware of what's "cool," he now chooses clothes that help him blend with style into the world of third grade. The Superman cape, the fireman suit, and the yellow trench coat have all gone the way of imaginary dragons and other "fancy stuff."

"And what about Gabe's mother?" you ask. "Did she ever leave her childish ways behind and acquire some fashion sense?"

Well, it's like this. I'm about to go out for a walk. It's a cold and rainy day, so I'll need my hooded coat—and, of course, a pair of wool socks for my hands and a red bandanna to secure the hood so my ears won't pound and hurt. My husband? These days, he's proud to take long, meandering walks with me—no matter what I'm wearing.

All he asks is that I give him a good forty-five-second lead before I begin my walk—preferably, a good twenty paces behind him.

> *Your beauty should not come*
> *from outward . . . clothes.*
> *Instead it should be that of your inner self.*
> 1 PETER 3:3–4
> ❧

I'm Sorry, Frog

Driving in the car last night, one of Gabe's little buddies, Dallas, was relating a scene from the recent *Little Rascals* movie.

"See, the Little Rascals had this 'He-Man Womun Hater's Club.' And the kid with the real deep voice, the one they call Froggie, was telling his friends about a girl that had played a mean trick on him. But he got back at her. He took out a lizard and showed it to the *girl!*" Dallas exclaimed.

"So?"

"So, it scared her."

"Why?"

"Because girls are scared of lizards."

"Why?"

"Because they just are."

"That's not true. I know lots of girls who like lizards. If somebody showed me a lizard, I'd reach out and pet it. I'd love it!"

After all these years, it is still incomprehensible to Gabriel that any sane person could dislike a reptile or an amphibian. Like the title of Arnold Lobel's famous children's book states, *Frog and Toad Are Friends*. And according to Gabriel, they are *our* friends.

Though much of Gabe's amphibian/reptile-loving history has already been well-documented, the stories continue to abound. I began writing the material for *Worms* when Gabe was about three years old. He's nine now, and still as critter-loving a kid as I've ever seen. On his desk I recently counted two turtles, one frog, two hermit crabs, and—oh yes—about a dozen tadpoles swimming in—what else?—my best crystal bowl. I put up with a lot when it comes to matters of the heart. And for Gabe, frogs and turtles and tadpoles and such are definitely affairs of the heart.

Once, just once, in an effort to be "cool," Gabe broke his own little frog-loving heart. And I'll never forget it.

That fateful afternoon, Gabe burst into the house and dived onto my bed, wrapping a sheet tightly around his head. Being the sensitive and observant mother that I am, I sensed right away something might be amiss.

"Gabriel," I coaxed, "what's the matter, Honey?"

Nothing. No response from under the covers.

"Gabe, you can tell me *anything*. Have you done something wrong?"

There was a slight movement in the affirmative from the mummified form.

"Well, there's nothing you've done that can't be forgiven. Come on out and let's talk."

When he finally unraveled himself from the sheets I was taken aback by the flood of tears on his face and the obvious agony of soul in his eyes.

"What, Honey, *what?*" I asked softly, shaking my head and searching his face for clues.

After a few gulps he finally managed to say, "I . . . gigged . . . a . . . frog."

"Oh, dear," I said, remembering that Gabe's big brothers had been into gigging bullfrogs for sport, and then cooking their game's legs for meat. I'd never approved of it, but I know boys will be boys, and I tried not to think about the "frog hunting" going on in nearby ponds. And now it was clear: Gabe, trying to be a big hunter like his brothers, had taken a fork and "gigged" a small frog—thinking he'd bring home frog-leg "game" like the big guys.

"Oh, Gabriel," I said, "did it surprise you when you realized you had hurt something you've always loved?"

"Mo-o-mmm," he sobbed into my shoulder, his small fingers squeezing tightly into my arms, "I didn't think about it hurting him until it was over!"

I found myself swallowing lumps in my own throat all the while I was trying to convince my son he could be forgiven for his mistake. In truth, I wasn't stifling tears for Gabe's "heinous crime." It was because I identified with him so much. Have we not all, at one time or another, hurt something we loved and held dear? Haven't I "gigged" the ones I love the most with my careless or hateful words? And then suffered the weight of my guilt, wishing—oh wishing so hard—that I could turn back the clock and erase something awful I'd said or done? Every child, every man, and every woman has at one time or another come face to face with the fact that they've just gigged an innocent frog—that is, if they are still tenderhearted enough to admit it.

What to do, what to do? Dry the tears. Have a proper burial. And go back to loving frogs—this time with a deeper awareness of how precious and dear and inescapably beautiful are all the things that have been created by God's hand.

A few months after Gabe's frog-gigging crisis, he and I were walking hand in hand along our country road. Out from the woods, a box turtle lumbered into view. Gabe looked up at me and grinned toward heaven.

"Oh, wow, Mom!" he exclaimed. "That's two turtles in one day! Man, God's being good to me."

Gabe knew, as only a child can know, that all had been forgiven. And he also knew, instinctively, that God loved nothing more than showing off His frogs and turtles and toads to him. For it is our children—tender of heart and low to the earth—who are, most assuredly, the connoisseurs of creation.

Be gentle and ready to forgive; never hold grudges. Remember, the Lord forgave you.
COLOSSIANS 3:13, TLB

S I X

Am I Cute?

G abriel has a friend living in the neighborhood now, which is a pretty big deal in this lonesome neck of the woods. Her name is Sarah, and she is eight years old. Now if someone asked me to choose a little girl who could epitomize my own "child within," Sarah would most definitely be in the running. Though she's a blue-eyed, cherub-faced blond—and I'm an olive-skinned brunette—I've decided we still have a lot in common. Our best hope of survival in this world is our ability to be really cute once we get ourselves into hot water.

Since Sarah's overactive conscience sometimes makes her honest to a fault, it is vital that she maintains her charm as she begins her truth telling. Otherwise, one might be tempted to wring her neck.

One April afternoon, the phone rang at my house and I heard Sarah's cheerful voice on the other end of the line.

"Happy birthday, Becky," she said.

"Oh, Sarah, how nice of you to remember!" I responded with genuine feeling.

"Well, I *didn't* remember." As I said, from Miss Sarah, one can always expect the unvarnished truth. I thought I'd help ease her conscience.

"It's OK, Sarah. You didn't remember yesterday, on my *actual* birthday, but you remembered *today* and it was so nice of you to call."

"Well, I didn't remember today or yesterday. Gabe just told me about it."

I was determined to be gracious about these belated birthday greetings, but Sarah was not making it easy.

"OK, Sarah, but you see, the fact is you called to wish me a happy birthday all on your own and that was a very nice thing to do. Thank you."

A loud silence followed. The angst on the end of the line was palpable, for Sarah is always compelled to tell the whole truth and nothing but the truth.

"Well, actually . . ." Sarah started. *Did I really want to hear what was coming next?* There would be no stopping Sarah until she had completely unburdened herself.

"Well, actually, Gabe *made* me call."

It was important that I get this straight. This child *was* telephoning me with a heartfelt and sincere-sounding birthday greeting. However, I was now to understand that Gabriel, my young son, was *forcing* her to do so. Silently I thought, *I get the picture, Sarah. No more explanations, please.* Anxious to put an end to this conversation before more true confessions poured across the line, I signed off in a hurry.

"Sarah, thanks for calling. You have made my day."

"Oh, you're welcome," came the sweet reply.

Not only are Sarah's "live" phone calls entertaining; the ones she leaves on my answering machine are equally popular. They bear perpetual testimony to her confused state of mind, with which I identify so heartily. When someone says, "Sarah left another message!" we all come running. For one thing, it took little Sarah a couple of tries to figure out that my voice on the other end was actually a tape recording and not me in person.

Her first recorded phone message went something like this:

"Can Gabe come over? What are you saying to me? Momma! Come here! Becky just picked up the phone and started talking to me, and I don't understand anything she said. *What?* Oh. *Is this a recording?* Oh. Well, I just don't know what to say. I guess I'm just pretty mixed up."

Ah, a girl after my own befuddled heart. If you know how to play your cards right, even confusion can be charming.

There was another message I almost couldn't bring myself to erase—it was left this summer while Gabe was supposed to have been over at Sarah's house playing. I later learned he had run home to go to the bathroom, but he'd neglected to tell Sarah he was leaving. When I checked the phone recorder later, Sarah's very serious message was blinking.

"Becky. I'm sorry to tell you this, but I lost Gabe. I can't find him anywhere. I'm sorry. He was here and now he is gone and I've looked everywhere. I don't know what else to do. We just lost him, that's all. I'm sorry, but he's gone. That's all I can say. I am really, really sorry."

Once again, I can relate to Sarah's message. If there is one underlying theme running through my own psyche, it is this: I am sorry. I am sorry I'm late. I'm sorry dinner isn't on the table right now. Or in the oven. Or even in little unprepared segments in the refrigerator. I'm sorry the house is a mess, and I'm sorry I've gained five more pounds. However, I am a Sorry Survivor. Let me rephrase that. I am a Survivor of Sorry.

How? I work really, really hard at being cute enough to compensate. Sometimes it does the trick; sometimes it backfires. But if you happen to be a child like Sarah, or an adult like me—if you find yourself being too honest for your own good, or in a constant state of confusion, or if you have a hard time keeping up with important things (like eight-year-old boys)—you may want to take careful notes. I recently pulled off a "coup de cute," and it probably saved my skin.

It all started after the Winnebago incident—the one that killed my once-spiffy Ford Explorer. Anyway, as I was rummaging through my purse after the accident, I came upon a tissue-thin piece of paper I'd forgotten all about. It happened to be a traffic ticket I'd received while driving on one of Gabe's field trips a few weeks earlier. (I had run a stop sign at the park.) Upon examining the fine print, I realized with some shock that I had missed the court date by ten days. Since Scott had recently bent another woman's fender, and I now had a major accident claim on my insurance, a thought occurred to me: *Maybe this is not the best time to have an outstanding warrant for my arrest.*

When I confessed my error to my husband, his expression didn't change—the way Clint Eastwood's doesn't change—and he retired to our bedroom to meditate. When he came out, his speech was prepared.

"Becky, listen. This problem could be disastrous. With another ticket, the insurance company could drop us and put us into a pool."

"Do you think they'll just throw us in with our clothes on and everything?"

"Becky, this is serious—you *know* what I mean. With Zach about to turn sixteen, our insurance will soar through the roof. I don't know how you're gonna do it, Honey. I know you're still shaken up from almost being splattered by a Winnebago, but you've *got* to charm your way out of this one. Godspeed."

The first thing that came to mind as I was receiving my marching orders was a bright orange billboard I'd recently seen on the highway. It read, "Traffic Tickets? No problem. Call 1-800-We-Fix-'Em." Or something like that. So my next move was to call a lawyer from the yellow pages whose advertising square looked most like the billboard. The deep male voice on the other end sounded fairly upbeat and hopeful as I described my case, until I told him the name of the judge on the bottom of my ticket.

"Ma'am," he quickly advised, "that's the toughest judge in the county. He doesn't cut anybody any slack once they've missed their court date. Just send 'em the money, and pray your insurance company has mercy on you."

I hung up, swallowed hard, and gave myself a pep talk. *OK, OK. So this judge is no soft touch. And sure, lots of women have tried and failed to cry or sweet talk their way out of a ticket in his court. But I must not give up. Scott's counting on me; he believes I can do this, and I have to give it my best shot.*

Just then my eyes fell upon a couple of my books and then to a chapter I had recently completed on the subject of my forgetfulness. It was called, "I Never Promised You a Rose Garden. Or Did I? I Can't Seem to Remember."

That's it! I thought, *I'll try to entertain him!* For the thirty minutes it took me to drive to the county courthouse, I conversed—nonstop and fervently—with the Almighty.

"God, grant me favor in the eyes of this judge and please, if You see fit, let him be a wanna-be writer." Human nature being what it is, I knew if the judge "had always wanted to write a book," he might very well be putty in my hands.

Upon arrival, I was ushered into the judge's chambers by a secretary in sensible shoes, who gave me little in the way of a greeting other than a pitying shake of her head. Sitting down on the edge of a cold vinyl chair in front of an expansive bench, I found myself opposite the Judge of No Mercy. Nervously, I cleared my throat.

"Your Honor, sir. First of all, I'd like to explain my situation—"

"Well, you can't," he said without looking up.

"Why not?" I asked, caught more than a little off guard.

"Because first you have to enter a plea. What will it be?"

"Insanity."

With that, he glanced up, and I thought I saw a glimmer of a smile. Perhaps I *had* found a soft spot after all. I settled on a more feasible plea of "no load contender"—or whatever it is—I told the judge I wanted the one that means "I'm not saying I did, but I'm not saying I didn't." This time he definitely smiled. Things were looking up, so I plunged ahead with my plan. I plopped two of my books, and the Forgetful Chapter, on top of the mahogany desk between us. His Honor's thick eyebrows stood at attention.

Thankfully, I had dabbled quite a bit in law, having read two John Grisham novels and viewed *The Firm* on video. And who didn't see more than their fair share of the O.J. trial? Patting the pile, and doing my best Marsha Clark imitation, I simply said, "Evidence."

Any balanced jury could have seen I was now on an unstoppable roll.

"You see, Your Honor, I'm sure lots of people come in and out of your office every day and *say* they forgot about their traffic tickets. But I have brought you undeniable *proof.* I actually make a living writing about all the things I've forgotten. Short and long-term memory loss is a handicap, as much as any other physical disability. But you can see from the evidence before you that I've determined to turn my disability into income and inspiration. So when I tell you that I forgot about the ticket in my wallet, you can believe, beyond any reasonable doubt, that I am telling you the truth."

He was quiet for a few seconds. Slowly, he eased his substantial body back in his black leather chair, scratched his chin, and sized me up with a raised brow. I gulped. What had I done now? Whatever it was, it was too late to back out. After what seemed like eons, he broke the silence.

"So you're a writer?"

"Yes, I am. I do so solemnly swear. I mean, I don't swear in my writing. I mean I swear I am a writer. Yes, Your Honor, I do . . . I mean, I am."

"You know, I've always dreamed of writing a book someday."

Oh, God, You are merciful to me! From that moment the judge and I were pals, friends—yes, even buds, if you will. He recounted tale after tale of life in a small-town courtroom. Why, before long we were laughing and slapping the bench and having a rousing good time. Then there was a knock at the door. The judge wound down a good story about a little old lady who'd told some amazing whoppers trying to squirm out of a delinquent ticket. Then good naturedly, he called out, "Come on in!"

The gentleman behind the door peeked in, his face a curious study.

"Thought I ought to check in on you, Judge. Sounds like you're having an awfully good time in here."

"Well, come on in," the judge said amiably. "Got a little gal here I want you to meet. She's real forgetful, so I've been trying to impress upon her the importance of putting outstanding traffic tickets at the top of her priority list. I'd sure hate to see her locked up in your jail."

With that, the judge smiled in my direction and said, "Mrs. Freeman, meet our chief of police."

Turning his attention back to the police chief, the judge spoke with mock sternness, "Listen, this young lady will need a police escort to the city limits. She's real accident-prone." Both men broke into a camaraderie of chuckles at my expense, but I couldn't have been more thrilled.

As I stood to shake the jovial judge's hand and take my leave, he informed me I could still take Defensive Driving to cover my ticket. I floated out of his office on wings of gratitude, but when I told the secretary outside that the judge had granted me mercy, she refused to take my word for it. She wasted no time picking up the phone and dialing his chambers. A few seconds later, the bewildered woman was staring at the receiver and then at me and back again at the receiver.

"Well, if that don't beat all. What in the world did you say to him?"

I shrugged and replied, "I just told him the facts, ma'am. Just the facts."

Not long after the incident, my mother sent me a greeting card in the mail. A note was attached to the front saying, "You might want to use this the next time you get in a fix with a judge." The front of the card shows a black-and-white photo of an adorable little girl, about five years old, wearing a rainslicker and a hat. She's holding an envelope in her outstretched hand.

———

Her facial expression is angelic, yet pitiful. Inside, the card reads, "Will you forgive me if I remind you how cute I am?"

Sarah, I have a feeling you and I will need all the "cute" we can get in this life.

Though there will be times when others may say we are maddening, I hope no one will say we are not entertaining. If we're very good, they might even say we have *charm.*

But just to be on the safe side, I think I'll tape the date for my defensive driving course to the dashboard of my vehicle. Now if only I can remember where I put the tape.

Standing in the court, she obtained favor
in his sight.

ESTHER 5:2, NASB

۶

Would You Rub My Back?

I t was another one of those over-my-head, insufferably long
church services. I was probably four or five years old. I laid
my head on my mother's lap and curled my patent leather shoes
up under the flounce of my dress. I remember Mother's lap
being extra firm because she was wearing her full-strength
Sunday morning girdle. My eyelids grew heavy as she absently
stroked my hair and played with one of my curls. I felt loved,
cuddled—her baby again. Then came—ahhhh, heaven in a
church pew—my mother's fingernails, gently etching circles and
curlicues and figure eights as they floated up and down my back.
Even Big Church preaching could be tolerated under the influence of those hypnotic maternal hands.

Touch—the soothing power of touch.

When I was thirteen, I contracted hepatitis while on a youth
trip—the form of hepatitis you get from drinking bad water in
Mexico. Back home, in the wee hours of the morning, I couldn't
eat, my side ached, I was weak. I had missed six weeks of school,
and now my skin was afire with a rash—a side-effect of the jaun-
dice. No amount of medicine, baths, or tears would halt the

burning itch as it spread from my head to my toes. My mother, in the early morning darkness, sensed my misery—with good old-fashioned mother radar, I suppose—and padded down the hall to my bedroom. Once here she helped ease me from my bed to a comfortable pallet on the living room couch. Then, having done all a mother could do, she began to pray. Her hands rested upon my back, her words pouring quietly into the darkness.

"Father, I come asking relief for my Becky. Please grant her a good night's sleep." After that, all I remember is sliding into sleep with Mother's fingernails gently etching curlicues and circles and figure eights onto my back. The insidious itching, miraculously, was gone.

Touch—oh, the healing power of touch.

Fifteen. Sick again from bad drinking water on a summer mission trip to a foreign country. But this time I was still *in* the foreign country: Guatemala. I was riding on a rickety bus, with Scott sitting next to me holding me upright as his arm encircled my shoulders. I was not so sick, however, that I couldn't appreciate the delicious feel of Scott's skin next to mine. We'd not been allowed to show any physical affection during the summer until now, when the leaders relaxed the rules somewhat for our journey home. I will never forget the precise moment Scott reached over and took my hand; it felt amazingly tiny threaded between his strong fingers. It was wondrous, this hand-holding business, and I recall wishing there was some way we could stay linked this way forever. Then Scott said something that we both remember vividly, even after twenty-three years.

"Becky," he said with a boyish grin, as he stroked the top of my hand, "I have a feeling the sense of touch will always be an important part of our relationship." Now I know what you are probably thinking: There's a sharp line to use on a sick, vulnerable teenage girl. Think what you like; I happen to know my young heartthrob had the most honorable of intentions.

Wait a minute. Hold on. My husband is informing me that maybe it was just a wee bit of a line. But it worked. And he was right. Touch has been a special form of conversing between us for more than twenty years, connecting us in times of confusion, heartache, anger, passion, and tenderness—when words are either too clumsy or inadequate for the task.

Touch—the communicating power of touch.

We read about it in psychology and medical studies everywhere—this powerful, God-given force called human touch. Babies thrive on it and shrivel up and die without it. A simple hug has been shown to lower blood pressure and to release feel-happy endorphins. Even stroking a pet is healthy, they say, because there's something about touching a living, breathing *anything*.

A couple of years ago, Mother and I were interviewed at a local radio station. The host asked Mom for her best advice on raising kids. "Well," she said, "you pray a lot. You laugh often. And you keep touching them. When they're small, rub their backs, stroke their hair. As they become teenagers a quick neck rub or hand on their shoulder may be all they will accept. But don't stop giving your children some measure of physical affection."

No mother is perfect, but in this area, mine scores especially high. She's been given lots of opportunity to practice—not only with her babies, teenagers, and grandchildren, but also with the elderly. As each of our grandparents took their turn being sick and, finally, dying, Mother rubbed their tired feet with warm lotion; caressed their weary, wrinkled faces; held their love-starved hands.

Touch—the compassionate power of touch.

Even unto death. Perhaps, in fact, it is especially during occasions of grief and death that we find our greatest comfort in the voiceless compassion of a caring touch.

It was last summer. I was sitting across from my friend, Ruth, sharing a casual lunch of hamburgers, spicy fries, and soft drinks. The setting was average, everyday—just two women enjoying a lunch out. Anyone looking at us would have no way of knowing that one of us had passed through the death of her one-year-old son a few days before—a parent's ultimate nightmare. Yet even in the midst of her grief, Ruth managed to smile and occasionally to laugh.

Baby Caleb had been terminally ill since he'd drawn his first breath, so the element of shock was not as strong a factor in Ruth's grief as it might have been otherwise. But grief still comes. Her nursery stood emptied of its precious smiling, reaching content. Even so, Ruth, a young woman of boundless courage and determined joy, presses on, looking for the "good" in "all things." Her faith through this season of trial leaves me stunned with admiration. Still I know she aches, and I want so much to be of comfort. What can a sister offer another whose world has just fallen apart at life's fragile seams?

"Ruth," I asked tentatively, "can you tell me, other than our prayers, what practical things help at a time like this?"

She smiled as she retraced the events of the last few days. "Becky, even though Lee and I knew the end was always one breath away for Caleb, his passing still came as a surprise. I was in a fog all that morning of his death. Friends came with food, the youth group dropped by to clean house, mow the yard, and generally offer their services. All of that helped tremendously. But I still felt so uptight—so *anxious.* Then a couple of my closest friends sat me down and said, 'Ruth, we want you to think for a second. What do *you* need?' Then out of the blue, I found myself saying, 'I think I need a massage.'"

I laughed. "Had you ever had a massage before?"

"No," she answered, "I don't know why or how I knew what I needed. But God must have known. My friends arranged an appointment that very afternoon with a massage therapist named Adreena. And Becky, it was the strangest thing. It turned out to be exactly what I needed. I laid down on the table and Adreena began kneading away at the stress and sadness in my weary body. It was *wooonderful.* After months of nonstop caring for a critically sick baby, stroking him, attending to his needs, now I was on the receiving end of care. By the time Adreena finished with me, an hour later, I found I had the strength to get up and complete the funeral arrangements. My fuzzy head was more clear, and I knew I was going to make it through the day."

Touch—the life-affirming power of touch.

Ruth's testimony piqued my curiosity. I'd never had a massage. The whole concept of a stranger pouring oil on someone's body and rubbing them down seemed a little weird to me. Yet in many, if not most, cultures this practice isn't given a second thought.

As a matter of fact, I'd just read a passage from Suzanne Lipsett's journal, *Surviving a Writer's Life*. As a young student, Suzanne had been raped and assaulted. Since that time, she stayed emotionally numb. Seeking escape from painful memories, she traveled overseas and ended up in Istanbul. A series of circumstances landed her in the company of an aged, wrinkled Turkish woman. Much to her surprise, the old woman insisted on giving Suzanne a massage. The mothering, caring touch from this foreign woman sparked a turning point in Suzanne's journey toward healing. She wrote, "There was little left in me but gratitude to the woman whose hands had taken time to stroke and knead me. I was clean and warm, a child in the hands of an old, knowing woman whose very body spoke survival of her own nameless ordeals."[3]

Massage has been used for centuries to keep skin and muscles healthy and to relieve the stress of weary minds. My own youngest child begs me nightly for a back rub because it helps him fall asleep more peacefully. There must be something to it. But still . . .

Ruth assured me that Adreena was a trained professional—like a medical doctor. "Massage is therapeutic," many of my friends kept telling me, unflinching in their insistence that I must try it. I worried about disrobing in front of a stranger, even with a towel covering me. I possess several lumps and bulges—not to mention road maps of stretch marks—I prefer to keep under wraps. But then Ruth told me that Adreena was blind, and my excuses ran out. I made an appointment for a Tuesday afternoon.

Adreena turned out to be a pretty African American woman in her early sixties. She wore a simple cotton dress with her hair pulled up in a bun. When I walked into the room, she greeted me in a lilting voice. "Well, hello! I'm over here, Hon, be with you in a second."

I undressed and lay down on the table, covered only by a towel, and growing more uneasy about this idea as the seconds ticked by. I told myself this was just an experiment; I would be like a reporter on assignment. Adreena walked into the room, turned the radio to an easy-listening station, poured lotion on her hands, and started in on my neck.

Whoa. I was putty. I was a lump of dough. *Yes,* I thought, *I believe I can probably handle this assignment after all.*

While Adreena kneaded my muscles, I started a conversation. I began by telling her how much she had meant to my friend Ruth on a painful, heart-wrenching day.

"Ruth?" Adreena asked enthusiastically. "Oh, Honey, I liked her right away. She told me she'd just lost her baby boy. What can you say to a mother at a time like that? I just tried to love and comfort her through my hands. I believe my abilities are a gift and every day I pray that God will use me to minister love."

"Adreena," I mumbled as my body unwound in places I never even knew were wound, "what made you decide to do this for a living?"

"Well," she began, turning around to gather more lotion, "I like people. One good thing about being blind is that I honestly never think about a person's color. Their looks don't matter to me at all; it's their personalities and voices I remember. Also, I knew I'd be good at this because I do sincerely care about people. I've had massages, and I can tell the ones that are given with a sense of caring and the ones that are given out of duty. Without sight, all your other senses grow stronger. So I can tell a lot about people from something as simple as touch."

I closed my eyes and listened as Adreena went on to tell me how, as a little girl, she lost her sight after a series of operations for a brain tumor. She told of a mother who had wanted the best for her and, even though life was hard, had found a way to send Adreena to one of the best schools for the blind in the country.

As I lay on that table, I was getting a double whammy—refreshment for body *and* soul. Adreena's inspiration was infectious as she continued talking and kneading.

"You gotta have faith—in God and in yourself. Set realistic goals. When we do something we're a little afraid of—but we believe in ourselves and have faith and get it done—it strengthens us. My mother and my teacher and friends at the blind school all taught me these things and I'm here to tell you, they work. They made me believe in myself—and I've never been afraid to venture out."

While Adreena massaged my shoulders, arms, and hands, I discovered more about her life. She had once been married and now had two grown daughters. She spoke with her grown children almost daily, she said, but she's quite content to live alone. She talked of the exciting occasion when as a teenager she'd taken her first plane trip—a trip to get her first seeing-eye dog, a collie-shepherd named Susan. When Susan died after fourteen years of faithful companionship, it had been like losing a member of the family. Her children were heartbroken as well. Adreena never replaced Susan. She said she just never saw the need to.

"Do you ever get depressed, Adreena?" I asked lazily, curious to know if this lively woman ever suffered moments of despair.

"Now, I'm not Super Woman or anything," she answered as she continued working away with her magic fingers. "Sometimes I get down in the dumps and then I have me a good cry. Then I say, 'Lord I don't want to feel this way.' I hate those times. It's like an artery is plugged up in my spirit and I can't give out all the love and joy I want to be giving. Every Sunday morning, it's my job to give an inspirational statement at my church. Oh, they seem to love it, but I love it even more. I've got so much inspiration coming my way now, with people handing me quotes and verses and such, that I had to ask them to let me give two a Sunday."

Adreena rubbed my feet with a circular motion, and applied long firm strokes to the backs of my ankles. I melted. I vowed to teach Scott how to do this.

"Adreena?"

"Yes."

"Why don't you go ahead and give me the full treatment. Inspire me with one of your favorite sayings."

"Well, all right. Here's one of my favorites." She slowed down for effect, "With God's arms under us and His love around us we can face anything before us."

"Oooh, that's good." I turned over like a chicken on a spit to get the other side done.

"How's 'bout this one?" Adreena paused from her work a moment, adopting her Sunday morning voice. "Earth's worst often turns out to be heaven's best."

"Your church must be awfully proud to have you there," I commented. "Adreena, can I ask you one more question?"

"Sure."

"If you had to choose between being blind or deaf, which would you choose?"

I was unprepared for Adreena's depth of enthusiasm on the subject. "I believe I would have to choose to be blind, because there are much too many things I love to hear. I *love* music. Oh, how I love music! And the birds! How could I stand it if I couldn't hear the birds? I hear them sing, and I'm so thankful for their cheerful voices in the morning. And the sound of a baby's coo, and the little noise my dog made when she'd hand me her paw or lay her head on my lap! And the voices of my children. No, I can't even *imagine* not being able to hear!"

The thought of her children and grandchildren led Adreena to one last piece of advice before she ended my "therapy" session.

"And about children. Hon, you have to *listen* to children. They want to tell you things you may not think are very important, but you really listen to them—because it's important to them—oh my, how children need that. I used to read books, from Braille, to my children. They *loved* that attention. And when they were babies I nursed them because I knew the closeness was good for them. Now my daughters want to do the same with their babies."

"Adreena," I observed, "because of your blindness I'm sure your children had more physical contact with you than most children have with their mothers, out of pure necessity. Maybe that's one of the many reasons you've had such great relationships with them."

She nodded and smiled as I rolled off the table, limp as a rag. I felt refreshed, renewed. I thanked Adreena for using her gifts—her warm, caring, mothering hands and her warm, caring, mothering words—to bless my day. I promised myself as I readied to leave, *I will definitely do this again.*

❧❧❧

That evening, at home, I noticed Gabriel tucked in his bed as I passed by his room. I paused to give him his favorite go-off-to-sleep back rub.

I also took the time to trace a few curlicues, circles, and figure eights on his back with my fingernails, which he liked very much. I told him he could thank his Granny. He looked up at me curiously.

Adreena told me she's flying up North to visit her grandchild this Christmas. I imagine her holding him close, reading to him from a book as her fingers fly across the colored pictures and dots of Braille. Just as she'd done with her daughters.

Touch—the cross-generational *blessing* of touch.

Paul went in to see him and, after prayer,
placed his hands on him and healed him.
ACTS 28:8
❧

EIGHT

I'm Gonna Marry a Hero!

Do you remember the first hero that made your little knees go weak? (Or, perhaps, inspired you to run through the house with your mother's lingerie secured around your neck with a large, pink safety pin?)

I was six when I found myself lovestruck over a cartoon rendition of Hercules. He was, I thought, the most handsome and well-drawn figure of a man I'd ever seen. I'd dream of being rescued from my kindergarten-small-potato life and swept away in the arms of my cartoon hunk. Even more interesting, I believed it could happen at any moment.

Then one day an awful thought crossed my mind. No, it wasn't that the man of my dreams was a comic-book drawing on a black-and-white screen. I never considered there could be any complications in carrying on a relationship with a cartoon. My concern went much, much deeper.

If Hercules flies out of the television set tonight to carry me off to Happily Ever-after Land, I can't even go! I don't have a single princess dress to wear!

STILL LICKIN' THE SPOON

So, in early fall, I began plotting how I might acquire a suitable gown should my Hercules come calling. At first, I tried getting a dress the surefire old-fashioned way: I whined. When whining failed to get the hoped-for results, I turned to my last resort: Santa Claus. On Christmas Eve, I don't think I slept at all. I was worried Santa might not be trusted to pick out a suitable princess gown. No matter how jolly and well-suited he was, Santa was still a *male,* and how could a man know what a little girl needed in a fairy princess dress?

Maybe Mrs. Claus helped him out, I don't know. All I know is that under the tree lay a perfect dress: silky blue and princessy pouffy with flounces of netting under the skirt. I nearly burst with gratitude. Thus, appropriately costumed, I spent many a happy hour imagining myself being carried away—all bedecked in princess blue—in the strong arms of my Grecian hero.

But then one day, as I was turning the channels (by hand—things were tough, kids, in the olden days before remote control), I found someone new. And suddenly, I realized my cartoon hero from Mount Olympus was much too one-dimensional. What I needed was a real man. A swinger. A man with minimal clothing needs. A man who knew how to hold meaningful conversations, even if they were with a chimpanzee.

During my Tarzan the Ape Man phase, I spent my summer afternoons imagining I was swinging from tree branch to tree branch with my hero of the month. I could perform a lovely female version of the famous "A-a-e-e-e-ah!!!" yell, accompanied by dramatic chest beating. I was sure if Tarzan ever swung by my backyard and overheard my mating call and saw how gracefully I could hang by my knees from the cross bar on my swing set, he'd drop Jane faster than a slick banana.

After Tarzan came Superman, then Prince Charming, and then the cute guy from "Lost in Space" took my fancy. Oh, I also took quite a shine to Robin. (Batman was too old for my taste.) From frontier survivalists to caped heroes leaping tall buildings in a single bound; from the adventurous to the supernaturally charming—I've always been a pushover for a hero.

Why this longing for a knight in shining armor? Feminists warn that these little-girl fantasies are harmful, leading us into womanhood with thoughts like, *I need to be rescued by a man* (thoughts from which, I suppose, we need to be rescued by feminist psychologists). Perhaps, to some extent, they are right. But how do you explain little boys and *their* worship of superheros? Seems to me both sexes dream of being rescued by a larger-than-life benevolent being.

Children realize early on that no mere mortal can save them from the evil forces in this world. The rescuer, the hero, the *savior* must be of supernatural stock. Is it coincidence that Jesus Christ so perfectly fulfills this childhood longing? (A longing that never, even in adulthood, really goes away.) The Book of the Revelation is, for the good guys, the ultimate fairy tale come true. Our Hero, the Royal Son, will come riding in on a white horse to rescue us from the evil dragon and take us to live happily ever after with Him—in a jeweled city of no more tears. Talk about the fulfillment of every child's fantasy. But while I wait along with boys and girls for my Heavenly Prince to come, I've been given the privilege of living with an average, everyday human hero.

Enter Scott.

From the moment I met my husband-to-be, I could tell he had the raw makings of a hero. Of course, in fantasy, it's romantic to be in love with a man who leans toward the heroic and adventure-esque. In reality, it's terrifying. There's not space to cover the Epic Adventures of Scott Man—so how about I lightly touch on the last six months?

Let's see, there was the day Scott was supposed to come home early to watch the kids while I went to a class. He breezed in about thirty minutes late, rushed me off, and offered no explanation for his tardiness. The next morning, over a leisurely cup of coffee, Scott mentioned—almost as an aside—why he had been late the night before. Seems he'd been helping a woman get her head together—literally.

———

The woman of which he spoke had been in a car accident near the bridge Scott crosses on his daily commute home. Our hero was first on the scene.

"So," Scott calmly related, "I crawled into the cab of the woman's pickup. The skin across the top of her head had split in two when it hit the windshield, exposing her skull. So I held the two flaps of skin together and put pressure on the wound with my shirt until the paramedics got there."

"And you call *this* an excuse for being late?" I teased, amazed he actually kept this story to himself overnight. "Is she going to be OK?"

"Well, it took some talking to calm her down, but I think she's going to be fine."

Now, I don't know about you, but if I had been in my husband's place, I would have found this turn of events incredibly newsworthy. As a matter of fact, as I told Scott, "If I had been the one to help that woman close her wound—shoot, if I'd Band-aid-ed someone's *paper cut*—I would have been tooting my own horn even as I pulled up into the driveway!"

Not so with my husband. He is understatement personified—which is, I suppose, the sign of a true hero. Strong. Quiet. Modest. A man of steel with just the right mixture of compassion. The sort of hero all little girls want to marry when they grow up.

Then there was this past summer with Scott, the Olympic Mountain Man. While on a business trip with my publishers in Denver, I let Scott off the "husband hook" for the day to do whatever he wanted—with assurances from him that he'd make it back in time for dinner with friends. True to his word, Scott met me at our hotel door just in time for dinner, though I noticed he was a little out of breath.

It wasn't until hours later, after the dinner, that I asked my husband for details on how he'd whiled away the afternoon.

"Oh," he answered nonchalantly, "I climbed to the top of the highest mountain in the Rockies."

"Come again?" I asked, blinking.

"Yeah," he continued, "I knew I didn't have much time, so I just started running up Mount Elbert. Without a coat or hiking boots or gear or anything, I figured I could make some good time."

"Wait," I stammered. "You hiked up a mountain without a coat? In your tennis shoes? No water, no food, no backpack, no emergency kit?"

"Yeah, it was kind of stupid I guess," he admitted. "Before long, I sort of felt like I was living through the ol' Pony Express motto. I ran through rain, then sleet, then snow. All I missed was the black of night. But it was kind of funny, too."

"Oh?"

"Yeah, when I reached the crest of the mountain, these two ice climbers coming from the glacier side reached the top at exactly the same time I did. They were dressed from head to toe in these huge Eskimo parkas, loaded down with climbing gear. Anyway, they just sort of peeked up over the side of the cliff as the snow swirled around them. And there I was in a summer shirt, standing in the middle of a blizzard on top of this mountain. All they could do was stare."

"No kidding."

"So I said, 'I guess this is the top.' They just kept staring, and then, finally, they sort of grunted. Then I said, 'You know, I'm not really dressed for this. I best be moseying along.'"

I shook my head and asked, "So, Mountain Man, how long did all this take you?"

"The whole trip, up and back only took a total of three hours and forty-five minutes. The guide at the bottom couldn't believe it."

"Scott, I can't believe you cut it that close!" I shouted incredulously. "You *had* to believe you'd make record time if you were going to keep your promise to me."

He looked at me thoughtfully as he brushed back his sandy blond hair with his fingers. "Yeah," he answered slowly, "guess I did."

Keep in mind, Scott reported all this in the tone of voice he uses for telling me he had the tuna on whole wheat for lunch.

Let's fast-forward now to as recently as a month ago. While our family was eating dinner, I happened to mention that I'd seen a huge garbage truck laying on its side in front of a local store.

"Oh, yeah," Scott said, taking a bite of his salad, "that happened right in front of me. This morning on my way to work, I climbed on top of the truck and helped pull the driver out."

"Oh, sure, Scott," I prodded. "Come on—this 'hero thing' is getting to be a bit much."

He just looked at me and shrugged as if to say, "I can't help it. I only do what must be done." Scott the Rescue Man, doing his good deed for the morning.

A mere two weeks ago, my husband strolled in the front door reeking of smoke. He headed to the freezer and made an ice pack, placing it between his blistered hands. His face looked as though he'd spent a week on the beach without sunscreen.

"So what have you been doing now?" I asked, inspecting his wounds. "Fighting fires?"

Again, he looked at me with those soulful brown eyes and nodded the nod of a little boy who's been into mischief. Scott had been driving along the road, minding his own business, when, he said, "I saw—off to the side—an older man in a panic. He'd been burning trash, and the flames had leaped out of the trash can and quickly spread to the dry grass and nearby trees. So I stopped my truck and ran out to lend a hand, and that's when I realized the flames were heading straight for the man's home."

You got it. Until the fire department arrived, Scott fought the fire back from the house by shoveling dirt on the flames. Scott, the Volunteer Fire Fighter.

I could go on and on with this man's adventures, both serious and frivolous. For a lark, while we were in Florida, Scott took the kids' dare and bungee-jumped. But no, he couldn't jump straight down like every other daring tourist. He had to do a triple back-flip on the way down. Scott the Man Who Can Leap from Tall Buildings in Three Backward Bounds.

We got a Christmas card last week from people I've never heard of, inviting us to come visit them anytime we might pass through Missouri. Curious, I asked my husband what it was about.

"Oh, yes," Scott said when he saw the card, "those must be the folks whose car broke down awhile back. They were from out of town and had some elderly relatives in the car with them, so I towed them to a service station. Nice people." Scott, the Good Samaritan.

As you know (but it bears repeating), sometimes it scares me to death living with an adventure/rescue-type guy. In all honesty, Scott could easily lose his life someday in the pursuit of a thrill or in trying to help someone. But the truth of the matter is, I married exactly the sort of man I've dreamed about since I was a little girl. And would I stay as fascinated with a book worm, computer nerd, or fellow couch potato? As things are, I got my Hercules, Tarzan, and Prince Charming all rolled up in one.

Oh, there's just one more heroic feat of Scott's I'd like to mention before I sign off and go join my husband (who's currently snoring away in our bed under his cape). Every holiday season my husband dresses up in full Santa Claus regalia and visits a school full of underprivileged children. Then he holds more than 150 of them, one at a time, on his lap while they whisper their most fervent Christmas wishes into his ear.

This year Scott was stretched to superhuman endurance. The day my husband was scheduled to don his costume of thick velvet and fur, we had one of those crazy Texas December heatwaves. The thermometer climbed to nearly 80 degrees. Ho, ho, ho, HOT! But this Santa would not be stopped. One hundred and fifty sweaty lap-sittings later, Scott the Santa Man came home exhausted but jolly. I greeted him with a hug at the door.

"So, Santa, how'd it go?" I asked, motioning for him to sit down while I went to the kitchen for some refreshments.

Scott heaved a sigh as he lowered himself into a recliner and answered, "Great."

"Well, Mr. Santa," I said, handing him a cookie and a glass of milk, "now that I have you all to myself, there's something I've been wanting to tell you for a very long time." I moved to his lap and then whispered in his ear, "Thank you for the pouffy blue princess dress you gave me when I was five. And I also want you to know I finally married myself a real, genuine hero."

"Well, little girl," my Santa-Hero replied, "I have a secret to tell you, too."

"What's that?" I asked, smiling mischievously as I playfully fingered his white fur collar.

"At least two of the children who sat on my lap today wet right on the spot where you're sitting."

I jumped up right away.

But I ask you, honestly, does a man get any more heroic than this?

Many times you have miraculously rescued
me . . . You have been loving and kind to me.
PSALM 18:50, TLB

Why Can't Everybody Just Play Nice?

N ot all of childhood is sweetness and light.
Especially if you are the new kid in school. Or if you wear glasses—glasses so large and round that kids joke about your giant "fly eyes." Or if your front teeth come in with brown indentions instead of pearly white enamel because of some medicine a doctor prescribed when you were an infant.

Childhood is not sweet when it is important to be athletic and you, most definitely, are not. Even if you can hang from a chin-up bar for a hundred hours, it is of no use if you can only manage to throw the softball twenty feet. Without a good throwing arm you cannot receive the Presidential Physical Fitness Award. And that means you not only become a disgrace to the entire physically fit fourth grade, but also to the president of the United States of America.

Childhood is not light when you have a really pretty voice and love to sing, but the music teacher only notices the popular, loudish-singing girls. It is also not fair when that teacher handpicks the cast for the school musical instead of holding open tryouts.

Childhood is not sweet or light when your last name is Arnold and one of the most popular characters on TV is a pig from "Green Acres" named Arnold Ziffel.

Then there was PE. Maybe it's no coincidence that recess sounds a lot like *abscess*. I find them equally enjoyable. I have too many memories of standing against a brick wall, breaking out in a cold sweat, and praying that some preadolescent captain would choose me before I fell victim to the torturous fate of being— horrors—the last one picked.

How about lunch? Or not. I tried to spend as many lunching minutes as possible hiding out in the bathroom to avoid the popular girls' favorite game: Who Does and Does Not Get to Sit by Me? Sweetness and light? Ha!

It was during those middle grade school years I learned that the safest route to survival for me was to pretend to be shy. Better to be nothing, to disappear, than to chance public humiliation by reaching out and being labeled a nerd for daring.

It didn't take long to uncover the fact that fourth through sixth grade girls can be carnivorous, eating each other alive to maintain their place on top of the food chain. Because of that fact, I also learned what it's like to spend some part of every day either fighting back or succumbing to tears, trying to gather the emotional strength to face the next school day's onslaught.

There were those times I couldn't contain it, and would find myself overflowing into my mother's arms. She comforted. She agonized with me. Yet there was little she could say but "I understand" and "I think you're beautiful" and "It will get better" and all the other things we count on mothers to say at such times. It was a horrible, trapped period of life and I, the female embodiment of Charlie Brown, felt sentenced to Grade School Prison.

But somewhere in those miserable years I said to myself, "If I survive this, if I ever get the chance to be pretty or popular, I will find others who are shy and wear glasses and get teased and I will stand by their side and say, 'See these kids here—they are my friends and I happen to think they're pretty cool. Oh, and by the way, they, and anyone else who cares to join in, are welcome to sit by me at lunch.'"

The summer before my first year in junior high, the miracle occurred.

It began when my parents—God bless them—took me to the optometrist, shelling out a wad of hard-earned money I'm sure. I came home squinting and glorying in my new contact lenses—forever free of ol' Fly Eyes! Then it seemed almost overnight that my figure began to curve in and out in all the right places. To complete the transformation, our family dentist painted the brown spots on my teeth with a new white wonder called "bonding." I could smile again—a great big open-mouthed smile.

For the grand occasion of the first day of seventh grade, my mom made me a "knock 'em dead" dress. Its sleeveless green bodice was crisscrossed all over with cheerful strips of white rickrack, and from an empire waist flowed a skirt in the perfect shade of a ripe watermelon. Over the summer, my olive skin had baked to a golden brown and my hair had grown dark and long—long enough to tie into pigtails with thick lengths of matching yarn. For the final touch, I smoothed a tinted gloss over my lips—my first hint of makeup.

On that bright September morning, I had the heady experience of knowing I looked *quite* a picture. I would have known it even if my daddy hadn't given me a mixed look of worry and admiration as I strolled out the front door toward the waiting world of junior high.

Junior high, for me, gradually ushered in a time of "all things new." Boys who once taunted me turned into admirers. Even the popular girls became civil. I found myself growing confident. Then my self-esteem gained a foothold on even more solid ground. I discovered I had value, not only because my parents said I was a great kid, but because I'd discovered that the God who created everything in the whole world loved me. He even gave His life for me—*me*, Becky Arnold, a speck of preteen flesh down here on planet Earth. How can I begin to express the impact this knowledge had on this awkward girl in her season of blooming? (Youth workers take note. Your life and your message of hope make a *difference*.)

Blossoming though I was, I never forgot my "lonesome lunchroom" resolve. I set out to notice the lost, the different, the lonely, dotting our school's crowded halls and lunchrooms. So it came to pass that during my junior high years, and on until I graduated from high school, I befriended the loners, nerds, dorks, dweebs, geeks, freaks, brains, foreign students, artsy-drama types, budding philosophers, "Jesus freaks," and one talkative Jewish kid. (The Jewish boy even sent me a telegram from Israel on my wedding day!)

Funny, now that I think about it, I've always preferred the company of those who are a little out of step, a little quirky, a little apart from the popular core. I simply find them more fascinating. So I have to confess that my desire to befriend the odd-guy-out wasn't completely altruistic; I have a built-in affinity for those who cha-cha to the beat of a different drum. (Note to my dearest friends: Yes, I'm sorry, but it is true. In some way, you *are* slightly odd. But remember, I love you more for it.)

By the time I reached high school, several girls and I ended up in a loosely formed group. Not a clique really, because we welcomed anybody and everybody. Two or three times a week we'd walk to my house during our school lunch break. My mother—grateful, I think, for the happy appearance of chit-chatty laughter in my life—put up with the mess and allowed us to freely forage her clean kitchen for snacks. Not only did I begin to form wonderful friendships during those days, but other grade school wounds found their healing during my high school years. (Yes, moms. Yes, suffering eighth graders—there is life after junior high.)

In spite of my less-than-loudish musical beginnings, I went on to join a choir, perform in ensembles, sing solos, and play major parts in school musicals. Unfortunately, I had less luck keeping my name from being associated with pigs and hogs.

My grand stage debut was as the character Moon Beam McSwine, from *L'il Abner*. My part required that I carry a rubber pig in my arms, walk center stage, and belt out, "Howdy, boys, I'm Moon Beam McSwine. Sleeping out with pigs is my line. The fellas admire me, but they won't squire me unless the weather is fine. But I does all right when the wind blows the other way." Enchanting, wasn't it?

In spite of my piggish preamble, the "fellas" indeed seemed to admire me—especially at dress rehearsal when I donned my skimpy hillbilly costume. Thus attired, I encouraged such admiration, in fact, that my mother took no time in sewing extra rows of ruffles to my shorts and neckline before opening night.

And how can I forget that opening night? Unbeknownst to me, as I scooted across the stage for my big entrance, a pair of pantyhose adhered itself to the heel of my foot. The stage hands tried unsuccessfully to catch me, but they were too doubled over with laughter to be of help. The audience laughed and hooted and I ate it up—even after my eyes focused and I discovered it was my pantyhose trail, more than my comedic song, that had them going. Oh, I'll go ahead and say it: It was the night Miss McSwine discovered she had some ham.

For me, this pantyhose event marked a transformation: Rather than shrinking in shame, I found myself laughing along with the rest of them. Liz Curtis Higgs, a fantastic humorist and sweet friend, often says in her talks, "The day we learn to laugh at ourselves is the day we begin to grow up." After years of introspective pain, I was finally on my way.

Besides the joy of uncovering the funny streak buried in my "shy" personality, in my tenth grade year I fell head-over-heels-and-pantyhose in love. Finding a soulmate in Scott left me with a general feeling of "the world is all aglow." I pretty much floated throughout my remaining years in school. In fact, I was so crazy in love that I doubled up on my classes during my junior year and graduated early to become Scott's bride. (See *Marriage 9-1-1* for the rest of *that* story.)

Looking back on it now I have to say that even though my school days ended on a high note, the years of pain left a couple of scars. To this day, my idea of a nightmare is having to "mingle" in a large crowd of people I don't know. Give me one on one, or a small group of new folk, and I'm in my element. But when I'm thrown into an unfamiliar situation where I am supposed to mix and mingle, tears often involuntarily spring to my eyes. I'll find myself, as if on autopilot, escaping to the bathroom or to a quiet spot outside where I can regroup alone. My personal theory is that these emotions are flashbacks to lunchroom days when I stood gazing at a sea of kids, afraid of what to say and wondering where I should sit and if I'd be accepted or rejected.

Yet it's important to note that scars aren't all bad. They serve as reminders of battles endured and of what we want to avoid in the future. I'm not sure I would trade those painful early experiences for easier ones even if I had the power to do so, for they graced my teenage years and adulthood with a heightened sensitivity to feelings of others. I believe the hard experiences in life often leave us kinder people than we would have been if all of childhood was pure sweetness and light.

As a sophomore, singing in a girls' chorus, we performed a beautiful poem by William Penn, set to music. Even then, the words struck a chord in my heart and have followed me all these years.

> I expect to pass through life but once.
> If therefore, there be any kindness I can show . . .
> let me do it now, and not defer or neglect it,
> as *I shall not pass this way again.*

We are given one, and only one, journey through this life. One chance to show affection. One life to give love. I often visualize the faded image of a little girl with thick glasses sitting all alone, her heart aching for friends and a bit of human kindness. Perhaps those of us who've warmed benches and been passed over for others more beautiful try a little harder to love the unlovely. Having experienced the sting of rejection, I now have a tremendous appreciation for those who honor me with their kindness—who add to my everyday humdrum life a touch of sweetness and light.

Today was a great example. I went to our small-town grocery store and was immediately greeted by several of my buddies who work there. Maybe it was because it's the beginning of the Christmas season and I'm feeling especially sentimental; but it suddenly touched me just how special it is to walk into a store where I'm known by name—where small kindnesses have been shared over the years until our over-the-counter experiences have turned into store-bound friendships.

I've come to love Robert, the mentally challenged bag boy who never fails to greet me with a hearty welcome like, "You sure look nice today, ma'am." This, even when I'm wearing my old faded sweats. I know he loves to help, so whenever I can't find an item I ask for Robert's assistance. Then he cheerfully escorts me down the aisle, triumphantly pointing to the desired product on the shelf and shouts, "There it is! You didn't know where it was, huh? Well, I sure found it for you, didn't I? Yep. There it is, right there, yes sirree." It's nice to be helped with such enthusiasm.

I also love the way Judy, my friend and checkout woman, hollers her series of run-on questions in my direction over the heads of other customers.

"Hey, Beck, howyadoin' girl? What've you been up to? Haven't seen you lately." It's nice to be missed.

Small-town kindness. Big-hearted acceptance. How could anyone ever take these things for granted? They couldn't. Not if they'd ever been without.

The highlight of today's trip to the supermarket was being escorted to my car by my favorite stocker. He is up in years; I'm guessing mid-seventies. Over the years, he and I have shared lots of small talk over bags of groceries. After his wife died, he took this job so that he could be around people.

This morning my grocery buddy sensed I was feeling embarrassed about my old station wagon, so he said, "Hey now, don't say anything bad about a good car like this. You need to hang on to it—it'll be a classic someday." He said it with such sincerity, I almost believed him.

As I ducked into the front seat and prepared to put my key in the ignition, I said, "Thank you for the pep talk and for unloading the groceries."

"Oh, you're welcome," he replied, "my pleasure."

But before I could shut the door I noticed my friend standing nearby, hands resting on the empty cart as if there was still something he wanted to say. I smiled up at him and our eyes met.

"And—*Merry Christmas*, Mrs. Freeman!" he said with heartfelt sincerity.

I returned the season's greetings in kind, but he had another gift for me. Something incredible. Something spontaneous. Something purely brimming over with kindness. He walked around the empty cart, over to my car door, ducked down, and gave me a terrific bear hug. I left the grocery store—the *grocery* store, mind you—feeling as though I'd been to a family reunion. And the little girl inside me, the lonely one with big round glasses, smiled clear down to her toes.

I drove home on air, happily stuck in a state of childlike wonder. And as I drove, I thought, *In a perfect world, a kind world, this would be the way a child would feel all the time: chock plumb full of "sweetness and light."*

Be ye kind one to another, tenderhearted.
EPHESIANS 4:32, KJV
❧

T E N

Come Watch Our Show!

I recently stopped by for a backporch visit with our neighbor, Mary Sue Gantt, and during the course of our conversation she asked, "Have I ever told you about the first time I ever laid eyes on Gabe?" I wasn't quite sure I really wanted to hear this story, but she continued anyway.

"Well," she said, settling into a lawn chair, "I was taking a walk along the road, when suddenly this little boy pops out of nowhere from a nearby field, grabs my hand, and says, 'Come on!' Before I could even think, he led me down to the edge of the lake. Then he plopped down on his stomach by the bank and ducked his entire head under water."

"That's my Gabe."

"That's not all. Then he lifted up his head, the water pouring in streams from his bangs, and hollered up at me, 'I learned how to duck my head under water today! Idn't that great?'"

Mary Sue said she thought it was terrific, indeed, and she and Gabe have been buddies ever since.

What struck me about that story was Gabe's attitude. He was not only excited about his newfound skill; he assumed others would, of course, want to see him perform it. Why wouldn't they? What happens between childhood and adulthood to dampen this natural assumption that we will succeed—what quiets our enthusiasm?

Zachary burst into our bedroom the other night with a story he swore was true, and it is a perfect example of the way many of us begin thinking as we move into adulthood, always futurizing worst-case scenarios. According to my son, there was a woman sitting in her car in a grocery store parking lot in Houston, Texas. Her head was resting against the steering wheel. A passerby observed that the woman seemed to be in distress, so he opened her car door and asked, "Ma'am, are you all right?"

"No," she replied feebly, "I've been shot in the back of the head. I think I feel a bit of my brains on my shoulder."

Of course the man wasted no time in calling 9-1-1. When the paramedics arrived on the scene, they immediately began checking the woman's vital signs, careful not to move her unnecessarily. That done, the paramedic drew a breath and asked, "Ma'am, what makes you think you've been shot?"

She repeated her tale weakly. "I felt something explode against the back of my head and I can feel some of my brains on my shoulder."

"Miss," drawled the paramedic with a grin, "what you've got on your shoulder is a canned biscuit. Looks like a whole can of them shot open from the grocery sack in the back of your car."

This was one of the funniest stories I'd ever heard, and I love to tell it to crowds of women. Who among us hasn't wondered if our headache might actually be a fast-growing tumor? Imagining worst-case scenarios is every mother's specialty.

As you now know, I spent my grade school years feeling like a little turtle—terrified to stick my head out of the shell. (Never, in my wildest moments, would I have dreamed of plunging it under water in front of a stranger!) But, thankfully, I had a cousin who shared Gabe's enthusiastic outlook on life. And she would pull me "onstage" with her now and then, without giving me a chance to say no.

———

My cousin, Jamie, was tall and lanky, and she wore her flaxen tresses pulled back in a yard-long ponytail braid. She also wore braces on her teeth, which she despised. But what I remember most about Jamie is that she was a royal hoot. She was the embodiment of Pippi Longstocking, almost a fantasy character who leaned toward eccentricity, always game for any adventure, and hovering about her, an air of supreme goodheartedness.

No matter what awkward stage I happened to be passing through, Jamie never swayed in verbalizing her high opinion of me. She told me I was pretty and smart and funny and talented. And whenever I got a chance to go visit my cousin, I felt all those things might, indeed—at least for the week—be true. Odd thing about human nature: It's not only how charming our *friends* are that causes us to love them, it's how delightful they make us *feel* when we're with them.

I arrived at Jamie's house an unassuming little thing; but soon after stepping into her world, I felt more like a star about to be born. I barely had time to throw my suitcase on Jamie's chenille bedspread before she grabbed a pencil and paper and began writing out our schedule.

"OK," Jamie said, chewing on the eraser, "the first thing I think we ought to do is put on a dance show." Her assurance was so contagious that I had no time for self-doubt or contemplating whether or not I had what it takes to perform. From Jamie's way of looking at it, *of course* we had talent—why waste it? Never mind that I'd never shuffle-ball-changed a step in my life. We simply had to get on with the show and give out whatever it was we had to the waiting world. As a matter of fact, Jamie explained that she had only just yesterday given dancing a whirl.

"Nothing to it," she assured me. Within an hour or so, Jamie had not only taught me to dance (admittedly it was mostly arm-waving, high-kicking, and twirling-around-and-arounding), but she'd gathered up an audience of little brothers and sisters and parents and neighborhood children—and charged them a quarter each to watch our show. In that one week, we also put on a magic show, drew portraits, performed roadside slapstick routines, held a gymnastics tournament, made cream puffs from a gourmet cookbook, and became accomplished beauticians (meaning that, armed with rat-tail combs and industrial-strength hairspray, we teased every inch of each other's hair into enormous balls of fuzz.)

I owe Jamie a lot. Not only were so many of my best childhood memories sweetened by her presence as a friend, she taught me what Gabriel seems to have been given from birth: the ability to *assume* one can learn a new skill, *assume* it will probably work out well, and *assume* others will enjoy watching the performance. And finally, to assume it will be more fun than—well, more fun than spontaneous head dunking!

One of my favorite speakers in the Dallas area is Susie Humphreys. Susie delivers a delightful talk entitled, "I Can *Do* That!" From her youngest days, with little education and no experience, Susie assumed her way from one fantastic job to another. One of her life's mottos is, "Volunteer it! You can learn it later!" The world is starving for more Gabes, more Jamies, more Susies, (and a few less Biscuit Brains).

August, 1995. Family Reunion. Houston, Texas.

Jamie strolls out into the sun from the open door, her arms open wide. Flowing mane of blond hair. Perfect straight white teeth. A figure I thought only came manufactured in Barbie Doll Dream Houses. Tan, dimples. Where, I wonder, did Pippi Longstocking go?

Not to worry, the heart of Pippi is still here—only now she's a little harder to detect under Jamie's startling beauty. But not for long. We are immediately both shocked and pleased to discover we own the same model car—both of us have been chauffeuring our four kids around our respective towns in old Buick station wagons. Yes, hers even has faded contact paper woodgrain siding like Sag's! We wonder aloud how many thirty-something women, besides ourselves, drive the same gas guzzlers our mothers drove in the seventies?

Suddenly Jamie remembers a story.

"Oh, Becky," she laughs, "can you believe I was stopped by a policeman awhile back, in that station wagon, for *weaving* on the road?"

My mouth drops open. I can't believe there's yet another coincidence. "Weaving?" I ask, my voice growing louder and more excited. "You've been stopped for weaving? *I've just been stopped* for weaving, too!" It is a touching moment. Like finding a long lost twin. I finish my story.

"The most embarrassing thing about it was that when the officer asked if I'd been drinking, Gabriel looked at the Coke I'd been sipping and assured him I *had been!*"

But Jamie can match this. She speaks with great animation, her slim hands flying to emphasize the highlights of her story.

"Listen: The policeman asked me if I knew, while I was weaving, I'd also been speeding. My little Jacob piped up, too, just like Gabe. He looked straight at the officer and said, 'Oh, yes. My mom *did* know she was going too fast. I've been telling her to slow down for miles and miles. Even stuck my arm out the window a ways back there and the wind nearly took it off!'"

Jamie and I laugh so hard we are leaning on each other's arms for support. We cannot believe we've both raised sons who will freely tattle on their *own mothers* to strangers in uniform. I cherish the kinship of laughter we've shared over the years, the music of little-girl giggles echos in my memory. And I realize, suddenly, that Jamie is my oldest friend and how special it is to share nearly forty years of history with her. A quote by John Leonard plays about my mind: "It takes a long time to grow an old friend."

Goodness knows Jamie cannot let our good stories go to waste. She's already pulling me by the sleeve toward the kitchen, urging, "Becky, come on. We've got to tell this to . . ." And once again, I've no time for self-doubt or wondering if I have the ability to perform. Jamie's sure enough for the both of us. After all, we have some great stuff to share; why waste it? So I smooth my shirt, stand a little taller, smile a little wider, and get ready to follow Jamie "on stage"—to give out whatever it is we've got to the waiting world. Or at least to our parents and brothers and sisters and aunts and uncles milling about in the kitchen.

And this time, we do not even charge them a quarter.

If you love someone you will . . . always believe
in him, always expect the best of him.
1 CORINTHIANS 13:7, TLB
❧

I Can't Wait 'Til Camp!

L ast summer, in East Texas, I drove Sag through a set of iron gates (thankfully, they *were* open) and cruised down a black-topped road. Just as I rounded a curve I encountered a large animal. The beast had planted itself in the middle of the road, and there it stood, methodically chewing its cud. Having grown accustomed to life outside the big city, I wasn't all that shocked to come upon a hoofed, cud-chewing animal sunning itself in the center of traffic. But this was a bovine of a different color. This creature had a hump on its back, and its legs rose to the top of my station wagon. It was a camel—of the Arabian desert variety.

The dromedary began eyeing my hood ornament hungrily and licking his chops in anticipation. Not knowing what to do, I honked the horn. All I got in response was the nonchalant blink of his ebony eyes. He would not be moved. *What? Had I thought he could be honked into action like some common Hereford or Jersey?*

Just then a long-legged cowboy strode by and tossed out some advice.

"I'd go around him if I was you. He's fixin' to spit."

And so I did. Speedily in fact, and—may I add—none too soon. Welcome to Jan-Kay Ranch—Detroit, Texas.

I came to this unusual setting to bring Rachel and her two girl-friends for a week of summer camp. Gabe tagged along for the ride. However, when he saw the camel, and then the llamas, ante-lopes, wild pigs, peacocks, monkeys—and of course, the tiger, bear, and baby elephant—it was all too much. How dare I bring him this close to Paradise only to take him home again?

What is a good, sensible mother to do in such situations? I haven't the foggiest. I only know that this mother ended up leaving her son at camp with a plastic bag full of clothes scrounged from the recesses of her station wagon.

Honestly, I knew Gabe would be fine at this family-owned camp. I went to this very same ranch with the junior high group from my church. The wild and exotic animals weren't around back then, but the cabins and rec hall and lake were exactly as I'd remembered them.

I had loved those church camp weeks at Jan-Kay Ranch. I loved watching the early morning mist rise over the lake as white-washed egrets flew from stump to fish and back again. I recall spiritual stirrings inside, as I read from Scriptures that were just beginning to make sense. I found, lying between those pages, fascinating situations involving what I now call "Camelots of the Soul"—stories where truth, goodness, mercy, and *right* stood its ground in the midst of cruelty, jealousy, confusion, and wrong. It was refreshing. I found myself, as a teenager, especially hungry for such shining visions. (One doesn't find many shining visions in the daily halls of public school.)

I also remember the beating of my heart as I stepped out of my cabin on summer evenings, just-showered and sweet-smelling after a day filled with team games and noise and sweat. I can almost hear the screen door bouncing closed behind me with its rhythmic thump, and feel the adolescent hoping-beyond-hope that a cute boy might walk by the porch, take notice, and smile in my direction. Evening hayrides. Midnight gossip. Morning walks. Afternoon swims.

Nice memories. Very nice.

About five years ago, I was invited back to Jan-Kay Ranch to attend a women's retreat. I rediscovered the mist and the lake, unchanged and serene. On this stay there would be no boys to impress, however. The boys had turned into husbands—*our husbands,* who were graciously staying home with our children so we could escape for a weekend. And we women had come, hoping to rediscover a bit of spiritual Camelot in the midst of our hectic, modern lives. Along with absorbing the Scriptures for their goodness and truth, we also played and yakked and laughed and ate goodies until the wee hours. To get to Camelot, m'lady, there needs be some fun along the way.

Seriously, every woman should have a chance to go back to camp again. For one thing, it's great for the ego to see other gorgeous, sophisticated women without their makeup, dressed in flannel feety pajamas. It has a way of bringing high church ladies down to my comfort level. With the makeup removed, masks also drop with more ease, and the resulting gab sessions can be the best. I, for one, didn't want to miss out on any late-night, impromptu round circles.

One night during the retreat, way past midnight, I was plagued with bunk-bed insomnia. Feeling slumber-partyish anyway, I climbed down from my perch and pulled a plate of brownies from my food stash. I was a woman on a mission. Confident I could find another night owl, I walked out into the darkness seeking a friend with whom I could share a chocolate conversation.

Without my contact lenses, it was a terrific challenge to feel my way through the blackness. Finally, I spotted a lone figure sitting on the front porch in the moonlight. I walked toward the woman, sat down beside her, looked up at the starry night, and said dreamily, "Isn't it beautiful out here? I guess you couldn't sleep either, huh? Listen—I come bearing gifts. Would you like a fudge brownie?"

There was no answer. The woman sat stone still, staring straight ahead. *Oh, great,* I thought, *she must have wanted to be alone.* But as I looked closer, I jumped back with a start. The figure was not a woman after all. I'd just offered my brownies to a wooden Indian.

As I rose to find more lively companionship, I patted the Indian's knee and offered him some free advice—"Fella, you really should loosen up." The incident was a big hit when I finally found a live, nocturnal audience to share my brownies with.

As much fun as it is to fellowship, there *is* one big drawback to camp: All camp directors seem to insist on organizing some form of physical group activity. It conjures images of that ugly childhood word: recess. And you know how I feel about *that*. After what happened at one retreat, though, I now like it even less. But, still, I know it's good for my character to be stretched beyond my comfort zone every once in a while.

The fateful physical activity to which I'm referring had ominous overtones from the start. The idea was for us ladies to participate in what is called a Ropes Course—a series of challenges involving wood and ropes and needlessly frightening tests designed to help bond a team together (from sheer terror, I assume).

The nightmare of tests is the trust fall. At this juncture in the course, each of us had to ascend a four-feet-high platform. Then we, being adults of sane mind, were to fall backwards—one at a time—from that height into the locked and waiting hands of our fellow middle-aged, baggy-armed comrades. I learned one thing from that experience. Peer pressure doesn't ever completely loosen its grip, even in midlife. To chants of, "Don't be a sissy, Becky," I climbed, I fell, they caught, it hurt like the dickens.

When it was my turn to join the "catchers," I was relieved. "Better to be a catcher than a fall guy," I always say. The next woman to climb the platform was rather large. When she plummeted, we did our best to break her fall, but down to the ground she went with a sickening thud. Stunned, the fallen woman shook her head as if to clear it. Then she uttered the bravest words ever spoken by a mere mortal.

"I want to try it again," she said. I couldn't believe it. We'd just dropped this woman, our friend, on a *trust* fall, for goodness sake. We had just proven we were not the sort to be trusted. But she believed in us, and she believed in herself. As our fearless faller began her climb, I locked arms with the woman across from me.

She whispered to me under her breath, "Becky, if you let go, I'll kill you. We have to make this catch."

Our Lady of Bravery, ready for her descent, stood on the platform and turned slowly around. She fell straight back, arms folded across her chest. We caught her! Hallelujah! (And it hurt!) But the whole experience resulted in a new hero added to my own personal vision of Camelot. In my eyes, this brave woman became a true knight in shining armor, for she was determined to see our ragtag group rise to the challenge. And even though we failed her once, she was willing to sacrifice her own body, King Arthur style, so our faith in each other could be restored.

Having learned such a significant moral lesson, I limped back to my cabin, warm with emotion. I had forced myself to experience the ultimate camp challenge—I had been part and parcel of a team's success, and I had to admit it was a good feeling. Wild horses couldn't drag me into doing a Ropes Course *again*—for I am now officially at the end of my ropes—but I'm proud to say, "I did it."

These types of experiences make up an unforgettable week of camp: conquering challenges, teamwork, beautiful scenery, nature's animals, late-night talks, spiritual refreshment, chocolate. Mulling it over, I knew that Gabe would be a natural for summer camp—even with nothing but a plastic bag full of old clothes. As it turned out, I couldn't have been more correct.

I made a mid-week visit to Jan-Kay, carrying fresh clothing rations for my little camper-to-go. Once I made it past the camel guard, and parked my car—hood ornament intact—it didn't take long to locate Gabe. He was happily feeding Eedie the baby elephant fistfuls of popcorn. As I strolled up to say hello, I saw Eedie stretch out her trunk, grab the popcorn bag Gabe was holding and in an instant, gulp it down, paper and all.

Gabe was startled at first and then he got tickled as only little boys can—breaking out in a gale of spontaneous giggles. The scene of Gabe bent over with laughter and the elephant scarfing down his bag of popcorn, went "click" in that place in my head where pictures I don't want to forget are stored. *At moments like this Gabe makes it look like so much fun to be a kid. And if I can't be one, at least it's fun to have one.*

Though he looked as happy as I've ever seen him, I wondered if my baby had suffered any gone-away-to-camp-for-the-first-time homesickness. I'd been reading Art Linkletter's latest edition of *Kids Say the Darndest Things* and had come across a letter written by one little homesick soul trying to keep up a brave-camper front. It read, "Dear Mom and Dad, I am not homesick. Please write to me. Are you coming Sunday? Please come. I need some clean towels. Write and tell me if you are coming. Please come and bring the baby. They keep us so busy here, I don't have time to get homesick. Please come Sunday. Love, Paul. P.S. Next year I think I'll come to camp for the shorter period."

After reading this pitiful letter, I wanted to be especially sensitive to my son in his first extended experience away from home.

"Gabe," I asked gingerly, "have you had any crying spells? At night maybe?"

"Yeah," he answered sheepishly, "last night I did."

I nodded sympathetically and rubbed his back. He continued, a twinge of bittersweet to his voice.

"I cried because camp only lasts for three more days, and I want to stay forever."

That did it. I was convinced. Every kid should get a chance to at least try a wonderful, healthy, eye-opening "camp experience." Especially kids like you and me, who still need excursions in nature, to laugh out loud in surprise, to have our faith refreshed and our friendships deepened—who are, forever and always, in search of whatever bits of Camelot can be found in this hard-edged ol' world.

He satisfies me with good things.
He makes me young again.

PSALM 103:5, NCV

—

476

Sorry Boys, This Is Girl Talk

I can no longer remember what my daughter's right ear looks like. As far as I know, she may not even have one anymore. How *could* I possibly know? The ear has been beneath a telephone receiver for at least the last ten months. Not only that, but the telephone cord has transformed into Rachel's umbilical cord—transmitting all the information needed to sustain life in junior high school.

Another interesting phenomenon: I only see my daughter these days as part of a pair. She's always with one of her best friends—namely, Michelle (whom Scott lovingly nicknamed, Miss Prissy) or Cricket (whom Scott insists on calling Grasshopper). I try not to look at the situation as though I've lost a daughter, but rather, as if I've gained a revolving set of twins.

It's imperative, of course, that Rachel and her girlfriends keep up-to-the-minute on the details of every aspect of each other's lives. The following are halves of actual conversations I've heard from Rachel's end of the phone chatter.

"That zit hasn't cleared up? Ohmgosh, how *awful!*"

"He did? He said he liked me? Liked me, like, LIKED me, or liked me, like, *likes* me?"

"Oh, yeah! I spilt Dr. Pepper on my Massomo shirt—*What?* Did I not tell you that?"

"He's the guy that threw a french fry at me in the cafeteria, and then I giggled like a dork and milk started spurting out my nose and I, like, thought I would *die!* You know—he's the one that used to go out with Chelsea, and just broke up with Heather, and I think he's really fine but I just don't know for sure, for *sure* if I'd go out with him or not."

Just as an aside—is any other parent out there stupefied by elementary and junior high kids saying they are "going out" with someone in their class? All I want to know is, where are they going out to? When I ask this question of my children they look at me as if I'm fresh from having my lobotomy done. "MUH-ther! They don't *go* anywhere. It's just what they call it these days."

"And they never actually go out anywhere together?"

"Nope."

"Do they talk to each other, or sit by each other, or hold hands or anything?" I ask naively.

This question always gets great laughs from Gabe. It is obvious that I am a confused old woman, so he explains patiently.

"You see, Mom, if a boy likes a girl, he gets his friend to ask the girl's friend if she wants to go out with him. If she tells her friend to tell his friend yes, then they are going out together. And they don't ever have to talk to each other or nothin' if they don't want to. Then when they get tired of going out, the boy or the girl gives a note to the friend of the other boy or girl saying they don't want to go out with them anymore and that's it! Then they can start all over again."

As my little nephew pointed out, I must be too old to under-stand—which is scary because it seems like only yesterday I used to be the *daughter* trying to explain what "going *with* someone" meant, to my mom. (I wonder if my mother went through the same conversation trying to explain what "going steady" meant to her mother. I can just hear my grandmother asking, "Going steady? What does that mean, 'going *steady*'? What? Are the rest of us going crooked or rocky or something?")

Perhaps Rachel and I aren't really so far apart. At least I still understand one thing: the need for girl talk. This weekend three of my old girlfriends and I gathered in Dallas and rented a hotel suite for a night. We arrived about 5:00 in the evening and talked and giggled until 2:00 A.M., slept a few hours, rose again at 8:30 the next morning, and continued nonstop chatter until noon when we practically had to pry ourselves away from the hotel. There were still stories untold, discussions left hanging, questions unanswered. My stomach, three days later, is still sore from hours of laughing.

"What in the world did you girls talk about for thirteen straight hours?" Scott asked in amazement when I arrived back home.

"Oh, I don't know," I said. "First, I guess, we told our 'cute kid' stories. Brenda told how she'd bought her little Ben a one-minute timer and told him to brush his teeth until the sand ran out of the hour glass. The next time she passed by the bathroom, Ben had thick foam all around his mouth, dripping all over his chin, his shoulder, and down his right arm. Bless his heart, turns out Brenda gave him a *three-minute* timer. And then Shawn told about her four-year-old decorating the floor of her car with hundreds of doodle bugs while she was napping."

"And this kind of stuff really entertains you girls?"

"Oh, we *love* it!"

"Did you talk about any current events or anything?" Scott asked, trying hard to understand.

"Of course. We discussed nutrition. Did you know that the Cabbage Diet gave someone an ulcer? We decided that diet must work by putting a hole in your stomach so the food can leak out. Then after we finished discussing all the diets we'd been on, we ate strawberries dipped in chocolate."

"Typical females."

"Then we talked about how to make ends meet. Crafts and stuff."

"How fascinating."

"Shawn won top prize with 'how to get whatever you want for pennies, with a bucket of paint.' She's painted her cement floor in her kitchen to look like grass and cobblestone, painted a fireplace on a blank wall—and get this, somebody gave them a white couch but it was all covered with stains so—"

"She didn't!"

"Yes, she *did!* She painted that sucker red with a gallon of water-based enamel!"

"Anything else?"

"Well," I replied, batting my eyelashes. "We talked about our husbands." This perked up Scott's ears.

"So, did you discuss everyone's marital problems?"

"Yes, as a matter of fact we did. But you will be pleased to know that we all decided to keep the men we married."

"Why?"

"Because you guys are so good at understanding us women—and playing Mr. Mom so we can get away now and then for a girls' night out."

I kissed Scott on the cheek. He grinned sheepishly and darted outside to do some man stuff. But before he closed the door I heard him say, "Women! I'll never understand 'em."

I didn't tell Scott that eventually our girl talk turned deeper: We talked of ongoing quests to find our purpose in life, what it means to really know God, to relax and be real. We each wondered if we'd ever overcome the pain of our imperfections as women, mothers, and wives. How could we learn to forgive more, holler less, love our families better? Women do this talking thing really, really well. Connectors R Us.

In contrast, Ray Ortland speaks to groups of males on the topic, "The Loneliness of Men." In a candid moment, so rare among men, Mr. Ortland even admitted that sometimes in rooms full of people he feels like a little kid with his thumb in his mouth, swinging his legs back and forth and wondering,

"What's going on?" Surveys from Promise Keepers reveal how few men, especially pastors, have even one close friend with whom they can be totally honest. This makes my heart ache. It also makes me want to burst into a chorus of "I Enjoy Being a Girl."

Ask any female—from age four to ninety-four—and she will tell you she understands *exactly* what Anne of Green Gables longed for when she said, "I've dreamed of meeting her all my life . . . a bosom friend—an intimate friend, you know—a really kindred spirit to whom I can confide my inmost soul."[4] No place is really home to a woman until she has a friend she can call up for no reason at all.

Scott stands in bewildered amazement as he observes my friendships and those of his blossoming daughter. As a matter of fact, he looks at us both as something almost alien. According to Dee Brestin's book, *The Friendships of Women*, "The friendships between little girls differ from the friendships between little boys."[5] She also points out that perhaps it is not always such a terrible thing, this lack of deep conversation between the males of our species. Some of it may just be a built-in difference between the sexes. Brestin goes on to quote Zick Rubin, author of *Children's Friendships*, as saying, "Girls not only have a much stronger need for friendship than boys, but demand an intensity in those friendships that *boys prefer living without*"[6] (emphasis mine).

Yes! Though my husband and my sons value their friends, they've got to be *doing* something. Conversation is on the side, rarely the main course. None of my three sons' friends call to find out what color socks the other is wearing to school the next day. There are no long chats between the males in our family over hairstyles and the latest school gossip. Hurt feelings between the boys and their friends are almost never a topic of dinner conversation. And frankly, they don't seem to miss it or need it. Yes, my daughter is unique among her brothers. She is in training for womanhood and honing friendships that will, hopefully, stay her over a lifetime. Just as women friends have sustained and nourished her mother and her grandmother, and her great-grandmother before her.

I just got off the phone a few minutes ago. It was Mary, one of my best friends. She said, "Becky, I just made a decision. But I need you to tell me that I'm doing the right thing." I listened to her story and answered her with exactly what she wanted to hear. "Absolutely, Mary. You are doing the right thing." (A man, you see, might want to point out miscellaneous logical options. This, of course, only serves to infuriate a woman.) "Thanks," Mary answered, audibly relieved, "that's all I needed to know."

After I hung up, Scott casually asked what Mary's call was about. I answered, "You wouldn't understand. It was girl talk."

Then I went on to discuss Mary's conversation with the only other person in my family who *would* understand—my daughter, my Rachel.

Some of our women amazed us.
LUKE 24:22
❧

Which Way Do I Go Now?

M y husband tells a story to each of our children as they pass from the gently flowing rivers of childhood into the treacherous waterfalls of adolescence. It is a story about a friend-ship—about a fork in the road and about simple choices that affect us for the rest of our lives.

But first, some background on my husband's foray into teen-agehood.

The first time I saw Scott, he was fourteen, and I, barely thir-teen. I was new to church, new to believing in Christ—new to everything. It took no time for the youth group to label me: I was cast as the Goody-Two-Shoes Ding Dong. (Funny how those teenage labels have such staying power.) I could hardly wait to go along with my youth group on an outing to the park—to get to know lots of wholesome kids my age who were as interested in "higher spiritual things" as I had become. Boy, was I in for a shock.

The old church bus pulled into the park entrance, and as soon as the kids unloaded onto the grass, I noticed one adorable guy, in particular, heading off in the direction of an arching stone bridge. I mean he was *gorgeous*. Doe-brown eyes. Tom Selleck–style creases along the sides of his wide smile. Perfect, white, straight teeth. Wide shoulders, arms that rippled with muscles—a body built better than any fourteen-year-old's I'd ever seen. And his hair was straight, thick, soft—the kind I would have loved to run my fingers through. That is, if I had not been a Goody-Two-Shoes Ding Dong.

I softly hummed a happy tune, checked to make sure my hair was in place, and meandered off in the direction of the cute boy. When I got to the bridge I gasped, turned around, and whistled off in the opposite direction. For there, beneath the bridge was Adorable Guy and a few other kids from the youth group passing around and guzzling a clear bottled beverage as fast as they could get it down. Adorable Guy, as you've probably guessed by now, was my Scott. And the clear beverage was straight vodka.

The next time I saw Adorable Scott, he was leaning on a rather sturdy girl's shoulder. She took him to the church bus where he promptly threw up all over the floor.

Scott was so ill all he could think about was getting home and into a bed. In the meantime, his parents heard of his adventure in the park. To this day, Scott is grateful for his dad's compassionate, matter-of-fact response to the embarrassing event. Jim (Scott's dad) walked into his son's room, where Scott was writhing from a terrific hangover, and said, "Son, I heard what happened. You know, I think the natural consequences of this are probably worse than anything I could do to you. Sleep it off. We'll talk tomorrow."

The next Sunday morning, the Under-the-Bridge-Drinking-Gang apologized to the entire youth group. Scott cannot speak for the other kids; he only knows his own apology was sincere. He desperately wanted to do what was right.

Sometimes I think I've been a "good girl" all my life (at least in the outward forms of "goodness") because I am a great big chicken. Sure, I'd rather say it was because I had such deep moral fiber that I fended off temptation by sheer courage and character. More truthfully, I was scared to death to "sin." If a TV commercial said that drinking, smoking, or taking drugs was an unhealthy thing to do, that it might could even kill you, I would have been terrified that one puff or one sip would put me six feet under. Those public school anti-smoking, anti-drug campaigns worked like a charm on me.

Scott, being a guy and being less naive about the ways of the world, and realizing early on that grown-ups don't necessarily know everything, was at a higher risk for experimentation.

And it is at this point the story that my husband tells our children begins.

During this "risky" time, Scott met Larry,* a boy his age who was in need of a friend. Scott's mom, unaware of the danger, even encouraged Scott to befriend Larry. He seemed like such a nice, lonely kid.

But Larry, at age fourteen, was already on a slippery path—drugs enticing him to escape from hard reality. For a while, Scott was tempted, too, still fighting the part of him that wanted to be one of the gang, to be cool. Back then, he even went by the nickname "Joe Cool." Often when I saw him around town, Scott would be wearing a striped tank top, a burgundy beret, and sunglasses—and he rode a motorcycle. I mean, he was one cool-looking dude. To keep up this reputation, Scott found himself denying his soul of souls and giving in to the stuff of illusion.

The inward struggle intensified until the day came to make a choice.

One afternoon, Scott and Larry went out riding their motorcycles.

They came to a literal fork in the road—a crossroads. Something clicked in Scott's head. He pulled over to the side of the road, turned off the engine of his motorcycle, and spoke. "Larry," he stammered, searching for words to accurately express what he wanted to say. "Look, I just can't do this."

"Can't do what, man?" Larry asked, his voice heavy and slow.

---

* Not his real name

"I can't go the way you are going. You're heading the wrong direction, Larry, and I'm not going down with you. Look, I'm going to drive over to the youth director's house—you know, that guy from my church—and I'm gonna talk to him. You wanna go with me?"

Larry looked sadly at Scott for a minute and then shook his head. "Do what you have to do, man. I've gotta do what I have to do."

Larry drove off one way; Scott turned in the opposite direction—for a visit with a man he could trust. A man whom Scott knew to have faith, character, courage, conviction—the things that had been knocking at his soul. And just that quickly, in the blink of an eye, the choice had been made.

We cannot deny the fact that some moments in our lives hold more significance than others. We mark the stages, the milestones, in our lives by small turning points. The scene of Larry driving off on his motorcycle is forever imprinted in Scott's mind. The memory marks a moment in time when Scott followed his inner convictions and let the pieces of Joe Cool fall where they may.

The man in Robert Frost's immortal poem, "The Road Not Taken," acknowledges that some moments in time are seconds of such significance, that years from now they will not only be recalled, they will also be *retold*.

> I shall be telling this with a sigh
> Somewhere ages and ages hence:
> Two roads diverged in a wood, and I—
> I took the one less traveled by,
> And that has made all the difference.

In time, Scott would realize more profoundly the full impact of his choice.

From that afternoon on, Larry took a fast ride toward darkness, deluded by the fog of revolving drugs into believing he was heading toward light. Larry had a precious praying mother, and God intervened time and again, but Larry always continued to make one disastrous choice after another.

Years passed, and every so often Larry would ride up on his motorcycle and shoot the breeze with Scott. Larry had plenty of drug buddies, but he knew Scott had been the closest thing to a true friend he would ever have. Scott lost count of the times he offered to get Larry some help. Finally, Scott gave up trying, and when Larry came by he just tried to be kind, to be a friend in the middle of all the darkness.

More years went by and Scott married me, and we had our first baby boy—Zachary. Life was good, the sun shone bright, we had moved into a pretty wood-frame home, and we had a healthy, adorable son bouncing in his Johnny Jump-Up in the kitchen. Then Larry showed up at our doorstep. I felt ill at the sight of him. He reeked of oil and smoke and leather. He was filthy and sullen, and—like a nasty animal—I didn't want him in the house, on my furniture. But Scott believed Larry was really harmless to others—he was too bent on destroying himself. And in spite of the fact that we lived next door to our church, Scott insisted we welcome Larry into our home. I wondered what sort of gossip might be flying with a druggie's motorcycle parked in our driveway. Scott's never been one to concern himself with gossip. He simply cares about people.

I'll never forget the look on Larry's face when he first saw our baby. It was like Zachary brought a brief glimmer of joy and light into Larry's cave-like existence. Larry would actually smile and soften and talk baby talk as Zach jumped up and down in his little seat, squealing with delight. I marveled at the contrast between the two of them and wondered what, in our baby's face, might be speaking to Larry. I kept a close and watchful eye.

One evening, Larry dropped by and I made him a simple supper. Then we all sat in the living room and Larry began to describe a nightmare he'd had the night before. It scared him so much that he wasn't able to get back to sleep and was afraid to go to sleep again. In his vivid dream he saw demons and evil and darkness and death. I could not hold my tongue.

"Larry," I said, "I really think God's trying to get your attention. Please, *wake up!* You've gotta get help. I know this may sound hokey, but I believe in the reality of evil forces, even satanic beings. You need to call out to Christ, Larry."

"Yeah," Larry slurred his thick words, "I believed in Jesus when I was a kid. Lot of good it did me."

"You know," Scott added gently, "you probably did trust in Jesus a long time ago. I remember that you once told me you had. But how you live your life is your responsibility. You make the choices. And your life is not only mocking God; it's killing everyone who loves you to watch you self-destruct."

Suddenly, the living room grew quiet.

"Larry," I said urgently as he started to get up, "I'm not playing around. I really think that dream means something important. For some reason I don't think you have much time left."

Larry moved to leave and said, "It scares the ———— out of me, but I think you're right."

Two days later, on a sunny Saturday afternoon, Larry dropped by again. He hadn't changed his clothes for at least a week. His face was covered with soot, the smell of smoke and oil filled the air.

"I'm really sick," Larry mumbled as he stumbled toward the living room. "I just need to lay down for a minute and rest before I drive the rest of the way home."

Scott nodded, got Larry a drink of water and a pillow, and let him rest on the couch. While Larry slept, I went back in the bedroom to nap with baby Zach, and Scott sat across from Larry in an easy chair working on some school papers. The house was quiet and serene—even in the back bedroom the stillness was palpable. Peace fell softly, like a warm down blanket around our home. Scott looked up from his papers at Larry resting and thought, *I think this is the only time I've ever looked at Larry and thought he looked at rest. I'll let him sleep as long as he wants.*

Several minutes later Scott looked up again and realized that Larry's chest was not moving. "Oh, God," Scott said quietly, moving to check Larry's pulse. There was none.

Two days later Scott and I stood arm in arm at the simple graveside service. Larry's mother, a woman of amazing strength and courage, cried silent tears. Larry had been her only son. Her heart was breaking, but then, her heart had been breaking for a long, long time. In a way, she was free—free from the torturous pain of watching her son walk a daily, living death. As we stood under the green canopy in front of Larry's casket, his mom encircled Scott with a hug and asked him to say a few words. Scott spoke of Larry's good qualities and of their friendship. Then he spoke of forks in the road, of significant choices, of human weakness and pain, and finally of eternal hope, and of God's mercy.

And so, with a sigh, I listen now as my children's father tells the story. The tale of two friends on two motorcycles and two roads that once diverged on a highway. Of a path that leads to life. And of another path—whose end is death. And he urges his children, as one who knows, to take the road less traveled by.

This is what the LORD says:
"Stand at the crossroads and look; . . .
ask where the good way is, and walk in it,
and you will find rest for your souls."
JEREMIAH 6:16
෨

F O U R T E E N

I'm Gonna Change the World!

B etween Scott's "wild" days and the time we would eventually fall in love, he and I became good "church buddies"—
both of us oozing with idealism. Other kids our age were just
kids. *We* were different; we were going to change the world. So
when we read about an organization that sent teenagers out on
summer work teams to make a real difference to needy people in
foreign lands, we signed up right away. A prerequisite for getting
to Central America (our chosen field) was to attend a week-long
boot camp in the swamps of Florida.

And so in the summer of 1974, a sixteen-year-old boy and a
fifteen-year-old girl ended up in an airport in Dallas saying teary
good-byes to their families for the summer. They each held a
squared-off shovel—donations for their work project. The thin,
blond boy also held a box of stationery outlined with the map of
the world; his mom hoped it would encourage him to write
home. The girl—a cheerful brunette—busied herself with alter-
nately losing and finding her purse. Oddly, the two teenagers
seemed to share a penchant for running into walls and tripping

on carpet. The mother of the girl turned to the mother of the boy, her eyes pleading.

"Is your son, by any chance, a 'together' sort of person? Because you see, actually . . . well . . . my daughter is *not.*"

The mother of the son swallowed hard and shook her head. Both mothers gripped the guardrail a bit tighter as the silver plane took off with their offspring—their offspring who could not be trusted to keep up with their own shoes, much less their passports.

That was the summer the fifteen-year-old girl fell in love with the sixteen-year-old boy, and together they grew up to be me and Scott.

Two weeks ago, Scott and I found ourselves once again walking around in the Dallas–Fort Worth airport. Our teenage son, Ezekiel, walked in front of us, shovel in hand. That's when the airport began taking on the feel of a time-warp tunnel.

You see, our lanky blond son was heading to boot camp in Florida and then on to Guatemala with the same organization his father and I had gone with more than twenty years ago. Besides the shovel, Zeke was also carrying a box of stationery, faded and outlined with a map of the world—a gift from his grandmother, Scott's mom. I silently prayed it would encourage him to write home. Walking beside Zeke was a fifteen-year-old girl, Rachel Morris, heading toward the same destination. She's just a buddy. Brunette. Winsome smile. I soon found Rachel's mother, Deborah, and cornered her with a question.

"Look, Deb, is your daughter, by any chance, a 'together' sort of girl? Because to tell you the truth our Zeke . . . well . . . he's *not.*"

Deborah shook her head. "Are you *kidding?* She's forever losing her purse. That's why I got her that little pack that attaches to her back."

Uh-oh.

An attendant asked the passengers to begin boarding, and I smiled bravely and walked with my son to the entrance ramp. But as soon as his back turned the corner, I ran to my husband's embrace and bawled like a baby. Elizabeth Stone once said, "Making the decision to have a child—it's momentous. It is to decide forever to have your heart go walking around outside your body."[7]

Had it been this hard for my own parents to tell me good-bye that summer of 1974? I only had to look over at them now—our parents, Zeke's grandparents—to see the answer to my question. Their eyes were pools about to overflow. Daddy stayed close by my side until his grandson's airplane disappeared from sight, offering a shoulder as I felt a big hunk of my heart take off with Zeke.

It was eerie and comforting, knowing my dad had been in my shoes. As a matter of fact, as we calculated the years, we figured out that Scott and I were the exact same age my parents had been when we had left for our trip. Funny. My parents had seemed so much more mature than we are.

On the way home I thought, *Seven weeks—seven whole weeks without my child! I will die, that's all, I will just die from this ache in my heart by the end of the summer.* Then I had a wild thought, and soon the wild thought took on a life of its own—shaping and twisting itself into a wild, full-blown plan. I broached the subject with Scott—carefully.

"Listen to my whole speech before you say no, OK? What if—now hear me out—what if we flew to Florida in a couple of weeks to see Zeke at his commissioning from boot camp? Before he leaves the country? I know it's expensive, but Visa would let us pay it all out, I'm sure about that. And we could see the old boot camp again.

"Remember how you led the obstacle course and were the big macho hero of our team? Remember how beautiful it was when all the kids lit candles on commissioning night? Remember the circus tent and the loud, wonderful songs we sang underneath it? The hopes, the prayers? Remember how we were so young and how we were going to change the world and how we ended up falling in love instead? But falling in love was pretty good, wasn't it? And maybe Zeke will change the world. Just in case he's about

---

to do it, we should fly down to Florida to see him, don't you think?"

I drew a deep breath and waited. Scott shrugged his shoulders.

"OK," he said.

"OK?"

"Yep. OK."

And so we did.

Upon our arrival, our son walked out of the jungle like Tarzan. Or maybe more like Cheetah. Anyway, he was filthy and happy. I'd written him that we might be coming, but I think he was still surprised to see we'd really come.

"Hey, Dad!" he said, giving us both an enthusiastic, grubby hug, "I'm leading our team in the obstacle course! We are *taking* this camp, man!"

The gleam of pride in Scott's eye did not escape my notice. Our son gave us the grand tour of the camp while mosquitoes enjoyed a gourmet meal on freshly-flown-in flesh. After a camp-style supper, Zeke cleaned himself up and together we headed for the big top and the big night—the last night of boot camp.

Almost 2,000 kids gathered under the giant tent—in our day there were only about 400, as I recall. But the lively choruses they sang were the same, and as we sang, I was fifteen all over again. An African youth choir shuffled rhythmically down the aisles in their native costumes, singing to the beat of bongo drums.

"I'm gonna shake, shake, shake de world! I'm gonna shake de world for Jesus! I'm gonna shake, shake, shake de world! Gonna shake de world for Him!"

I remembered. I was, too. I was going to shake the world. Me and God. And Scott.

Bob Bland, the ordinary looking but amazing founder of Teen Missions, stood to speak. He hadn't changed at all, other than the silver in his hair. We'd seen him earlier—riding around the camp on a bicycle, wearing jeans, a T-shirt, and his famous wide smile. And, of course, he was barking orders as he sailed by.

Yet we knew he must be in his mid-sixties. Over the last twenty-five years Bob and his precious wife, Bernie, have given more than 30,000 teenagers the opportunity to serve and grow in other countries.

As Bob asked former team members to stand up and shout out the year and country they had visited, Scott and I obliged. In unison we yelled, "El Salvador! 1974!" It was soon apparent that we were both so—so *old.* No one else even came close to our decade.

Moving toward the final ceremony, the floodlights were turned off, and blackness settled over the tent. Reverently, Bob Bland recited one of my favorite quotes, "It is better to light one candle than to shout at the darkness." With that he lit his candle and others followed one by one, as the teens accepted the challenge to be lights in their world. Our loving, giving, incredible son was among them. Just yesterday, it seems, we were too.

That night we said good-bye to Zeke for the second time in two weeks, and my heart tore once again. This time he would be flying toward a land of volcanoes, lush foliage, and gentle Mayans. He would be helping to construct a building and working with handicapped Guatemalans—wonderfully and terribly exciting.

I remember how it felt. I was there, Zeke. I was fifteen once. Only I am a mother now, and along with the excitement and joy, I will worry about your safety and I will ache every night missing you. It's what mothers do, and it seems nobody can help that.

But I will let you go, and I will pray for you, because I have no other choice. You are our child, and what beats inside our hearts now beats inside yours. Go forth and make a difference. Shake the world upside down, our son.

Your life is already shaking ours. All over again.

Back home we soon got a letter from Zeke. It read,

Mom and Dad,

I guess you should know me and Rachel have fallen madly in love and that we hope to be just like y'all and marry as soon as we arrive.

Love all y'all!
Zeke

He's quite a little kidder, that boy. (You *do* think he's kidding, don't you?)

> *Even youths grow tired and weary . . . but . . .*
> *the LORD will renew their strength.*
> *They will soar on wings like eagles.*
> ISAIAH 40:30–31
> ❧

Hey, Mom!
I've Got a Job!

A couple of springs ago, some good friends of ours, Karl and Terry Kemp, sent us a graduation announcement in honor of their son, Joshua. Inside was a dashing picture of Josh, age seventeen and wearing a tuxedo.

The fancy script engraving on the card read as follows:

Whereas
Joshua Adam Kemp
has completed the course of study required of him
pursuant to achieving mastery of matters academic; and
Whereas
he has a job, pays for his car insurance,
pumps his own gas and eats out
when he jolly well pleases; and
Whereas
He is able to converse at the dinner table with wit and
erudition

without even mentioning boogers,
Let it be known henceforth
to all peoples that
he is a big boy now.

I reread the card several times, laughing out loud.

Joshua was the first baby born to our circle of college friends. It wasn't long before the rest of us followed suit and began having babies of our own. This baby-birthing period was sort of like a popcorn machine: First, one baby kernel popped. Then after a while, another burst forth. Then all of a sudden it was poppoppoppoppop—and soon there was popcorn (or, in this case, babies) everywhere we looked. Then, eventually, it all slowed down. Pop-pop. Pop. Pop. Pop. We looked up one day and, suddenly, none of us were popping out babies anymore. We were having teenagers instead.

Which brings us to the present. When I realized that Joshua was a full-fledged teenager on the verge of graduating and leaving home and all the things that go with these emotional rites of passage, I knew our turn to watch our own kids take flight was up next. Josh simply blew the whistle of "things to come." It won't be long before my oldest son, Zachary, is officially a big boy too—heading out the family door to the waiting world.

Zachary just turned sixteen. The number's still pretty new to me. I'm having a little difficulty even putting it down on paper, since he's only been carrying this age around for a month. The age of sixteen, as you know, traditionally ushers in a new driver and, hopefully, a job. Zachary just began pumping gas at a local convenience store. Bless Zach's heart, when it comes to learning a new job the transition from childhood to adulthood is more than just a rite of passage; sometimes it's more like a riot of passage. As a matter of fact, Zach's boss just called last week to warn us that our son would be coming home early, and then added, "Now don't be too shocked when you first see him. It's not as bad as it looks."

As Scott and I sat on the back porch puzzling over what this might mean, our teenager rounded the bend and our mouths simultaneously dropped open. Zach was literally covered from head to foot with great globs of dripping black grease. He looked like a toxic waste accident in Nike tennis shoes. Scott handed him a bucket of grease remover, and after he'd cleaned up the worst of it, the story unfolded.

Seems a customer had pulled up to the station and asked Zach to put a couple of quarts of oil in his car. Zach cheerfully agreed to the task. When the man came out of the store and saw what Zachary was doing (which was in truth, simply following orders) the man yelled, "Son, you didn't put all of the two quarts of oil in there did you?"

Puzzled by the man's rage, Zach answered, "Yes sir, I did."

"Well," ranted the irate customer, "you've got to get under there and take out the plug and let some of it out right now. You overfilled it."

Zach, being young and still of a mind to try to please the man, obliged. It might have worked, had the plug not broken loose while Zach was twisting it off the bottom of the oil pan. (Zachary would like me to point out, in his defense, that the plug coming loose is a common occurrence in these situations.) As things were, Zach ended up on the receiving end of an oil bath. Only a few weeks earlier, Zach had accidentally poured a quart of oil in a customer's radiator. Needless to say, he was pretty discouraged.

I identified with Zach's troubles because I also had a miserable time adjusting to new jobs as a teenager. Actually, come to think of it, Zach's already much farther along than I was at his age.

The first job I ever held was a summer baby-sitting job for a family with a brand-new home. I was fifteen. Wanting to impress them by baking a hot apple pie, I opened the preheated oven door (which was so new it still had a sticker on it) and a hot skillet slipped out. Then it fell with a sickening sizzle-thud onto the freshly laid floor. When I pulled the skillet up, a big gooey circle of melted vinyl came up with it. Crying profusely, I telephoned the father to prepare him for the decorating adjustment I'd just made to his two-week-old home. I could barely talk between sobs, and by the time I finally got the story out, the poor father was simply overtaken with joy that no one had died.

Eventually I graduated from baby-sitting to a secretarial position at a health club. One day my boss called me into his office, and I was certain he was going to offer me a raise. After all, I was "friendly" personified. Instead he said, "Becky, you are a nice receptionist, with a lovely phone voice and all—but I can't have an employee who consistently hangs up the receiver on my clientele three to four times an afternoon. Giggling 'Ooops, I'm so sorry, I did it again' just isn't cutting it anymore. I'm afraid we're going to have to let you go." I couldn't believe it. I'd been fired! And me, such a nice girl.

Then there was my short stint as a pharmacist's assistant. (I know what you are thinking. Now there's a scary thought: a teenage girl who can't handle phone buttons dispensing prescription drugs.) I'll never forget the time a customer walked up to the counter and asked for Neosporin. I thought he said his name was Neil Sporin, so I came back with, "I'm sorry. I can't find it. How do you spell that last name again?" On another occasion, the pharmacist caught me typing up instructions for a patient to "Take one suppository, two times a day, by mouth." At that point, he and I both came to the conclusion that my talents might be better placed elsewhere. Far, far elsewhere.

And so, when I received yet another call from Zach's boss this morning, I was more sympathetic than the average mother might have been. Thankfully, she was laughing this time. "Becky," she said, "you haven't finished Zach's chapter have you? Because I've got another good one for you."

"No," I answered, grabbing for a pen and paper. "What do you have on him now?"

"Well," she answered, "Zach accidentally left his application for a D-FY-IT card here at the store. (A D-FY-IT card is a discount card the teenagers in our school district can receive if they pass a drug test and promise to stay drug-free.) The questionnaire asked for the students to describe any prescriptions or over-the-counter pharmaceutical products they may have taken in the last twenty-four hours. Zachary, wanting so badly to be conscientious, made sure he'd covered all the bases. His drug list? Aspirin, Crest, Speed Stick deodorant, and Barbisol shaving cream. (I can see some police officer chuckling, "Son, when was the last time you got high on toothpaste?" or even better, "I'm sorry, Mr. Freeman, but I'm going to have to book you for possession of deodorant.")

As time passes I'm sure Zachary (and his mom) will survive all the rites, and the riots, of teenage passage. He's well on his way to becoming a big boy. Mistakes, unfortunately, are a necessary part of the journey. All of us had to learn our share of lessons from them.

It seems to encourage Zach, somewhat, to know that even his mother, once a scatterbrained teenage girl, arrived safely to scatterbrained adulthood. Of course, I never did succeed at holding down a regular, steady job. I'm still in the embarrassing position of having to explain, "Yes, I have a degree in elementary education and taught first grade. But I'm a retired teacher now—after nine long months of faithful service." There is a happy ending to my job search, however. I finally figured out a way to make a modest living—writing about the very messes I've been accumulating all my life. ("See, Mom and Dad, there was nothing to worry about all along.")

George MacDonald wrote, "When we are out of sympathy with the young, our work in this world is over." Well, George, looks like I can relax. Because with all the sympathy I have for teenagers, I'm going to have steady work in this world for a very long time.

Being confident of this, that he who began a
good work in you will carry it on to completion.

PHILIPPIANS 1:6

SIXTEEN

I Don't Wanna Go
to Church Anymore!

"What is it? What's wrong with me?"
I set my cup down on the coffee shop table as I rested the side of my face on the palm of my hand. As long as I was in this far, I went ahead and unleashed the rest of it. "I can't stand church."

It was a childish statement—exaggerated, to be sure—but it welled up within me in a candid, unguarded moment and spilled out into the atmosphere. And there my confession hung for a few seconds, suspended, like a soap bubble before it bursts. My three girlfriends blinked in unison around the table and took deep consecutive breaths before diving into the interrogation.

"What's there not to like, Becky? Is it the color of the carpet? the song selections?"

"I don't know," I fumbled. "Yes. No. I don't know!"

"Is it the people? Are they not friendly?"

"Yes. No. Oh, I don't know!"

"Are you OK with your relationship with God?"

"Yes—oh, *yes!* It's wonderful—He's wonderful. I'm more assured of God's love than I've ever been. I'm especially enjoying reading slowly through the Gospels, but I'm finding more and more that I want to read them *alone*—not be involved in a study group. I have you guys and other Christian friends I love to be with—you know that. We lunch, we pray, we share each other's lives. I come away filled and renewed. But for some reason, lately I'm wanting to hibernate from church. I come away empty and relieved that the ordeal is over. What is wrong with me?" We talked around the subject for nearly an hour.

This morning, I sit alone, sipping my coffee and staring out the window at the overcast coolness of the morning. I mull over my unenthusiastic feelings about going to church. I find, surprisingly, there are stirrings inside me similar to those of an angry little girl. The grown-up part of my head argues back with plenty of "shoulds" and "oughts"—like that Frosted Mini Wheats commercial where the "adult" on the outside battles emotions with the outspoken "kid" inside.

But this time, the childish feelings prevail—strongly. I read two things that made me feel a little better. One is from Paula Hardin's book, *What Are You Doing with the Rest of Your Life?* "In middle adulthood," she writes, "the inner child long denied becomes increasingly insistent. It wants to be heard."[8] Now, I've not completely bought into this "inner child" stuff—much of it smacks of New Agey egocentric mumbo. But something in my soul warns, *Don't throw out the inner child with the New Age bathtub. For inside everyone there is a child who needs to be loved and accepted. We are, eternally,* children *to our Heavenly Father. Not only is this concept biblical, it is a childlike part of us we can never outgrow. Nor should we want to.*

Second, something a young boy said in Sunday school brings the corners of my mouth up in a weak smile. "When Jesus was my age, He went to church with a bunch of people and got lost. It happens."[9] I think Jesus understands what is happening to me. I'm probably one of thousands who've felt lost in church. It happens.

Still, I'm alarmed to find I am close to tears. What if I were ten years old, headstrong, honest, and outspoken—what would I be bursting to say right now? Imagine . . . if I were to take Jesus at His words this morning and come to Him as a child, what would I say to Him? How would I express my feelings about church, about Him? How would it all come tumbling out? I might ramble. I might say things I shouldn't. If I were a child, sitting on the grass having a conversation with Jesus, what would I say? Perhaps I'd start with something like . . .

Jesus, I love You—but can we talk about this "church thing" for a minute? First of all, I do not understand why I'm supposed to dress up fancy to come to church. Why do I have to wear dresses that itch and shoes that hurt, and curl my hair to come visit Your house? Who made up Sunday school clothes? If you meant what You said—if You want people to come to You as a child—how come everybody doesn't just wear overalls and T-shirts and Keds and ponytails and baseball caps, or even feety pajamas, to church? and maybe even run through a mud puddle on the way in the door? I'd like to wring the neck of the person who came up with the big idea that we should all look la-di-da-dressy for church.

Another thing. In the Bible, You got to have church *outside.* Oh, You visited fancy temples now and then, but maybe just to keep Your foot in the door. When it was up to You, You had church out under the sky by a lake or on a grassy hill or in a boat. You didn't need fancy banners or stained-glass windows—Your sun painted the background with bursty oranges and purples and reds. You didn't need an organist playing worshipy mood music—Your Sea of Galilee made pretty, smooth sounds with its waves dropping onto the shore. And Your birds sang from the trees in between Your words. I wish I could have gone to Your outside church.

There's another thing I don't like about church: the sermons. I especially don't like the little outlines with every point starting with the same letter of the alphabet. Who teaches this stuff to preachers anyway? I don't want to hear about The Position, The

Principles, and The Promise anymore. (And is there really even supposed to be just one "big teacher"?)

What I really want to know is what happened to my brothers and sisters this week. Where were they when they met with God? What words did He say to their hearts? And did they laugh, did they cry, did they sing or dance with the joy of it? I also want to hear stories. Short ones. Like the ones You told, Jesus. Children like little stories a whole lot. I'll tell You another secret: I think their parents do too.

And by the way, in every church there should be lots of nice old people—the kind whose skin has gotten too big for them, so it kind of hangs wiggly under their chins. The kind who are especially nice to children. It's especially good if they keep gum or candy in their pockets to hand out after church, if moms and dads will let their kids have some. (And their moms and dads should let them have some.) I wonder, did You carry treats around in Your robe pocket, just in case? It probably didn't matter if You did or not. The kids all loved You anyway, because You were kind and noticed them.

By the way—do You know what my favorite miracle is? It was the time that all those gobs of people were listening to You, and they loved Your stories so much they forgot to stop and eat. Remember that time? And remember how those grown-up disciples of Yours were all worried and stressed out because there wasn't any food? I think it is funny that You had to find Yourself a calm, quiet little boy to help You out. Sometimes grown-ups just get in the way. I would love to have seen the big people's faces when that boy's lunch just kept growing and growing and growing. I wonder if somebody put up golden arches later that said, "Over 5,000 served from five loaves and two fishes." I wish I could have been the kid with the lunch that day.

This is kinda off the subject, but I'd just like to mention that I think food's a good thing to have around at church. I've always liked church suppers—where everybody brings something to share with everybody else. Especially the coconut cake and the

Mexican salad. I get really, really thankful for lunch when there is coconut cake and Mexican salad.

OK, back to the part I hate most about church, if You want to know the truth. Church reminds me too much of school. It's too big, there are too many people, there's too much sitting and listening. I'm not good at trying to squeeze into talking groups of people or wandering around in halls hoping I look like I know what I'm doing. I think certain grown-ups feel really bad admitting they don't like to go to church a whole lot, because they are supposed to love being around people so much. But the truth of the matter is, even grown-ups sometimes feel lost and alone in the middle of crowds—and would like to just go get donuts and go home.

Sometimes, I wonder how people who aren't born and raised in church ever get the gumption to go visit the first time. And lots of them *actually come back again.* I think probably it is the real strong talkers and good dressers that get most gung ho about it all.

Why couldn't we just skip Big Church? And then everybody who loves You could just get together at the donut shop. And they could tell each other where they met God last week, what His words sounded like to them, and whether the words made them laugh or cry or sing or dance. Share stories, You know. Then they could pray, sing a song, and go home. If church were like this, I might even could do it every other day.

"Oh, grow up," I can hear someone out there saying. Well, I have just one thing to say to that someone: I think you are mean and ugly, and I don't like your shirt.

Tell you what, I think I need a time out or a nap or some juice and cookies. Can we pick this subject up in the next chapter when I'm not feeling quite so sleepy and grumpy?

> *He went back to teaching by the sea. . . .*
> *He taught by using stories, many stories.*
> MARK 4:1, THE MESSAGE

SEVENTEEN

Jesus Is Easier to Love
Than His Kids

All right, all right. I've had my cookie break and nappy time.
I'm feeling more mature, and the child in me has had her
big say. I'm teasing about it, but truthfully it is a big relief to get
those pent-up childish "whines" out of my system.

Alas, however, the grown-up left in charge of my mind is
wondering, *What now?* The solution is not to change churches.
All of them, every single one of them, has its own set of problems. People tend to be very candid with me, so this much I do
know: I am not alone in my frustration. Church rejects, outcasts,
and misfits are everywhere and are immensely relieved to find a
sympathetic ear. In my humble opinion, we should listen to
them every once in a while, that is, if the church truly wants to
understand and love people.

One of the most obvious problems in all denominations is
that church people are capable of inflicting so much pain on one
another.

This week, I visited with two other precious women who have burgeoning ministries in writing and speaking. We each shared our own "horror stories"—the occasional nasty letter or rude verbal rejection they receive from, of course, well-meaning church ladies. We all admitted we sometimes struggle with the pain of these comments even months and years later. Though it was strangely therapeutic to know our experiences were not isolated cases, it saddened me to realize the sort of grief the church is capable of imparting to its own.

I also had an interesting conversation with a complete stranger in a public rest room a few months ago. I had just picked up a dress from the dry cleaners, and since I had to hurry on to a speaking event, I decided to change into the dress while in the rest room of a local grocery store.

As I was digging into my makeup bag, a woman walked in, observed my dolling up, and commented, "Nice dress. You going to church?"

"No," I answered, "but I'm about to go somewhere and give a little talk, and I'll probably say some good things about God. Does that count?"

She laughed a little and said, "You know, I'd like to believe in a good God." Then quickly she confessed, "I used to go to church every Sunday. But I was so hurt by some of the people there, I've never gone back again."

I turned toward her as I finished tightening the back of an earring and gently, *carefully* said, "Did you ever read that story in the Bible where the mothers took their children to Jesus to be blessed? I always thought it was kind of ironic that it was the disciples, Jesus' followers, who almost kept those kids from running into Jesus' arms."

"I never thought about it that way, but it's true. And it's *His people* that make me want to avoid everything having to do with Jesus and His church."

"Just remember, Jesus is really, really different than many of His followers act. They often mean well. But lots of us still don't know what we are doing, and the church has a lot of growing to do. Please don't let Christians stop you from running to Him like a kid needing a hug. He loves you so much."

She smiled, and as she turned to leave, she said, "Thanks, I needed to hear that."

I wondered, *Is it possible this woman found more compassion in our over-the-sink encounter than she'd been able to find from her years in an organized church?* The thought frustrated and then angered me. It is so easy to understand why so many people do not feel that the benefits of belonging to church are worth the pain involved. And many feel that if they left, they wouldn't be missed—like taking a teaspoon of sand from the desert. "The professionals are in charge anyway. Who needs me?"

I know a wonderful, God-fearing woman who grew up in a wonderful, God-loving, church-going home. She also adored her father, who pastored one of the most well-known churches in America. Today she's married to a wonderful, God-loving, church-going man. However, the "church-going" part is something she no longer feels an obligation to do. I also know a terrific marriage counselor, a deeply spiritual, compassionate man. God's love pours through him as he comforts hurting people in his office every day. But he's also said, "Thank you, but no thank you" to much involvement in a regular, formal church. Been there, done that, got burned, gonna avoid it.

I have to admit there's something about their decisions I admire. I think sometimes I, too, shall simply cross church off my "to do" list and be done with it. And yet . . .

What would happen if the traditional, organized church disappeared from the American scene? I must confess, I'd be devastated. It would be a terrible loss for our country. I think of my friends, Igor and Elaine, who grew up in the days of a "godless, churchless" Russia. (This was, what? A handful of years ago?) To attend an organized, underground worship service might, at any time, turn into a life-threatening event. Elaine's father, the pastor, was dragged away to prison twice for his faith. There was only one Bible in their church, and it had to be passed around in secret from family to family. When Elaine's family got their turn at the Bible it was like Christmas and New Year's all rolled into one.

I think, sometimes, I am spoiled, not remembering what a privilege it is to assemble en masse, openly, to worship. My husband hastens to remind me that one of the main purposes in coming together in a "Big Church" setting is to honor God and worship Him as a whole; it is not simply about getting *our* human needs met. *Oh, yeah,* whispers the little girl in me, *I forgetted that part.*

Also, I must admit, with all its faults, the structure of a formal church gives our children healthy places to go and sweet, decent kids with whom to hang out. Because of the youth group, my oldest boys have had opportunities to minister to orphans and the poorest of the poor on summer mission trips. I met my own husband, twenty years ago, in a church youth group. Come to think of it, I've met most of my best, lifelong friends in some pocket of a church setting. Even the women to whom I made my horrible I-don't-like-church confession are friends I made—you guessed it—at church.

There is no easy answer to the complexities in the Christian church today. The bad news is: Church is imperfect; it does not meet everyone's needs; it sometimes does more harm than it does good. I don't even know why they call it the "organized church" because it usually appears anything but organized with its members fussing and fighting and pulling and pushing—often on front pages of newspapers for all the world to see and cluck their tongues at. Let's face it: Sometimes it's plain embarrassing to admit holding membership in this God-ordained family of feuders.

The good news is: Since the church is imperfect, it won't shake things up much if the likes of you and I join in. Often, too, there are moments of glory when the church responds from its heart and does a great deal of good. Mother Teresa and her tender work among lepers is sanctioned and funded by a church. (Maybe not your particular denomination, but still, part of the Church Universal.) During the Nazi reign, Corrie ten Boom and members of her church risked and gave their lives to save Jewish families and friends.

Ironically, my hometown of Greenville is suddenly being blasted across national headlines and "honored" with visits from the New Black Panthers and the Ku Klux Klan. (I've yet to hear of one citizen, black or white, who welcomes either group here.) I stood in a stadium Sunday night, looking out over a salt-and-pepper sea of thousands of black and white Christians praying together as Dr. Tony Evans led us in a call to unity and peace. There were very few dry eyes as the crowd joined hands singing, "Bind us together, Lord." It is in these shining moments that I know that this mystery called "the body of Christ" has all the potential of being the eyes, hands, and compassion of Jesus to a confused and angry world. If only church happened like this every Sunday. If only it did not take an enemy's assault to "bind us together with love."

Last night I came across a well-worn book, authored by Philip Yancey. Actually, I didn't know it was a book—at first I thought it was a lump. I felt something stuck down the side of my mattress and, curious as to the origin of the lump, I fished around and pulled it out and discovered it was, after all, Yancey's book. (Whole libraries of used books and drawers full of socks and bags full of cookie crumbs live between the mattresses and under my bed. We could sustain our family for months from the haphazard rations pushed, swept, shoved, and stored there.)

Anyway, I've become a huge Philip Yancey fan since having heard him speak and having read his books. I am so grateful for this thoughtful, honest, intelligent, fuzzy-haired brother in Christ. He has a way of putting so much that is puzzling—about the Christian life, about God, about pain, about the Bible—into meaningful chunks I can slowly, methodically digest. I just finished his latest book, *The Jesus I Never Knew,* and believe it is perhaps the most significant book I've ever read. But the worn-out Yancey book under my bed happened to be one of his earlier classics, *Disappointment with God.*[10]

I try not to quote extensively from the writings of others. This practice is often a tactic for writers too lazy to fill empty pages with their own thoughts. (I think my mother told me this; it sounds like one of her Momilies.) However, I'm going to make a small exception. For those among us who admit to episodes of being disappointed, not only with God, but also with church, I do not think I can possibly offer more wisdom and insight than Yancey's observations on this subject. To begin with, he raises a series of rhetorical questions that I could easily "Amen."

> The manifold wisdom of God being made known through the church? Have you been to church lately? Jesus would have been impressive; the shekinah glory cloud would have stopped you flat; but the church?

Yes, Philip, I am as stumped as you are. Maybe the problem is that our modern westernized American services have strayed from the original guidelines of the early church. Mr. Yancey gently, but firmly, protests that argument.

> I cannot agree. The Epistles were written to a motley crew of converted angel worshipers, thieves, idolaters, backbiters, and prostitutes—those were the people in whom God took up residence. Read Paul's descriptions of the supposed "ideal church" in a city like Corinth: a raucous, ornery bunch that rivals any church in history for their unholiness. And yet Paul's most stirring depiction of the church as Christ's body appears in a letter to them.

But look what a mess the church has left in its wake throughout history! On this point, at least, Yancey agrees.

> The church's obvious defects would seem to be the greatest cost to God. Just as He committed His name to the nation Israel and had it dragged through mud, He now commits His Spirit to flawed human beings. You don't have to look far—the church in Corinth, racism in South Africa, bloodshed in Northern Ireland, scandals among U.S. Christians—for proof that the church does not measure up to God's ideal. And the watching world judges God by those who carry his name. A large measure of disappointment with God stems from disillusionment with other Christians.

That's exactly what I have been saying! Have you been reading my mind? Then why, for God's own sake, is He allowing holier-than-thous, nitpickers, wimps, odd birds, etc., to go on making an embarrassing wreck of things, misrepresenting His nature? Surely there's a better way. Yancey explains that God's way rarely follows earthly logic in His passionate pursuit of reconciliation with humankind.

> Dorothy Sayers has said that God underwent three great humiliations in His efforts to rescue the human race. The first was the Incarnation, when He took on the confines of a physical body. The second was the Cross, when He suffered the ignominy of public execution. The third humiliation, Sayers suggested, is the Church. In an awesome act of self-denial, God entrusted His reputation to ordinary people.

Oh.

So, let me get this straight: God Almighty is trusting ordinary quirky people like me? Whiners like me? A woman/child like me? To represent the love and compassion of Christ? Wow. The little girl in me raises her tiny wavering voice to say, I think maybe God should know I'm not big enough for this important of a job.

It dawns on me, astonishes me, as I realize we humans not only place our faith in God; He has also chosen to place His faith in *us,* His church.

OK, Lord, then show me what it is You see through my human eyes. What is it You want to say through my faltering voice—this peculiar Texas accent of mine? Where do You want me to go? To church? To bathrooms of grocery stores? You show me, I'll go.

I can't believe this. As I'm writing, the phone rings. It is a woman from my church wanting to know if I'd emcee the Ladies' Camp Retreat this year. How about that? I haven't been completely written off as potential church material in spite of my less-than-stellar attendance.

So, Lord. Are You saying You want me to go to camp? OK, I can deal with this. I like camp. I can wear sweatpants and feety pajamas and eat donuts there. Unlike formal church, everyone's not in a big hurry to rush off to the next service. I can take time to get to know a few ladies, one at a time, at my own snail's pace.

I say to the woman on the phone, "Yes, I'm honored to be asked."

Next day. Still editing, finalizing this chapter. The phone rings again. "Becky?" I recognize the voice immediately. It is another friend from church whom I've not seen for a couple of months. I remember now that I miss this friend's voice. She and I have prayed each other through valleys of tears. She also makes me laugh with a funny story about her daughter's latest antics. Then she gets right to the point. "Becky, I've been elected to call you because I'm the only one on our committee who's not afraid to ask you to speak at our October women's event. Here's the catch—we have no money for a speaking budget. It would have to be a freebie."

I laugh. Offend me? Little does my friend know that it is the *committee ladies* who are encouraging *me* with this invitation. I'd never consider taking a fee for speaking at my home church. Oh, now listen to me. My *home church.* Just a wee bit of encouragement and I'm already making noises like a church lady again. Perhaps, the greatest need in the body of Christ is very simple. All of us—in some way—desperately need to feel that we are needed, that we *belong,* and that we are at *home.*

Lord, just promise me one thing. If I ever start giving high-sounding speeches with three little points that all start with the same letter or start dressing in sensible shoes and button-up flowery dresses with lace collars—instruct a brave, honest little kid to come up to me, pull on my knee-highs, and say, "Lady, you wanna go for a walk outside? The sun is real pretty right now."

Then I'll also know it's time to kick off my shoes, put on my overalls, go for a walk outside in the grass or mud, and watch a sunset filled with bursty oranges and purples and reds. Time for a heart-to-heart talk, little girl to loving Father. Time to gain a bit of childlike perspective again.

Lord, teach us—Your Body, Your Church—
for Your Sake and the Sake of a Hurting World
to mature, to grow up . . .
into Children again.

All the believers . . . broke bread
in their homes and ate together with glad
and sincere hearts, praising God and enjoying
the favor of all the people.
And the Lord added to their number daily.
ACTS 2:44, 46–47

I Do It Myself!

The French writer Collete hit the proverbial nail on the head when she wrote in *Earthly Paradise,* "There are days when solitude is a heady wine that intoxicates you with freedom."[11] One of the things I most looked forward to, as a child, about someday getting to Grown-up Land was that I knew I'd finally get to do stuff *all by myself.*

This old daydream of mine is leading up to a small confession: I'm feeding a childish indulgence on a regular basis—acting out, I suppose, the desire to prove I can do whatever I want to do, whenever I want to do it, and do it all by myself, thank you very much. At least, in one small area of my life. I have to admit that nearly every day of my adult life I stop by a convenience store to buy myself a little "treat"—a Coke, a Reese's candy bar, a stick of beef jerky, a box of Junior Mints, or some such delicacy. Or if I'm on a diet (which averages about every third day), I'll buy bottled water or a cup of coffee and simply sniff or gaze longingly in the direction of the candy bar aisle. Most often I wind up purchasing nonsensical fluff, completely void of nutritional, educational, or spiritual value. Though it is thoroughly politically and nutritionally incorrect, I'll confess: I adore these goody-seeking jaunts. I look forward to them as much as a nap in a hammock or thirty minutes alone with a good book.

I know, I know. It's probably a power issue fraught with a myriad of dangerous physiological, not to mention, psychological implications. Yet from earliest childhood, I've dreamed of the day I could be on my own, driving my own car, carrying my own coins, and buying my own treats sans the hassle of begging or pleading or finagling my parents. I'd fantasize of marching headlong into the corner store any old time I pleased, relishing the control I could wield over my own destiny. Would it be a soft drink, a snack cake, a candy bar, or a pickle today? *When I get to be a grown-up,* I'd think with abandoned glee, *why, I can go to the store all by myself! Without asking a single adult for permission or loose change!*

I must say, this is one of my few childhood fantasies that has actually panned out to my expectations. Of course, my requirements for what qualifies as excitement are admittedly low, but every day I so look forward to declaring this tiny bit of independence. Yep, a real rabble-rouser, that's me.

And if I have my druthers, I prefer the local out-in-the-sticks convenience stores—Big Daddy's, The Village Bait & Tackle Store, Get-It-Kwik. Sure, they are filled with the aroma of stale smoke and their offerings often consist of petrified edibles and RC Colas with aluminum lids doubling as dust catchers, but I get a kick out of these hometown mom-and-pop operations.

Why? Because I can walk into any one of these places with my baggy purple shorts, my old red "Go Lone Oak Buffalos" T-shirt, my hair pulled up with those squeegee contraptions, bare feet, no makeup, and of this I can rest assured: There will be someone in the store who looks even worse than me. All in all, I believe this ritual to be a relatively harmless addiction.

It is extremely important, of course, that I get away for my excursion—*all by myself.* I'm sneaky when the kids are home and it's time to head out, solo, for my treat fix. I've even been known to put the car in neutral and let it slide backward out of the driveway so as not to alert the troops I'm about to escape for a few moments' respite. Otherwise they start running out of the house like orphaned children stranded on a desert island, begging—as if for their life—to "go with." I used to relent and take them, but after umpteen fights over "he gots more stuff than me" and twenty dollars down the drain trying to even it all out, I realized one day I was *not* having fun anymore. So these days, I make my getaway quickly and quietly.

Besides, I sooth my conscience, *my kids will have to wait their own turns to be grown-ups and buy junk food whenever they want. I had to wait all my childhood for this coveted reward.*

Now that my oldest child, Zach, has been driving for nearly a month, I'm enjoying watching him discover the joy and privileges of semi-adulthood. It's been surprising to discover how beneficial it is to have an extra driver around the house. Zach no longer begs and prods me to take him from point A to points B through Z and back again. He can get there in his own car now *all by himself.* Not only does he take care of his own transportation, but also his snacks, his entertainment, and—more and more—his general all-over life, *all by himself.* Which means I get more luxurious time to spend *all by myself.*

My mother phoned the other day. She has a new car phone, and I can always tell when she is using it because she's convinced she must shout in order to be heard way out there on the highway—seeing as the cellular phone's so far from her telephone lines and all. She cannot believe the small receiver actually works—looks too much like a dime store toy, she says.

Anyway, via the cellular airwaves, I could hear Mother's hollering loud and clear. "SO SISTER, HOW ARE YOU HANDLING YOUR OLDEST SON DRIVING A CAR?" (Mother always calls me "Sister" whenever she talks to me via telephone. I have no idea why. I think it's a generic name system, a holdover from her West Texas roots where everyone coming in and out of the house was a sister or brother to somebody.)

"Mother," I answered in a voice I knew bordered on that of a preschool teacher's, "let's try to talk just a little more softly, please. I promise, that toy phone of yours works really well. But back to your question—I am *thrilled* that Zach's driving. This is one time in my life when my forgetful nature has been a real boon. I keep forgetting when Zach is gone, when he is supposed to be home, and what time I'm supposed to start worrying. The other night, I didn't even know he'd gone out—and I was taken completely off guard when Zach walked in the front door and apologized all over himself for being an hour late. Because I didn't want him to think I'm not a conscientious mother, I scolded, 'Son, you had me worried sick! What's the matter? You didn't have a quarter to call home?' Of course, I really should have added, 'Next time pick up the phone and let me know when you aren't in your bedroom!'"

Mother laughs so loud I think my eardrum will burst. "WELL, HONEY, THIS MAY BE A BIG LOAD OFF YOUR SHOULDERS, TO HAVE ZACH WITH WHEELS AND ALL!"

"Mother, I love you. But if you don't tone down that volume I'm going to have to put the phone down on the floor."

"Oops. I forgot. I just can't believe—"

"—that little toy phone works so well. I know. But trust me, it does. Now back to Zach again. My life has simplified overnight since Zachary got his own car. You know how he's always been chomping at the bit to do his own thing; and with his new freedom, our relationship has really relaxed and improved. I only wish I'd thought about getting him a driver's license when he was two!"

Our conversation wound down, but I can't say the same for the volume. After yelling good-bye (if you can't beat 'em, join 'em), I hung up from my conversation with Mother, massaging my right ear as I walked from the bedroom to the kitchen. Then I began pondering the all-by-myself experiences that mark our children's lives as they move from childhood into adulthood.

One day a newborn arrives into our arms. So helpless, needy. In the space of a few months, however, our baby is holding a bottle or cup—all by himself. The next thing we parents know, our once-helpless infant is crawling, toddling, breaking eggs, and pouring milk into cracks in the floor—all by himself. Then comes the tearful day our pint-sized children insist on walking into a brick building and down the hall into a school classroom—all by themselves—where some teacher forever takes over our position as Primary Daytime Adult Companion.

Other "solo" rites of passage come so quickly the rest of childhood flies by in a blur. They learn to ride a bike—alone. There's the milestone of watching our children insist they go can into the doctor's examining room—unattended by Mom. Next, they're driving a car by themselves. Out on dates, without a chaperone. Then, hopefully, they'll find and hold down a job—all by themselves. All by themselves, one day, our kids will choose a mate, set up housekeeping, and begin having babies of their own—babies that, in the span of a few short months, will be holding their own bottles, all by themselves. And the cycle will repeat itself all over again.

This process, though poignant, does not make me sad. It is a good thing to grow up comfortably with all our scheduled "premier solos," and to learn to be content in our moments alone. While working on my degree in early childhood education a few years back, I was asked to write and illustrate a children's book for a class assignment. I read my little book to classroom after classroom of children; they loved it, identified with it, and begged me to read it "just one more time." Without benefit of my lovely homemade fingerpainted illustrations, I will attempt to describe the pertinent scenes as I share the text. The title of my book was—appropriate to the topic at hand—*All By Myself.*

All By Myself

Sometimes when I am happy
and want to sing and dance

I'll find a place
A quiet place
To hide
All By Myself

I sing, I twirl
I put on a show
Where no one else
But me, will know

[scene of a tree house, little girl dancing and kicking up her heels]

Sometimes when I'm upset
and want to cry or scream

I'll find a place
A quiet place
To hide
All By Myself

I'll fuss, I'll stomp
I'll SHOUT, SHOUT, SHOUT!
Until The Mad is all yelled out.

[scene by trees and pond, little girl having a royal fit]

Sometimes when I feel crowded
and want to get away

[little girl surrounded and squished by numerous siblings]

I'll find a place
A quiet place
To hide
All By Myself

[little girl in bathtub, pink bubbles everywhere]

I hop in the tub
and scoot down low
And pop the bubbles
With my toe

Sometimes when I am tired
and want to fall asleep
[she's yawning]

I'll find a place
A quiet place
To hide
All By Myself

Then snuggle deep
inside my bed
My pillow sinks
beneath my head

[scene of pigtailed little girl, sitting on a window seat,
contentedly looking out at the world]

I like Myself
I'm nice to know
So with Myself
I like to go

Sometimes you see
I like to be
All by Myself
With only Me

© Becky Freeman

Funny. These all-by-my-lonesome ponderings have caused me to work up an appetite. Perhaps I should get up and move around a bit. Or better yet, run to the corner store and get an ice-cold RC Cola. I bet The Village Market has some unpetrified Moon Pies in stock. Did you know that a Moon Pie, placed in the microwave for just a few seconds is . . . mmmm, a convenience store junkie's gourmet delight? OK, that does it. Got my own car keys, got my own quarters. I'm outta here. But don't tell anyone.

I'd really like to get away for a few minutes *all by myself.*

Then shall he have rejoicing in himself alone.
GALATIANS 6:4
❧

Has Anybody Seen Our Brains?

I am not exactly what one might call a Mountain Woman. Or even an Outdoors Woman. Oh, let's be frank here. I'm not even what one could call a Lawn and Garden Woman. And I'm not even remotely what one could call a Ski Buff, Bum, or even Bunny. However, I suppose I could be called a Ski Barely. (Not as in "Skiing Sans Clothing," but as in "Skiing Just Enough to Endanger.")

However, on this Colorado getaway with my husband, Scott, I was—shall we say—feeling my Cheerios. It was late March, and the sun was shining. I was soaking up the joy of this outdoor adventure vacation after having been holed up all winter writing. This tightly wound spring chick had been sprung!

Scott, being of the athletic ilk, enthusiastically encouraged me to try it all: hiking, rock climbing, snow skiing. I am sorry to report that my number-one vigorous outdoor sporting event turned out to be Quaint Little Shop Browsing, but I did engage in a little husband-coerced snow skiing. And it did this middle-aged mother a world of good. With every push of the poles and swish of the snow, my self-esteem climbed. Why, I could almost feel the muscles growing in my biceps and triceps and, yes, even forceps. One might say there's even a little rugged tinge now to my previously ruffled personality.

So when I spied a telephone attached to a tree, right smack in the middle of a nature trail, I was overcome with one desire. I felt compelled to call home and brag—loudly and obnoxiously—to my teenagers. I thought I'd toss out something casual like, "Hey guys, how's it going? Yes, it's your ol' geek mom. Just thought I'd stop on top of this snow peak, gnaw on some beef jerky, and give you guys a quick call before helping your ol' dad down the next slope."

I giggled as I dialed the number, listening impatiently to the rings. It was not one of my teenagers, however, who finally answered the phone. It was my mother, who had graciously volunteered to watch over our four children during our absence. Before I could even say, "Hi, Mom, this is your daughter, Snow Queen of the Mountain," she breathlessly replied, "Oh, Becky, I am *so* glad you called." Then I heard her yell in the background to my fourteen-year-old son, "Zeke! Have you been praying?"

"Mother?" I asked, a little shaken. "What's going on? Are the kids OK?"

"They're fine," she answered quickly, "but we do have a little crisis on our hands."

"What's up?"

"You know Zeke's leaving, in one hour, for that Mexico mission trip with his youth group?"

"Uh-huh."

"Well, a few minutes ago he informed me that he needed a copy of his birth certificate in order to cross the border."

"Oh no!"

Immediately I understood my mother's panic. She knows that if I should die, no living *sane* person could hope to understand my filing system. Without my guidance, she and Zeke would never locate the certificate. But now that I had astutely placed this phone call, everything was *under control.*

Of course, to me, my organization has always made perfect sense. My tax forms are tucked away in a pink rose-covered hat box. (Logic? Put ugly IRS forms in something pretty and feminine. How can one be intimidated by papers in a flowery hat box?) Notes for my books are scattered on pieces of napkins and old envelopes in every room in the house. (I like to surprise myself.) Birth certificates are located—well, your guess is as good as mine. The time my youngest child, Gabriel, needed a birth certificate to get into kindergarten I ended up pleading with the principal to let me drop by and show her my stretch marks instead.

"Becky?"

I was brought back to reality by the way Mother spoke my name, oh so tentatively—I knew she was contemplating all those years she ran around in a mild state of panic, picking up after her absentminded teenage daughter. Now *I* was the mother of my very own absentminded teenager, and my son was in need of a little parental encouragement.

"Mother," I said, "tell Zeke to pick up the phone in my office."

As soon as my mom was safely off the phone and Zeke had picked up the line, I let him have it.

"Son, son, son, son, son! When are you *ever* going to get your act together? I can't believe you've waited until the *last minute* to tell us you needed an important paper! Again! How many times is this going to happen before you realize that you need to think ahead?"

After venting the standard get-your-act-together lecture, I asked my son to follow my careful instructions in order to locate the desired document. After ten minutes of searching, Zeke and Mother methodically dismantled my office until they found (Hallelujah!) the treasured certificate. They finally discovered it in a large brown envelope labeled "Wrist X-Rays." (Logic? Sorry. Even *I'm* stumped on this one.)

Eventually Zeke made the bus to Mexico, and our remaining getaway days in Colorado passed all too quickly. On the plane ride home, Scott and I settled into seats near the rear of the plane. We held hands as we talked about missing the kids, and then laughed and shook our heads over Zeke's near fiasco—confirming once again that we *must* find a way to help our children get their acts together, to teach them to plan ahead, keep up with their things, become more responsible about communication. Otherwise, people would be picking up after them for the rest of their lives. Teenagers!

Just then, a voice broke over the intercom, interrupting our conversation. It was the flight attendant.

"Did anyone on this plane, by any chance, leave a jacket and a red plaid coat in the airport waiting area?"

On the long walk from the back to the front of the airplane to retrieve my belongings, passengers chuckled and picked on me. I played it up, using theatrical gestures and teasing about how I was actually picking up these items for someone else—some crazy, absentminded *friend* of mine. I, of course, had everything *under control.* More laughter broke out up and down the aisle, and then spontaneous bursts of applause.

Ah, well. If I'm not qualified to teach my kids how to get their acts together, perhaps I can at least teach them how to make their acts *entertaining.*

Within a few hours, Scott and I arrived back home in Texas to our children and one kind-hearted but exhausted Granny. After saying our thanks and good-byes, we sent my mother on her way—for the hour-and-a-half drive back to her home near Dallas. She wanted to leave in plenty of time to meet my father for lunch before he flew off on a business trip to Canada.

Later that evening we received a phone call delivered via a French-sounding telephone operator who put us through to my father. Even through the fuzzy connection Daddy's voice sounded worried. He went on to explain that Mother had never shown up for their lunch date. He had gone ahead with his trip, expecting she would call him later to explain her delay. But he'd never heard from her, and she had not answered the phone all day. Had we heard anything?

We had not.

The circumstances grew more and more suspect. Her close friends had not heard anything. Neighbors were alerted. The health club where she faithfully performs her daily workout said she had not signed in. ("Oh, yes," they said, "we know your mother well. She's the one that comes in to walk the treadmill in her high heels and handbag." Obviously, my athletic genes did not fall far from my mother's tree.)

At this point I begged Scott to call the police and area hospitals. In the meantime, we also telephoned Mother's best friend, Almedia, who happened to have a key to Mother's house. She volunteered to drive over and check out the circumstances. Within minutes, she'd called us back.

"Scott and Becky, I'm a little boggled here. All the lights are on, the television is blaring, and groceries are on the counter, still in their bags."

"Scott!" I yelled hysterically. "My mother's been kidnapped!"

About that time, Mother walked through her front door, totally unaware of the panic she'd left in her wake and shocked by the sight of Almedia sitting in her house using her telephone. As it turned out, Mother had been delayed by traffic and had decided, as long as she wasn't going to make her lunch date with Dad, to take in an afternoon matinee. It had been her understanding that the lunch date with Daddy was more of a loose we'll-do-lunch-if-I-can-make-it-back-in-time sort of an arrangement.

Once we knew Mother was all right—and after shedding a few tears of relief—Scott and I sat down at the kitchen counter and sighed. He was the first to speak. "I tell ya, Becky, these fifty-nine-year-olds think they can just take off gallivanting around the country without letting a soul know their whereabouts!"

"I know," I replied, resting my chin in resignation on my palm. "It's totally irresponsible, that's what it is."

Then simultaneously, we both smiled and asked each other, "When do you think our parents are ever going to get their act together?"

A few days later, Mother and I reunited over a cup of mocha latte at Hav-a-Java.

"Mother," I said, "I can't believe I blew up at *Zeke* for being irresponsible. Then within twenty-four hours, *I'm* being paged—to the front of an airplane, like some unruly girl, for not keeping up with my things. Then *you* have the *entire city* in a panic because you neglected to tell anyone about your change in plans."

"Well, Beck," my mother replied, sipping at the foam rising over the top of her cup, "look at the bright side. These events really close the generation gap—because it sure seems to me that kids, parents, and even grandparents have at least one thing in common: None of us have our acts *altogether* together."

"Yep, you're right," I sighed, stirring my coffee. "And anyway, if we ever do get it together in this family, I have a funny feeling we'd just forget where we put it!"

For you were like sheep going astray.
1 PETER 2:25

❧

Will You Go *with* Me?

A magazine caught my eye the other day. And even though it's so politically correct it is nauseating, I bought it because the cover intrigued me. On the front was a photograph of a little boy and girl, both dressed in grown-up attire: business suits, briefcases, the whole bit. The question across the top of the picture asked, "Are you grown-up yet?" Then, in parentheses, it also asked, "Do you know anyone who is?" I don't quite know how to answer those questions. I think it depends on your definition of the word *grown-up*.

If grown-up means that you have your own quarters and can eat dessert first, hey, I'm as adult as they come. If being grown-up means you can snow ski, I'm now snow plowing with the Big Dogs. (I'm still pretty proud of this.) But if, by any chance, being grown-up means you are a responsible, competent out-of-town traveler, bring me my blankie and a pacifier.

Middle-age has brought so many "firsts" my way. (Why doesn't the above-thirty crowd get baby books—with blanks to fill in for our First Gray Hair, First Pair of Bifocals, First Hot Flash, and so on?) One of the biggest challenges and changes in my life is that I've become a real, live author; and because of this, I'm getting some invitations to travel and give real, live speeches. The first obstacle I had to overcome was my fear of flying. Of course, it wasn't so much that I was afraid of *flying;* it was the *falling* part that always got to me. But I'm much, much better. (In my imaginary baby book I could sign and date a category for First Airplane Trip Accomplished without Embedding Fingernails into Arm of Passenger Sitting Next to Me.)

The second hurdle has not been as easy for me to jump. Because of what Gabe so succinctly pointed out at the start of this book—the part about my having no sense—out-of-state travel poses a special challenge. There are a few basic skills that would, I'm sure, increase my confidence level as I try finding my way around a strange city—for instance, the ability to read a map.

I've been blessed thus far to have friends who are so desperate to get away they've been willing to take me on as a traveling companion. Little did they know what they were committing themselves to. My problem with traveling is this: Once I hit the airport, I transform—responsibility speaking—to a child of about five years old. Thus, the person traveling with me begins a subtle development into the parent.

Tina Jacobson was one of my first traveling buddies. Tina owns a burgeoning home-based business called Books and Bookings, and has arranged all the radio publicity for my books. The first time we ever talked on the phone, we hit it off and since have become good friends. We even make regular lunch dates to discuss publishing and marketing, and wife-ing and mothering, and what it is like to try to operate a professional business with kids wandering in and out of our offices asking, "What's for dinner?" So when we both had business to conduct in Nashville, Tina agreed to go with me to help me learn the ropes of travel savvy.

I met her at the Dallas-Fort Worth airport. When it was our turn to board the plane, Tina asked, "Becky, now where is your ticket?" Already, her voice had picked up a faint maternal quality.

"It's in my purse. Don't worry," I replied with a grin.

"OK," said Tina. "Don't get offended by this, but I *have* read your books. Where is your purse?"

"Well, it is right—*oh no!* I don't know! Oh, my goodness, it has over three hundred dollars in cash and my airplane ticket in it!"

Tina swallowed hard, checked her watch, and then asked me very carefully where I had been in the last few minutes.

"The rest room! I was in the ladies' room!"

Running full speed ahead I darted to the ladies' room and there—miraculously—sitting in the sink was my open purse. Right where I'd left it. Not one penny was missing. I praised God from the top of my lungs and caught up with Tina just in time to board the plane.

I learned my lesson right away and held on to my purse from then on, as if my life depended on it. I did very well, too, until we went out to eat at a restaurant in Nashville. We had a delicious dinner, and as we turned to leave, I double-checked to make sure I had my purse swinging over my shoulder. Then Tina asked calmly, "Are you missing anything?"

"Nope," I answered, with childlike confidence. "See, I've got my purse right here. My head is attached to my body. Everything is *under control.*"

"Why don't you check under the table, just in case."

And there, where I had been sitting, lay five twenty-dollar bills.

"Oops," I apologized, sheepishly retrieving the cash off the floor. "Guess I should start *zipping up* my purse, huh?"

"Becky," Tina asked as we started to leave, "you *are* older than me, right?"

"Yeah, by a couple of years, I think."

"Then why do I suddenly feel like your mother?"

"Don't worry. This always happens when I go on trips with people. I should have warned you."

"Well, then, I must ask: Do you need to go potty before we leave?"

My next willing travel victim was my neighbor from the boonies, Melissa. Our first out-of-town trip started off smoothly enough. We boarded the plane without a hitch, laughing and talking the entire first leg of the journey. However, the challenge began when we had to pick up our luggage before changing planes in Phoenix. We retrieved our bags without a problem, but then we had to descend an escalator—and both of us were loaded to the neck with luggage. I do not know what possessed Melissa to do this, but she insisted I go first.

When I reached the bottom of the escalator, I managed to step off fairly gracefully. Unfortunately, my suitcase was heavier than I realized and I couldn't drag it off with me. There it sat, like a road block, stuck on the bottom step. Which meant that Melissa had to descend the escalator with bags under each arm and *straddle* my suitcase to keep from tripping over it and falling on her face. She was also, I might add, wearing a dress.

This scene—like something out of an "I Love Lucy" rerun—struck me as *hilarious*. Unfortunately, when I get really, really tickled, something horrible happens: I become completely incapacitated. I was literally sprawled on the airport floor, laughing so hard that tears were falling down both cheeks. Melissa, on the other hand, did not seem to find the situation quite as amusing. That's when she began to adopt the mother role.

"Get up off that floor and come help me!" she ordered. (I really expected her to add, "young lady!")

Eventually, I pulled myself up and managed to offer some weak assistance. Thankfully it didn't take long for Melissa to get tickled, too, and she forgave me. From there, our trip went relatively smoothly until the airplane ride home. I boarded the plane with several pieces of take-on luggage and one shopping bag full of huge cinnamon rolls, each of them the size of a cantaloupe. We'd promised our children a treat, and these monster rolls seemed the perfect answer. As we were squeezing down the aisle, trying to locate our seats, the bottom of my shopping bag broke loose.

"Uh-oh," I said quietly. Melissa's eyes widened with disbelief. Like a dozen bowling balls gone wild, the cinnamon rolls began veering crazily down the alley and under the seats, with passengers yelling, "Catch that big roll coming toward you!" and "There goes one under your feet!" Melissa looked at the flight attendant and rolled her eyes upward. As I scrambled around on my hands and knees, I believe I overheard Melissa say, "Kids! Whadaya gonna do with 'em?"

A year later, Melissa's memories of traveling with me had faded somewhat, and besides, she was desperate to break loose from the boonies again. This time, we were heading to sunny California. We adopted our Lucy and Ethel roles right away, humming bars of "California, Here We Come" as we stepped off our plane at John Wayne Airport. After I finished my speaking engagement, we checked ourselves into a budget hotel and spent the next few days doing the tourist thing: Universal Studios (where we lingered for an hour at the "Tribute to Lucy" display), Mann's Chinese Theater (where I had my picture taken with John Wayne's boot prints), and Beverly Hills (where we ate lunch and gawked). Amazingly, I managed to behave like a responsible adult the entire trip, and Melissa was even able to relax. Well, almost.

Our budget hotel turned out to be the epitome of economy (the swimming pool was the size of my kitchen table), but we did get an in-room whirlpool bathtub. And after a long day of touristing, I was eager to give that whirlpool a whirl. So I flipped a switch on the wall, positioned myself in the tub, laid back, and let the steaming water pour in. I couldn't wait to feel those little scrubbing bubbles work their magic on my aching muscles.

Then something unusual happened. Something for which I was totally unprepared. Water began shooting out of the little holes on the side of the tub like a fountain. As a matter of fact, the jets began propelling eight-foot streams of water upward and all around me, hitting the walls, the ceiling, soaking the floor. And then, that horrible thing happened again. I got tickled. I could not move; I could not speak. I could hear Melissa pounding on the door, but I could not answer her. All I could do was cuddle up in a ball and snicker and snort.

"Becky! Answer me!" Melissa was yelling outside the bathroom door. "Are you OK? I hear something splatting against the wall! Becky! There is *water* pouring out from under the *door!*"

Still I could not catch my breath as I sat like one of those cherub statues encased in a huge fountain of water. The noise of the whirlpool drowned out my feeble attempts to communicate. Finally, Melissa opened the door a couple of inches. Streams of water hit her—splat—in the face. As a matter of fact, the water shot out so hard and so high that it arched over her head, soaking one of the headboards and bedspreads out in the *room!*

"I won't look," promised Melissa as her arm stretched toward the whirlpool button on the wall, "but I'm coming in and turning this thing off!"

Immediately, the indoor hurricane died down and we surveyed the damage. An inch of water puddled on the floor, and beads of water dripped from every conceivable surface. The towels were useless—completely saturated. Melissa smoothed a lock of damp hair off her forehead. The maternal voice returned. "Becky, did you read the instructions?"

"What instructions?"

"The ones on the bathtub that say, *first* fill the tub up with water until it covers the jets. *Then* turn the whirlpool button on."

"Oh, *those* instructions."

Melissa made me promise not to touch any more buttons without her permission. For "tomorrow, if I were very, very good," she said she'd to take me with her to Disneyland!

> *Entreat me not to leave thee, or to return from*
> *following after thee: for whither thou goest,*
> *I will go; and where thou lodgest, I will lodge.*
>
> RUTH 1:16, KJV

533

Is There Really
a Magic Kingdom?

W alt Disney once said, "I myself have been flattered by the reputation for never having quite grown up."[12] And I must say, having recently visited Mr. Disney's fantasy world, this reputation seems pretty accurate to me.

Though you walk through the gates of Disney's Magic Kingdom an adult, everyone comes out a child on the other side. Melissa and I flew above rooftops in Never, Neverland. We sat entranced at the intricate detail and diversity of the famous "It's a Small World" ride. (Though I believe if I had to hear the chorus of that repetitive song one more time, I might go out of my small, small mind.) I wondered, perplexed, at the new virtual reality rides: I mean, how do they *do* that? How do they make you feel as though you've just sped through galaxies in a star ship?

But my favorite part of all was the parade. Not just any parade, but the Lion King Parade—Disney style. Never in all my life have I seen such a gorgeous display, such beautiful music, right where I could reach out and touch it. I found myself caught up in it all. I was incredibly moved as dancers of all nationalities in brilliant costumes ascended poles and floats and swayed to the beautiful rhythms of the song "The Circle of Life."

By evening, I was a grinning fool, sporting a Mickey Mouse shirt and a matching beanie complete with propeller.

"Melissa," I said to my friend as we stopped for a rest and a bite to eat, "I've been suckered into this whole commercial theme park deal. Look at me! Can you believe it? I've bought the entire enchilada."

"I noticed," said Melissa, aiming a camera in my direction. "It happens to the best of us. You've been thoroughly Disneyed."

We found a table near a jazz band and dance floor and propped our weary feet on a nearby chair. The band started up, playing the romantic, toe-tapping music of the 1940s era. Melissa and I visited with some teenagers during the break, who were elegantly dressed in forties regalia. They'd been having a ball, swing-stepping together under the stars. A new trend among teens? I hope so. They told us they come out several times a week just for some good, wholesome fun. (I know, you could have knocked us over with a feather, too.)

The breeze was soft around my face. The gentle wind-caress gave me a twinge of homesickness. I wished—OK, yes, *upon a star*—that my husband could have been there with me at that moment. He'd have had me out on that dance floor in no time. And we'd have given those young whippersnappers a run for their money.

From the corner of my eye, I could see a young father buying his little boy some ice cream. The child reached up for the cone, his chubby hand eager for the cold, dripping sweetness. Then the band, in the background, began playing what is, perhaps, my favorite song. Slow and sweet, its melody melted the simple smile of the evening into my memory. For I believe Louis Armstrong captured for all time the essence of childlike joy when he flashed his famous grin and gifted us with "What a Wonderful World."

As the last strains of the music wound down, the little boy finished off his last bite of ice cream. Then just as the crooner sang the final, "What—a-won-der-ful—world," the child—as if on cue—clapped his sticky hands together, grinned for all he was worth, looked straight at me, and shouted, "Yeah!" And I looked at him and shouted, "Yeah!" right back at him. And for that enchanted moment, connecting on some special frequency with this child, the world indeed seemed sparkling and amazing and completely wonderful. Louis would have been pleased.

Ironically, I understand some people have called for a boycott of Disney. There is cause for concern. Disney, the multi-million-dollar company, has certainly wandered far from the type of entertainment that Walt Disney, the creator, originally envisioned for children and their parents to enjoy together. But I have some personal misgivings about the value of boycotts. I believe it is usually more effective to spend our time lighting candles than shouting at the darkness—throwing more effort into applauding what is beautiful and right rather than acting appalled when man does what man-without-God will naturally do. But that's just my Mickey Mouse opinion.

I've been pondering something since my day at Disneyland: I noticed it is *grown-ups* who buy the tickets for their *children* to enter into the Magic Kingdom. Parents are the ones who drive the little tikes there, guide the way through the gates, and take them on the rides. But in the kingdom of God, according to Jesus, the roles are reversed. It is the *children* who point the way for us grown-ups to enter in to all the Kingdom's riches: humbly, delightedly, and wholeheartedly.

Part of the Kingdom can be experienced here and now as we ride the roller coaster of life—from infancy, to toddlerhood, to grade school, adolescence, young adulthood, middle-age, and old age. Depending on the Creator of it all to teach us, to help us, to love us, to comfort us around each curve, each bend, each thrill, and each terror.

And then, one day, the roller coaster will plunge into that mysterious dark Tunnel of Death. But death is only a temporary door—opening and birthing us into a magnificent world beyond our wildest dreams. "Yes," I can tell my children, "there really is a Magic Kingdom."

Sometimes, when I'm all alone, I try to imagine what that Kingdom might be like. Surely delighted giggles of children will be among the parade of singing angels as we gather around our King's throne. And I think to myself, *What a wonderful world.*

But Jesus called the children to Him and said,
"Let the little children come to me,
and do not hinder them,
for the kingdom of God belongs to such as these.
I tell you the truth, anyone who will not receive
the kingdom of God like a little child
will never enter it."
LUKE 18:16–17
છે

Can You Come Tuck Me In?

"**N**ighty-night, sleep tight. And don't let the bedbugs bite."

How many of us were tucked in bed and left with this parental sign-off ringing in our ears as we lay in the darkness? I loved it, but why I loved it I can't quite fathom. Interpreted literally this night-night farewell says, basically, "Sweet dreams my little one—by the way, I'd keep a sharp eye out for biting insects crawling under the covers if I were you." How did a message that sounds like it sprung from a twisted mind end up part of our "comforting" bedtime routines?

Perhaps this is only one example of many pre-bedtime activities that elude all logic. Back when the children were tiny, we had quite the involved bedtime routine. I read to them, bathed them, rocked them, sang to them, prayed with them, nursed and/or watered them, diapered and/or pottied them, hugged them, kissed them, and stopped often to gaze at them—cute as baby bunnies in their soft feety pajamas. Then I repeated many of these things several more times throughout the evening before they actually fell asleep. By that time, I was wiped out—too exhausted even to cry, much less marvel over how cute they were. So why, thinking about it now, do I suddenly miss it all?

As I ponder childhood bedtime rituals, I realize that I still have several of my own nighty-night traditions I've carried into adulthood. Almost every night, I grab a good book or magazine and head to my tub full of hot-as-I-can-stand-it water. When I've steamed and read long enough that my eyes refuse to decode another word and my toes have turned into ten wrinkly prunes, I know I'm preheated and ready for bed. Once snuggled under the covers, I spoon into the curve of my sleeping husband and drop contentedly off to sleep. Unless my sleeping husband is just pretending and not actually ready for full-fledged sleep. But I . . . um, digress.

As far back as I can remember, a hot bath, a good book, and snuggling up (with a pillow or comforter in the days before Scott was handy) have been part of my nightly routine. On the other hand, Scott has his own method of going off to dreamland. As soon as he realizes it is a proper time to retire, he stumbles toward the bedroom, peeling off excess garments, and *while* he is actually plummeting toward the bed, he falls asleep—mid-air—before his head hits the pillow. It never ceases to amaze me.

As one might imagine, our diverse bedtime routines have also been the cause of some ongoing conflict. Not long ago, after a rough night's sleep, we tried to discuss our sleeping preferences rationally. I opened the debate.

"Scott, I understand that you like to have some fresh air coming in the room. All I'm asking is that it not be of the arctic variety. I honestly think I saw snow flurries drifting out of the air vents last night."

"Becky," Scott calmly replied, "just because your feet never thaw does not mean the rest of us like to sleep with the temperature set on broil. What you need to do is tuck your head under the covers, like me, and you'll be warm as toast."

"I can't! It makes me claustrophobic. Look, I'm gasping for air just thinking about it." I clutched at my throat for effect.

"Do you think you could possibly be a little more melodramatic?"

"And besides, O Toasty One, you wouldn't even let me warm my feet on your calves last night."

"That's because you kept pinching my leg hairs with your toes."

"OK. Let's move on to the next subject. What I want to know is why you and the kids go so ballistic whenever a teensy, weensy shred of light slithers its way into your rooms?"

"Shred of light? *Shred of light?* Beck, you leave so many lights on in the house every night, the neighbors must think we never sleep. Which isn't too far from the truth. The only thing we're lacking is a rotating searchlight in each closet!"

"Now who's being dramatic? Look, I *need* lights on in the house so I can see my way to the children should they need me in case of fire. Or a burglar. Or a stomach virus."

"That's ridiculous."

"Yeah, well obviously you've never groped in the darkness for a nauseous child. Believe me, mister, it only takes once."

There is no end in sight to these debates. Amazingly, I keep loving Scott in spite of his weird habits. (It's so nice to be the one in charge of the slant this book takes.) Somehow we've managed to get in at least a few hours of sleep each night for the past twenty years.

As I'm writing this, it is after 10:00 P.M. Fighting off yawns, I'm still in my office taking advantage of the unusual quiet, but I'm not completely alone. Zeke is in an easy chair beside me, silently reading his homework assignment. Zachary, our eldest, just opened the door to "check and see if Zeke was ready for bed yet." The boys still share a room (they have no choice). *Their* bedtime routine consists of listening to music, discussing stuff they think adults are too old to understand, and arguing about whose turn it is to turn off the light.

Zachary looked so forlorn just now, peeking his head around the door, dressed in his boxer shorts and baggy T-shirt. I couldn't resist teasing him a bit. "Poor Zachary," I said in my syrupy-mommy voice. "Can't you get off to sleep without your little brother and your nighty-night pillow talk?" Zach stifled a sheepish grin while unconvincingly denying my charge. He's already checked on Zeke once more to see if he was "done yet." Despite Zach's protests, it's obvious that he enjoys his nightly chats with his brother.

Scott and I usually have our pillow talk before he goes to bed. Unless I'm simply in the mood to hear myself chattering a soliloquy, I have to catch my husband before he begins the descent toward his pillow. Thankfully, I still get a chance to enjoy a little pillow talk with the youngest children, Rachel and Gabe. My Rachel, bless her heart, can always be counted on for a nightly hug and kiss and quickie chat. And to her everlasting credit, she'll even come to find me before heading to bed instead of relying on her absentminded mother to remember to tuck her in.

Then there's Gabe, the Champion Pillow Talker of the Western World. If only I had more time to lie down with Gabe before he drifted off to sleep, I could gather enough material to keep me writing for a lifetime.

During one of our recent going-off-to-bed talks, I discovered Gabriel has an unusual, secret nightlife. During the ages when most kids are supposed to be afraid of the dark, I discovered that Gabe was actually roaming from room to room, where he would collect things from underneath the beds of his sleeping siblings. He was, simply put, a nocturnal treasure hunter.

"Gabe," I asked in surprise, "aren't you afraid to put your hand under a bed at night?" Psychologically speaking, I know that's a dysfunctional question for a parent to ask a kid— especially a child so obviously well-adjusted to the dark. But as a little girl, I used to be petrified of the make-believe alligators roaming under my bed. I was sure they hid there every night, waiting for an opportunity to snack on my toes or hands. Remembering this, the question slipped out before I thought better of it. In any case, I needn't have worried. Gabe simply looked at me as if I'd lost my mind.

"No, Mom! Are you kidding? You can get some really good stuff under there." As proof, he showed me his stash: a tennis ball, a pile of rubber bands, an old piece of candy, and a Frisbee. He went on to say that he also talked to his drapes at night, pretending they were his friend. "Oh, really?" I asked him. "Do you have a name for your little imaginary friend?" Of course he did. How silly of me to ask. His friend's name was "Curtain."

There is no telling what we might learn about the intriguing private worlds of our wee ones if we lingered a little longer at the edges of their beds. Or as they grow up and their bedtimes begin to outlast ours, I think teenagers should be obligated to come to tuck *us* into bed. And, since turnabout is fair play, we parents ought to refuse to go to sleep until they bring us three or four drinks of water, read us a story, sing us a song, rub our backs, listen to our pillow talk, and help us say our goodnight prayers.

Well, it's bedtime. And I've spent my "pillow talk" moments with you, my reader friend, tonight. So to all a good night. Please do sleep tight. And even though I think it might be psychologically destructive to say this—don't let the bedbugs bite.

I will lie down and sleep in peace, for you alone,
O LORD, make me dwell in safety.
PSALM 4:8

I'm Just Fixin' Stuff

L ate tonight, after a long day of playing handyman around
the house, Scott plopped his tired body down in the old
green rocker in my office. Ever since he was a little boy, Scott has
been "fixin' stuff." And Lord help the woman who ever so much
as suggests he might hire a professional. Fixin' stuff is my man's
sacred territory—*his* boyish realm of "I can do it all by myself."

For a few seconds Scott just sat and rocked, grateful for a
respite, as I finished some editing. I typed in the last correction,
swiveled my chair around, and propped my feet up on my husband's weary knees.

"Tired?" I asked.

"Exhausted," he answered, staring blankly ahead.

"So now that you are here, I suppose you'd better go ahead
and tell me the news. Do we have water? And if we do, is it hot,
cold, or lukewarm? And, I'm almost afraid to ask but . . ." I gazed
upward at this point, my hands folded together. "Lord have
mercy on us, do we have a clothes dryer yet?" I crossed my fingers and shut my eyes tight as I waited in suspense for the reply.

I should explain that for three weeks now, we've been without a clothes dryer. Actually, we've always been without a *legitimate* clothes dryer. I bought the machine used—well used—from a local laundromat for the bargain price of twenty dollars. For our "twenty big ones" we got a harvest gold machine that looked and sounded more like an enormous rock tumbler than a clothes dryer.

In the beginning, the dryer sounded as if it were tossing, say, a few small pebbles. Then it went through a period of time when the pebble-tumbling noises actually came to a halt—which would have been a relief, except that our mechanically deranged friend had other tricks up its belts. At this point our clothes tumbler went from merely drying our clothes, to baking them. Honestly. White dress shirts began popping out of the steel door the color of perfectly browned toast. During this awkward stage of dryerhood our clothes always smelled suspiciously as if they'd been dried at the end of a coat hanger over a campfire.

Finally, Scott figured out how to adjust the temperature from bake/broil to normal, but then the rock-tumbling noises started again. Only this time, the sound had graduated from mere namby-pamby pebble tumbling to serious boulder grinding. We knew our dryer's days were numbered when Jim Ed, our next-door neighbor, came over and asked Scott if we could hear the horrible noise our "air conditioner" was making outside. (I love the way folks out here get some use out of the middle names. Jim Ed's my favorite, but we also know and love Mary Sue, Ida Lou, and Sue Ann.) Scott had to confess that the ruckus Jim Ed had heard was not emitting from an outside air conditioner unit, but our inside clothes dryer. I was sure it would blow at any moment, but for several more weeks it noisily, but efficiently, managed to keep drying our clothes. Finally, the hunk of metal clanked to a grinding halt. But hey, we figured we had squeezed our twenty bucks out of it.

You aren't going to believe this, but about six months ago, we had actually purchased a nice, almost new, dryer. It's been sitting on my back porch just waiting for the old machine to give up the

——

ghost so it could move in on its territory. *Why in the world,* one might be wondering, *did we wait so long to replace Old Yeller?*

I'll tell you why. Because the new, improved dryer must run on propane. And before we could install it, for reasons only completely understood by my husband, we would have to let our butane tank temporarily run out of fuel. *Why?* So he could move the tank over to the side of the house. *Oh.* And if he was going to move the butane tank over to the side of the house, he would also like to go ahead and move the water tank from the bathroom to the laundry room. *I hope this makes sense to you.* And if he had to do that, well then, all sorts of plumbing lines and gizmos and connectors and such would have to be moved and welded and soldered and piped. This could take days, Scott had been ominously predicting. Faced with this scenario, I agreed with my husband that the most logical thing to do under the circumstances was, of course, to stall—as long as humanly possible. This weekend, however, the jig was up.

For the last four days—in addition to air drying our laundry on the back porch like a family of hillbillies—we've also been coping without benefit of hot water—in January.

Over this weekend I've not seen either of Scott's hands without tools attached to them, and I've only caught brief glimpses of his face from behind bars and under pipes. He's grown the scraggly beginnings of a beard. His eyes have taken on a hollow, haunted look and all his attempts at conversation have started with, "Becky, please tell me you've seen a little piece of metal that looks like an elbow," or "a donut," or "your grandfather's nose."

"Becky," he confessed at one point, "I think I've had my fill of fixing stuff now."

"Do you want me to hire a—"

"Don't say it! Don't even *think* it. Give me time. I'll get my second wind."

And me? Oh, I've been pressing bravely on. I've devised an ingenious system, I think, for still managing to get my daily hot bath. I can go without almost anything, but anyone who knows me well, knows I will *not* be deprived of my daily hot soak in the tub. My system?

First, I begin by putting four of my biggest pots on the stove top to boil (we have an electric stove, thank goodness, that is unaffected by the empty butane tank), and then I heat one big bowl of water in the microwave.

Then I take off all my clothes (so as not to waste precious time when the stage is set), wrap a towel around me, and shuffle back and forth from the kitchen to the bathroom until I've emptied three gallons of boiling water into the bathtub. (Of course, the neighborhood kids have been a little curious. "Hey, what's your mom cookin' up in the bathroom? Does she always wear a towel when she boils water?")

Then I refill the pots, set them all back on the stove to boil again, and jump in the tub before the water cools off. Midway through my bath, when my hair is all lathered up with shampoo, I pop out of the tub, repeat the running back and forth with hot pads and pots of boiling water, in order to reheat the two inches of bathwater that have now begun to cool.

Just call me Pioneer Woman. If I am anything, I am adaptable.

So now you understand how much I had vested in the answers I was about to receive from my bone-weary husband. The news was mixed.

"Becky," he began solemnly, as if he were giving a battle brief, "as it now lines up—yes, we have a working clothes dryer."

"Hallelujah!"

"Yes, there is hot and cold running water in the bathtub."

"That's my little handyman! I knew you could do it!"

"However, there is no water at all in any of the bathroom sinks."

"Yuuuuck . . ."

"In the kitchen, I have hot water only coming out of the faucet."

"That I can live with."

"No water to the dishwasher."

"That I cannot. What about the washing machine?"

"Cold only."

"All in all, sir," I replied with a dutiful salute, "not too shabby. The troops will survive. For a couple of days. But I cannot write another word tonight. May I be dismissed now? I have an appointment with a tub of steaming hot water."

The next morning.

It was rather amusing this morning to watch the kids fighting over who got to use the bathtub first—to brush their teeth and wet their combs. I went to the kitchen sink for a cold drink of water and forgot that today's option from that particular faucet was limited to hot liquids only. Resigned, I put a tea bag in a cup of steaming water from the hydrant and let it steep. Then I sat down on my living room couch—the only neat, new piece of furniture we've ever bought—and began a melancholy muse.

Sometimes I think our lives are so very strange—surely I'm stuck in an ongoing sitcom from the Twilight Zone. Or maybe we're really on Perpetual Candid Camera.

I can't help it. Sometimes, I confess, I compare. Not our family's lifestyle to other people's, really—at least not often. What I compare is my neat, clean suburban upbringing to this wacky, country, live-by-the-seat-of-our-pants life we are giving our children. I do laugh about it. This house-building project provided much of the inspiration for my first three books.

We still chuckle at the time when we'd first moved to this dilapidated cabin and our Gabriel, at about age three, grabbed his coat and started out the door. When we asked him where he was going, he answered, "I'm goin' home now." I informed him that this new "house" was now our home. That's when Gabe cried out—on behalf of us all, really—"But this house is broken!" However, I would not change our decision to move to the country, building as we could afford, even if I could. But I'll be honest; there are times when it gets awfully tough.

My mind drifts back to an evening two weeks ago. . . .

I am sitting at my big, round kitchen table. The dining room set is used furniture, too, of course; I found it at a bargain shop.

But I love this table with its nicks and character lines. It's a deep honey-colored maple, like the Early American furniture you see in old magazines from the fifties. It's a table meant for turkey and stuffing and coffee and cookies and family and conversation. Norman Rockwell would have loved my table, I think. But this evening, there are no turkeys or chocolate chip cookies on my honey-colored table. Instead, the maple surface is covered with bills, bills, and more bills. I *hate* bills.

We've come so, so far. We really have. From a one-bedroom cabin to a gorgeous two-story shell, at least, of a home. Built, every board, by my husband, with occasional help from his sons. In the last few months, Scott & Sons have managed to finish our beautiful living room—giving us much-needed space for our sprawling family. But still, on this night of bills, Scott and I admit we are not where we had hoped we'd be at this point in time. We face the possibility of not being able to give our children what we so desperately want them to have before it is too late and they are grown and gone. Our fixer-upper might not get fixed. Zach's best chance at a room of his own may be a college dorm. Still, my husband refuses to dig deeper into debt to finish the house. In my heart I know he is right. But this is hard truth, still, for me to swallow.

Our oldest son and his brother still share a small room. Gabriel sleeps in a makeshift hall. Rachel must crawl over Gabriel's bed to get to her bedroom. My kitchen cabinets are held up by a two-by-four. There's still only one bathroom for the six of us. These things eat at us—the parents, the *providers*.

Sometimes I wonder if they bother me even more than Scott, though I know he agonizes too. But Scott was the youngest in his family, and his household was, for most of his life, in some state of remodeling flux. His dad was ever the tinkerer in his off hours, and his mom the creative type—knocking down walls on a whim, redecorating with antiques and sentimental finds. It honestly never bothered Scott that his bedroom was, for a few years, a walk-in closet. His parents have a lovely home on a lake now, but it is ever-evolving into new form too.

My parents, on the other hand, were the typical seventies couple who bought into the concept of new, neat, simple: the gift-boxed suburban dream on a cul-de-sac. Perhaps I feel the guilt about the state of our home more acutely because it contrasts so sharply with what I knew as a child.

By the time I was in third grade I had a large, bright bedroom of my own with new ruffled white curtains and sunny yellow furniture. The carpet matched and flowed smoothly from one room to another. We had two bathrooms and a huge kitchen with built-in coppertone appliances. There were two living areas, a laundry room, a two-car garage, and a bedroom to house each sibling, along with my parents' master bedroom. The paint was fresh, the caulk was neat, the trim all finished. It was such a neat little package. I even had a neat little yard, with real grass that got mowed and watered, and a porch swing and a fence. Today, my parents own a similar home—only prettier, neater, more polished, and beautifully decorated.

I have to admit, though, even as a child growing up in a "perfect house," I dreamed of living in the country, with woods and water and picket fences all around. I'd ride my bike out away from the subdivisions until I found myself a tree to climb or a pond to read by.

My husband breaks my reverie, sitting down beside me at the table and pouring me a cup of coffee. Then, one by one, our children file in from the front door and from various rooms in the house and join us around our table. As if by instinct, they seem to know I need their strength. The coffee and my family softens the sight of the monster bills. Then Scott speaks.

"Kids," he says, "we love you guys. We moved to the country because we chose to give you nature and water and woods over a nice, modern home. Sometimes we wonder if we've done the right thing. And I want you to know that your mother and I want more than anything to finish this house. We want you to each have a bedroom of your own and we all want the privacy an extra bathroom would give us. I want your mom to drive a decent car. But I refuse to go deeper into debt. Times, right now, are a little tighter than they've been for a while. We need to slow down our spending, and we need you guys to be understanding."

One by one, each of our children offers words of comfort. "Mom and Dad, you've given us a great life." "Dad, we're not in a big hurry. We're OK." "Look at our beautiful living room! At least now there's room for parties and kids to come over and spend the night on the floor." "We'd rather live like this and be in the country any day than one of those perfect houses in the city."

The tears fall freely down my face. Scott takes my hand and offers his other hand to the child beside him. One by one each brother or sister takes the hand of the other until the circle closes. Then Scott prays for us to be satisfied and grateful, as a family, for what God has given us. Out-loud prayers are not frequent occurrences in our family—other than at mealtime. It means the world to me that my husband senses I need this. Maybe moments like these are what growing up is all about.

Later, Scott catches me in the hall and says, "Becky, Zachary just offered to sell his car if it would help out. Maybe we came across a little too pitiful. But we've got a good bunch of kids, don't we?"

I nod slowly. We are wealthy.

Back to early this morning . . .

Comforted by that memory, I got up from the couch, walked out the front door, and could hardly believe my eyes. There, in front of God and the neighbors and everybody, sat a white commode. As columnist Dave Barry is prone to say, I am *not* making this up. I did an about-face and marched back into the house.

"Look, Scott," I stated in no uncertain terms, "I'm a very patient woman. But this is where I draw the line! I'm OK with table saws and towers of pink insulation stacked on my front porch. I can even handle a dryer on the back porch. But I refuse—for even one second—to have a *potty* in my front yard!"

"Gee, Becky," Scott said calmly, "I just needed to spray it off. No need to cry about it!"

"Hey, Buster, it's my potty and I'll cry if I want to!"

One look at my face and he knew I'd reached my limit. As the kids and I loaded up in the station wagon for the drive to their school, I saw Scott run out the front door (in nothing but his boxer shorts), pick up the commode, and drag it to the front porch. Then he threw a blanket over it, in a futile attempt at camouflage.

Zeke couldn't resist a comment. "Hey, Dad, try putting a hat on it!"

I finally got tickled and hollered out, "And a carrot nose and corncob pipe!" Scott just grinned and darted back in the house.

He is taking off a few days to work on the house and get it in shape for Friday night when the kids' youth group comes over for a game night and pizza party. Hopefully, all our faucets will be running hot and cold again by then. (If not, it is safe to assume that my blood will be.)

Learning to be content with where we are and with what we have is one of the most difficult lessons I'm having to learn. In reading through a little book called *Kids Say the Greatest Things about God,* I came across a child's interpretation of heaven that my children could probably "Amen." The little boy said, "When you get your room in heaven, you don't have to share it with any of your brothers. Or, if you do have to share, God makes it so you don't mind sharing."[13]

It is a child, once again, that puts life back in perspective for me. Nothing will ever be "just right" here on earth. It isn't really supposed to be. But one day we'll have a home that is absolutely perfect, where everything is working—or even if it isn't, God will make it so I won't mind. And Scott, I'm sure, will be tinkering on the mansions—having the time of his life just "fixin' stuff."

I have learned to be satisfied
with the things I have
and with everything that happens.

I know how to live when I am poor.
And I know how to live when I have plenty.
I have learned the secret of being happy
at any time in everything that happens.
PHILIPPIANS 4:11–12, NCV
୬

Let's Go Muddin'!

Mud . . . glorious mud.
Remember the feel of squish-squashy stuff oozing up
between your toes? Who knows how many chefs began their
careers by decorating fancy mud pies with chocolate dirt and
candy rocks and twig candles. When asked what God did with
His time, one youngster replied, "God makes bees with little
wings all day. Probably out of mud."[14] Since God created Adam
from the dust of the earth, this child must have concluded that
God continues to create masterpieces from dirt, eternally up to
His elbows in mud. Who knows?

I'd almost forgotten what wonderful amusement a bit of dirt
and water can provide for a child. And how *large* pools of gushy,
goopy, glorious mud can entertain children of all ages for hours
at a time. That is, until last week, when a little boy down the
street reminded me what excitement awaits those who take the
time to go outside and play in the mud. I should probably mention that "the little boy down the street" is six feet tall, and a
grandfather of seven.

First, let me set the stage before I give you the scoop on this story. Our family lives on the banks of a small lake, in a neighborhood of about a hundred cabins that dot the surrounding woods. Living near water has been an adventure in and of itself, but one of the most interesting events in our neighborhood happens when the board members of our community decide it is time to drain the lake—for dock repairs, or to plant fish-attracting algae or, I suspect, simply to satisfy curiosities about what's lurking under the water. One thing is certain: The best thing lurking is mud; the thickest, goopiest, doggone best mud a young boy or old man could ever hope to squish-squash around in.

Our kids—from nine-year-old Gabriel on up to sixteen-year-old Zach—have invented a new sport of their own to play during these times of forced lake drought. Although, temporarily, there is no boating, skiing, fishing, or swimming, our children are far from depressed when the water is drained. They now have—muddin'. "What's muddin'?" you ask. Perhaps I should simply explain how muddin' is carried out, and I think you'll get the general idea.

To get the most from the muddin' experience, you first pull on the tallest pair of rubber boots you can find—hip boots are best. Then, starting from the shore, the object of the game is to wade toward the middle of what used to be the lake, venturing out and in as deep as you dare. Our teenagers routinely make it clear up to their necks in black goop. And that's about the gist of it.

"Why would anyone in his or her right mind want to do this?" you may ask. I don't know; believe me, I don't know. I was a child of more dainty constitution, myself. But my kids absolutely love this activity, and since muddin' keeps them happy and busy and out of my hair—and since I suppose it's an invigorating form of isometric exercise—I hold my tongue. As long as they spray off with the hose in the yard before setting a toe on my carpet, I'm pretty easygoing about such things.

I inherited this attitude, I think, from my own mother. She never blinked about letting us kids play outside in the rain. In reference to such leniencies (or lunacies, as the case may be), one of my boys once complimented me by saying, "Mom, I'm so glad you aren't sensible like other mothers." "Thank your Granny," I said.

There is one thing I protest about the muddin' days, however. Every now and then, one of my children will dig up and bring into the house a horrible, vile-looking, hissing eel-like creature—about a foot long and an inch and a half thick. They find them burrowing into the mud along the banks. The critters go by the name of "mud puppies" around here, much too sweet a name for these miniature horror monsters if you ask me. They give me the heebie-jeebies and look just like offspring of those blood-sucking earth-eels from the movie *Tremors*.

Once Gabriel brought a mud puppy into the bathroom and left it unattended in some tap water in the sink. I didn't realize it was there, came along, and reached into the sink to the plug. Before that fat eel disappeared down the drain like slick fettuccine, he managed to slither around my hand just to let me know he was there. As you might expect, I screamed until there were no screams left in me. Now I have a *permanent* case of the heebie-jeebies. I keep expecting that someday a slimy black creature will return and pop its hissing head up out of the sink, just when I least expect it. And I will simply die. That's all. I'll just die.

Now back to the little boy/grandfather. His name is Wally. Wally decided the other morning that it would be a great idea, while the water was down, to dig some deep pools around the edge of the lake—pools where fish could eventually congregate so fishermen could eventually do the same. In truth, I strongly suspect Wally simply had a hankering to dig a big hole with a great big tractor. And so, when his wife went shopping and promised to be gone for the entire morning, Wally set out to go play in the mud with his man-sized Tonka truck.

In our neighborhood, the sound of a tractor or backhoe's engine is like the call of a roaring pied piper to every machine-loving male within hearing distance. So it wasn't long before Wally had a crowd of playmates around him, eager to help, or at least to provide him with an audience. It goes without saying that as soon as the sound of a heavy-duty engine drifted through the back door, Scott walked outside toward the noise like some beguiled sleepwalker in a cartoon—not blinking, not uttering a word. On his hypnotic trek toward the big-machine noise, Scott ran into Jim Ed, our no-nonsense, laid-back neighbor.

"Hey, Jim Ed!" Scott called, "What's goin' on down there by the lake?"

"Wally thinks he's going to dig himself a fishin' hole," Jim Ed replied. "I tried to tell him it was still too muddy."

"So what are you going to do now?" Scott asked.

"Well," drawled Jim Ed, "guess I'll pour me a cup of coffee and come sit out here on the porch. Then I think I'll watch a tractor sink."

Jim Ed's not only no-nonsense and laid-back—he's smart. He sat down just in time to see Wally drive the tractor six feet out from the edge of the mud and watch it sink nearly six feet under. Talk about your mud on your face. Wally was in it at least up to his hip boots, and Scott walked back in the house to give an updated blow-by-blow report.

"Becky," he informed me, "Wally's going to have to rent a big diesel truck to come pull that tractor out. Can you believe it?" I could tell my husband was working hard at trying to disguise the little-boy excitement that kept trying to creep into his manly, serious voice.

"Honey," I answered brightly, "I think it is just wonderful of Wally to do this on a holiday, so all you neighborhood guys can be in on this while you've got time off to enjoy it. You couldn't pay for a better male-bonding experience than this—men, mud, big tractors, trucks. Shall I make popcorn?"

"No time," Scott answered, no longer even attempting to hide his grin. "I gotta get back out there! Tell the boys to get out of bed; they'll want to see this!"

That evening I visited with Wally's wife. She was sitting on the couch, staring off into space, shaking her head back and forth, and mumbling. "Five hours," she said over and over again to herself. "I only left him alone for five hours. . . ." Bless her heart, we women are going to have to pull together, I can tell. Until that mud is covered up once again with lake, I'm afraid none of us can completely relax. All we can do is try to keep a better eye on our kids—large and small—while they play in the mud: goopy, squishy, gushy, glorious, eternally magnetic mud.

Post-Script: After reading this story and admitting to finding it a mite funny, Wally wrote me the following note. "I do want to set the record straight, however. WE DID GET ONE FISH-ING HOLE! When that big diesel truck upsurged the tractor, it left a pretty nice bass hole. Not a big one and we don't want to estimate dollars per cubic feet—but it will provide a home for several lake bass." Consider the record straightened!

God, save me. The water has risen to my neck.
I'm sinking down into the mud. There is
nothing to stand on. I am in deep water.
PSALM 69:1–2, NCV

🐸

T W E N T Y - F I V E

Can I Hug the Bunny?

During their third-grade year at school, each of my children colored and cut out a large paper-doll-sized boy and named him "Flat Stanley." Then, along with all the kids in their class, they mailed Flat Stanley to an adult friend or relative to take on an "adventure." The adult was then to take the "paper boy" along for the day, write about what they did together, take pictures if possible, and mail him back to the child's school for "show and tell."

This year, Gabe had his turn at making a Flat Stanley. But then Gabe was faced with a dilemma. Who on earth could he trust to be an adventurous companion for his paper boy? Only one person, Gabe realized, might be up for the task. It had to be someone who knew how to handle a camera. It had to be someone with a vivid imagination. It had to be someone who still liked kid stuff. It had to be Grandma.

I don't know much about the childhood of Gabe's paternal grandmother, Beverly. Oh, here and there she's shared some scattered memories of sunny days growing up in California. But I've had the feeling that Bev's childhood went by way too fast for her liking. Like a piece of gum one is forced to spit out too soon, childhood often disappears before we have a chance to chew all the "goody" out of it.

So, over the last few years, I've been casually observing my mother-in-law as she paints more "childlikeness" into her adult days—using colors of her own whim and fancy. I, for one, think it's marvelous.

One childlike, fun thing Bev has started doing over the past few years is collecting teddy bears. This Christmas, we gave her a tapestry teddy and a teddy bear wreath. Other grown children and grandchildren gifted her with a leather-attired motorcycle bear and a ready-for-the-slopes snow ski bear. Bev's now acquired more than fifty-seven bears—enough to decorate a Christmas tree from top to bottom. Though it is now the end of February, the Bear Tree is still up, and I have a sneaking suspicion it is not coming down anytime soon. The nice thing about getting old is that you can eat dessert first and keep a Christmas tree up until July if you jolly well please.

And so it followed quite naturally that when Flat Stanley arrived in Grandma's mailbox, she'd choose to take him along on an adventure with her bear friends. The result was not just a quick letter and a handful of pictures. Oh, no. Grandma wrote and photographed an entire book about Flat Stanley's adventures. Flat Stanley on the Bear Tree. Flat Stanley sailing in a basket with the Quadruplet Sailor Bears. Flat Stanley on Grandpa's motorcycle with Motorcycle Bear. Flat Stanley cooking beans with Chef Bear. Gabe was delighted.

As I read through Beverly's wondrous book, I thought of a passage I'd read recently about mid-life choices. Paula Payne Hardin has a chapter called "The Child of Yesterday, The Adult of Today" in her book, *What Are You Going to Do with the Rest of Your Life?*

"One day," she writes, "I realized I wanted to go to a toy store and find a teddy bear. This may appear foolish to some—a woman in her fifties wanting a teddy bear, but it was my desire. I found a wonderful furry creature who called out to me from his deep-set brown yes. I was so excited!" She even wrote a sonnet of her experience called "In Praise of Teddy Bears." In the sonnet she expressed how her bear comforted her with its soft, accepting presence. "So grown-ups, hug your bears with heart's delight!"[15] the sonnet encourages.

"Come on," I'm sure some calloused soul out there is protesting. "We're talkin' about a stuffed piece of fluff!" My answer to this logical argument is, "Never underestimate the power of fluff."

Even my upper-level business executive father still keeps his old, pitiful, adorable, gray stuffed elephant in the top of his closet. The fur has mostly been rubbed off. One of its button eyes is—sorry to say this, Daddy—a socket of stuffing. But don't make fun of this stuffed baby elephant around my father. He transforms instantly into a boy of about five. "That was my Dumbo," he softly reminisces. And I can almost visualize a hazy image of my daddy as a little boy going off to sleep with his arms around his baby elephant.

On my trip to Disneyland, I bought a brand new stuffed Dumbo and mailed it off to my father. I wasn't back home in Texas for long before my parents showed up for a visit. When I opened the front door, there stood my dad, stroking the velvet pink ears of his new baby elephant toy. In his classic "little boy" voice he said, "I like my Dumbo." Mother shook her head in mock worry.

"Becky," she said, "he's been under so much stress at work lately, I'm a little worried he's going to take that elephant into a board meeting."

When Scott was young, he had a stuffed monkey. He also had an imaginary friend named Joe, who lived in the closet. When Scott talks of Joe and his monkey, his voice also slides back in time until he's sounding like a small boy. Funny how people do that. Everyone I ask about their special childhood companion begins to revert, without thinking, to using baby talk as they describe their treasured friend.

As an adult, my husband continues to keep friendly stuffed animals around. But now, the more macho name for them is "his truck mascots." He has a soft, squishy, stuffed cow with long spindly legs. Ingeniously, he named her "Cow." Recently, he added a stuffed moose to the front-seat menagerie. You guessed it. "Moose."

My children have also had their assorted stuffed "friends." Zach took lots of teasing over it, but when he was a little tike he toted around a "Buddy"—a stuffed boy dressed in overalls and a cap. Zeke had a fluff-and-battery-filled Glo-Worm that lit up the dark night. He called it his Glo-Buggy. Scott and I secretly called it his Bed Bug. Rachel, at age twelve, is completely enamored with her stuffed Pooh Bear. We even had a Winnie the Pooh birthday party for her this year. I'm amused to see toddler toys are "in" with teens right now. Have you noticed? In the malls more and more teenagers are sporting Piglet watches, Mickey Mouse shirts, and Tweety Bird ball caps. It sure beats satanic rock group attire all to pieces, I say.

Gabe has Big Bear, a huge, floppy, huggable bear, three feet tall and three feet wide. Even when Gabe was only three feet tall himself, he'd insist on taking Big Bear everywhere. (I even let him take Big Bear to the grocery store with us. Where, I now wonder, did I ever put the groceries? Desperate moms will find a way to put up with *anything* if it keeps their preschoolers quiet on shopping trips.) Seven years later, Big Bear still occupies one-fourth of Gabe's bed. Says he still loves his bear and "will never ever get rid of him."

This Valentine's Day, Gabe wanted to give his little girlfriend the best present his savings could buy. So he gathered up all his dollars, quarters, dimes, and pennies and bought her the biggest, softest, fluffiest, white teddy bear he could find. She loved it and told him so. He was so touched he wrote her the following note, which I found on my computer.

> I'm glad you liked you'r teddeybear. I rote a rime
> for you it goe'es like this I think you'r grandey I

think you'r handey & I like to give canddey. I
know it's short but you know I love you & that's all
that matter's. love, Gabe

(They also had to write what they liked most about Valentine's Day. I got a kick out of his paper.)

I'm polst to tell you good things about Valen-
tims. They are giving presents becouse it's fun to
watch them open it. I usually give my friends stufft
bears & chocklets. The party's are fun becouse we
get cookies, candy, Sprite, & I can be with my
friends. I just flat out like Vallintines.

(I can't help myself. It's hard not to smile when you've got a
frog-loving, bear-hugging kid around the house.)

As my sweet grandmother, Nonnie, moved into her eighties,
someone gave her a pretty, soft doll with flaxen hair and a pink
folk-style dress. Nonnie named the doll Ursula and kept her
primped and propped on her bed. Grandchildren and great-
grandchildren could freely play with anything in Nonnie's
house, but it always made her nervous if little grubby fingers got
too close to her Ursula.

One day Nonnie had a stroke and had to enter the cold stark-
ness of a hospital. Ursula came along too. I remember Mother
commenting on how bittersweet it was to see her aging mother
comforted, in strange antiseptic surroundings, by the presence of
a familiar doll.

What about me? Well, I never had a special stuffed piece of
lovable fluff as a child. I had a doll that I loved, but no soft bear
or monkey or elephant that stole my heart. As I was writing this
chapter, I realized this made me a little sad. Then one day I was
in a toy store, around Easter, and I picked up a stuffed bunny
with big floppy ears and huge feet with calico pads. And it fit
perfectly in my arms.

So, at age thirty-seven, I marched up to the counter and
bought myself a bunny. I took him home, put him on my bed—

and I absolutely love him. It's become a sweet family joke. When one of the kids is sick or needs some TLC, they'll pitifully moan, "Mom, can I borrow your bunny?" Scott came home once after an especially grueling day, stretched out on the bed, and stared at the ceiling. When I asked him what I could do to help, he gruffly replied, "Bring me that bunny."

This very afternoon I met a precious woman who often hosts women's retreats in her log home. She also collects teddy bears. "Becky," she said, "one time I was preparing for the ladies to come, and I felt the Lord wanted me to give away three of my bears. So I set them aside, thinking to myself, *Oh, they are going to think this is so silly.* But during a sharing time, three of the women shared heartbreaking stories of childhood abuse. Then I told them what God had impressed upon me earlier and handed each woman a bear, saying, 'God wants you to enjoy your child-hood starting *now.*' They couldn't say anything. They just hugged those bears and bawled. It was beautiful."

Every grown-up who has ever been a child—or is part child still—understands that there is more to bunnies and bears and monkeys than fluff and stuff. In a popular story about a little boy who was afraid of the dark, the mother tells her son that he can rest assured that God is always with him, even in the night.

"Yes," the little boy answers, "but I need somebody with skin on." And in the absence of "somebody with skin on," I believe the next best thing to snuggle up with in the dark is something soft and fluffy—with fur on.

The poor man had nothing except one little ewe lamb he had bought. . . . It grew up with him and his children. It . . . slept in his arms.
2 SAMUEL 12:3

But I Don't Wanna
Go Home Yet!

I am bummed. I mean, I'm *really* bummed out. I just got home from summer vacation, you see, and I'm not quite ready for life. It's like I found the most perfect, peaceful place to hide. Then just as I settled into a calm "ahhh . . .," big, clumsy ol' Real Life shouts, "Ready or not, here I come!" And within seconds, I am discovered and hauled by the scruff of my neck into the game against my will.

This morning, life forced me up early and into a game of Follow the Kids to the Station Wagon. Upon my offspring's arrival at the car doors, all four of them broke out in a rousing chorus of "I Get the Front Seat." The participants then began to battle each other in what looked like a wild game of Twister— all tangled up trying to reach the coveted seat of honor. At that point I changed the game to Let's Make a Deal, claimed Monopoly on the front seat, and refused to move until all children were ready to participate in Sorry. (OK, enough of the game motif.)

After finally depositing the children at school, I drove back home, and it was then I realized the horrible truth. Today, all by myself, I'd have to clean the whole entire yucky house; cook supper—from scratch, mind you—and *then* make wild after-school zigzags all over town picking up my umpteen kids from every conceivable form of "practice." Not only that, but I'd also have to sit down and work, which means actually *using my brain* to make sense of the little black marks floating across the computer screen at the tap of my fingers. Am I starting to sound just a wee bit ugly? Forgive me, but sometimes I get so frustrated. Can you indulge my tantrum just a second longer?

Here's the news that really rots my sandals: Waiting to greet me on my office desk is IRS Form 1040A—the incredibly, unbelievably looooong version, along with all of its tricky little friends—8898, 4562, and Schedules A-Z. (Yes, I should have filed them in April, but I always file for the extension. Never do today what you can put off for four months, I always say.)

As a result, I'm cross-eyed and bewildered and, yes, even para-noid. I just know there is an IRS agent with beady little eyes and an evil sense of humor sitting in some government office waiting for me to misplace a decimal. (Um, just in case an IRS agent is reading this—I'm just teasing with the "beady little eyes, evil sense of humor" bit. But according to line 42, section b, page 55-A—I believe "teasing about the IRS" is "allowable.")

I want you to know that all of this nonproductive whining does have a point—*but what was it?* Oh, yes. The transition from play time to clean-up time is the *pits*. I hated it in kinder-garten, and I don't like it any better as an adult. Visualize a tod-dler wailing—one of those open-mouthed, out-loud whines—and you'll have a perfect picture of how I feel right now.

I don't wanna go home yet! I'll do my chores next month! I wanna go back and play some more!! WAAAAAH!!!

But maybe [sniff, sniff] if I could tell you how much fun I had on my summer vacation [pitiful swallow], and about the good time I had with my friends, maybe I'll feel all better again.

First and foremost, I've got to tell you about the great big ocean. (Hang on to your visors; I'm about to wax poetic.)

I could sit for hours near the sea, watching her emerald waves toss up soft foam toward sandy shores, then pull it all back out again—as if reluctant to hand over such lacy treasure. Show and tell, take it back, then show and tell again.

The beach is also a rather noisy place. Yet the noise of the waves is another thing I love about retreating to the sea. I don't believe people usually come to the ocean to *sort through* complicated problems. The din of sloshing sea water assures active thinking will be kept to a minimum, at best. I believe, instead, that people come to the ocean to be *swept away*—to let the crashing, repetitive sound of the pounding waves wash out tired, muddled heads. The laborious swooooosh . . . swooooosh . . . swooooosh . . . leaves you empty, limp, and clean. Like a head massage. Or a mental rinse. I guess you could say it's a lovely experience in brainwashing. And the sheer gift of a nonthinking day spent watching the gentle tug of war between sea and shore, and of listening to the white noise of the playful struggle—well, that's only the *beginning*.

It is at night, after the sun makes its crimson bow, all glitter comes out for display. On this particular trip, a full moon dropped by for a welcome visit. I'd never seen a full moon over the ocean at night, and I almost ached with the beauty of the thing. Luminescent, with its eye wide open, hovering over the dark velvet waves—like something wise, gentle, maternal. In response to the glowing roundness in the sky, thousands of diamond lights danced their gratitude from tops of rolling sea water.

Walking over a dune that night, unprepared as I was for the gorgeous panorama rising before my eyes, I understood the old expression, "It takes my breath away." When I found my breath, I whispered quiet praise to the Artist of the masterpiece.

Isn't this a good vacation story so far? My brow is already beginning to unfurrow. By the time I'm finished recounting

"My Summer Vacation," I may even feel some measure of warmth toward the IRS.

Right about now I suppose you might be asking, "Just exactly what did you do on vacation besides participate in poetic waxing?" OK, OK, I'm getting to that. I did absolutely anything I wanted to do at any given moment. For days—six of them to be exact.

Actually, I did do *some* things. I made our bed once or twice, but I must confess—I enjoyed it. Even housework can be fun in tasteful surroundings belonging to wealthy, yuppy-condo-landlords. The furniture in our bedroom was white wicker, the walls pale green, the bedspread thick and covered with fat pink roses. And there was a lovely balcony where I could slip out at any time to rest between the exertion of fluffing pillows and tucking in coverlets.

I also did a little cooking—toast, salad, and cold cereal. Seriously, I did manage to whip up some real live meals. There are witnesses that can testify that I also made chili dogs, Bisquick biscuits, and coleslaw from a mix. Somehow, we managed to eat well.

One of the best parts of our annual vacation is that we always go with two sets of old friends—Ron and Gail, and Dean and Heather—and their children. Luckily, Gail can cook—rich treats like pecan brownies and sour cream coffee cake—from *scratch*. And Heather—well, Heather knows how to both buy and boil shrimp. And because she's got just the right touch of obsessive-compulsiveness, the kitchen stays spotless. Culinary matters aren't of much consequence anyway, since eating out at oceanside cafés has become our group's favorite all-weather water sport.

When vacationing with others, we've found it's important to have similar likes and dislikes. For example, Gail and I are always on a budget, which we don't like. But then there's shopping—which we do like. Very much. Luckily, for determined bargain hunters like Gail and me—with little to no sense of pride—there's always a way to get our shopping fix. You should see the great stuff we've picked up from resale shops, Goodwill, and Salvation Army stores along the coastal highways!

One of our "finds" on this trip was a used bookstore. This particular bookstore was in a converted upstairs apartment. It seemed odd that the young proprietor was wearing a tie with his shirt, but he had recently retired from military service. He greeted us warmly and apologized for the mess, not knowing how really low our standards of neatness are. Since I read at least five books during vacation week, I love browsing for reading treasure—especially something that will touch my heart or lift my spirit. In the stacks of dusty books lining the floors and shelves, I found a couple of pearls: a fifty-year-old copy of *The Robe*, by Lloyd C. Douglas, and a thirty-year-old copy of *Gifts from the Sea*, by Anne Morrow Lindbergh.

When it was time to pay for our books, the military-type shopkeeper surprised us with a serendipitous method for determining the price. Flashing a smile, he asked, "Do you know the game 'Paper, Rock, Scissors'?" Puzzled, we nodded. "Well, here's the deal: If *you* win, you can name the price. But if *I* win, I get to set the price." He continued, "Fair enough?"

We were game. Why not? Unfortunately, Bookstore Man won. I held my breath, waiting to hear his price.

"How does two dollars sound?" he asked. *For two hardback books? Are you kidding?* I thought. He charged Gail an entire $1.50 for her small stack.

As we turned to leave with our bargains, already tickled with our good fortune, our young man pulled fresh flowers from a nearby vase and handed each of us one as a parting gift. We felt like school girls.

A surprising number of the people we met in Florida went out of their way to be pleasant. Maybe it's the climate. Maybe it's the simple way of life—shorts and sandals are standard attire in even the finest of restaurants. Perhaps it's just that people in Florida stay in an eternally pleasant state of mind. We even came upon a nearby town called Niceville. *Niceville?* Gail and I had to check it out. We found a native Nicevillian working behind a convenience store counter and plied him with all sorts of questions.

"Are people really *nice* here? Is there always a breeze? Do you ever see mosquitoes? What are the schools like? How's the crime rate? Do you just *love* living here?"

I never thought I'd ever consider moving from our East Texas home, but I was tempted for the first time in years to pull up anchor and move to the oceanside.

If Gail keeps me company on shopping sprees, then Heather's my comrade in devouring books and also in the quest to know the answer to everything there is to know about everything—especially about the true meaning of life. One night, the rest of the clan went out for a while, leaving us bookworms alone in the living room. But as soon as the door slammed shut, Heather sat up with a start, put her book down, and fired her opening sentence.

"OK, Becky, let's catch up!"

And we were off! At the end of an hour, we'd only hit the tip of our theological/philosophical icebergs. But just as we were getting warmed up, kids of all ages began pouring through the front door eager to share their latest adventure, and our time was gone.

Yes, it was a good vacation. Good friends, good conversation, good shopping, good food, *great* schedule.

And this year we also had lots of teenagers among the children in our group—our Zach, Zeke, and Rachel; Dean and Heather's nineteen-year-old, Jarin; and Ron and Gail's girls, Mandie-Lee, Laressa, and their friend, Amy. I must admit that much of my luxurious sense of freedom was because my children are entering a wonderful stage of independence. Those long years of having to be constantly on the lookout for little ones is fast coming to a close. (A wonderful consolation prize for failing my pregnancy test at the outset of this book!)

Our teens were amazingly uncomplaining, polite, fun, and just plain *good* this year, if I do say so myself. After watching them together this summer, I'm convinced they'll be friends for life. Just as we, their parents, have been all these years.

As an added bonus, a couple of our teenagers now drive. However, the only vehicle that would hold them all for their short excursions about town was poor old Sag. One year, within three hours of the resort, Sag suddenly expired on the highway. But after about ten minutes rest, he gathered up the strength to start his engine again and mosied on down the highway for another hour, whereupon he felt the need for another roadside break. At the time, none of Sag's weary contents found this amusing. But a couple of days after we'd said our "good-byes" to the beach and unpacked our bags in Texas, I found a letter in the mailbox addressed to "Sag & Those Within." It said,

> Dear Sag, We wrote this in your honor.
> Thanks for the memories.
>
> Sag, the Tragic Wagon
> Traveled to the sea
> And weaved all over I–20
> As far as we could see
>
> Sag, the Tragic Wagon
> Had traveled there before
> But previously had to stop and rest
> Every hour, and sometimes more!
>
> Sag, the Tragic Wagon
> Had many squished in the back
> Including one lonely watermelon,
> Gabe, Zeke, Rach-el, and Zach!
>
> Love,
> Mandie-Lee, Laressa, and Amy

Is this not *moving?* Brings tears to a mother's eyes. The ocean has now even inspired our children to wax poetic!

Well, that's pretty much the end of my summer vacation story. Wow. I feel so much better. I really do. Thanks for hearing me out. I think I may have the strength to tackle ol' 1040 and 8898 now.

Wait a second. One last thought. Since vacation did me such a world of good, I wonder if people who may be thinking about checking into a mental hospital ought to try "six days of doing nothing at the beach" first. It would be much less expensive over the long haul, a lot more fun, and honestly, what harm can it do? After all, if you're still nuts at the end of six days, the mental ward will always be there.

I know one thing for sure; every chance I get I plan to do more Nothing. As that wise old philosopher, Winnie the Pooh, once said, "Don't underestimate the value of Doing Nothing, of just going along, listening to all the things you can't hear, and not bothering." If I do not take periodic getaways, I'm afraid life will leave me playing "Ring Around the Rosie" at some loony farm way before my time. And I need my faculties in working order so I can enjoy the golden years with Dean and Heather and Ron and Gail in our Florida retirement villa—where we'll play in God's giant sandbox all day and watch the moon pour over His wave pool at night. (How long does it take to reach those golden years anyway?)

Hey, since you've been such a great help to me today, please feel free to call us in about twenty-five years and drop by for the fun. I'll even make chili dogs and Bisquick biscuits and coleslaw for supper. And it goes without saying, you'll find us listed in the Niceville directory.

"Come to me, all you who are weary and
burdened, and I will give you rest."
MATTHEW 11:28

❧

Old People Can Make Pretty Good Kids

I met a kid yesterday at a local folk festival. He was having an absolute ball playing around with a couple of sticks—in front of anybody who'd pause long enough to watch the show. So I asked this kid, "How old are you anyway?"

"I turned seventy this year," he answered with a grin.

This gentleman was one of *several* lively senior citizens Scott and I met yesterday. They didn't appear to be ready for retirement homes, although several seemed likely candidates for kindergarten—especially a kindergarten that allowed for plenty of play time. Now I'm *really* ready for retirement!

The "stick kid's" real name turned out to be Donald De Camp, but he goes by the name of "Mr. Bones." This was evident because the word *Bones* was engraved on the back of his leather belt. (Leather belts substitute for business cards and billboards among folk festival types.) He goes by "Mr. Bones" because he *plays* the bones. Not the ones attached to his skeleton, but two pieces of bird's-eye maple carved into the shape and size of a couple of thick bookmarks.

Held loosely between the fingers, they snap out infinite and complicated rhythms to the harmonies of guitars, banjos, dulcimers, and such. Mr. Bones played his sticks two sets at a time—a pair going in each hand. I must say it was an awe-inspiring sight for all who watched this performer at work.

Scott and I took advantage of an opportunity to visit with Bones during a break. As the old gentleman wiped the sweat from his forehead, he said, "Man, oh man. I *love* that rhythm!" Now he wasn't referring to a particular rhythm in a particular song. He loved the big idea of rhythm, the entire *concept* of rhythm, any regular beat that allowed him the chance to get out his sticks and go play.

He told us that years ago the "bones" were originally made from animal bones. He'd even found some evidence that the bones, as musical instruments, had been in existence some 1,500 years before Christ. Young Donald De Camp had picked them up as a child for the pure fun of it and has been playing them ever since. That's all the information we could squeeze out of our conversation, because the band started again and all his friends began begging him to come out and play with them some more. He bowed his apologies to us young'uns, shuffled to center stage, closed his eyes for a moment, then went to tapping and dancing and playing those bones. He was wild joy on the loose.

Scott's eyes followed Bones' every movement—my husband has always been an admirer of old codgers, especially the sort with plenty of twinkles left in their eyes.

I imagine if Scott were to write a male version of the famous poem, "When I Am Old I Shall Wear Purple," it might go something like this:

> When I am old, I shall wear my hair in tufts of
> sweepy silver 'round the perimeter of my
> head.

> I shall wear old boots and faded jeans and a
>   tanned leather belt with my name on the
>   back.
> I shall own a crisp white shirt, a black string tie,
>   a handsome vest and a pocket watch, with a
>   gold chain that loops in front.
> I shall close my eyes when I hear the band start
>   up and I shall wander toward
> the sounds until the beat collides with the joy in
>   my heart.
> And I shall dance.
> Alone, or with a pretty gal, or with my best set
>   of bones.
> And I shall make all the young ones wish they
>   were old—
> old enough to shuffle centerstage and play
> with the abandon of an uninhibited soul.

Sometime after our encounter with Bones, we heard the sound of a soulful tenor drifting above the crowd. It was accompanied by an instrument that sounded something like the warble of a bird or a woman's voice. Following the beautiful strains, we came upon a most unlikely sight. A rather dapper looking gentleman (even though clad in overalls) was sitting and playing a handsaw. He held the handsaw tucked under one thigh and ran a violin's bow across the smooth side of the blade, producing an almost other-worldly melody.

This unusual musician was also the source of the incredible tenor voice. Many of us in the crowd stood misty-eyed, listening to that voice tenderly pour the words to "Danny Boy" from his soul to ours. Only a true Irishman could evoke the sort of emotion this man pulled from the small audience around him. He finished up the last strains a cappella, ending the final notes with a gallant sweeping of the black derby from his head and over his heart.

We gave the Irishman our compliments during a break and discovered he went by the name of Ramblin' Ray Rickets. He hailed from Arkansas, so his Southern accent left no hint of an Irish brogue. But, sure 'n' sure, he was Irish of soul. Said he could sing "Danny Boy" every day of his life and never grow tired of it.

As we had done with Mr. Bones, we asked Ray how he came to play his unusual instrument. He smiled and smoothed back his hair with his hand before replacing the derby atop its silvery perch.

"It was real simple. I heard our preacher play the saw one Sunday in our li'l ol' country church, and I went up right after the service and asked him if he'd show me how to do it. Right then and there, the preacher sat down and gave me a quick lesson—and I was hooked. Took it right up and never put it down."

I could see Scott making a mental list—a list I knew he'd eventually bring to a hardware store: bird's-eye maple, new handsaw, violin bow. Later in the afternoon, we passed table after table of wood carvings, and visited with elderly craftsmen as they carved their works of butternut, maple, and other delicious-sounding woods. These men, too, were a friendly, most contented looking lot. Scott added "a porch swing, butternut, and a whittlin' knife" to his growing list of necessities. (He plans to get a running start on ol' codgerdom.)

Watching all the fiddlin' and whittlin' and cloggin' and sawin' made us suddenly aware we were hungry. Two dishes of homemade vanilla ice cream hit the spot and satisfied our hunger. Well, almost. Of course, there was no way I could pass the funnel cake booth—with its swirls of fried bread piled high with fresh whipped cream and juicy strawberries.

Moments later, Scott instructed me to wipe the bits of berries and cream off my face, then asked me to dance a couple of impromptu waltzes and a schottische with him—right there on the street. After all, we'd just seen ol' Bones take off with his sweetheart and twirl her around to a western swing. We couldn't let the old folk beat us completely into the ground. Scott and I were getting more childlike and frisky by the minute. Being around happy, unrestrained people over the age of sixty was beginning to have a youthful effect on us.

As the sun began to fade and the autumn air cooled, we found ourselves wandering back in the direction of our Irish friend. As we'd hoped, Ray was still happily "sawing" away. The crowds were gone, so Scott and I sat down, propped our feet up on empty chairs, and listened to the music serenade the nightfall. A younger man on Ray's left was doing a fine job of picking his banjo, a woman to his right was belting out an old mournful ballad as she strummed her guitar. After a couple of melancholy tunes, Ray looked up at us and winked.

"These old songs are so sad, it's a wonder we're not all depressed."

I laughed and said, "It's OK. Just sing us a 'hallelujah' song in between the depressin' ones now and then."

"I'd like to do you one better than that, right after we finish this next heartbreaker."

Scott put his arm around me and stroked my shoulder as we waited, peacefully, for our love-graced day to come gently to its end. The group sang their last sad song for my husband and me, their only audience. No matter. These artists performed for the simple pleasure of sending their music into the air. Finally, the young banjo player set his instrument down, looked at the woman, at Ray, at us.

"Now this has been what I call a *festival*," he declared.

Scott and I rose to give the group a two-person standing ovation, but Ray asked us to sit for just a minute longer.

"I'd like to say an Irish blessing for you two."

With that, he stood, swept the derby from his head, and placed it over his heart once more, pronouncing a benediction befitting the day.

"May the road rise up to meet you, may the sun shine warm upon your face, the rains fall soft upon your fields, and, until we meet again, may God hold you in the palm of His hand."

What a wonderful thing it was to be blessed in such a way. How precious, how rare.

"Thank you so much," I said, standing to leave with Scott. "You've made our day."

Scott nodded in agreement. "Yes, it's been an honor."

"No," Ray leaned a little on his saw, placed one knee up on a chair, and argued, "*you* have honored *us*."

It's not easy to find childlike fun and thoughtfulness in and among human beings these days. Yet all in one day we were privileged to witness those very qualities in several fine people—the likes of Bones and Ramblin' Ray.

Victor Hugo once said, "Winter is on my head, but eternal spring is in my heart." Or as my eternally young mother puts it, West Texas–style, "Just 'cause thar's a little snow on the roof, don't mean there ain't a fire in the furnace."

They will still bear fruit in old age, they will
stay fresh and green.
PSALM 92:14

Hey, I've Got a Great Idea!

S eeing a book nearing its end is a little like watching a first
child go off to kindergarten (especially, this *particular*
book). The ending of an era is always fraught with ambiguity.
On one hand, I'm ready to let 'er rip, fling this prose out the
door, and get on with life! On the other hand, I worry there
might be just one more thing I need to say before completely letting go. I've only just begun to scratch the surface on the benefits
of behaving like a child! Inevitably, as soon as my manuscript is
cuddled, bundled, kissed good-bye and deposited at the post
office, I'll remember another story or think of one more piece of
advice that would have been "just perfect" for the book—if only
I could climb into that little mailbox slot and retrieve the package.

But I must begin to let go, for my sake and the sake of my
family. The other day Scott drove our family through Burger
King (the drive-thru, not the building) and placed an order for
french fries. He also asked for some ketchup, and on reflex, I
found myself bouncing up and down in my seat chanting, "Ask
for bunches and bunches and *bunches* of ketchup!" Like robots,

my entire family stopped moving at once, slowly turning all heads and eyes on me. Finally, Scott spoke on behalf of the group.

"Becky, *where* did *that* come from?"

"Um," I replied sheepishly, "from the little girl inside me?"

"Becky, this childlike stuff is getting out of hand. You're acting so young you're embarrassing the *children*."

"Okeydokey," I said cheerfully, as I twirled my hair around my finger and stared wistfully out the window.

Perhaps I am getting a little carried away. But in my own defense, the idea of staying childlike into our adult years has been around for a very, very long time. Mencius from the third century B.C. wrote, "The great man is he who does not lose his child's-heart." I think ol' Mencius knew what he was talking about.

How do we turn our mid-life crisis into kid-life creativity? I have a great idea! How about starting a list, maybe even keeping it up on the refrigerator, of things we can do to help us find our child-heart when it wanders too far down Growing Up Lane. Here are a few suggestions to get you started, off the top of my wee little head.

Keep Asking Questions, Even If It Drives People Crazy

As you may have already guessed, Gabriel is—hands down— our family's top Weird Question Asker. A couple of weeks ago, he called me to the living room with an urgent, pertinent question: "Mom, what is that little dip called on top of your upper lip and under your nose?" I had to confess, once again, Gabe had me stumped. In my thirty-seven years, I can't say I'd ever, even once, given a thought to the dip above our lips. So I asked Scott to relay the question to a friend of ours, a physician.

"The medical term?" our doctor friend asked after Scott described the part of the body in question.

"Yep," Scott replied, "Gabe needs to know."

"Beats me," the good doctor replied. "But my best guess is that it's probably known as The Lip Dip."

It's questions like this that keep medical science on its toes—
and the curiosity of a child alive in your heart.

Never Outgrow Children's Books

Just as children give us wonderful excuses to go see animated
movies, they're also great reasons to reread favorite books from
childhood (or discover new ones for your second go-around at
kidhood).

I remember my third grade teacher as being pretty and young,
but so, so sad. We found out later in the year that her husband
had been killed in Vietnam just before she came to our school.
The one bright spot of those melancholy classroom days was listening to her read from Laura Ingalls Wilder's *Little House in the
Big Woods*.

During those fifteen minutes, while my teacher read aloud, I
could escape the classroom for the hearthside of Pa and Ma
Ingalls, Mary, Laura, and Baby Carrie. I'd feel cozy and happy
and warm inside, as my mind drifted to the little log cabin in the
big woods. Not surprisingly, this was the first "chapter book" I
read to my own children, and I must admit I read it for my pleasure as much as for theirs.

Other classics I've loved and reread to children are: *The Box
Car Children; Pippi Longstocking; Charlotte's Web; James and the
Giant Peach; The Lion, the Witch, and the Wardrobe.* There are
so many wonderful, *unforgettable* children's books worth reading
with or without kids nearby, simply to keep a fresh, child's-eye
view alive and well. Some of the most beautiful artwork anywhere can be had for the price of a children's book. I've collected
about a hundred illustrated books. They're a treasure I can share
with children now—and look forward to sharing with my
grandbabies-to-be someday in the future. (Note to my teenage
sons: in the far, far distant future.)

Don't Be Afraid to Be a Little Goofy

I have in my repertoire several examples of personal goofiness
to choose from—as you might expect—but I'll narrow it down

to one recent example. About a month ago, I had a flat tire. Well, it was more like a blowout—the steel belt had popped open but the tire still had air in it. When I drove the car forward, the belt made a horrendous sound as it flopped and slapped against raw metal. But when I drove it in reverse, the sound was much more subdued. So, to my children's horror and my neighbors' amazement, I drove all the way home in reverse. Five miles. All backwards. The funniest part was when we passed a poor, bewildered German shepherd. The pitiful thing really wanted to chase the car, but you could almost see him thinking, *Gee, which direction should I run?*

I must admit, I was not as embarrassed as most people might have been. There's a touch of little-kid mischief in me that enjoys keeping the neighborhood guessing about my sanity.

Be a Bubblegum Philosopher

As part of my journey to becoming a deeper thinking woman, I recently purchased a book written by Ravi Zacharias. In case, like me, you've been wading shallow intellectual waters the last few years and have not heard of him, Dr. Zacharias is a brilliant Christian philosopher who travels the world arguing for the existence of God in cerebral settings like Harvard and Princeton University.

I must confess, I've remained in a suspended state of insightful confusion throughout the first half of Dr. Zacharias's book, *Can Man Live without God?* Heavy reading is a lot like eating spinach: I know it's good for me, but hey, it's not chocolate cheesecake.

Then, just as my neurons refuse to stretch one more dendrite, Ravi breaks through with an easy-to-read story that even a kid like me can understand. Dr. Zacharias points out that G. K. Chesterton once "unabashedly proclaimed that he learned more about life by observing children in a nursery than he ever did by reflecting upon the writings of any of the philosophers."

This comforts me because I've been so busy changing diapers and wiping runny noses the last sixteen years I've had precious little time to delve into the great philosophies of the ages. Then Ravi proceeds to tell a remarkable story that points out exactly what I've been trying to explain for, lo, these many pages: There is a lot to be said for behaving like a child.

As the story goes, Ravi and his family were crossing from Jordan to Israel by way of the West Bank. Ushered into a highly secured immigration building to procure a visitor's visa, they had been warned to expect a long and grueling morning—in fact, the process might take all day. On every side, Dr. Zacharias, his wife, and his two-year-old daughter, Sarah, were surrounded by soldiers toting machine guns, "whose glares led us to believe that we were all guilty of something." From there, the scene Dr. Zacharias describes takes on an almost storybook quality.

> Finally it was our turn to be interrogated. Unknown to me, as she surveyed the room filled with armed guards, Sarah had locked eyes with a young Israeli soldier who was staring back at her in eye-to-eye "combat." Suddenly and strangely there was a moment of silence in the room, broken by the squeaky little voice of my daughter asking the soldier, "Excuse me, do you have any bubble gum?"
>
> Words alone cannot fully express to you what that little voice and plea did for everyone in the room, where hitherto the weapons of warfare and the world of "adult ideas" had held everyone at bay. All who understood English knew a soldier's heart had been irresistibly touched. All eyes were now on him.
>
> He paused for a moment, then carefully handed his machine gun to a colleague. He came over to where we were standing, looked endearingly at Sarah, and picked her up in his arms. He took her into a back room and returned a few minutes later with her in one arm, and in the other hand, he carried three glasses of lemonade on a tray—one for my wife, one for Sarah, and one for me. We were in and out of the immigration office in twenty-five minutes. In fact, the soldier brought his jeep to the door and drove us to the taxi stand, sending us on our way to Jericho.[16]

Leave it to a two-year-old to make lemonade out of machine guns—with bubblegum! So learn! Stretch! Grow intellectually! But don't forget to chew bubblegum while you're at it.

Be Aware of Guardian Angels

Cousin Jamie called the other day with a story about her youngest child, four-year-old Martha—a delicate, sweet, and shy little girl with soft blond hair and beautiful blue eyes and an adorable way of talking. Little Martha is even more precious to all of us after a recent close call.

Jamie and her mother (Martha's grandmother) had taken Jamie's four young children along on a shopping trip to a mall in Houston. When they were pooped out, they stopped to rest a moment near the bottom of an escalator. As kids will do, little Martha leaned her arms over the escalator's handrail, as she stood on the floor beside it watching people going up, up, up.

And as the railing also rose, Martha lifted her feet off the ground for a ride and before anyone knew what was happening, her small body began rising above the mall floor. She was dangling only by her tiny arms clinging to the escalator handrail. It all happened so fast that by the time Jamie looked up, screamed, and began sprinting up the steps to help her daughter, it was too late. When little Martha reached the top—twenty feet above the ground—she also hit the wall. Her grandmother watched in helpless horror as she saw one little hand let go and then the other.

And that's when the angels took over. A woman standing below the escalator happened to see what was going on, positioned herself, said a silent prayer for strength, and opened her arms. As Martha fell from the full height of twenty feet above the mall's tile floor, the woman made a successful catch. Both woman and child went down with the impact, but thankfully, both were unhurt. Of course, they were stunned.

Martha lay there in the woman's lap on the floor, perfectly still, not saying a word. Nothing seemed hurt, but she might have been in shock. After a long while, she wriggled and tugged at her rescuer's shirt. The woman leaned down closer to hear the quiet little voice. In the midst of noise and turmoil and Jamie's crying and the grandmother's sighs of relief, Martha had one concern on her ladylike four-year-old mind.

"My unduhweauh is showing," she whispered.

Jesus said, "Beware that you don't look down upon a single one of these little children. For I tell you that in heaven their angels have constant access to my Father" (Matt. 18:10, TLB). That's why the child in me *has* to believe that somewhere, watching over a Houston mall, unseen to the naked eye, a couple of guardian angels gave each other a high five and laughed a hearty chuckle.

This list could go on forever! I've not even touched on coloring with crayons, watching clouds float by, climbing a tree, eating popsicles, skimming stones across the pond, telling a knock-knock joke, running through a sprinkler, making up a silly song, decorating with wit and whimsy, going barefoot, or saying prayers like ,"I love You, Jesus. Amen"—and meaning it, and leaving it at that. The world is so full of simple, childlike joys. Why leave them behind when we can carry them with us?

It is no wonder we adults are stressed beyond reason. We've lost our child-heart! When was the last time you laid back in the grass, propped one foot over one knee, and made imaginary pictures out of clouds? Oh, the money we waste on spas and psychologists and pills, when time to meander and ponder and lay back in the grass is all most of us really need to get balanced again. I believe people today are *starving* for unscheduled blocks of precious time to *waste*. We know, instinctively, that our children need *time to be kids*.

But what about you? What about me?

My son just burst into my office, a baby turtle along for the ride in his grubby outstretched palm. He comes bearing important news. "Mom!" he says. "Remember that little seed that I planted? Well it plunked up from the dirt into leaves! Come see!" Now, should I keep writing or go outside with my child?

See ya later. I just made an appointment with a kid and some plunked-up leaves. Oh yes—and a sky full of clouds.

———

*"I praise you, Father, Lord of heaven and earth,
because you have hidden these things
from the wise and learned,
and revealed them to little children."*
MATTHEW 11:25
❧

Look Daddy, I Can Fly!

Although I love the slinky, silky gowns my husband gives me every holiday season, this year I asked if he might give me something a little less breezy. I was particularly interested in sleepwear that would wrap warm and snugly around my cold, cold feet.

Thinking it would be a cute joke, Scott gave me a pair of "woman size" pink and white feety pajamas—in a teddy bear print. Christmas evening, I stole away to the bedroom and tried them on just for fun. As I put one foot and then another into the pajama legs, I drifted back to the very first memory I have as a child. I could almost hear my daddy—as he sounded nearly thirty-five years ago—softly singing, "Put your little foot, put your little foot, put your little foot right here. . . ." as I stood on my bed while he helped me into my feety pj's.

My father is one man who has managed, all his life, to keep his child-heart pumping strong.

One rainy spring afternoon, when I was about eleven, I went out in the garage to find my father ascending a ladder into the attic. Though Daddy was sentimental, he was *not* a handyman, so the sight of a ladder provoked my curiosity. Then he crooked his finger in a silent gesture that I knew meant, "Come along, but be quiet."

I followed him up into the attic and sat down beside him, curious as to the nature of our exploration. But all my dad said was, "Shhh . . . listen." Then I heard it. The rain, pattering overhead—amplified by our nearness to the rooftop.

"I come up here whenever it rains," Daddy said softly. It was cool and comforting, a tender moment caught—like a snapshot—in my mind.

To my pleasant surprise, my husband turned out to be a rain-on-the-roof kind of guy, too. He even built our bed so that the head of it fits snug against a large picture window. At night, if the full moon is shining or a soft rain is falling, Scott pulls up the blinds and raises the window and whispers, "Shhh . . . Becky. Listen." And this, I believe, is part of the reason why the two men I love most in the whole world are my daddy and my husband.

Another thing I love about Daddy is the way he gave us kids silly nicknames. My little sister, Rachel, he nicknamed "The Bunky." Or sometimes he called her "Yupupuh." (Don't ask me where he got the inspiration for these.) When my brother, David, was small his word for "horses" came out as "saucies." Thus he earned the nickname "Saucy." When I was small, I wore a red ruffly nightgown, which I adored, and whenever I wore it Daddy called me his "Red Arriba." All of us kids collectively were dubbed "sproogins."

Another amazing thing about Daddy: In all my years, I cannot ever recall my father criticizing me. Not once. Always, he would praise and encourage my efforts—however crazy, however childish.

Not long ago I had a dream; it is a reoccurring dream I've had for years. In it I can fly. I love these dreams, and while I'm in them, I cannot understand why other people don't just float themselves up to the sky and join me. It is so easy, nothing to it at all. Most of the time I just spread out my arms and take off, but in one of my dreams I piloted a Frisbee. Now *that* was fun!

But the last dream I had was especially realistic. Once again I was flying, and in my dream I thought to myself, *This is ridiculous. Nobody else is flying except me. I need to find out if this is real or if this is just my imagination.*

So I flew to my parents' home, knocked on the door, and floated up to the ceiling. Then I hovered over my father, who was looking up at me, not at all surprised to find me up there, and I said, "Daddy, listen. You've *got* to tell me the truth. I really think I'm flying. It feels so real. But I'm worried that this might just all be a dream."

My daddy's answer was swift and sure. "Honey," he said, "it's no dream. You're flying all right."

When I woke up I laughed, but then tears welled in my eyes. *How marvelous,* I thought, *that even in my subconscious, in spite of all logic to the contrary, I have a father who believes I can fly.*

For Father's Day last year, I could not find a card that seemed to fit how I felt about Daddy. However, I came across a scene in a children's book that turned out to be perfect. It was a scene with Piglet and Winnie-the-Pooh, walking side by side toward a setting sun. Their short conversation summed up exactly how I felt about my father through the years.

Piglet sidled up to Pooh from behind.

"Pooh!" he whispered.

"Yes, Piglet?"

"Nothing," said Piglet, taking Pooh's paw. "I just wanted to be sure of you."[17]

My dad has been like Pooh to me, his Little Girl-Piglet. Oh, we don't chit-chat a whole lot, not like my mother and I anyway. But in every memory involving my father—from the time he sang, "Put your little foot" as he helped me into my feety pajamas, until this latest dream where he assured me that, yes, I could really fly—my father has been there in the shadows, cheering me on. He has given me the steadfast assurance that always, and forever, I can be sure of him.

And so it is, oh Piglet-Children everywhere, with your Father in heaven.

> *This resurrection life . . . is adventurously*
> *expectant, greeting God with a childlike*
> *"What's next, Papa?"*
> *God's Spirit touches our spirits and confirms*
> *who we really are . . . :*
> *Father and children.*
> *With God on our side like this,*
> *how can we lose?*
> ROMANS 8:14–17, 31, THE MESSAGE
> ❧

Growing Up to Be a Child

BY BECKY FREEMAN

Mud-puddle miracles
Doodle-bug designs
Bursts of fun with bubblegum
Oh, to see life as a child!

"I love you's" big as rainbows
"I'm sorry's" from the heart
A kiss goodnight, a bear hug tight
To love as would a child!

"Let the children come to Me,"
He said with arms flung wide
Don't stop me now—
I'm coming, too
For I'm a child *inside*

I want to laugh from the belly
Risk playing a clown—
I'm giving up on growing up
Think I'll just start growing

d
  o
    w
      n

Oh, yeeaahh.

*"Any of you who welcomes a little child like this
because you are mine,
is welcoming me and caring for me."*
MATTHEW 18:5, TLB

Notes

1. Art Linkletter, *The New Kids Say the Darndest Things!* (Ottawa, Ill.: Jameson Books, Inc., 1995), viii.

2. Karol A. Jackowski, *Ten Fun Things to Do before You Die* (Notre Dame, Ind.: Ave Maria Press, 1989), 13–17.

3. Suzanne Lipsett, *Surviving a Writer's Life* (San Francisco: HarperSan Francisco, 1994), 58.

4. L. M. Montgomery, *Anne of Green Gables* (Boston: L. C. Page and Publishers, 1940), 75.

5. Dee Brestin, *The Friendships of Women* (Wheaton, Ill.: Victor Books, 1988), 10.

6. Zick Rubin, *Children's Friendships* (Cambridge, Mass.: Harvard University Press, 1980), 108.

7. Billy and Janice Hughey, compilers, *A Rainbow of Hope* (El Reno, Okla.: Rainbow Studies, Inc.), 198.

8. Paula Hardin, *What Are You Doing with the Rest of Your Life?* (San Rafael, Calif.: New World Library, 1992), 170.

9. Dadi Daley Mackall, *Kids Say the Greatest Things about God* (Wheaton, Ill.: Tyndale House Publishers, 1995), 27.

10. Philip Yancey, *Disappointment with God* (New York: HarperCollins, 1988), 163–64.

11. Colette, "Freedom," *Earthly Paradise*, ed. Robert Phelps (1966), 2; as quoted in Rhoda Thomas Tripp, *International Thesaurus of Quotations* (New York: Harper & Row, 1970), 601.

12. Linkletter, *The New Kids Say the Darndest Things!*, vii.

13. Mackall, *Kids Say the Greatest Things about God*, 73.

14. Ibid., 7.

15. Hardin, *What Are You Doing with the Rest of Your Life?*, 174–75.

16. Ravi Zacharias, *Can Man Live without God?* (Dallas: Word Publishing, 1994), 76.

17. A. A. Milne, *The World of Pooh: The House at Pooh Corner,* "Tigger Unbounced" (New York: Dutton Children's Books, Div. of Penguin USA, 1957; copyright renewed 1985), 261.